GROUNDTRUTH

groundtruth

NICK HERSHENOW

FIRELAND
PRESS

This is a work of fiction. Names, characters, places, and events are either the products of the author's imagination or are used fictitiously.

COVER PHOTO: Nick Hershenow
MAPS: Nick Hershenow and Max Hershenow

BOOK AND COVER DESIGN: Sarah Bennett
shbennettbookdesign.com

ISBN: 979-8-9942178-0-1

TWISP, WASHINGTON

FIRELAND
PRESS

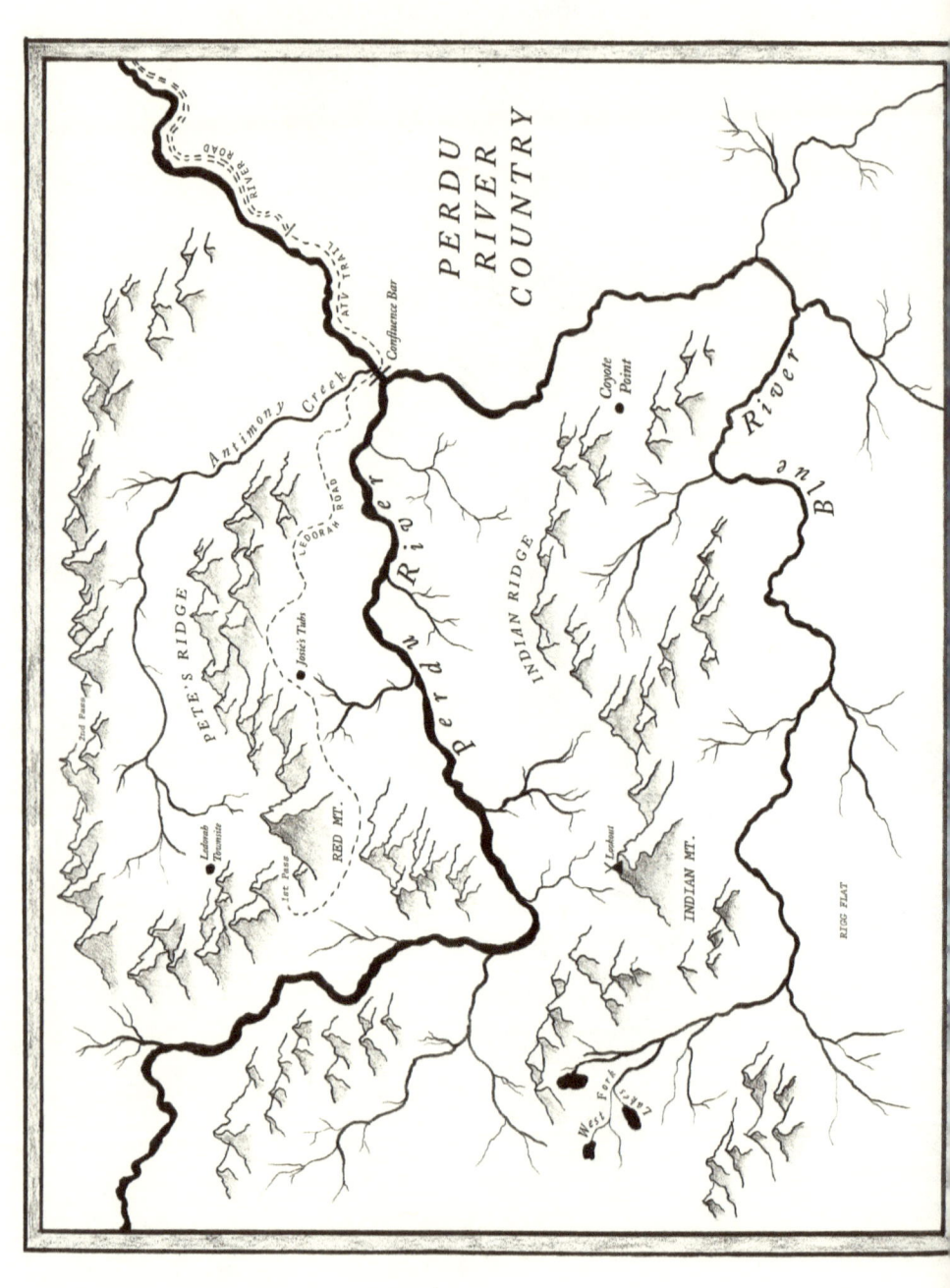

Table of Contents

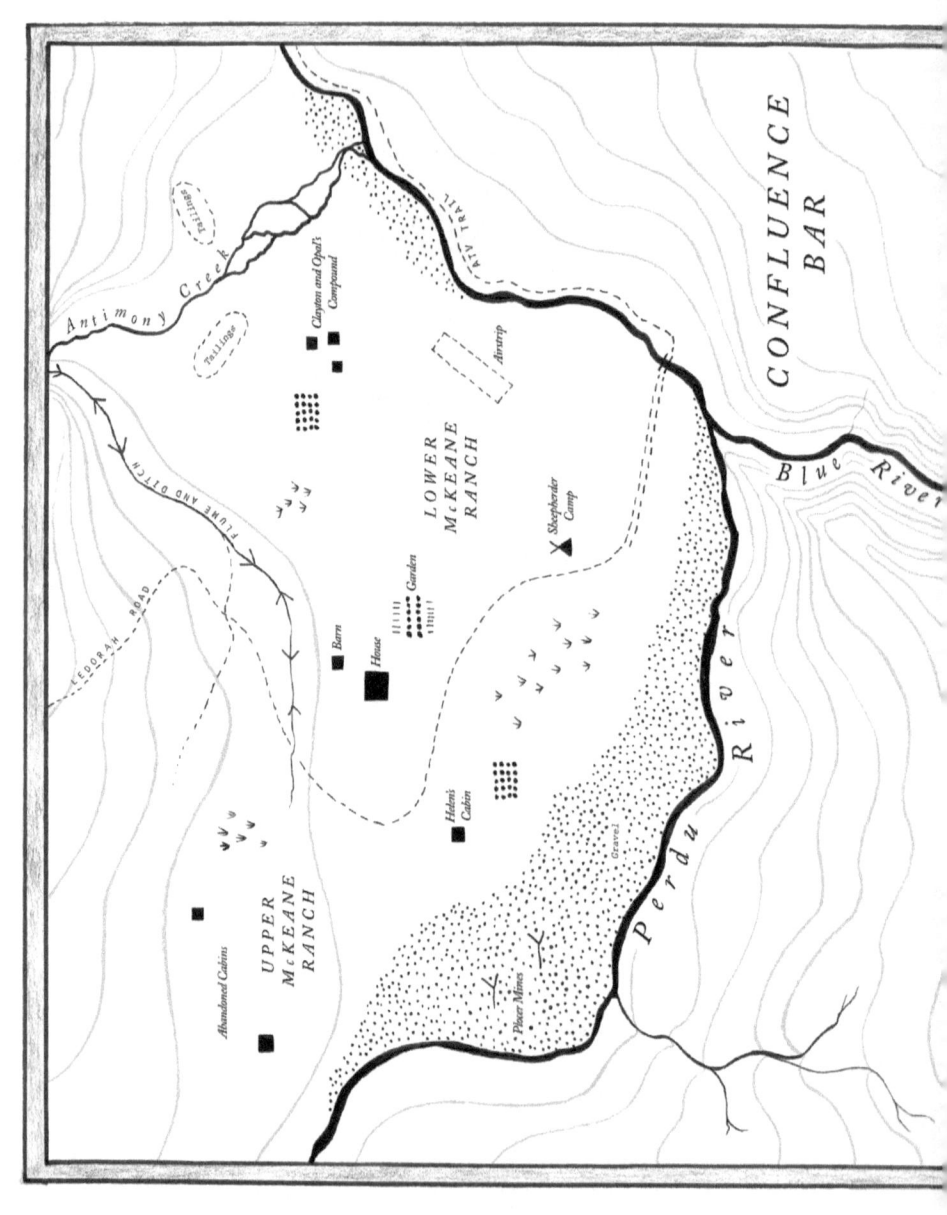

She's in a tower on a mountaintop at night, inside a bubble of light. She hears footsteps coming up the stairs.

She opens the door. The sheepherder is standing on the catwalk, holding something in each hand. Two cans, an offering.

They eat the fruit cocktail sitting at her table under the propane light, in the center of an immense darkness. His smell fills the small room. Sheep, horses, pine sap, cooking oil, smoke, sweat, what else? She opens a bottle of wine.

De dónde vienes?

Her Spanish is not so good, she understands only fragments of his answer. A tale, or it seems like a tale, of a journey over mountains and rivers, bright meadow, sunless forest, ghost forest. Four passes. One horse, two mules, three dogs, two thousand sheep. One sheepherder though he counted for two. In the darkness behind them, the hunters, cazadores: coyote, lobo, oso, león.

And behind them something else, solo Dios sabe.

In his camp the dogs begin to bark. Cazador, he says. He takes up his coat. She leads him down the stairs. At the bottom she stops and turns.

León, she says with certainty. Then tells her own tale, or tries to. A mountain lion, a journey... she falters. She doubts he understands, though he says something in reply. The dogs bark, the sheep wail. She whispers, kisses his mouth in the dark.

In the morning she's awakened by a sound like thunder.

I

something else hovers out here, not
color, not outlines or depth when air
relieves distance by hazing far mountains,
but some total feeling or other world
almost coming forward, like when a bell sounds
and then leaves a whole countryside waiting.

—William Stafford
(Is this Feeling About the West Real?)

1

NUCLEUS

WHEN HE WAS three years old, Chele Cruz' whore mother sent him on a bus to his grandma in the campo with an envelope pinned to his shirt and a deadly virus in his blood.

He had no memory of his mother or the bus ride or the envelope or the virus, but he remembered his grandma. She lived in San Miguel in a house surrounded by orange trees and sweet lemons, mangoes, papaya, banana, everything prospered in the ideal climate of his grandma's country, where rain and sunshine fell in equal abundance. She passed out bags of oranges to even the most casual visitor. If he needed something—a piece of string, a pocketknife, a coin, a pencil—she would rummage around in one of the many pockets of her lace-fringed apron and likely find it, or find something he needed more. Amulets and rosaries hung on a stand on the dresser in her bedroom, beside a painted wooden statue of the Black Madonna and different-colored candles she lit at different times for different reasons. Magazine ads and pictures of saints and Virgins and the Holy Infant were taped to the walls; plants and ears of corn hung drying from the rafters. His grandma had a garden of medicine plants and knowledge of others growing in the wild, and she stood for hours at her clay stove in the smoky kitchen, boiling herbs and turning out stacks of thick tortillas with her arthritic hands, while grandchildren and great-grandchildren played on the floor or watched from the shadows.

In his earliest memories he was one of those children. 'Mateo' was his name then, though hardly anyone used it. His grandma called him *Leche, Nieve* or, mostly, *Chele* or *Chelito,* nicknames given to light-skinned boys. His skin was a shade or two lighter than the others, but nothing remotely like milk or snow.

Other kids came and went but there was always a small pack of them and he was always on the outside. The others crowded into bed with his grandma, but he slept alone in a cot in the storeroom. He bathed and mostly played alone. He had his own towel and his own plate and spoon and his own bitter medicinal teas to drink, to fortify his kidneys and quiet the fever in his blood, she said.

Yet he was the one who accompanied her when she went to gather plants in the surrounding hills. She rode her little bay mare and he walked beside her carrying her walking stick. When she tired of riding she'd get down off the horse and shamble along with the stick and Chele would ride. Always she would stop first at the river to bathe. To purify, she said. Chele played in riffles and shallow pools while she stripped off her many layers of clothing down to her underwear and eased herself into the turbid water. She'd stretch out her stocky, swollen legs, skin cracked and mottled with great varicose veins, and sit in the shallows splashing water on her shoulders, and talk. She was a great talker. She talked constantly while she rode, to him or to the mare or the Virgin or some other angel or spirit, or to the plants themselves. She would point with her lips and call them by their common names and their names in Indian languages and speak softly of their intimate parts and the virtues and perils associated with them, while Chele scrambled around harvesting whatever leaves or flowers or roots she told him to harvest. She spoke to the ghost plants, that had grown in the forests around San Miguel when she was a child but were lost when the mining company came with promises of riches and then cut down trees and set fires and tore into the earth and did a more subtle violence to the town, corrupting young girls and drawing the boys into the mines to exhaust their bodies and turn old and broken before their time.

Now the mines were closed and the miners gone, leaving behind dead waters and soils that grew only this bitter and stunted vegetation. Anyone who wanted paid work went elsewhere, to the city or abroad, to Spain, New Jersey, Los Angeles. San Miguel was abandoned to the old and forsaken, to the very young, the sick, the intoxicated; its woods and fields left to ravens and vultures and wild dogs and phantasms who preyed on careless children. Hairy Sisimiti with his monstrous penis and backwards feet that left giant prints in the fresh ash of wildfires; the dog-like Cadejo, with matted, filthy fur and eyes burning red-hot like embers, emerging from the mineshafts at night to feed on the dead.

When the swelling moved up her legs and the varicose veins broke out and ulcerated these expeditions became impossible for her. Then she sent him out alone to gather plants, complaining that he brought back the wrong ones or the wrong parts or harvested them too young or too old. Mostly she sat with her legs squeezed into tight stockings and resting on a low table in front of the TV that was always on. Tele-novelas, reality shows, the news programs she called her *sucesos*, that told no complete story but were rather a perpetual stream of horror stories and freak shows and violence and the aftermath of violence, police and soldiers standing around dead bodies, naked bodies, the camera panning splatterings of blood on the streets and walls. None of it seemed real but when he asked her if these were true stories that had really happened she said of course they were true. *Suceso*, she said. *Algo que sucede.*

Something that happens.

The other children drifted back to live with their mothers or rela-tives. Then at night it was just him in his cot and his grandma in her bed alone, and all day his grandma talking—to the TV, the Virgin, to him, it was getting hard to tell which. She grew more remote, absorbed in her monologues and her physical suffering. A woman, a daughter or granddaughter, returned from abroad and moved into the house with her children. Sometimes a man stayed with them. The children scarcely spoke to Chele and often there wasn't enough food and more than once when the man drank he hit or threatened to hit him.

He began to stay away from the house. He rode the mare into the hills, when he could catch her. She'd gone a little wild; she'd jump fences or slip out of enclosures and he'd have to go after her, though sometimes he'd just let her range while he played by the creek or around the mines, building forts and hideouts and studying the ground and the tailings for tracks, tools, some treasure the miners might have left behind. He stuck his head into tunnels and called out for an echo, half-hoping, half-afraid to catch a glimpse of Cadejo, of Sisimiti. But the air was dead, unless a whirlwind of bats sent him scurrying.

The mare disappeared; he searched farther and farther afield but could not find her. Then he began to spend more time in the town, wandering the streets looking for a chance to steal or beg some food, or just an unlocked shed or hidden corner where he could curl up beneath his horsey blanket and sleep. Not easy on Saturday nights, when two neighboring bars blasted competing music all night and into the dawn, though patrons and proprietors had long since staggered off or collapsed unconscious in their chairs or on floors or tabletops or the street.

But mostly San Miguel at night was dark and quiet and shut down. One or two shadows moving quickly through the streets, footsteps sounding on the cobble, low muttering voices, silence. A campfire or trash fire glowing in some dead end or alleyway. Once, skirting the edges of what looked like an abandoned fire, his foot crunched on gravel and a giant shadow rose up. Firelight flashed on ape-hairy shoulders, a malevolent bearded face. A stick or club swung from the brute's hand or waist, blunt and threatening. Or was it…? Chele turned and ran, forgetting to look at the feet.

Certainly he was afraid of his grandmother's demons, even if he didn't quite believe they were real. They seemed real and unreal at once, like the *sucesos* on her TV screen. In any case, his fear wasn't great enough to keep him off those empty night streets, a spooky playground he had mostly to himself. He played stalking games, hiding and spying games, hunting games. He moved quickly and silently in and out of streetlights, house lights, firelight, the shadowy places in between. On the far edges of town, mine tailings spilled into the streets and there were no electric lights at all, though the pale ground still gave off a faint glow—the refraction of starlight and moonlight in the shattered crystals, or some extracted incandescence from deep inside the earth?

But even a town as demoralized as San Miguel could not permit a seven year-old to indefinitely prowl the night streets and wander hills where mine tunnels had never been closed off and explosives were left lying around to blow people up. Twice a priest came to talk to his grandma. The second time she gave him a knapsack and told him to put his things in it and made him promise to say his prayers. Then she lit a candle and he got in the priest's car and they drove into the city and the priest left him with some nuns in a Home. There was enough to eat and no one was mean to him and he lived in the Home until Alvaro came.

Alvaro squatted down and looked straight at Chele. His eyes were very black. He had a thick mess of hair, also very black, and a thick black beard and thick eyebrows and, when he finally talked, a voice so thick and deep it was hard to understand, at first.

"Chele. Where's your home?"

"San Miguel."

"Which San Miguel?"

"San Miguel in the mountains."

"Okay, which mountains? It doesn't matter." Alvaro smiled. He opened his arms and Chele ran forward and Alvaro folded him into his chest. His beard was soft and scratchy at once. His voice rumbled, Chele felt as much as heard it. *Do you miss the mountains?* He didn't think he missed the mountains but he couldn't remember anyone ever holding him like that, or speaking so softly into his ear. Then Alvaro said he was building another Home in other mountains and did he want to live there, and Chele said yes.

That was the first year of the Gardens and Chele was one of the first dozen children. A seed, Alvaro said. A nucleus. What's a nucleus, he asked, and Alvaro said it was the central and most important part of something. A solid body in the center, pulling other bodies close.

Alvaro's Home was called *Los Jardines de Santo Jerome*. St. Jerome was the patron saint of orphans. But the place was nothing like a

garden, not at first. Just a barely flowing creek and hills of scrub pine
and brush, a few clearings with cement slabs and a couple of unfin-
ished cement block buildings barely distinguishable from the blocks
of crumbly bedrock surfacing here and there in the thin soil. Poor
land, and isolated, at the dead end of a steep, windy, gullying dirt road,
miles from the highway. Which is why we could buy it, Alvaro said.
And for us, isolation gives it value.

The land might be poor and the gardens non-existent, but somewhere behind St. Jerome's Gardens there was money, a church foundation, wealthy donors. Alvaro brought in construction crews and
heavy equipment. They reengineered and graded the access road,
carved out more building sites, dammed the creek to make a reservoir, built a pumping system and water storage tanks on the low
hills. Hauled in truckloads of building materials, cement and lumber and brick. The cement slabs expanded, became foundations for
dormitories, workshops, a chapel, a school. They cleared brush and
forest for more buildings and for pastures and planted fruit trees and
vegetables in bottomland soils tilled up and enriched with compost
and manure.

Kids were expected to help where they could. There was school,
playtime, and worktime, in more or less equal balance. And always
there were more and more kids. Alvaro was constantly hustling off
to meetings and hearings, to barrios, villages, backcountry ranchos.
Often he returned with kids, sometimes entire families, a half dozen
brothers and sisters whose parents had died or gone to jail or were
too sick or poor or intoxicated to care for them. There seemed to be
an infinite supply of children like that and Alvaro had tremendous
energy for seeking them out and triumphantly bringing them back
to the Gardens, as if he'd recovered a lost treasure, not some litter of
sickly children no one else wanted.

He had people helping him, of course. Cooks and gardeners, teachers, counselors, nurses, caregivers, house parents they called *tío* or *tía*.
Many were actual parents themselves, leaving their own children with
relatives while they earned a livelihood caring for children who had
no parent at all, and no relative willing to claim them. Others came

from far away. Alvaro had some kind of Scandinavian connection and he recruited a succession of pale, earnest, and empathetic volunteers, mostly young women, who crossed the ocean to teach and love orphan children. Chele sat in their laps, held their hands, listened to their music, parroted their English. He fell easily in love with them and his love was easily reciprocated. And quickly, though never painlessly, transferred to new ones when they moved on.

Though the kids at St. Jerome's were orphans, or effectively orphans, most still had people on the outside, family or close to family. They had occasional visitors, letters, phone calls. But for others there was no one. Chele was one of these. He had come without papers, Alvaro said, other than the paper his grandma had illegibly signed, giving him over to the priest. That priest had gone back to Spain and they could only guess at his grandmother's name. She lived in San Miguel, was all anybody knew. But in every *cantón* there seemed to be a little town or village called San Miguel, baking in dry hills or glimpsed through sheets of rain.

So Chele's beginning was hard to see, full of mist and shadow. But Alvaro said that didn't matter, for he had now found a clear and solid place and purpose. And Chele knew that was true. He felt solid with Alvaro, who pretended to be impartial but took a special interest in him, that was obvious. He felt connected and supported. He did well at school, worked and played hard, set an example. Teachers praised him, adults trusted him, kids were drawn to him.

A nucleus, pulling other bodies close.

Many bodies. He was never entirely free, never *alone*, that was impossible. Sometimes he longed for a taste of the solitude and freedom he had known as a small child, wandering the hills and streets and alleys of San Miguel. At St. Jerome's the only way to be alone was to run away. Or rather, to pretend to run away, a game. It was easy. You slipped under a couple of barbwire fences and followed paths that went off through pine woods and arroyos into the hills and eventually into the mountains.

The farthest he actually went, though, at first, was the Overlook—a big chunk of exposed bedrock protruding from a steep slope a short walk up the hill behind the Gardens. It was easy to walk out on it from above, but standing on the far edge you found yourself on a vertical cliff, looking down on treetops and buildings, fields and reservoirs. Beyond, a vast rolling plain, little hills and valleys, towns, villages, ranches and farms. Here and there a column of smoke rising, the glint of water or metal, rivers, highways. Shadow and light shifting with the clouds and seasons. Patchwork of field and forest and settlement, greens and browns and yellows that washed out in the distance into a hazy glare, cement and metal and glass—that was the city where Alvaro had found him. On every horizon, cordilleras. Looking out from the Overlook you could imagine you were high on one of them yourself, and San Miguel was hidden somewhere in those hazy mountains.

But the Overlook was not far and other kids occasionally did go there, so it didn't really feel like running away. He started venturing farther and the game got more exciting. He followed a trail that climbed steeply through the forest and then over a narrow saddle in the ridge, a pass. At the saddle the ground rose up on either side, or the path sank, becoming a long, narrow slot incised two or three meters deep into the earth, practically a tunnel, with a hardpacked floor and high walls of pale soil and a green roof of leafy plants and overhanging pine branches.

How many years, centuries, had it taken to grind down that earth, how many walking feet? And now there were no footprints at all. Maybe it wasn't a human path and never had been. Maybe it had been dug out and pounded down by wild creatures, who might travel through it still.

Sisimiti. He imagined his grandma hissing the word, backing her horse out of the ambush.

The path emerged from its canyon and he looked down on a pocket valley with pastures and corn fields, rock walls, whitewashed houses, cows, chickens, gardens. A building with a flag—a tiny school? A man hoed a cornfield, kids scrabbled around kicking a deflated soccer ball up and down the sloping dirt yard. A dog barked and kept barking.

No one looked up. Beyond were high, dark mountains, dark forest, thunderclouds gathering.

What if you ran away and this was as far as you got, the end of the game? Suddenly he didn't want to play anymore, or to be seen playing. He hurried back through the mini-canyon and down the paths home. His absence had been noted. He was reprimanded and put on garbage duty for a week. The most menial and disgusting job, supposedly, but Chele didn't mind. He pushed a big wheelbarrow around from courtyard to courtyard, calling out: *Basura! Orgánicos!* People brought out their kitchen slops and household trash, and he wheelbarrowed it down a road and dumped it onto a stinking pile beside a big rusty burn barrel with a chimney that put out a permanent smudge of foul-smelling black smoke. The Transfer Station. They called it that as a joke, though it was true that nearly everything dumped there was sooner or later transferred elsewhere, if not trans*formed* into some other physical or chemical substance, smoldering for days in the incinerator or rotted or carried away by human or animal scavengers or blown by the wind into surrounding woods and fields.

Black vultures perched on the chimney or in nearby trees, or stalked about in the sun, spreading their wings and closing them again. *Zopilotes.* Wrinkly, ash-colored heads, stench of rot and shit and carrion, ingested, metabolized, excreted. He dumped the wheelbarrow and hurried away. Immediately the zopilotes swooped or hopped in and stabbed their long hooked beaks into scraps of carcass, blood, bones. *Theirs* was the most menial and disgusting job. But they didn't mind either. They clawed, hissed, snarled. He wouldn't have believed a bird could snarl but the zopes did it all the time.

Sometimes when he was pushing the wheelbarrow down the road the zopilotes fell in close behind, hopping along so fiercely and aggressively that he began to wonder what was keeping them from coming after him with their bloody beaks and talons. He took to carrying stones. When the birds drew too near he whirled and threw one as hard as he could. They scattered at the motion but miraculously the stone caught one in the skull and it fell over. He dumped the wheelbarrow and circled the long way home. Later he looked down the road and saw the zopes standing around the body of their companion exactly as they stood around any other body, waiting for it to finish dying, to start rotting.

Whatever part of the *orgánicos* the zopilotes didn't eat the horses mainly did. There was a herd of eight or ten feral horses that came down out of the hills to range the property, drawn to gardens and irrigated fields and garbage. To human smells and voices, maybe. Whoever they belonged to must have had no use for them, or had never trained them to be useful. They were scrawny and bony, except for their swollen bellies. Flies and gnats buzzed and swarmed across their scabs and scars. Even standing still they were agitated —eyelids blinking, tails swishing, bellies twitching—and they bolted, practically stampeded, if you got too close or moved too abruptly in their presence.

Yet they loitered around the buildings and paths of the Gardens. They kicked over garbage cans and broke through fences, trampled gardens, crowded onto dormitory porches to get out of the rain. They rubbed against drying clothes and pulled them off clotheslines and embedded them with horsey smells. No one knew what to do about them, everyone was a little afraid of them.

Chele had a name for them. *Mesteños.* He had read about the feral horses of western North America, who ran in great wild bands and were captured by the Indians and turned into war ponies. It was from these mustangs of the Texas plain that the bloody Comanches had drawn their fearsome power. From horses who knew they were wild, and later knew they were Indian horses.

But these *mesteños* didn't know what they were. They didn't know what their connections were, with humans or the land or maybe even other horses. They were like the orphans—they didn't get all they needed from the Gardens but they got some part of it: food, shelter, society, the freedom to dream of another reality, maybe the open range of the Texas frontier.

He thought of his grandma's mare—how far might she have wandered, what if she were running in a feral band like this? He started taking the garbage down voluntarily, every chance he got. When the horses were there he approached them, spoke or sang quietly to them, fragments of songs his grandma had sung to her horse. Gradually they allowed him to approach. One mare, slightly less skittish, took apples from his hand, rotting bananas, old tortillas. Eventually he got a rope around her neck. She struggled but only a little, he sensed she had some memory of doing a thing like this before. Soon he was leading her around, the other horses following at a distance. He and a couple of other boys led the band down to some neighboring ranchos, where a man said he knew the people who owned them. They lured them into his little corral with handfuls of grain. The owners would come for them later, the man said.

Within two days they were back at the Gardens. Chele caught the mare again and they led the band in the opposite direction, down the mountain and across the highway to a wide plain where they found people willing to claim them straight out, squatters living in window-less mud houses and hoeing rocky, exhausted fields.

A week later the horses were back, except for the mare. She had been killed crossing the highway. For weeks she lay bloating on the edge of the pavement, with the zopilotes standing by.

Don't get sentimental about those horses, Alvaro said. They had come with the land; the previous owner supposedly had sold them but no buyer ever appeared to take them away. That owner had some idea of raising horses and he'd ended up with these pests, that could not be fenced or ridden or driven off. Trespassers, vandals. No doubt the man had treated them poorly. No doubt they suffered from PTSD. And no doubt someone would eventually come along to buy or steal them for slaughter, there was always a market for horsemeat.

Sometimes at night the smell of horses came through the window and into Chele's sleep. Hooves clattered on cement paths, large bodies bumped and jostled, grass hissed with the passage of the herd. Then he remembered a night gallop through tall grasses, heat lightning going off behind mountains and night birds scattering before him and his horse weaving in darkness among trees and buildings, with a band of yet-unbroken horses galloping behind.

But how was that a memory? The only horse he'd ever ridden was his grandma's mare—a slow, sleepy, swaying ride on the worn roads around San Miguel, heat coming up from the road and off the horse's sweating back. He'd never ridden at night, never really galloped. Yet that night ride felt like a thing that had actually happened, or that might happen yet.

He was spending most of his free time with the horses. Eventually he managed again to get a rope around the neck of one, a stallion, swaybacked and black. The horse fought the rope but Chele hung on, talking softly and walking him in an endless circle. A worker loaned him a bridle and he persuaded the horse to accept it, too, and finally to allow him to get up on his bare back and ride.

The power Chele gained over those great, nervous beasts set him apart from the other children and gave him a freedom and mobility none of them could imagine. But the horses also gained a power over him. Unguided, they carried him into epic daydreams far from St. Jerome's Gardens, off the mountain and across plains and valleys and over more mountains and finally to the ocean he had never seen, and on its shores a city that was like the only city he had seen, but darker and more terrible and unfathomable.

On horseback he entered a labyrinth of streets and buildings, narrow passageways, tunnels, bridges, high walls and cliffs. He galloped through empty streets, reined the horse in, called a name into the darkness. A girl emerged from a doorway and he pulled her behind him onto the horse. Shouts, footsteps, gunshots. The horse wheeled and galloped back through the tunnels and passageways and leapt over walls and broke through ambushes and swam a pestilent river to escape at last into the forest, where they rode slowly through groves of giant trees with her arms around his waist.

He inserted different faces into these fantasies; most of the girls he knew wanted rescuing in some form. The stories evolved and developed subplots and variations but eventually he outgrew and nearly forgot them, childish and fantastical as they were, and in the end made from elements that were lost to him. Whole neighborhoods were obliterated and the city revealed to be a darker labyrinth than he could bear to contemplate. Even dream horses refused to enter such a place. Horseless and not in a dream, he did at last go into that labyrinth and snatch a girl from its depths, but that was a bitter rescue that ended not with her body pressed against his back as they rode beneath the leafy canopy, but with burnt trees, broken faith, solitude, exile.

One hundred years after the Louisiana Purchase, the McKeanes, a last, lost band of Jeffersonian yeomen, came into the Perdu River Canyon. They turned off rutted wagon roads to follow Indian trails into a maze of canyons cartographers had yet to trace on a map. Coming to a dead stop at the confluence of two unfordable rivers, they gazed across the mingling waters at the broad delta of a third stream. Gravel bar, cottonwood bottomlands, high terrace of green grass and pine. Confluence Bar: a piece of level ground at the bottom of the steepest and deepest canyon; a few strips of fertile soil among rockslides and gravels on the shores of an unnavigable river; and one of the last places on the continent Jefferson would have imagined his yeomen settling.

> Crack Between Mountains: a History
> of the Perdu River McKeanes
> —Helen McKeane

2

THE KNIFE RIDGE

ONE HUNDRED MORE years, a dozen linear miles, and 7000 vertical feet from that homestead ranch, Galena McKeane, great-great granddaughter of homesteading yeomen, walks backwards along the spine of Indian Ridge on a path made by wild goats.

At her feet the country falls away into distances and depths. Dying forests and birthing forests and splintered outcrops of rock. Landslides, fire scars, alluvial fans, moraines. The deep shadow of the inner canyon, the bright and dark walls and spires of rough and wandering ridges.

At night black ridgelines are silhouetted against a less-black sky. She sees the prows of ships surging from a tumultuous sea. The broken frozen surface of the sea itself. The parapets of a foreign city, high buttressed walls topped with shards of metal and glass.

By daylight these mirages disappear and another country comes into focus, foreshortened in the compression of the telephoto or divided into thin slices by the vertical slot and hair of her firefinder. Or just spread out at her feet, nothing between her eyes and too much country for her eyes to take in. She breaks it down with maps and photos, histories and natural histories. She sketches points and angles, arcs, distances, memorizes azimuths and place names, invents names for the nameless places. She has a map in her head of everything she sees.

But now that map is blurred. Now she's focused on a single point fifty yards down the trail, a binary focal point she's locked onto and is resolved to stay locked onto for however long it takes to walk back-wards along the knife ridge of Indian Mountain and cross the saddle to her lookout tower, a half mile away.

The ridge is steep-sided and narrow but traversed by multiple rough paths, skirting rock outcrops, cliffs, fields of talus and scree. A dull knife. And the paths are worn into the rock less by wild goats than by errant domestic sheep, wandering up from the dry meadows they graze every summer on gentler slopes to the south.

She's wearing shorts, tank top, hiking boots. Full sun on her sweat-ing shoulders and her legs. Skin starting to burn, tan as it is and in spite of the sunscreen applied a few hours back. Radio silent in her knapsack, binoculars swinging pointlessly from her neck, sunglasses trapped in the v-collar of her shirt while her squinting eyes hold the focus and her body proceeds in a manner contrary to the engineer-ing of its muscles and joints. Assbackwards, which is to say, ass for-ward, ass leading the way up the goat path, a task nothing in its design or experience has prepared it for. Back muscles tense and cramping, knees and quads killing her. Sweaty strands of hair falling across her face, obstructing her critical line of vision, the connection between her eyes and the eyes of her pursuer.

Her pursuer. This deliberate, hypnotic pace, no distance closed or advantage gained or lost, this is *pursuit*? This blind, tedious, assfirst one-tentative-step-at-a-time propulsion is *flight*?

She reaches up slowly to push the hair back under her baseball cap. Through hard rubber soles her feet feel their way over loose rock, gnarled root, boulder and ditch. A foot lifts, hovers—over the abyss, or over skittery ground, hard rock? The foot won't know until she brings it down, makes renewed contact with the trail. Or not.

The eyes had materialized out of rock and bush. She was on the ridge trail, home stretch of a long ramble on her day off, pleasantly worn-out, spaced-out, when something made her stop, some presence or sub-audible sound activating sensors on her neck and back. She turned slowly to see a cougar on the slope below, in mid-step but not moving. A paw suspended in the air, yellow eyes fixed on her.

Cougar. Mountain lion, catamount, panther, puma. The most solitary and secretive of the large mammals, abruptly emerged into the open, watching her.

A rare sighting, first in many years for her. And a modest adventure, more thrill than fright. Cougars pose little real threat to humans, she knows that much. Actual attacks are rare, usually occurring in suburban edge country, as often as not involving an overly curious pet or unlucky jogger in a park or wooded trail of a subdivision. In the wild, the lion still mainly retains the run of its territory and feels little pressure to confront the humans—gunbearers, firestarters, casual noisemakers—who blunder through.

Yet the thrill had an edge on it. Lena and the cougar stared at each other. She turned and took a few steps up the trail. When she looked back the cat was still motionless, still holding a paw in the air. But a different paw, and a third of the distance between them closed.

A cougar not just observing but actually tracking her, *stalking* her—that was an adventure of a different color. A reminder: big cat versus human, an adversarial relationship with a long history. For most of it the human has been prey. Maybe this cougar also needed a reminder. That the tables have turned, and the human is now by far the more dangerous animal. But how to demonstrate that? Swell up, wave her arms, pick up some scraggly pine branch and wave it around? Yell, sing, dance? Get out her radio, turn up the volume and the squelch, blast the cougar with a territorial shriek of static?

Or—maintain eye contact. Stare it down, dominate it with the fierceness of her gaze. As long as their eyes are locked the cat will keep its distance. She knew that too, or thought she did. Probably she'd heard it from one of her brothers, Ben or more likely Jimmy, or years ago from her father or her uncle Clayton. Or read it in one of the natural histories or pioneer memoirs in her small summer library. Maybe even somewhere in the sprawling pages of her mother's unreadable book.

The last thing you want to do is show it your back. Which just seemed like good sense.

She edged away, tiptoed backwards a few tentative steps. When they were maybe fifty yards apart the cat made a move—one deliberate step, freeze, one paw easing forward, then another. For ten yards, twenty, they matched steps: backwards feet, forwards paws, a choreography. Impossible to travel far like that, over rough terrain. Impossible, but here she is—a half hour later? One hundred yards up the trail?—eyes still locked in, same distance between them, traversing the knife ridge, the steepest, most exposed part of the trail. Assbackwards, blindfooted.

But ass and feet are not going into it completely clueless, without at least some inkling of what they might encounter. A trail sketched out by goats and sheep, maybe, but reengineered to more human specifications. Over the course of the summer, out of that network of wandering paths and guided by roughly parallel bands of rock, Lena has defined a single trail, smoothed out tread, engineered waterbars and switchbacks, stabilized skittery outslopes with rock walls and logs, wrestled big flagstone slabs into place to make steps.

So she has some visual and tactile memory of the path ahead. Behind. She shuffles, lifts a foot, forces herself to bring it down on the unseen ground. She edges away from the escarpment, stumbles into rocky brush, scratches up against the twisted skeleton of a dead pine. Snagged by a snag. Extricates herself but loses the path entirely, bumps up against rocks and brush in all directions, with no idea where either is, trail or cliff.

She's thinking of a certain kind of drunk, profoundly impaired yet painstakingly cautious. Inadvertently she glances at her feet. When she looks up the cat has closed a little more distance between them. Could it be true, only her eyes are holding him back? Or is that just superstition, viral folk belief? Maybe looking into the eyes is a challenge, a provocation. Maybe she's just egging him on.

Cougar, the most solitary mammal. Seldom seen. Kills a deer a week. A prodigious leaper, it can leap over a bus. The long way, she has a hard time believing that.

But say it is her gaze keeping him at bay. Then what are her chances, with two or three hundred more backward paces along a rocky, cliff-hanging path still to go, then a quarter mile of somewhat easier trail crossing the saddle and climbing to the sanctuary of her lookout tower? Her muscles cramp, her eyes strain. One misstep and the game is over. How long before she catches her heel on a rock and goes down, flailing on her back exactly like wounded prey? Before her quads seize up, legs give out, she sits or drops feebly to her hands and knees, a compact, four-legged, more familiar-looking target in the cougar's crosshairs?

What she wants to do is just break off and run for it. A mad dash to the saddle, then up the summit trail to the lookout, maybe he won't follow. Or, maybe the last sound in her ears will be the whoosh and snarl of the leaping cat. The blow at her back, hot rake of claws, heat of a slobbering mouth on her neck.

Or—what if she takes one backward step too far? Her foot comes down on—nothing. She pulls back but the foot's already committed, her balance shifts, she wavers a moment on the edge then drops over the cliff, flips, tumbles, bounces, freefalls, shatters her skull and bones on the rocks below.

A misstep, or just fate? Fulfillment of destiny, prophecy, legacy. RIP Galena McKeane, born with a genetic predisposition for going backwards off of cliffs.

WWJD. What would Jimmy do. Jimmy who's spent much of his life in wild places, working offbeat jobs or hunting or fishing or just wandering around finding things. Animals, rare plants and rocks, arrowheads. Radio-tagging wolves and bears, spying on mountain goats, sitting up all night hooting at owls. Jimmy, lone male unconstrained by law or territory, who's stalked or been stalked by any number of predators. Who stands on the porch of the ranch house at night howling for his brothers, the wolves. Who can think like an animal, still remembers that he is one.

What he *wouldn't* do is freeze up fatalistically among the rocks, hard gaze gone squishy, eyes fixed with increasing desperation and fuzziness on the cougar's unblinking stare. Somehow he would engage the cat. Negotiate. Call its bluff with his own, more audacious bluff. He would know, or know how to determine, if the cat was truly hunting or just teasing, testing.

From the radio in her backpack comes a harsh sputter of static, then bits of conversation. A field crew, trying to find each other in the woods somewhere. The cougar's ears flicker. But it's the nostrils that are really going at it, sniffing and twitching, deciphering the chemistry of her body, her blood, the trail of exotic fragrances left in her wake. Sweat, sunscreen, moisturizers, hormones, pheromones. The common oozings of the adult human female, enriched and refined. She hasn't had a real bath, with soap and extended soaking, for many days.

But at least she's not on her period. She's taking full-cycle birth control pills, not so much to foil any hypothetical sperm that might wriggle up to her nest of eggs as to avoid the hygienic complications of menstruation in a place without plumbing, trash pick-up, scarcely any water. Not to mention the predation complications. Menstrual blood, not a scent you want to waft in front of a stalking cougar's nose.

Male or female? That would be Jimmy's first question. She'd have to admit she hadn't noticed. By default she'd been thinking he. But now the cougar is crouched too low to the ground to tell, too deep a shadow between its legs.

She inhales deeply and, projecting a confidence she in no way feels, takes a long, definitive, backwards step towards, she hopes, the trail. Her foot comes down on a solid, perfectly flat rock. The other foot joins it. One foot slides along the rock to another edge, ventures again into the treacherous air.

She brings it down slowly, toe first, a long, stretching distance before it meets a second flat and solid surface. Lowers the other foot beside it, inches it back to another edge, hangs it in the air again, brings it down onto yet another smooth, flat rock.

Steps. Her little handmade stone staircase beneath her backwards feet. Her steps still have a raw look, they haven't fully settled in. But to her feet they feel as if they've been in place a long time. As if they're connected to things, laid down by the pioneers themselves, or some earlier company of stoneworking humans.

So Lena comes down backwards off the knife ridge, winding between fractured slabs of granite, guided by the curve of the rock and her own smooth trail tread. A slow, sinuous descent toward the saddle and the aspen grove, canyon and mountains falling away in the distance as if with the measured turning of the earth. In the foreground the cougar still trailing, still staring.

Off the crest there's less wind. Approaching the saddle she hears scattered birdsong, the watery croak of a raven, a distant airplane engine, the light fluttering of aspen leaves. A softer and deeper sound or vibration, a low, feline rumble.

Cougar, the largest cat that purrs.

The aspen grove is a simple woodland, with few low branches and little understory or debris. Leaves tremble in a gentle breeze, half-filtered sunlight ripples across the ground. A sharp but mercurial contrast between sunlight and shadow, no place fully lit or fully shadowed, everything dappled, interchangeable, impermanent. She glides through slowly, still backwards, weaving among smooth and pale trees. Smooth but not flawlessly smooth—the trunks have been cut over the years by the blades of sheepherders, carving brief messages and pictographs that go back over a century. She skirts the edge of the empty sheepherder camp—tumbledown rock fire ring, crude log furniture, bare ground powdery with decades of fire ash and horseshit. She hardly sees it. Camp and carvings both are absorbed into the receding layers: woods and mountain and sky, shadow and glare, periphery and background. The foreground occupied entirely by the cougar. Staring eyes, twitching nostrils, thick black-tipped tail curling high into the air. Precise, beautiful movements, beautifully synched with hers. She steps backwards, the cougar steps forwards. She freezes, the cougar freezes. Eyes linked to eyes, to muscle and blood. Neither of them can break away. Maybe neither wants to. Maybe she *wants* to draw him with her along the trail. Maybe he wants to follow her into this tremulous light beneath the aspens.

The light glares and blinds, the shadow blinds too. The cougar shimmers, breaks apart, vanishes into the textured background. Then reappears beneath a different tree. The black snout gleams, the eyes glitter and dim. Hair and flesh melt away, the skeleton glows, irradiated bones. The articulation of bone, the cat walking in death, through Time.

Then it's gone. Or at least, her eyes can no longer assemble a cat-like form out of the dappled mosaic. She turns and half-walks, half-runs, up the trail to the lookout.

3

THE FUTURE

P EOPLE LOOKED at him differently when he was up on the horse's
back. Small boys trailed along behind, older boys watched from
a distance. Girls working in the garden yelled and hooted, or stood
with their hoes and stared in silence.

He'd named the black stallion Tuc-tuc. Along the roads and trails
of St. Jerome's he kept him to a trot or walk, but farther afield were
stretches of empty road or track where he could urge him into a full
gallop and feel, for a moment, untethered to any place. Tuc-tuc responded to the most subtle shifts in weight and pressure. The more
perfectly Chele balanced on the horse's back the more perfect the
horse's balance, the two of them weighting and unweighting together,
synchronized so seamlessly the earth itself seemed to shift its weight
with theirs.

But not always. Once he got thrown hard and returned limping,
with raw, stinging roadburn on his shoulder and face. He acted as
though it were nothing. After dinner Alvaro took him for a walk.

"Looks like maybe your horse isn't all the way tamed," he said. "Or
maybe it's the rider? Why not give him a rest tomorrow, and come
ride with me?"

That ride was in Alvaro's Mazda, a shortbed, extended cab pick-up.
Alvaro drove them—a half-dozen kids—to the crematorio, a giant
incinerator, landfill, and scavenging ground on the edge of the city's
sprawl. The crematorio was Alvaro's favored community service outing. You could be invited for all sorts of reasons, but this was the first

time for Chele. Not a punishment but a privilege, Alvaro said—the privilege of service, which is ultimately of greatest benefit to the person who serves.

From a distance the crematorio looked like a great white mountain, with gulls and zopilotes swarming. But the mountain was built of trash—how was it possible that so poor a country could generate such an immense quantity of trash? It was not a single mountain but a more complex terrain of multiple peaks and valleys and hills and plains, an evolving topography created by dump trucks, bulldozers, and excavators. The ground glittered with tiny fragments of glass and metal and plastic and gave off a powdery, metallic dust in the dry season that turned to a pale and greasy mud when it rained. The crematorio was a bright, glaring space among hills of dark pine and scrub, and squeezing your eyes you could blur out all detail and pretend it was something else entirely: an Egyptian desert of white quartz sand, an island of coral beaches in a dark sea, a miraculous tropical snowfall, a white city overlooking the darker city that had spawned it.

One thing it actually was: a barrio. A place where people lived and made their living. Scavenging, sifting through and extracting some final value from what others had cast away.

On a broad flat near the summit were a few dozen oversize cardboard boxes draped with tarps and plastic sheeting. The smoke of cooking fires hung over the place, but only when he saw people emerging from the cardboard did Chele understand that he was looking at houses, a settlement. People came out of the boxes and from across the open expanses to converge on the bed of Alvaro's Mazda, where Chele and the others stood passing down packets of food and clothes and bottles of drinking water.

That was their mission: to deliver food, clothes, and clean water to the crematorio people. But it wasn't the actual point of the outing. It wasn't the lesson. The lesson was about humility and perspective and empathy. It was about gratitude for their own great good fortune. They might be without family or possessions, sleeping in dormitories and working in fields and mopping floors, compelled to fall again and again into line, at school and church and pretty much wherever they went. But here was a place without beds or fields or floors or churches or schools. No lines to fall into. A place any one of them could have easily ended up inhabiting, and might inhabit yet.

Some kids just put their heads down and waited it out, let the lessons of the crematorio wash over them and quickly recede. But for Chele those lessons seemed profound, and he returned to the Gardens in a strange confusion of euphoria and horror. The fog of normalcy and routine had burned away and he saw St. Jerome's as Alvaro must have first envisioned it: a sanctuary of hope and light in a darkening world. Bumping up the gullied road through forest and pasture, he felt he was climbing to a holy mountain. A cloudburst had passed over and the land was fresh and clean. Trees heavy with epiphytes shone in a celestial light, sounding the calls of invisible birds. The gates swung open and they drove past freshly-painted buildings, cement pathways, lawns, groves of trees, rows of green corn and vegetables sprouting from black soil. Clean, healthy children, salvaged from the pits below.

He was at the center of it, a seed, a nucleus.

And somewhere in the crystalline distance: the crematorio, a different kind of nucleus.

The light faded, the vision gradually lost immediacy. He climbed to the Overlook and gazed into haze and glare, searching for that white mountain. Egyptian desert, tropical snow. He pestered Alvaro to take him back. Soon he was going voluntarily on every crematorio outing, no longer escaping with the others into the cab after they'd handed out donations, but staying outside with Alvaro and the crematorio people, listening to their complaints and supplications. Less for their benefit than for his own. Filtering their misery as they filtered trash, extracting from it an exaltation of his own circumstances, and—he hoped—an immunization against theirs.

Lying in his bunk at night he tried to imagine saving a girl from the crematorio, but the usual rescue fantasies didn't apply. Any girl there seemed beyond rescuing, transformed by her residency in the crematorio into something more like a zopilote—a human zope roosting in the shadow of her cardboard hovel, fanning black wings. Hopping and lurching along the ridge of garbage, taking flight, then swooping down on an emptying dump truck or pick-up full of involuntary philanthropists.

Worse than the crematorio in the rainy season was the crematorio in the dry season, and worse than that was the crematorio after a year of drought. The nearby mountains disappeared behind smoke and haze. Permanent fires smoldered in the garbage. Range fires blackened the surrounding ground and the unburnt scrub became a leafless desert of thorns and tangled branches. The light dulled. Trash skittered about on random gusts of wind and accumulated against the sides of the cardboard houses. Sometimes a dust devil blew up, sucking dirt and smoke and trash into its vortex and moving across the mountain as if it were going somewhere, until it faltered and dropped its dust and bits of paper and plastic and dissolved into nothingness.

The human zopilotes, parched and coated with a fine gray dust, also veered about on bursts of energy that were quickly exhausted. The orphans thrust food and clothing at them and retreated to the cab, but Chele remained outside, talking with a few kids. He could make little sense of what they said, yet somehow their voices conveyed absences and longings that stabbed at his heart. He squatted before a couple of little ones and immediately they surged into his open arms.

Others followed, piling on, shouting, laughing, jabbering. The smell was overwhelming. Alvaro called out but his voice was lost in laughter and gibberish, chanting, a sudden onslaught of zopilote children. Some nearly as big as he was, where were they coming from? They pulled his clothes, stroked his arms, his hair, breathed sweet and sour breath into his face. They hugged, stroked, pinched, tickled, scratched, tugged, punched. They clung to his legs, climbed onto his back. Someone bit his ear. He tried to stand and throw them off but faltered under the weight, lost his equilibrium, and went down beneath them, slow motion, into the pale yellow dust of the crematorio.

Then Alvaro was pulling them off and sweeping him into the truck. The zopilote children stood watching as they drove away. A girl in the back seat muttered something about the stench. Alvaro glared fiercely at her in the rear view mirror. "Yes they stink," he said. "They're the untouchables. And they are the future. We'd better watch and learn from their example."

What did he mean by that? All the long drive back to the Gardens no one spoke. Alvaro's eyes locked on the highway and he drove faster than ever and a heavier silence than ever settled into the truck cab. A truer silence, the lessons of the crematorio were nothing that could be put into words.

Alvaro took him on a walk.

"I found your grandma."

He'd ended up going to a half dozen or more San Miguels before he found the right one. *San Miguel de las Minas,* the most distant and remote San Miguel, among desert mountains in a far corner of the country. He found Chele's grandma's house but the people there said her family had moved her to the city, to an apartment in *Colonia El Porvenir.* Alvaro had found her there and spoken with her, and now he would take Chele to visit her.

They left Alvaro's car in a *parqueo* below the barrio, a dirt lot with an armed guard at the gate and a chainlink fence topped with razor wire. A man sat in a little hut behind what Alvaro said was bulletproof glass. Alvaro gave the man his car keys and the man handed him a slip of paper and they climbed the muddy street on foot. From the main road they had seen where the city abruptly ended on the steep, bare slope above the gulch of *Colonia El Porvenir,* but once they started up the street all they saw of the horizon were tightly packed houses and apartments and walls lined with metal spikes or broken glass and a sea of antennas and satellite dishes and tangles of wires on metal roofs weighted with old tires and bricks, and there seemed to be no end to it.

On the street, kids played jump rope, marbles, soccer, though there was no field or even much open ground. They stopped playing to watch him and Alvaro. Boys and men were working on cars or motorcycles or other machines, or watching others work, or just hanging around. Some were shirtless, with tattooed chests and backs, tattoos winding around their necks and onto shaved heads and faces. Alvaro said don't look. The tattoos were the mark of a *mara*, a gang, he said. But it was impossible not to look, also impossible to decipher the tattoos—a blur of labyrinths and hellscapes, pornography, violence, devotion, blasphemy. Chele both looked and didn't look, somehow, then put his head down and tucked in behind Alvaro when he felt the *mareros* looking back. Or not looking back, in a way that seemed even more menacing.

At the top of the barrio the gulch narrowed and houses and apartments were even more crammed together, rocky bluffs perforated with shallow caves on one side and on the other a steep-sided gully, where beneath improvised pilings and bridges a dark creek trickled and stank.

El Porvenir. The Future.

"I guess somebody had a different idea of how things were going to turn out," Alvaro said.

His grandma lived with a niece and the niece's family in a brick apartment built right up against the cliff, a place with no growing things or even soil. Yet her skin still smelled of plants. She rolled down her knee socks to show him her legs, all blown-out veins and ulcers, purple and black streaks and blotches. Tattoos he *could* stare at, and did. Her walking stick was gone; she shuffled around her apartment with a walker. She had allowed them to move her once, she told Alvaro. Only by the hand of the Blessed Virgin would she be moved again.

Alvaro talked with her in a tiny room in the back, while Chele sat with people he didn't know in the living room and watched TV, a movie he didn't understand. Alvaro came out, somber-faced. His grandma called him to pray a rosary for his mother. Her room was hot and smelled bad. She handed him a rosary and made him kneel beside her on the cement floor before the same Black Madonna from her house in San Miguel. Her TV was on, *noticias, sucesos.* Police and soldiers wearing black hoods pointed their guns at prisoners filing out of a house. The same short clip played over and over while the newscasters babbled on in great excitement and his grandma muttered inaudibly and shuttled her beads along.

"Are we praying for my mother."

"We're praying for you, that you don't grow up to be an addict and fornicator and blasphemer like your father and his father and all your fathers before him."

He had to pee. The toilet was in a little shack outside, on the roof. After he peed he didn't immediately go back inside. There was a view up the mountain to where the colonia finally ended. An excavator was working on the slope above. Beyond that, a man led a burro loaded with firewood down a trail, though as far upslope as Chele could see there were no trees at all, nothing to stop the expansion of the city, just as within the neighborhood there was nothing to stop its contraction: the further compression of low, compressed buildings, streets and passageways pushing like tunnels between buildings, houses built within houses, rooms further subdivided, more people crowding into smaller rooms. All of it connected—the weight of each new building on the slope above borne by the buildings below, so if you pulled a single brick out of the bottom house all of *Colonia El Porvenir* might come tumbling down on top of you.

The incinerator smoldered. Black zopilotes roosted in the pines. Gardens lay fallow, the reservoirs were fields of caked and cracking mud. There was scarcely water for cooking and bathing, none to irrigate gardens or douse the wildfires that instead they beat back with shovels and leafy branches. No one could say how those fires started. Discarded cigarettes, burning slash, a piece of glass refracting sunlight onto dry grass or paper. Spontaneous combustion in a pile of oily rags. Arsonists. Terrorists. His grandma would have blamed the Sisimiti, who loved destruction and flame and burnt hills where he could endlessly prowl and range. She herself had seen him as the fires cooled, loping across scorched ground. To Chele, riding over newly blackened fields under a smoky sky, the Sisimiti began to seem real again, and he half-expected to come across huge, backwards footprints in the powdery ash.

They cut a fireline around the perimeter of the property. They swept and mopped the dust and ash that accumulated on floors and tables. They prayed for rain, and when no rain came a few wondered aloud what were prayers for, what was God for?

A blasphemy God answered with a hurricane.

No one had seen one like this. Hurricanes pounded the coastline with wind and waves, but this one did its work almost entirely with rain. It stalled in place for days, pumping water out of the warm ocean and dumping it over the mountains, where the rivers sent it raging back to the sea. A brief and terrible hydrologic cycle that collapsed mountainsides, scoured streambeds and valleys into wide plains of rubble, carried away highways, bridges, neighborhoods, and villages, and sent a churning, muddy, impassable river through the heart of the city.

The reservoirs at the Gardens filled and overflowed in less than a day, flushing whole trees and the swollen bodies of drowned cattle over the dam. But the rocky stream channel mainly held, and most of the land at St. Jerome's was stable enough to escape serious damage. When the cloud finally lifted, the drab countryside everywhere had turned a luminescent green, streaked by red slashes in the mountains where the earth and vegetation had slid away. The road from the highway up to the Gardens was blocked by mudslides. But most of their vehicles were parked below, in a garage near the highway, and now Alvaro and some of the older kids hiked down and drove into the city to help deliver food and drinking water.

Water, the first necessity for people whose lives had been upended by an excess of water.

They drove slowly along streets narrowed by mud and wreckage and people who waited in lines or formless crowds, or walked numbly along the roadside carrying suitcases and bags. Bodies were stacked in plastic bags along the road. The air was crystal clear, and stank.

A naked woman stepped out into the intersection in front of them. She weaved around gridlocked vehicles, potholes, mounds of garbage, asphalt chunks, mud: beneath matted black dreadlocks a completely naked woman, with full bobbing breasts and great black nipples and a dark, shocking triangle of pubic hair. Through his open window Chele stared at her. As she passed before them she looked straight back at him but kept walking, her head turning to hold his gaze, until she reached the sidewalk and broke off and disappeared into the crowd.

"Another one lost to the flood," muttered Alvaro grimly. The traffic cleared and he drove on. As if he hadn't noticed how she'd locked eyes with Chele. As if he'd seen only another nameless lost soul in a lost city, not the actual woman, not the miracle of her sleek and glistening body, perfectly erect in a street where everything had collapsed.

In the Parque Central the fountains were silent. Statues of liberators and martyrs tilted and slumped in the saturated ground, as if their monumental pride had finally yielded to their monumental failure. Now they seemed to huddle in belated solidarity with the people wrapped in blankets or sitting on plastic tarps beside little bundles and piles of belongings. Chele and his companions went among them with food and water. They told terrible stories. How they'd been trapped in houses and apartments for many days and nights, desperately praying, hearing only the ceaselessly pounding rain and the roar of rushing water. That sound was everywhere—the sky, the arroyos, the streets. It seemed to come from beneath the floor, from out of the ground itself. Then within buildings of solid cement block and brick there arose a sudden smell of wet earth. Cracks appeared in floors and walls, water seeped through, they were staunching it with towels and clothing but the cracks widened and suddenly the wall or the floor burst open and a blast of muddy water, or watery mud, surged into the room to drown or smother or flush them into the streets.

The earth that had seemed so solid, a woman said to him, had turned out to be so soft.

The river that divided the city was a churning brown flood. All the bridges were gone. On the opposite side, buildings teetered on the edge of a wide gash of raw, red earth. Chele stared for the longest time before he understood that he was looking at the exact place where he and Alvaro had walked up the street in *Colonia El Porvenir*, with kids and *mareros* watching and the blackwater stream trickling below.

The mudslide had come down two days before. He was looking at the aftermath: dead mud, the living barrio flushed away in the viscous river. He could not stop looking. He made a circle out of his fingers and thumb and held it up to his eye, a monocular, a telescope. In the framed and sharpened image he saw that he was wrong. It was not yet the aftermath. The mud was not dead but oozed and churned and roiled, while pieces of his grandma's neighborhood—houses, automobiles, motorcycles, laundry, people?—heaved up and sank away again into the earth, that had turned out to be so soft.

It was horrible. Though maybe not so horrible for his grandma. Hadn't she been asking the Virgin for deliverance for years? And now the Virgin had come through for her—literally, coming through the walls of her apartment to mercifully suffocate her in the night. That was how Chele wanted to think about it. His grandma had not suffered. She had never even awoken. Gently smothered in her sleep and taken by the Mud Virgin into Her dark and eternally peaceful realm.

But Alvaro said it was more instructive to think of the underground flood not as the hand of the Virgin or God or even Satan, but rather as a consequence of the work of men, unforeseen like so many consequences. The city itself was an unforeseen consequence, growing up without design around the rich gold and silver deposits that first drew Spanish settlers to the mountain valleys. Indian and African slaves tunneled into the rock to bring the ore to the surface. Later, engineers arrived with explosives and machinery and sent new generations of workers ever deeper into the mountains. The mines gave out and were replaced by new enterprises and constructions. Improvised barrios spread up the mountain slopes, built on seemingly solid ground that in fact was just a thin crust of rock and soil and cement, covering a forgotten maze of buried mines and runoff channels that in the hurricane deluge became a system of accidental diversions and aqueducts, delivering pressurized floodwaters into the barrios built over them.

Now pumps and hoses drained the tunnels; later, bulldozers would cover them again with rock and soil and broken concrete. Which was what people did with the past, said Alvaro—sealed it off and went on living on surface networks of streets and buildings, with no thought for the networks buried in darkness below.

GROUNDTRUTH

The McKeanes did a rough survey of Confluence Bar. They filed home-stead claims, blasted and bladed in a road along the old Indian trail up the Perdu, and built a cable crossing over the river. They built dams and flumes and ditches and delivered water to land cleared of forest and rock and planted with pastures and orchards and gardens. They put up barns, houses, workshops, corrals, roads, trails. Out of purely wild ele-ments they created a fresh configuration of nature—then fell under some enchantment in their remote dominion, triggering cycles of desire, dis-illusion, and decay that have yet to run their course.

4

THE ELECTROMAGNETIC OCEAN

LYING ON HER BED in the winter mid-day dusk, Lena read these words in the manuscript of her mother's book and felt an unexpected stirring of her pooled blood. Outside, gray rain fell on pavement and dark trees and flowed in concrete channels to an inland sea, but closing her eyes she saw far below and in the summer light of twenty years ago a country of forest and stone, slashed and warped by the convolutions of canyons. And in its center, on the shores of converging rivers, that same reconfiguration of nature, still fresh to her.

She was flying with her father over the mountains to Confluence Bar. Ethan liked to fly close to the ground, following the contours along the crests of the ridges. Staying under the radar, he said. Or: I'm afraid of heights. Deadpan, ironic, his words always meant something more than they said, or the opposite of what they said. They skimmed the rocky ridgelines, the old fire lookouts and the newer communications towers, and shot through gaps where the ridges dropped off into cliffs and nearly vertical fields of shattered rock. Then that ground dropped away and all around was sky and mountains, the river and its canyon far below. The plane banked into a steep descent. Lena, on the inside of the turn, was pressed against the vibrating window, her father suspended above her and the engine howling in her ears and the earth below turning in the arc of their spiral.

Through it all she kept her head. She was just a child, spiraling fearlessly into the canyon in a tiny airplane, and everything she saw she loved without restraint, without irony. The Creation as it was manifested in the canyon and the ranch, the way it would always be wild and the way it could be worked by human hands. The alpine snow that melted into streams and rivers and was channeled into irrigation and electricity. The darting shadow of their plane on the pinegrass slope where the elk were galloping. The clear waters of the Blue River, churning out of its gorge to mix with the green Perdu and the darker flow of Antimony Creek. And directly across from that confluence, what remained of the McKeane homesteads: barns and houses and the ruins of barns and houses, orchards, gardens, glades, pastures, ditches, brown figures in the pasture that might be horses, or deer, or maybe wild boys—her woods-roaming, fish-stinking, blackberry-stained brothers, a part of the configuration.

Just above the sinuous course of the river the plane finally leveled out. Her father's voice came through the roar of the engine into her headphones. *How about a little peace and quiet.* He cut the throttle. The engine was silent. They glided. *It's always a glide,* he said. The wind howled, rapids churned below. *Flight is gliding.* At every bend the river was louder, closer. The plane rocked and bounced, as if riding the turbulence of the rapids beneath its wings. *If you have control with power, you have control without it.*

Then the engine kicked back on.

Helen had been working on her book for about as long as Lena could remember. There was no expectation on anyone's part that she would finish, and no warning, or none that Lena heard, that one dark midwinter afternoon she would come home to find on her doorstep a UPS package containing a binder stuffed with 800 double-spaced pages. On the cover page, pasted beneath the title—*Crack Between Mountains: the Story of the Perdu River McKeanes*—a sticky note, one sentence, asking Lena to please edit.

There was no chance of that. The opening pages triggered the memory, or vision, of flying with her father over Confluence Bar, and she came upon other evocative or lyrical passages, but mainly she bogged down in the density, the clutter and confusion. She couldn't bring herself to take much interest in the details of her ancestors'— or her mother's—ancient grudges and obsessions, or to sort through the tangled and fractured storylines. She had her own clutter to sort through, her own cycles of desire and disillusion. The manuscript stayed on her bedside table, mostly unread, and gradually disappeared beneath books and magazines.

Yet after she got the lookout job but before she actually came to Indian Mountain, the vision came back to her in a new context. The ranch far below; the green fields and floodlands; the confluence of three streams—seen through the window not of a spiraling plane but of a mountaintop fire tower. Motionless, flightless, but with a *sense* of motion and flight. Of centrifugal force, the suck of gravity, the lift of air.

One of several misfirings of her imagination. From her tower on Indian Mountain she had a view in all directions of mountains, forests, canyons—the country of her mother's book. And beyond, on a clear day she might see for a hundred miles. But not so much as a glimpse of the river below or even its inner canyon. Sometimes in a glaring or flat light she could scarcely even tell the canyon was there—the panorama lost its depth and the land falling away at her feet fused almost seamlessly with the land rising in the distance. She had to look hard to perceive the discontinuity, the thin seam where the canyon split the ridges.

Crack between mountains. At any moment smoke might come rising out of it.

The tower was a single wood and glass room raised on timber girders and tethered to the mountain by steel cables bolted to the rock. Windows on all four sides, more window than wall. A narrow wooden wraparound porch, the catwalk. You'll be the cat, pacing, Ben had told her. A trapdoor in the floor opened onto steep stairs, more ladder than stairs. Inside, the tiniest wood stove ever, also a propane cooking stove, propane refrigerator, propane lights. No plumbing. A small table, chair, narrow bed with a set of drawers beneath, and in the center of the room a high square table, with sliding shelves below for books, maps, sketchpad and pens, a visitor log, and a radio. On the tabletop the brass firefinder, with its circular topographical map and rotating sighting apertures, to pinpoint the location of lightning strikes and any smokes that followed.

To go anywhere she had to descend the stairs, three flights, and skitter down a rocky path through talus and wind-battered firs and twisted snags of pine to where four paths diverged. One led to the helispot and beyond to a chain-link fence enclosure on the edge of the cliff, where a microwave tower and telemetric weather station glinted in the sun and made thin, metallic sounds out of wind. Another to the outhouse, tucked away among some firs. The third went to the spring, gushing out of the ground amid ferns and flowers in a gulch a steep quarter mile away.

Two or three times a week she strapped a five gallon jug to a backpack frame and went for water, filling the jug from a short pipe that tapped the springwaters, then hauling it back uphill. Five gallons, good for three days drinking, cooking, sponge-bathing, at the cost of a quart or two of sweat.

The fourth path led to the aspen grove and sheepherder camp at the wide saddle in Indian Ridge a few hundred yards below the lookout, where the old sheep driveway came up from the Blue River highlands. Gouged into the biggest aspens, some now lying on their sides, were dates, initials, names of herders, their wives, girlfriends, children, hometowns in Spain or Mexico or Peru. Pictorial carvings both crude and skilled. Animals—horses, dogs or wolves, deer, cougars. Human faces and bodies. Breasts. Genitalia: penises; fierce scribblings of pubic hair; dark, disembodied vulvas gouged into the cambium. A hundred years of desperate loneliness and horniness on display beneath the aspens.

Beyond the saddle, the driveway took a long, meandering loop away from the jagged ridgeline, crossing open grassy slopes and shallow drainages to rejoin the main ridge two miles away. Her shortcut trail—the cougar's trail—cut off almost a mile of that, following the narrow, rocky crest until the ridge broadened and met the main driveway. That was a vaguely-defined strip of permanently trampled ground descending the spine of Indian Ridge—deep canyon of the Perdu on one side, open cirques and broader valley of the Blue on the other—down to the confluence, the bridge over the Perdu, and the McKeane Ranches on Confluence Bar.

Lena had not followed any trail far. She'd come to Indian Mountain by helicopter, stepping out onto a small piece of leveled ground in the center of a circle of painted white rocks. The helicopter departed and there she was in the midst of sky and mountains, alone.

Now, standing on the catwalk or sitting on her stool inside the lookout cab, she studied those mountains, through binoculars or wheeling her firefinder around and lining up in its sights feature of her Seen Area: the country she could see most clearly and in greatest detail and was charged with watching over, to keep any more of it from going up in smoke. She divided it into thin, triangulated slices, memorized points and lines, azimuths, distances, place names, the names of fires that had already burned.

Flying with her father, she remembered solid green forest extending to the horizon, interrupted here and there by a patch of meadow, modest fire scar, rocky ridge, clearcut. That world had seemed stable, constant. But the country she now looked out on was fire-scarred everywhere: black from recent burns, and older burns where stark, pale snags emerged from the brush. Even the green forest was mottled with the grays and browns of dead trees, primed to burn.

Beyond her Seen Area, seemingly endless layers of mountain and valley. Silhouettes, shadows, strips of shifting light. The far horizon indistinct, hazy, brownish, and thick, even on the clearest days. She had a name for that, too. The Smudge. Territory extending indefinitely in all directions which no power of magnification could bring into focus. A dead-looking place, remote. Yet out of it rose a constant, silent wind. A gush of electrons, photons, quanta. High on Indian Mountain, she was submerged in an oceanic flood—data, news, lies, rumor, illusion, speculation, music, dream, formula, desire, superstition, propaganda, manifesto, hallucination, noise—all ceaselessly issuing from the Smudge, saturating the atmosphere, radiating into space.

Submersion in an electromagnetic ocean—it hadn't been like that on Indian Mountain for long, and certainly nothing at all like it a century ago, when the McKeanes laid claim to the country. The effects were unknown. Submersion, and disconnection. She tapped into none of it. There was no internet connection, no wires or wireless, no cell phone. She had a work radio, tuned to narrow frequencies and narrow concerns. A pair of binoculars, pulling things a little closer while she looked for smoke, motion, a clue.

She was in high school the first big fire year, when a half million acres of forest burned and it seemed the green country of her childhood had been reduced in a matter of days to ash and charcoal. For most of the summer those fires burned. She'd meet with friends at the lake to swim, hang out, sometimes drink or smoke something. They'd sit on the beach and gaze past the chaotic weave of motorboats and jet skis at three huge smoke plumes boiling up into a perversely clear, blue sky. The largest to the northeast, over the Perdu country, in the exact line she'd flown with her father to the ranch.

The unreal sky, the frivolous trajectories of the watercraft, the mushrooming smoke—it was as if an apocalypse were upon them. The smoke plumes looked like explosions that had already happened. Like screen images, remote and static. But tightening her focus she could see the ongoing eruption, smoke churning violently out of a dark glowing core.

Town traffic was heavy. Trucks, buses, engines, crew cabs, heavy machinery. Retardant planes rumbled through the passes and over the lake on a low-angled landing trajectory. Red-stained bellies passed low overhead. The sky boomed. On the near hills, runners of smoke and flame streaked the ridges. Trees exploded as if drenched in gasoline. Helicopters swooped in to drop water from dangling buckets, hundreds of gallons but absurdly tiny against the scale of the blazes they were attacking.

A great mustering of forces to defend her forest, her town. But she had no role in the defense. Stunned, stoned daughter of a country that in living memory has known only peace, she could only sit on the beach and watch as war and ruin finally and inevitably bore down on her.

But in the end neither town nor ranch burned. The winds carried the fire elsewhere, through mid-slope chaparral into the dense, half-dead forests in the higher country. Ben, a smokejumper in those days, returned from the fires awed and exhilarated. He described a wall of flame 200 feet high, entire blazing forests laid down in corkscrewed patterns by superheated cyclonic gales. Apocalyptic. But it was no apocalypse, he said. These fires were not harbingers of catastrophe but simply repetitions in a natural cycle. Carbon shuffling, the business of nature. Humans meddled and muddled, for one hundred years we'd suppressed fire and as a consequence the forests had grown dense and flammable until, inevitably, fire could no longer be suppressed. Now accounts were coming due. But the math was the same as always. Everything fell within some range of 'normal', as long as your timeframe was broad enough.

And now Ben himself was doing the math. He had study plots and field crews all over the national forest. He had databases, models, maps. He was a fire ecologist, probing fire, seeking to understand its nature, he said. The nature of the compound organism that was fire and man.

But three mushroom clouds exploding on a clear horizon. How was that normal? How was that not a harbinger?

5

BOOK OF QUESTIONS

COLONIA EL PORVENIR was gone, flushed away or buried in mud, yet Chele's thoughts kept going back there. Before the mud, to his grandma's apartment, where *sucesos* played and replayed on the TV screen while she pulled him to the floor to pray an interminable rosary. Not for his lost mother but for him, an innocent child.

He should have stopped her. He should have said: why not my mother? Then demanded that she tell him something real about her. All he had was her name, Maribel Cruz. Alvaro said that of course he'd asked about her when he was in San Miguel. People remembered her but no one could say what had become of her. The little he knew he'd learned from Chele's grandma, when they visited her in *Colonia El Porvenir*.

"My grandma told you about my mother? Why didn't you tell me!"

"There was no point. You weren't ready. You never asked."

"I'm asking now."

Alvaro watched him for a long while in silence. Finally he spoke.

"She told me that she first saw you, first knew of your existence, when you were three years old. You got off a bus in San Miguel, alone, with an envelope pinned to the front of your shirt. Inside were your birth certificate, medical papers, and a short letter. She gave them to me. I still have them. There's no father's name on the birth certificate. Just your mother's—Maribel Cruz. A single last name, the same as yours. But not the same as your grandma's. Because she *wasn't* your grandma. She was your mother's *godmother,* not her mother. When you got off that bus, it had been years since she'd seen Maribel. The smartest, most beautiful girl in town, she told me. Too smart, too beautiful. The town couldn't hold her. When she was fifteen she ran off with a miner. That letter on your shirt was the first your grandma had heard from her in years. She wrote that she'd had the virus—HIV—but was feeling better now. That she was starting a business on Calle Cortez, in Barrio Colón. But living in that city was not healthy for a child. She was sending you to the campo to live as a child should, and would come for you as soon as she was able.

"The medical card was from the public hospital. It showed you'd had a positive test for HIV at birth. To your grandma—who's not your grandma, right?—that meant you had the virus too. Which at that time meant you'd get sick, infectious, probably die. But she took you in all the same."

"I have AIDS?"

"No. We tested your blood when you came here and you were fine. We've tested it several times since, to be sure. The hospital test may have been a false positive. Or you were born with the virus in your blood but it went away. That can happen with young children. You were lucky, it seems."

"But my mother had it. And then she was better. So she was lucky too."

Alvaro sighed. "That's what she wrote. Who knows. Your grandma never heard from her again. But this virus usually *doesn't* just go away. And back then there was no cure. No treatment even, or none for people like her."

Late at night Chele got out of his bunk to pee, then slipped out of the building and made his way through the woods to sit on the hill above the dark courtyard of the girls' compound. A place he mainly avoided during waking hours, when it was common to hear from behind the high brick wall melodramatic wailings, squeals of false hilarity, a shrieking and clamoring that brought actual physical pain to the ears. Advertisements for a female chemistry of caustic and abrasive substances. Even when the compound was more or less quiet it gave off a sense of agitation; in whatever small sounds escaped he heard intimations of discontent, trouble brewing.

Yet at night the place fell truly silent and all that noxious energy went out of it. Under the unreal moonglow of security lights courtyards and dormitories seemed to pulse slowly. They seemed to breathe, as the girls themselves were breathing: asleep in their bunks, stacks and rows of beds and girls, breathing the only motion. Brown arms and black hair thrown back across white sheets and pillows, tongues slack in soft mouths, mouths open and exhaling an odorless, intoxicating gas—product of an entirely different female chemistry—that drifted over his own sleeping dormitory to draw him out to his hillside vigil.

There was a rustling of grasses and the horses appeared as shadows weaving among the pines and tall grass. They stopped abruptly. It was too dark to see but he sensed their heads were up and nostrils open; they'd caught his scent and were trying to determine the nature of the trespass into their nocturnal territory. He whispered and the horses hesitated, started at some other sound, broke away. He heard more than saw them trot down the path, then coming out onto the road above the dormitory for a moment they became visible against the light-colored gravel, a single fluid and shifting shadow that fled clattering down the road and went silent and invisible into the darkness.

The bicycle that had spooked them stopped on the path below.

"Chele. What the hell are you doing here?"

He might have asked the same of Alvaro. What are you doing, riding your bike out here at this hour, always vigilant, how did you even see me sitting motionless on the hillside in the dark?

Alvaro got off his bike and walked him back to the boys' compound. What was he doing out there? Who was he waiting for? Chele made no answer. How to explain that he wasn't waiting for anyone, there was no particular girl, it was the entire colony drawing him in. The narcotic reach of female sleep, the buildings themselves breathing and dreaming. The horses passing through night grasses like spirits escaped from the girls' dreams.

Well, he couldn't say anything like that. But Alvaro's silence he could stand only so long.

"I like being around the horses at night," he finally blurted.

There was a computer lab at school but in those days nobody had their own computer. They were still writing in notebooks, *cuadernos*. He kept a stack of them in his locker. Over the years he'd filled them with questions and answers copied from blackboards or teachers' dictations, and memorized verbatim for exams.

What are the principal muscles in the human leg?

The principal muscles in the human leg are the Gracilus, Sartorius, Rectus femoris, Vastus lateralis, Vastus medialus, and Tibialus anterior.

What is the symbolism of the stars on the nation's flag?

The blue star indicates the principle of sovereignty and individual liberty. The red star represents the principle of sacrifice in defense of the homeland. The white star stands for peace.

Define Chastity.

Chastity is the virtue of using the gift of sexuality in the right way, regardless of whether one is single, married, or vowed.

What was the achievement of the indigenous warrior Lempira?

Lempira was a Lenca cacique who unified Indian resistance against the Spanish invaders and successfully defended, for a time, the great rock fortress of Cerquín, until he was assassinated by a Spanish sniper.

State the purpose of the mouth.

The purpose of the mouth is to ingest food, aid in respiration, and emit sounds and speech.

What is the Law of Supply and Demand?

The Law of Supply and Demand states that demand for a commodity or service, and correspondingly its price or value, is inversely proportional to its supply.

He mostly didn't mind school. He was good at it—a rare reader of books, quick with answers, routinely praised for his dedicated pursuit of knowledge. But at some point it occurred to him that there had been no pursuit. School was mainly a question of absorbing the information you were fed and regurgitating it when called upon. The more you absorbed, the more you understood how insignificant it all was beside the vast body of information left unabsorbed. And the more you contemplated the depth and breadth of your own ignorance, the more you understood how much deeper and broader was the ignorance of your teachers, who were just regurgitating something *they'd* been fed, with no thought for why they were feeding it back to you or what use it might ever be to you or how any of it might connect to the actual heat and tumult of the world.

Alvaro gave the teachers pep talks that turned into lectures. He sent them to workshops, took them on retreats. They returned with awkward games and a lot of talk about creativity and critical thinking. And kept writing more or less the same stuff on the blackboards, that kids kept copying mindlessly into their *cuadernos*.

Alvaro decided to set an example. Chele's last year of high school he taught his own class: Reason and Discourse. An honors class, only top-ranked students.

The first day he wrote on the board.

Thinking.

That's the subject of this class, he said. The subject of school. Or should be.

Then he wrote:

Thoughts become words
Words become actions
Actions become habits
Habits become character
Character becomes DESTINY

They copied this in their *cuadernos*.

"Now," said Alvaro, "put the *cuadernos* away. You're not going to be copying stuff down. What I want you to do in this class is more difficult. I want you to listen. Truly listen. If you do that, you'll begin to think.

"I'll ask questions, lots of them. But don't think that means I'm looking for some 'right answer'. There might not be one. Or the right answer isn't what's interesting. What's interesting is how you look at the question. Is there a better way to ask it, is it even the right question, what other questions follow from it? What analogies, examples, counter-examples? Is there some failure of logic, a fallacy, a contradiction? Is it part of an algorithm, a syllogism? Syllogism, who can give me an example of a syllogism?"

Nobody had any idea what Alvaro was talking about. He wasn't looking for the right answer, what could that mean? Wasn't that the reason they were all sitting there, in Alvaro's special class, because they had a history of producing right answers? Not that anyone could think of one now. Analogy, they drew a collective blank. Syllogism, a total blank.

Everybody looked at Chele. He was looking at the blackboard.

Thoughts become words

Words become actions

Actions become habits

Habits become character

Character becomes DESTINY

Was that a syllogism? An algorithm? How about a fallacy or contradiction? Like claiming you aren't looking for an answer, then turning around and demanding one.

He was nineteen years old. He had gotten a late start but had now been in school for a very long time and was only at this moment realizing just how sick of it he was. Sick of cramming his knees under a desk, of staring at blackboards, whiteboards, *cuadernos*, computer screens, it didn't matter. Sick of copying, absorbing, regurgitating.

Sick of the casual hypocrisy of school, that corrupted thinking, even Alvaro's thinking. Maybe *Reason and Discourse* would be different but Alvaro was too late, and starting off on the wrong foot besides.

So Chele was silent. For the entire semester of Reason and Discourse he said nothing, wrote nothing. He passed the time daydreaming, or drawing pictures in his *cuaderno*, or writing down questions. His own, not Alvaro's. No answers.

> *What does the crematorio smell like to the zopilote people?*
>
> *Would a zopilote die of starvation before it kills to eat?*
>
> *What became of the gold they took out of the tunnels beneath the city?*
>
> *Where had the naked lunatic come from, where was she going? Why had she stared at me so hard, for so long?*
>
> *What does it mean for a deadly virus to 'go away'? Where does it go? What does it leave behind?*

GROUNDTRUTH

The McKeanes came into the Perdu country and opened it up, put it to work. But now that country has closed back in. Travelers are few and mostly unseen, making their way through hidden canyons and dark forests, past great rotting saw-cut stumps, decaying log decks and firewood rounds, overgrown trails and roads, strands of rusty cable. Burned-out cabins, stone walls buried under fallen timber and flood debris. Mounds of dirt and rock. Shallow pits. A name scratched onto a rock. A few older artifacts: shards of pottery, an arrowhead, a smooth stone that could have been a tool. Or a grave marker. But no burial grounds. Yet people lived and died here, where are the bones?

The bones are scattered; they died already buried, or in unburiable ways.

6

OPTICS

S UMMER OF LEARNING to see. A practice, a meditation. To see like a child or an animal, no filters of history or culture. To see surface patterns that reveal the subsurface, to see anomalies in the patterns. To see what happens when you see nothing happening.

To see without eyes. She'd felt a shiver of electricity along her back, turned—a cougar. She'd walked the knife ridge blind and backwards, how? Had the cougar somehow guided her? When she tried it now on open, level ground she shuffled, stumbled, could barely force herself to move.

Summer of pick and shovel, muscle and sweat. Summer of excavation—earth and stone, mountain path, something in the core of her being that over time had been buried beneath confused and inauthentic versions of herself.

She rebuilt the ridge trail, scraped and painted the lookout, whitewashed the rocks that defined the helispot. She split and stacked firewood and carried it by the armload up the nearly vertical stairs. She arranged and rearranged her few pieces of furniture, scrubbed the floor, washed windows, swept the cab and the catwalk and all 35 steps daily, gathered fresh bouquets of wildflowers for the table and windowsill.

On her days off she ranged, following old paths or game trails down into the huckleberry patches of the mid-elevation forests, scratching her arms and staining her clothes and gorging herself on the small purple-blue berries, tiny, tart jewels of concentrated flavor.

She trekked out to the previous year's burn in Finney Creek in search of morel mushrooms. She took a fishing rod up into the cirque lake basins at the head of the West Fork and caught trout, laid them on the coals of an open fire and showered them with salt and ate them with her fingers, as she'd done with her brothers years ago. She dove into icy turquoise water, scrambled out, lay naked in the sun on polished granite slabs. Polished by ice, warmed by sun.

Pikas and marmots whistled among the rocks. Hawks, ravens, vultures glided out over the escarpments. Small bands of elk cows and calves emerged from forest shadows at dusk to graze the meadows beyond the saddle. An owl swooped beneath the aspens. One night, four black bears shambled into the open under a bright moon, stopping here and there to flip over a rock and graze on whatever they'd uncovered.

She heard airplanes. Birdsong, birdwing. Coyotes wailing. In the distance, wolves? The radio crackling, disembodied voices talking. The wind, almost a constant. The river—was she really hearing it, or just the wind again? Or something else? It was hard to distinguish foreground from background, the outer world from the inner. Sounds impersonated each other, ventroliquized. Sometimes the wind was calm and still the air hummed.

She saw no cougar or cougar sign. But at random moments on the periphery of her vision she caught some motion or anomalous color or pattern. Or felt, more faintly, that electric tingle on her back. But when she turned, nothing. Once, returning to the tower, she put a hand on the rail and heard a rustling overhead, felt a shadow fall. Then looked up two flights of stairs to see for a split second through the iron grill of the walkway a shape pacing the narrow, wraparound porch that all summer she'd been calling—mindlessly, prophetically—the catwalk.

Hallucinations, visualizations. Her own mind trying to spook her. Or maybe just habituate her to the presence of the cougar, who in truth *was* out there somewhere, moving in perfect stealth and camouflage, never seen and therefore present at any given moment, watching from any shadow or mask of leaves and branches, the cougar's eyes now the eyes of the country.

She read. Kept a journal, sporadically. Collected plants and seeds, listened to the calls of birds, imitated them. She had a book on how to draw and she worked on that some, exercises in perspective, shading, pure observation. She studied Spanish—workbook exercises, children's stories, conversations with a dialogue program downloaded to her computer.

> ¿Cuánto tiempo piensa quedarse en la isla?
> No sé, todavía no he comprado boleto de vuelta.

> Oye, ¿te gustaría probar una copa de vino?
> Gracias, muy amable, pero tengo que estudiar.

> ¿Piensa usted que va a llover?
> ¡Ojala que no! Se me ha olvidado mi impermeable.

She scanned for smoke, that was the job. Methodically moving around the catwalk, breaking her Seen Area into quadrants and scanning through binoculars along invisible transect lines, back and forth over ridges and valleys, forest, brush, rock, a dozen times a day. Every now and then something would catch her eye. She'd hold the binoculars as still as possible, tighten the focus, and gradually perceive the illusion that had deceived her. Not smoke caught in a slanted light over the West Fork but just a dusky stand of dead trees, killed by insects or wildfire. Not smoke choking the Red Mountain saddle but the great pile of unmilled ore left behind when Galen McKeane's Ledorah Mining Company suffered its literal and figurative collapse. Not smoke rising from the hidden cleft of Poison Springs but the sulfurous steam of hot springs, where a row of algae-stained bathtubs and shallow travertine pools were all that remained of Olympus Springs, Josie McKeane Pratt's visionary spa resort. Not smoke hanging over the Blue River highlands but a dustcloud kicked up by the sheep and horses of Peruvian herders, moving their bands along the old driveways into summer pastures. Not smoke but a strand of mist rising out of the canyon above the McKeane Ranch at Confluence Bar, where Jimmy McKeane was resurrecting the homestead, or pretending to, moving irrigation pipe and pasturing horses and trying to make up his mind which of the thousand or so things that were broken he would try to fix next.

In the evenings, under a propane light, she began to read her mother's book. Her *book*—the manuscript had metamorphosed and there now existed an actual artifact, a book. Self-published, but still. Quality paper, readable font and formatting, acknowledgments and references and a couple of simple hand-drawn maps. Serviceable if uninspiring cover art—a slightly schematic pen and ink map of Confluence Bar, with a generic-looking homestead cabin in the foreground.

It was dauntingly thick. Dense. No mention of an editor. But there it lay on the pine crate that served as her bedside table: *Crack Between Mountains: a History of the Perdu River McKeanes.* A catalyst, hadn't it in some way taken her to Indian Mountain? She would read it all the way through over the course of the summer, whatever the challenges.

7

HORSETAMING

CHELE WAS clearing his plate in the dining hall when Alvaro appeared.

Vamanos, Chele. Bajemos la comida un poco.

He took his time cleaning up and making his way outside to where Alvaro waited. They walked in silence for what seemed an especially long time. Digesting. Finally Alvaro spoke.

"I hear you're going around saying you're done with school."

Chele shrugged.

"You'll graduate in a year. But fine. Don't go. You don't like school, you don't have to go."

What did that mean? It was okay with Alvaro if he dropped out of school? Another long silence. Excruciating pace. Finally Alvaro spoke. But now he wanted to talk about the horses.

"They've changed. They're calmer. Less destructive, less panicky. You're riding that black one, amazing. He was wild and you tamed him. You seem to have a gift. But what to do with it? The horses still have nowhere to go, no purpose. The gift is wasted."

More silence. Then Alvaro changed the subject again, or seemed to:

"You know how certain kids here never find their way? Never come to terms with whatever happened to them before they came here. What they came out of. Maybe they barely remember it. But the trauma stays with them. The fear, anger, the wildness. PTSD, like the horses. And no one's dealing with it. No one's taming *them*. We don't have the time. Or the skill, maybe. But—what if you do? You came out of something like that yourself, we don't know exactly what. And here you are, horsetaming. Maybe it has other applications."

They kept walking. Chele waited.

"You don't like school. Okay. What about a job instead? What if you became—a kind of peer counselor? A mentor. School time you spend with these kids. You work, play, watch TV, study, read to them. Most have never opened a book. Talk to them, *listen* to them. No one's ever done that. Just *be* with them, the way you are with the horses."

From tamer of horses to mentor, tutor, companion, and tamer of half-feral kids. Mustangs. *Mesteños*. He helped keep them on track with schoolwork and chores. They played cards, chess, listened to music, practiced dance routines, brought pails of *orgánicos* down to the horses. He read to them, fantasies, kid stories. They swam or played in the reservoir shallows. They hiked to the Overlook to get some geographic perspective on the little world of St. Jerome's Gardens, and to gaze out on the large world they'd come out of and to which someday they were bound to return.

At first he did most of the talking. Later, some of them opened up and he did as Alvaro said, just listened. Other times there were no words at all. You could calm a *mesteño* with a gentle touch, sometimes. Or a gentle touch might just set it off.

He and Alvaro took them on service trips. To the crematorio. To a home for brain-damaged children, where they sat on the floor and pretended to play with kids who could hardly sit up or hold a toy. To *Ciudad de Luz*, a care center for the destitute and incapacitated, hidden in a scrubby urban wilderness on the outer edge of the city, where the *mesteños* spent the afternoon whacking grass and brush with machetes while demented old people lurked about making bird calls and sounds of distress and set out across the bush in wheelchairs until they bogged down and were rescued by a finger-wagging nun.

They went on cultural excursions. To the National Library, the University, the palaces of government, the National Gallery. On the trip to the Gallery something came up at the last minute and Alvaro couldn't go, but he told Chele to take them on his own. So he and a half dozen *mesteños* hiked down to the highway early in the morning and flagged down a bus and rode it all the way into the colonial center of the city, the *Ciudad Vieja*.

The National Gallery was a restored eighteenth century villa in the middle of a city block, a rectangular stone building of ten or twelve high-ceilinged, plastered rooms wrapped around an interior courtyard and garden. There were no other visitors. The woman who sold them tickets barely looked up from her computer. Two guards with automatic rifles wandered in and out of the rooms. A man wearing a suit emerged from a back room and followed them around.

If Alvaro had been there maybe it wouldn't have all felt so intimidating. The rifles, the suit, the antiquity and emptiness and hushed solemnity of the building. The ancient creaking floorboards, mahogany, teak? The paintings and artifacts themselves, enclosed in giant gilded frames or sealed off beneath thick glass. There was a room of Indian stuff, pottery shards and baskets and clay masks and little handworn stone tools and animal totems scratched into the face of a rock. A dusty diorama of an Indian village. A cutaway scale model of a thatch dwelling, no windows, smoke and shadow, shriveled plants hanging in the doorway, shrivelled tortillas on the stove. A more primitive version of his grandma's house, lit not by votive candles and a TV screen but by fake candles and a fake fire.

There was a profusion of angels, saints, Virgins, Christs. A series of paintings told the story of the suffering and exaltation of Jesus at the Stations of the Cross. Rooms or sections of rooms were devoted to the Conquest, the colonial era, the wars of independence and other wars and battles, revolutions, counter-revolutions. Fantastic landscapes, Indian cities now lost if they'd ever existed, armies poised for victory or annihilation on the battlefield. Portraits of presidents, emperors, chieftains, governors, noble savages and ordinary savages and the mustachioed and epaulleted conquerors and liberators of America. Princesses and concubines and matrons, *quinceañeras* in velvet and lace, virtuous and poised and a little stunned-looking, as if they'd just stepped out of High Mass in Madrid to find themselves on a muddy street in America, swarming with Indians and Africans.

The *mesteños* lost interest in the paintings and waited awkwardly in the courtyard under the mistrustful eyes of the guards. Chele wandered into another room. A painting of a nude woman covered half a wall. She leaned back against a table, downcast eyes, hands on a tabletop, smoky hair falling over pale breasts, pale thighs coming together in a shadowy blur of even more ethereal hair. He stepped closer and the light and shadow shifted, the painting blurred, smeared, disintegrated into coarse brushstrokes and globs of paint, a mess. As if the painter had set out to strip the layers of clothing off the regal *damas* and *quinceañeras* and Madonnas of earlier centuries, and streaks and blotches were all he'd managed to reveal.

"What are you looking at, Chele?"

A *mesteña* had slipped into the room to stand beside him. Tania Torres, a recent arrival. Skinny, watchful, quiet. She pushed some hair out of her face and looked sideways at him.

"I bet if Alvaro was here you wouldn't be studying that picture so hard."

"It wouldn't make any difference."

"Do you ever make pictures, Chele?"

"Some. When I was little."

"Naked ladies?"

He just looked at her.

"Maybe you should try. You couldn't do worse than this: all washed-out and blotchy and lumpy and saggy, makes you want to just turn off the lights."

Behind a curtain of greasy hair her black eyes glittered strangely. The man in the suit was watching from the doorway.

"It's time to go," said Chele.

But already he was imagining his painting. He'd paint the only naked lady he'd ever seen—the *loca desnuda* crossing the intersection in the aftermath of the flood. Her hurricane eyes, looking straight into his eyes even as she passed him by. A sheen of sweat or floodwater on her dark skin. The curve and shimmer of her neck. Black-nippled breasts, counterbalanced by a black wad of dreadlocked hair. By the whorled black triangle at the center of her symmetry. The world around her a hopeless mess, washed-out, smeared, all sags and lumps, but her shape and proportions perfect—perfect alignment, perfect geometry, perfect textures.

He'd put her in a gilded frame, hang her on a wall in the National Gallery.

When new kids came to St. Jerome's you usually didn't hear much about their previous lives. The focus was on moving as quickly as possible beyond whatever wretched circumstances had brought them there. But the story of the Torres girls everyone had watched on television. *Las huerfanas de la mara*: three motherless, fatherless girls who had lived with the *mareros* for years, cooking and cleaning and performing who knew what other duties, prisoners and servants and maybe accomplices, hidden away in an apartment complex the police knew better than to enter. Nobody knew where the girls had come from or what had become of their parents or whether Torres was even their real name. Alvaro had heard about them from a social worker and had argued with and threatened and finally shamed or bribed people in the Ministry into giving him custody. But on the appointed day no one showed up at the apartment except Alvaro and a TV camera crew. So there he was on the six o'clock news, making his way unarmed past hard-looking men and women who turned away from the camera or stared defiantly into it. He entered the *mareros'* building with nothing in his hand but a paper from the Ministry. The camera panned the building and the neighborhood, to show how rough and dangerous they were, then zoomed in on Alvaro emerging with two girls, while the reporter told how the *mareros* had stood by and watched him take these two youngest Torres girls away, though the oldest, the 16 year-old, refused to leave. Or the *mareros*, still having a use for her, refused to allow her to leave.

It was all over the TV news for a couple of days. So everyone knew the story.

Nobody knows the story, said Alvaro. You're watching *sucesos* on trash TV, you think that's the story? But you don't need to know it. It's up to Tania and Paola, if they want to tell it.

It turned out that Tania did. Gradually she began to talk. Soon she was talking all the time. Her voice was strangely deep, throaty, slack. She dropped her s's and left words half-pronounced, sentences half-formed, as if open to alternative meaning and possibility. An image of the girls' apartment took hold in Chele's mind, almost as if he had been there himself, inside the windowless room where Tania and her sisters watched TV for long tedious days with little food or company, followed by sudden unpredictable gluts of both. People, mainly men and boys, came and went, some familiar and others she'd never seen before and never saw again. Sometimes they appeared in the house and you didn't know how they'd gotten in, not through the front door. The rooms were full of smells: fried food, cigarettes, alcohol, marijuana, chemicals, men's bodies. Doors opened into rooms the girls never entered, that the *mareros* kept locked with electronic locks no one could pick, you had to know the code. They went about shirtless. They exchanged things: passwords, money, packages, weapons. They lifted weights. They took her older sister into a room behind the locked doors. They stood around with their hands on their own junk. They sat on the girls' bed watching movies: martial arts, cartoons, *lucha libre*, sex. A *marero* sat motionless for hours on the edge of the bed, while another tattooed on his chest a man strapped to an electric chair. Jesus on the cross was already on his back, barbed wire coiled around his nipples, snakes and skulls climbed his neck and onto his face.

Once a dead man was laid out on the bed all day. At night they carried him off.

He didn't know what to believe of it, the way he'd never known what to believe of the *sucesos* on his grandma's TV, no matter the graphic evidence, the footage of exploded faces, dismembered bodies lying in a field. *Suceso, algo que sucede.* That had been Tania's life, supposedly: one *suceso* after another, blood and sex all over her screen, right from the start. Though you had to wonder how she'd witnessed so much drama in her shrunken territory, no windows, or the windows blacked out. Her window was the television. Or maybe through gaps in doors and curtains she really did have a larger and truer view of the world. St. Jerome's was not the real world, Chele understood that much, notwithstanding Alvaro's field trips to the crematorio and refugee camps and homes for spazzed-out kids and castoff old people. The real world was disfigured with bodies and blood. With apartments like Tania's, *mareros* with their hands on their own junk, muttering passwords, carrying guns and packages, emerging at night from barrio pits and crevasses, from storm drains and sewers and the pressurized labyrinths beneath the city. Conducting business, driving the economy of the country.

Tania had seen all this; she was street-smart. Apartment-smart, anyway. On the other hand, she was possibly the most ignorant person he'd ever met. She'd never been out of the city before, knew nothing of forests, animals, water. How to grow things, where food comes from, electricity, what happens when you flush the toilet. Chele took her around, showed her the reservoir and irrigation canal, the brick-making, composting, sewage treatment and water purification systems, the dairy, vegetable gardens, pig and chicken operations. The slaughterhouse with its death smell and basins of blood.

Chicken blood, she said, unimpressed.

But she liked story hour, *Harry Potter* held her attention for at least a little while.

Meanwhile her complexion had improved, she'd put on weight and muscle. Almost ovenight she'd developed breasts, hips and buttocks, the contours of a woman's body. The same transformation was happening to lots of girls, sure, but it seemed to Chele that in none was the contrast so dramatic, and the effect—the work-in-progress—so beguiling. So unsettling. Tania herself seemed unsettled. Or maybe energized, animated. She'd cleaned herself up, washed and brushed her hair, trimmed her bangs. Sometimes she wore make-up, eye shadow and mascara and a light scattering of glitter around her eyes. Or had the glitter always been there? But still she did not quite meet his gaze. Even looking straight at him her eyes seemed to bypass his, as if she were looking through his eyes into the unfocused distance.

Her stories about the *mareros* kept evolving. Now she said her parents had been addicts who had sold their daughters to the *mareros* as slaves. But it wasn't so bad, being a slave. They didn't have to work too hard, a little cooking, a little cleaning. The *mareros* brought them presents, toys, dolls, when they remembered, and treated them kindly, even tenderly. They were like uncles or big brothers, sometimes. They taught them dance steps, martial arts moves, wrestling holds, a little schoolwork, even. They spoke a gangster language, hard to understand and full of codes and secret messages, she listened to their speeches and arguments and was beginning to figure things out, lots of things, when Alvaro showed up and took her away. She knew she'd been sold again. Alvaro thought he had some special power, he thought he was paying a bribe to the *Ministerio* but in fact he was buying a slave from the *mareros* and didn't know it. A slave who wasn't ever going to so much as lift her little finger for him. Maybe a different finger.

She talked and talked. Sometimes maybe mixing in some of the *mareros'* language and that was one reason he couldn't really understand her? But still he paid attention. Of course he paid attention, Tania was riveting. Her voice. Her metamorphoses. From silent to talking, talking, talking. From shy and brooding to extravagant, audacious. The obvious metamorphosis of her body, impossible to not pay full attention to *that*.

"How's the horsetaming going?" Alvaro said.

"Great."

But in Tania's case, not so great. A *mesteña* who spit out whatever bit and bridle anyone tried to put in her mouth. She was contemptuous of everything at St. Jerome's: the compulsory communal gatherings for lectures, prayers, sports, camaraderie; the chores everyone was expected to do; school most of all. It was all a lie, she said flatly. Nobody was learning anything remotely useful. They'd all be helpless when the train *really* fell off the tracks—terrorism, refugees, random violence, starvation, civil war. You thought that stuff happened far away but what about when there's no such thing as far away, everything happens everywhere and at the same time, everybody gets hacked and blackmailed and everything is held for ransom or destroyed or broken and nobody survives who doesn't have the right skills.

"But for you it's different. You do have skills. You can tame wild horses, use a machete, hush a baby. Live off the land. Or on the street. Disappear. Hide. Wait. Defend yourself. Fight, but only when you have the advantage. You're a *guerrillero*, Chele."

What was she talking about? Were these somehow her own ideas or was she regurgitating something she'd heard from the *mareros*?

"What about you?"

"Oh, I'm learning to defend myself, too. I'm learning all kinds of stuff in your club."

"My club."

"Your club of fuck-ups and retards. Did you pick me? Or does Alvaro just decide?"

"It's not like that. It's not a club."

"Sure it is."

Her eyes glittered. Her breasts were mesmerizing. Her lips, the way the words dripped out of her mouth. But she was wrong about everything, except one thing: it was Alvaro who decided. And what he now decided was that horsetaming had run its course and Chele needed a different job. Something structured, and supervised.

So he became an *ayudante*. A helper, he helped with everything. One week tagging along with the carpenter or mason or electrician; the next slicing vegetables and washing pots in the kitchen; the next working in the garden or chicken farm or slaughterhouse. He wrangled kids and changed diapers in the babies' house, learned about spreadsheets and inventories and contracts in the business office. Alvaro called him in to meet benefactors and church people. He took him out on the back roads and taught him to drive, grinding the gears of the old beater Toyota flatbed used for shuttling stuff around the property.

Now and then he caught from far away a glimpse of Tania. Just a glimpse, but he could tell at once that it was her by the way she moved. Or by the way she stood still. Sometimes he heard in the distant background her low, hoarse voice. Talking, talking, he could not catch the words. Or saw at night in the periphery of his vision a spark or tiny shower of sparks. But when he turned there was nothing, just shadow and deeper shadow.

Once or twice a week he would catch Tuc-tuc and ride around. Sometimes he'd turn him out to run along a stretch of dirt road, or they'd venture up into the hills and explore, paths worn into the ground by who or what he still didn't know. He seldom saw another human or animal. But one time he came around a bend at a hard trot and there was Tania, standing with her sister at the bridge below the reservoir dam. He pulled up on the reins. Tuc-tuc reared and skidded to a dusty, hoof-pounding stop. He skittered around and blew out his nostrils. Paola squealed and fled to the far side of the bridge. Tania just looked up at him.

"It's Chele. Who we never see anymore. What happened to orientation? Our club?"

"I guess it's over. You're oriented, I guess."

"You guess. Wow, a graduate of the Fuck-up Club. Where's my certificate?"

Tuc-tuc tossed his head and snorted. Tania edged back, barely.

"Where are the other horses?"

"I don't know. Around."

"All those horses, how come you're the only one riding one? And always the same one."

"These horses aren't really for riding."

"So what are they for?"

"They're for—nothing. They're too wild. Alvaro doesn't want kids around them."

"The horses are Alvaro's?"

"Not really. They're nobody's."

"So nobody cares if we ride them."

"People care. Listen, Tania—"

"I really want to ride one, Chele."

"Well, the *horses* don't care what you want. Have you ever even ridden before? Because you don't want to start by getting up all by yourself on a horse that doesn't care what you want."

She was stroking Tuc-tuc's flank lightly with one finger. Then in a single motion she stepped up on the bridge piling and grabbed the horse's tail with one hand and Chele's belt with the other and vaulted up behind him. Only she didn't make it. Instead of kicking her leg over the horse she ended up just hanging off his flank, clinging to belt and tail while Tuc-tuc reared and spun. Chele somehow managed to stay on and haul himself upright, leaning out against the flailing counter-weight of the shrieking and wriggling Tania and keeping up a steady stream of words, trying to calm both horse and girl. Finally he just reached back, grabbed the waist of her pants, and hoisted her up to straddle the horse.

He'd imagined it a thousand times, sweeping a girl up in a horse-back rescue. But never at a dead stop, without momentum or fore-thought, the girl just throwing herself at the horse and then hanging there, shrieking and thrashing. And now giggling.

"That's not how you get on a horse, Tania! And Tuc-tuc's never had two riders."

"You said not by myself! Anyways now I can't get down. Make it stop bouncing! I'm going to pee my pants."

He felt her arms around his waist, her giggly spasms against his back. He got Tuc-tuc mainly under control but had to let him go kicking up the road a ways, then settle down at his own pace. Tania's giggles finally subsided. Her fingernails stopped digging into his stomach. He eased Tuc-tuc to a stop and helped her down.

"Okay, well, that was fun, sort of. Also painful." She made a face and put her hands between her legs.

After that he again didn't see her for awhile, just now and then from a distance. It was too hot to walk anywhere, better to just ride. His route varied but he generally made a point of passing by the bridge below the dam. Then, one hot April afternoon a few weeks after he saw her there with her sister, Tania was standing on the bridge again, alone.

"I want another riding lesson, Chele."

He shook his head.

"I really want to learn how to ride! Just tell me, I'll do whatever you say. Exactly."

"Do your homework. Your chores. Go back to your house."

But a couple of minutes later she was up on the bridge piling and he was nudging Tuc-tuc in. With a little assistance she clambered on behind. Tuc-tuc snorted his disapproval but soon settled down. Tania kept squirming.

"Sit still!"

"I'm trying! There's nothing to hold onto back here!"

"You hold onto me."

She put her hands on his hips and braced herself, keeping a little space between them. He pointed Tuc-tuc up the dusty trail to the Overlook.

"It's so *hot*. Can't we find some shade?" she said.

At the Overlook, the distant plain and mountains were shrouded in haze. Streams of smoke rose from forests and fields. The air thrummed with a low rumble that seemed to have no particular source, like the sound of the earth itself laboring.

"Ugh. Not much of a view, Chele."

He urged the horse as close to the edge as he would go.

"Look down."

Below, through the treetops, were the red tile roofs of their dorm complexes. The chapel spire, the playground, the gardens she was probably supposed to be hoeing. That lurid green stain was the algae-choked reservoir they had just ridden up from. Small dark figures moved along the dam. A dust cloud rose from a vehicle grinding up the road from the highway, barely visible where it emerged from the mountains and crossed the smoky plain below.

But even diminished by smoke Chele found the view from the Overlook inspiring. A little altitude, a shift in perspective, and places he took for granted, that close up he hardly saw anymore, were made fresh and new. As if he were seeing for the first time his own small piece of the smoky, rumbling, dangerous world, which was also a shelter from that world. A shelter he had helped create. They'd sown a garden in a desert. Seeds that had been scattered and lost were taking root, sprouting, growing, blossoming.

"There was nothing in the beginning," he said over his shoulder. "A wasteland. But Alvaro put us to work. We picked up construction trash, that was my first job. We raked up about a thousand little piles of rocks. Raced around with wheelbarrows delivering cement. We gave each other joy rides, we were eight or nine years old! Alvaro was fine with it. You're doing your job, he said. You crash a wheelbarrow, maybe you'll learn something, that was his attitude. The job was as much play as work, we hardly noticed the difference. What's going on back there?"

"Nothing. Still trying to get comfortable."

"It's still like that. You have chores, you do homework, you stand in line, but you're not stuck in line. You have space to explore, to grow things. You're at the center of something growing. A seed. A nucleus."

Alvaro's words sounded contrived and false in his mouth. He felt Tania's breath in his ear. Her voice, low, raspy, whispery.

"Mmm, a nucleus."

"Yeah. Do you know what a nucleus is? What are you *doing*?"

She'd slid all the way down the horse's back so that there was no space at all between them. Her bare arms came around and held him tightly against his chest and stomach. Then she put one hand on his shoulder and the other on the side of his head and cranked him around until his head was cradled in her arm. Cradled maybe wasn't the right word. Immobilized. Trapped. Held in something like a full nelson. Small hard bicep tightly pressed against one cheek, soft breast against the other. Her smell was incredible. The feel of her breast squished against his cheek, the firm little nipple poking into his ear, also incredible. Her breath in his face. Her open mouth descending. Her lips, easily the softest flesh he had ever touched. Her wet mouth fused to his mouth. Her warm, slippery tongue, a naked little animal sliding and slithering against his own animal tongue. He closed his eyes.

The purpose of the mouth is to ingest food, assist in respiration, and emit sounds and speech.

Her free hand trailed down his chest and stomach. Unbuttoned his pants. Slipped *inside* his pants, inside his underwear. Seized the instantaneous hard-on that seemed to have sucked every drop of blood from his brain. It was impossible to think, move, do anything at all. Tania was the one doing things, with hand and arm and breast and lips and tongue. Actually he *was* doing something. Completely immobilized yet every muscle engaged, pushing back with equal and reciprocal pressure against each point of contact. Especially her hand, now extracting his fantastically swollen penis from his pants, laying it out in the open air, right there on Tuc-tuc's back, on the Overlook cliff above dormitories and soccer fields and people moving along the embankment of the reservoir.

She'd shifted her hold; now the nipple poked his eye. He opened the other eye and saw, close-up, her t-shirt tight against her other breast. In the background Tuc-tuc's tail, swishing flies from his butt. Horse butt, buzzing flies, perfect breast. He closed his eye again and concentrated on her hand, petting and stroking and squeezing and caressing with a vigor and softness far beyond anything his own hands had come close to achieving in the dormitory darkness, where jiggling and creaking bunks discouraged experimentation and made the indiscreet masturbator the target of hysterical ridicule from the other masturbators. Tania pumped and shimmied, rubbed and squirmed. Her body rose and fell like a wave against his spine, against the horse's spine. And still old Tuc-tuc just stood there in the sun, tail swishing autonomously. He smelled smoke, horse, Tania's skin, her breath, tasted her mouth: all a single smell and taste.

Her mouth went slack against his. From her throat came a low, sustained vibration/moan. A new smell arose—chemical, fermenting, coming from deep inside her. Deep inside but altering her on the surface everywhere. She writhed and twisted. Spasms of electricity passed through her body into his. Her holds tightened: thighs clenching the horse, arm and breast clenching his head, hand clenching his cock, cock shooting blast after blast of semen out across the horse's neck and into the valley of St. Jerome's Gardens.

Less than a minute later he'd turned Tuc-tuc away from the over-look and pointed him toward the Gardens. The afternoon continued as before—hot, dry, hazy. Yet everything was different. Not just in him and Tania but in the earth itself something had shifted. But he was dis-tracted from the seismic implications of what had just occurred by a painful and debilitating kink in his neck. For how long had Tania held him in that wrenching headlock? He'd felt no pain but now his mus-cles seemed to have seized up, the nerves, his vertebra felt displaced. He couldn't straighten his head or turn to fully face forward. He gave Tuc-tuc the reins and watched the bushes pass by. Tania moaned or grunted sleepily with every jolt of the horse's gait. Her full weight, hot and sweaty, slumped against him, as if she'd fallen asleep.

They came out of the pine woods into the clearing by the reservoir. He heard a voice in the distance and sat upright, forced his head to pivot. People were working on the dam, the same tiny figures they'd seen from the overlook.

"Get down," he said.

She mumbled something.

"Get off the horse, Tania."

"What the fuck, Chele." Her voice was thick and slow. She had, she'd actually fallen asleep.

"Get down. Just go away, quick! Tío Alvaro's right there!"

"Do I give a flying fuck where Tío Alvaro is? Hey, fuck off, Chele!"

He half-lifted, half-pushed her off the horse. As soon as her feet were on the ground he turned Tuc-tuc off the path and began to cut across the clearing, away from the reservoir.

"Chele!

He still could not turn his head. He was stuck looking sideways, away from Alvaro and back towards Tania, standing all sweaty and di-sheveled and indignant on the edge of the pines. Alvaro called again, louder, and Chele pulled back on the reins and slowly turned Tuc-tuc until he and Alvaro were looking straight across the field at each an-other—Alvaro on the dam in muddy work clothes, Chele on horse-back holding his head at a bizarre twist. Alvaro looked a little bizarre himself, standing in coveralls and muddy rubber boots, muddy hands, beard splattered with flecks of greenish mud, smiling quizzically at Chele. He skidded down to the base of the dam and waited for him to ride up.

"What's with your head? "

"I got a kink in my neck."

"It's awful warm for just riding around, Chele. Hard on the horse."

"Yeah. Well, I'm going in now."

"We could use some help here. We're trying to get these filters cleaned out. All kinds of slime and goop washes down in there."

A snort of laughter escaped Chele, with no warning and for no reason. Other than that it was preposterous, to be holding his head cockeyed while Alvaro in his campesino boots chattered on obliviously about slime-clogged filters, within plain sight of the overlook where fifteen minutes earlier Tania had wrapped her hand around his monumental hard-on and sent blasts of slimy, goopy semen shooting out into the desiccated valley.

The irony, thankfully, was lost on Alvaro. But he'd stopped smiling, wasn't even looking at Chele. He squinted into the distance, toward the pines. His voice went hard.

"How old is she."

Chele didn't answer.

"How old is Tania, Chele."

"I don't know. Fifteen, sixteen."

"She's fourteen, you know that. But that's not even the point." Alvaro's voice trembled. He stepped closer. Something on the horse's neck had caught his attention. Flies buzzed and Tuc-tuc's belly twitched and spasmed and Alvaro's face also went through a series of weird contortions, while Chele waited for what seemed a very long time for some signal that the conversation had ended so he could ride away.

The true irony was revealed a few minutes later, when he was lifting the bridle over the horse's neck and saw what Alvaro had been staring at with such intensity and, he now understood, such dismay. Much later, recalling the evolution of that terrible stare, he thought he could also see the rapid calculations already taking place. Even as he considered the dribbles of pale semen that had not, in fact, showered out on the valley, had not even cleared Tuc-tuc's black neck, already Alvaro was improvising his punishment and cure. Thinking of Ciudad de Luz. Thinking: *so, Chele, you think you're ready for sex? Fine. I'll show you sex.*

With the freedom and purity of their canyon homestead came a sever-
ity of isolation the McKeanes hadn't bargained for. They built the first
road and waited for someone to build another, for a railroad spur to
come up the canyon. But corridors of transportation and commerce
were established in places of less resistance and the McKeane home-
steads cut off from the new towns and cities. Congress repealed the
Homestead Act and set aside the surrounding land as forest reserve.
The mines played out or were exposed as delusion and swindle, and the
settlements that overnight had risen up around the mines were aban-
doned. The river itself was a disconnect, as the early explorers discovered
when, ignoring the council of the Indians, they attempted to float it out
to sea and found that the stream percolated off through basalt fissures
and lava tubes and flowed underground to its confluence with larger
rivers, leaving their rafts and pirogues washed up on a desert plain.
    Perdu.

8

SULFUR AND LEAD

L ENA HADN'T BEEN to the ranch in maybe fifteen years. But as a child she'd spent many long weekends and summer vacations there with her family, and when she was eight they'd lived in the canyon for over a year. Homesteading, just the five of them. At first they had some help from Clayton and Opal, who scratched out a sort of living at their sort of ranch, Lower McKeane, on the downstream end of Confluence Bar, along Antimony Creek. They called Clayton 'uncle' but really he was a second cousin or something like that. Family anyway. The hardscrabble, hillbilly, white-trashy side of the family, her mother said.

When it was all five of them they had to drive to Confluence Bar, but that was a long, slow way around and when the weather was good and he had fewer passengers her father preferred to fly, a straight line over the mountains. Though he seldom flew a straight line. He followed ridges and rivers, fault lines, rift valleys, basalt flows. Or an even more meandering course, attempting to track the obscured and wandering boundary of the suture zone, where continental plates had slammed together and generated earthquakes, tidal waves, explosions of magma, hydrothermal infusions and depositions, the metamorphoses of rock and mineral.

Molybdenite, azurite, stibnite, cinnabar, galena.

They'd named her after one of them. Galena, a compound of sulfur and lead. Dense, gray, metallic. Not showy. The primary ore of lead, sometimes silver.

Her father had chosen the name. She was named for the rock, he said, but also for his great and her great-great grandfather, Galen McKeane: farmer and sheep rancher turned prospector, hardrock miner, roadbuilder, entrepreneur, visionary. Con man and fugitive, Helen added. Philanderer. Deadbeat dad. Let's just name her for the rock.

But in any case it was a beautiful name. Graceful and elegant. Except to her it seemed there wasn't a graceful or elegant way to say it aloud. That hard G ejected from deep in the throat, rocklike, with some clumsy or jarring word sure to follow: galoot, gall, golly, galumph, gullet, goddamn. But instead the lena part came trilling along, the tongue lapping softly on the roof of the mouth. She couldn't reconcile the two parts. A good name for a rock but not a person, was her feeling. Eventually she dropped the Gal entirely and was just Lena. Only her father continued to call her by her full name, though by then they were seeing little of him and the name was just a confirmation of the distance and strangeness lying between them.

Eventually—long after it no longer mattered to him—she came to terms with the name he had given her and the elements associated with it. Sulfur and lead and a harsh Germanic sound, coming from deep in the throat but ending on the tip of the tongue, lips open. Softening vowels, lightening consonants—a Latin sound. A hybrid, then. She liked the heaviness and density and utility of lead, shielding things from radiation and resisting corrosion. The mysterious alchemy of sulfur, its potency, its softness, even its stench, which she associated with Poison Springs—a terrible misnomer—where the family often went in the winter of their homesteading year to escape the shadowed canyon and temporarily immunize themselves against the cold, soaking in bathtubs that 75 years earlier Josie Pratt had hauled upriver and up the Ledorah switchbacks and set down on a flat gouged out of the mountain slope beside the travertine depositions of the hot spring. Each in his own tub, five enamel bathtubs lined up above a mountainside gulch under a strip of winter sky. You smelled sulfur on your skin for days afterwards. Now there's a perfume, Ethan said. Your mother calls it Spanish Fly.

Lena was eight or nine years old, it would be years before she understood what Spanish Fly was supposed to be and even then she wasn't certain of her father's meaning or whether her mother had truly ever said such a thing. Where the irony lay, again. And even more years before she considered that there might be no irony, that under the right circumstances and with the right olfactory tuning even the smell of sulfur might work as a perfume and an aphrodisiac.

That year in the canyon they homeschooled. Helen was their teacher, though often she just assigned them something to read or write and disappeared into the attic or basement to work on her own projects. Mostly they were free to do as they liked. They ran pretty wild, with forts and hideouts and secret paths all over Confluence Bar. They were Indians, prospectors, hunters, human families and animal families. They occupied the gold dredge abandoned in the Antimony Creek floodplain. They played hide and seek in Uncle Clayton's junk-yard, exciting, scary, so many spooky places to hide, and what if it was grumpy old Clayton who found you?

Now and then Ethan would come by to see what they were up to. Sometimes he'd give an impromptu lesson of his own. Geology, evolution, lectures that devolved into rambling meditations that Lena couldn't really follow but that nonetheless left her feeling dizzy and uneasy, vaguely aware that her own seemingly placid surface was not unlike the surface of the earth, subject to unpredictable disruptions by violent stirrings in the depths of her being.

But mostly Ethan left them alone. He was always working—in the fields and outbuildings, or down on the gravel bar poking around the old placer drifts his predecessors had tunneled into the cobble. He and Clayton cleaned out and reinforced the dry ditch line all the way down to the lowest pastures. They shored up the trestle, patched the flume, and put in a new headgate on the diversion on Antimony Creek. The day they opened it, Lena followed Ben and Jimmy up a rocky slope to stand on the cliff above the trestle and listen to the unseen water surge around the point of the mountain, then glimpse through the gridwork of the trestle a bright gleam and flicker as it gushed over the creosoted planks of the flume.

In September the sky began to close in. Each morning the sun cleared the canyon walls a little later, a little further south. By November the house went into a three month shadow and you had to hike up the Ledorah Road halfway to the first switchback to feel the weak sun, if it managed to shine.

A gray sky lowered, bringing snow flurries and cold rain. In the higher country creeks froze and quieted and snow brought calm and stillness and an illusion of inviolability to the land. But in the canyon the snow was seldom deep enough to fully hide weeds and scars and debris, and the river that had sounded so soothing in summer became an irritant, an unintelligible voice that never went silent and seemed to come from all directions, echoing and reechoing between canyon walls.

It felt like they were trying to live too deep inside the pressurized earth. Too close to the core, the crush of nickel and lead.

There was little society. All summer Ethan and Clayton argued over fencelines and irrigation water and whose cattle or horses were trespassing on whose property or on the game refuge and the National Forest. By autumn they had fallen out entirely and Clayton and Opal kept to themselves.

The mail plane flew when weather permitted, buzzing low to drop a packet in the pasture. It dipped its wings and disappeared around the bend. In the time it took them to run out and retrieve the packet the sound of the engine faded entirely.

She went walking in shallow snow with her father. They heard hounds baying in the distance and followed fresh tire tracks through an open gate and came upon Clayton and two men in a field. The men were wearing holstered sidearms and standing next to four-wheelers with packs and hunting rifles on the cargo decks.

"Somebody's dogs running themselves in circles up there," Ethan said.

The men were silent. Clayton straddled his four-wheeler, his eyes fixed straight ahead.

"Public right-of-way is behind you," Ethan said to the men. "So is the national forest. This is private property. Trust land. Game refuge, no hunting. Maybe your guide didn't tell you."

The howling grew louder. Then the dogs broke out of the woods and were running straight across the field towards them. Her father's hand squeezed her shoulder. "They won't hurt you," he said, and they didn't, just swept in close, breathing hard, leaping and snapping at each other, barking, baying, streaming saliva and kicking up showers of snow as they tumbled and swirled around the humans. The dogs' teeth flashed, the men spat brown stains into the snow. Then Clayton whistled sharply and the dogs were gone into the woods again and Clayton and the two men got on their ATVs and drove after them. Her father asked her how much money she thought men like that might be paying Clayton to have his dogs run down a cougar for them. Not that anyone was making assumptions about Clayton's clients, he said. Not even the assumption that they were clients, they might just be hunting buddies. Might be only half as ignorant and violent and lowdown and inbred as they looked. No one was making assumptions about the hounds, either; whether animals that unhinged could even get near a cougar, and if they could how many the cougar would manage to kill before it took a bullet. An ugly business but if Clayton wanted to run cougars down with his dogs and kill one now and then no one was objecting to that either; it would serve if nothing else to remind the big cat that the human was a brutal and violent animal and it was best to give him room.

Two stovepipes. Two separate smoke strands, rising into a blue winter sky on either end of the bar. An unbridgeable territory lying between.

In *Crack Between Mountains* she was reading the history of that territory. A history of argument—over boundary lines and airstrip access and water rights and ditches and roads and bridges and weed management and timber and mining claims. A history of litigation or the threat of litigation, of sabotage, violence or the threat of violence, of contradictory documents, records, surveys. Of the fragmentation and reconstitution and refragmentation of property, and finally of its consolidation into a trust, with just two trustees, representing the two known branches, hereditary factions, of the family, and their two ranches, Upper McKeane and Lower McKeane—not legally separate holdings but rather an unofficial but strictly adhered-to division of a single property.

Her father had been one trustee and Clayton the other, but at the time she hadn't known a thing about it. For her there were just the two ranches, with an increasingly uneasy truce along their border. For weeks after the incident with the cougar hunters, the only visible sign of Clayton and Opal was the smoke rising out of their chimney and off their smoldering burn piles. The only sound an occasional saw or hammer or some machine coughing to life in Clayton's bone-yard—a greasy, rocky field covered with old machinery and vehicles, water tanks, barrels, construction materials, miscellaneous junk. The hounds were mainly quiet.

Then one day in February Clayton took a long-barred chainsaw up on the steep slope above Antimony Creek and in a matter of weeks cut down every mature tree in that woodland. He skidded the logs down to a landing on the tailings ground below. All day they listened to the noise of his machines, chainsaw or tractor, an occasional brief silence when the saw shut down. A couple of long seconds later a 400 year-old ponderosa pine came crashing to the ground. Then the hounds started up, and a while later the saw joined in again.

Ethan said that when Clayton got a fever like that there was no way to stop him, short of murder. It was to avoid that temptation, he said, and to get a little peace and quiet, that he went down on the gravel bar and began to excavate the old placer drifts. He had a theory about how the stream course on Confluence Bar had shifted over time and what that meant for the placers. The depositions of Antimony Creek were not merely the modest delta they saw now at the mouth of that creek, but the entirety of Confluence Bar—a much larger delta, he said, where the creek had dropped its bedload over millions of years. As in any delta, channels had fanned out and moved around. Now the stream flowed through Lower McKeane and straight down the east side of the valley, but that was a recent development, geologically speaking. The miners had gone after those shallow placers, low-hanging fruit. They'd ripped up the floodplain and sucked the gravels through their sluices and taken out the gold. But not all that much gold, Ethan said, considering how deeply Antimony Creek had incised into the heart of Red Mountain and how much gold-bearing sediment must have flushed down to the delta over time.

On the upstream end of the main bar it was different. Ethan had flown over and walked or ridden the snakey bottomland pastures of Upper McKeane enough to understand that they traced the abandoned meandering channel and floodplain of Antimony Creek. Upper McKeane was now a higher terrace cut off from the creek, but for eons, he said, the stream had flowed out to the river there, depositing its bedload and building up the terrace and gravel bar below. The soils were deep, the overburden deep, the bedrock deeply buried.

Slow, careful, patient. That was how you worked a placer drift. Far enough in, there was no sound. That silence was beautiful. The stones were beautiful. They came from so many places, each smooth, river-borne stone a story in itself. And somewhere beneath them lay bedrock, and resting in pockets of sand and gravel on the bedrock, gold.

Toward the end of their second summer in the canyon Helen announced that the homesteading experiment was over. An experiment in social deprivation, light deprivation, sky deprivation, that had been going on now for a century and that she saw no point in continuing for yet another generation.

She had been a willing enough participant, at first. But she had not fully considered the extent of the isolation, or calculated the seasonal geometry of sun angle and canyon wall, or understood that the atmosphere of abandonment and decline would persist no matter how hard anyone worked. She had not fully weighed the implications for her children, growing up with Opal and Clayton as their only society. Hearing always the hateful baying of Clayton's hounds, gazing out at the smoke of his perennially smoldering burn piles, or smelling in the air the toxic combustions of his boneyard.

So they moved back to town and started a different experiment. They got food stamps, shopped at thrift stores, grew a big garden. Helen worked as an aide at the school and a reporter at the weekly newspaper. She wrote a lot of poetry. It wasn't clear to Lena how they had gotten by. Her father worked sporadic construction jobs and had a little air taxi business, flying hunters and fishers into the backcountry. None of them Clayton's clients; the rift between the two men had only deepened.

Ethan continued to spend much of his time at the ranch, repairing fences, irrigating orchards and hayfields, and keeping an eye on Clayton, he said. Working the placer drifts a little on the side. But Helen said the hayfield were just an excuse, it was all about the placers. And who needs excuses. Why not just stop pretending you're there to do anything with the earth but rip under its skin and take out a few flakes of gold. Why pretend that seasons even matter. What difference does a winter shadow make to a man burrowing into a hole?

No difference, Ethan said. The weather was always the same. The darkness the same, the mission the same: to bring light into the earth and shine it on rock that had not been illuminated since the beginning of time.

Molybdenite, azurite, stibnite, cinnabar, galena.

9

CITY OF LIGHT

CHELE SPENT THE FIRST half of his nineteenth year—nineteen, the age of peak testosterone production in the human male, he'd read or heard somewhere—with Padre Jaco and his angels in the City of Light, amid the wreckage of the hurricane and a host of other disasters, where he and two nuns-in-training were the only people who were not old, insane, terminally sick, brain-damaged, or terribly deformed. Or all of those things at once. In a previous era Ciudad de Luz had been a convent and a single old nun, Hermana Belén, still resided there, caring for the infirm, overseeing the novices, and shuffling down to the gate each morning to squint through a peephole and see what fresh human calamity had washed up on her shores.

I'll show you sex. During his first weeks at Ciudad de Luz, Alvaro's words played over and over in Chele's head, until he practically forgot they *weren't* Alvaro's words, but words he'd only imagined him saying. Alvaro had especially fierce and uncompromising ideas about sex. He invariably saw sexual irresponsibility and immorality somewhere in the evil chain of circumstances that had deprived an orphan of his parents.

To keep sex at a distance was one reason for the intentional isolation of the Gardens. To keep at a distance for as long as possible a decadent and promiscuous culture that scorned the virtue of chastity—*using the gift of sexuality in the right way, regardless of whether one is single, married, or vowed*—and did everything it could to sexualize children at a very early age. A culture where sex was so cheap it lost all value and purpose, heedlessly producing unwanted children who would inevitably come to believe they too were without value.

Don't blame it all on the culture, Chele wanted to say, thinking of the extraordinary metamorphosis of Tania's fourteen year-old body. But there was no denying the central role of sex in the wreckage of society. A furtive shadow humping away in tiny bedrooms and dark corners, a grinding axis on which the cycle of poverty turned. Alvaro had founded St. Jerome's Gardens as a sanctuary from that culture, on the hope of breaking that cycle. And now Chele, handpicked seed and nucleus, had ridden up to him in a daze on a semen-splattered horse, with his head twisted grotesquely to the side and a gangster girl skulking on the edge of the woods behind him.

The next morning Alvaro took him on a walk. He counted off on his fingers the failings Chele had demonstrated. Poor judgment in general. Poor self-control. He'd yielded to carnal temptation and blind desire. He'd abused privilege and trust and, incidentally, put himself in a potentially precarious legal position, since the girl was only 14 and he was of legal age. Alvaro ran out of fingers, or lost count, waved his fingers away. There would be no punishment. Instead there would be a choice and an opportunity for service: to work for the next year as personal assistant to Padre Jaco, the director of Ciudad de Luz. A job, but it wouldn't pay. Work, live, sleep at Ciudad de Luz. 24/7. A job and continuing education. Studies in empathy and humility. In the dignity of work and the fundamental worth of human life. In a year, he'd have earned his high school diploma.

That was the opportunity. The choice was the same he'd had since he'd turned 18. Not really a choice. To accept whatever opportunity Alvaro offered, or leave St. Jerome's Gardens and strike out on his own.

Ciudad de Luz was the home for abandoned and incapacitated adults that he had briefly visited on a service trip with the *mesteños*. A sanctuary, like St. Jerome's, but of a different order. Sanctuary and crematorio at once, wasteyard for sex and most other forms of pleasure.

Residents lived in three wards: geriatric, medical, and psych, though certainly there was much overlap between categories, especially among the congenitally deformed or brain-damaged: people born limbless or with a crippling excess of limbs, the hydrocephalic, microencephalic, imbecilic, dystrophic, psychotic, palsied, retarded, cretinous. Products of incest and masturbation, fornication, rape, sodomy, fellatio, and other perversions, according to Padre Jaco. The iniquities of the fathers visited upon the children, who are themselves without sin, and live among us in a blessed state, as angels.

Como ángeles. If angels drooled, twitched, babbled. If angels stank of urine and shit, shook with spasms and tics and tremors, flapped stumps not wings, convulsed and contracted deep in cots and wheelchairs. A far cry from the celestial angels pictured in the paintings hanging in the National Gallery, and hard to distinguish from the non-angels—the head traumas, hemiplegics, amputees, and lunatics who had been whole once but were now broken by some terrible misfortune or series of misfortunes or just the long stretching rack of poverty. Though more often, said Padre Jaco, their wretchedness was a disaster they'd brought down upon themselves. Here were lives distinguished by abuse and depravity. Bodies maimed in some drunken accident, or in battles with police or *mareros*, or shriveled and rotted from disease and poison and the acidic corrosion of their addictions and sins.

"But now look at them," smiled Padre Jaco. "Those unholy fevers are exhausted, banished. They are innocent children again, weak, helpless, but purged at last of evil. Destroyed, that they may be renewed."

Yet somewhere behind their stupors and agonies the same fevers still festered, beyond the reach of the lance. Or so Chele imagined. More dimly, he understood the stunned resignation of the novices and the hardened devotion of Sister Belén. But Padre Jaco he couldn't make out at all.

Padre Jaco is a very pious man, Alvaro had told him. Maybe with the slightest ironic flicker of his eyebrows. But within hours of meeting him Chele decided that he was in the presence of an actual saint—a being entirely different from the mute icons and heavenly abstractions who for as long as he could remember had loitered irrelevantly on the periphery of his life. The padre's bottomless gray eyes locked onto his, probing hidden places that Alvaro, for all his penetrating gazes, had never seen. Yet Padre Jaco was no mystic, but rather entirely frank and open and guileless. He spoke of God and Jesus with casual familiarity, as if they were as much a physical presence as himself. Maybe Jesus too had gone about with a greasy combover and unshaven jowls, sweat-stained armpits in a shirt stretched over his paunch, gaping pores and psoriasis and permanent blackheads in a great swollen nose. Maybe Jesus' hands weren't delicate and elegant as they appeared in paintings, but calloused and coarse like Padre Jaco's, immersed in the physical world—drilling and sawing, hammering and digging, dispensing medications, cutting off casts, changing bandages and diapers, administering enemas, palpating diseased flesh, keeping records and arranging hospital visits and burials and finances and managing discarded lives as if there were some point to it all. As if he truly believed his own claim: that the existence of Ciudad de Luz was testimony to the sanctity and value of human life.

Chele believed that too, at times. Other times he believed that Ciudad de Luz made an entirely convincing argument for the utter cheapness and expendability of human life. And sometimes he believed that the argument was not for sanctity or cheapness, but only for the permeability of the thin film separating the two.

The novices were young but in no way compromised Alvaro's cure. Stiff, grey habits obliterated the contours of their bodies and also, it seemed, their personalities. At dusk they went into darkness and silence and at the first birdcall emerged from pre-dawn shadows to set about their endless and repetitive chores. They washed clothes, dishes, floors, bodies. They drew water out of cisterns in the back of their compound and poured it into barrels and sinks to store against the time when the cisterns would surely go dry. With kitchen knives and machetes they chopped at things—vegetables, chickens, firewood, the encroaching bush. They read the Bible, or just sat motionless in the garden, eyes closed, lips moving, silently praying—for a way out of their circumstances, or a way deeper in?

On the steel gate hung a rusted and barely legible sign: *Welcome to Ciudad de Luz. Through many tribulations we must enter the Kingdom*

of God. No acknowledgment of financial supporters, no logos or plac-
ards or brochures, no evidence at all of the sort of benefactors Alvaro
was always escorting around St. Jerome's. Where does the money come
from, he asked Padre Jaco, and the padre merely smiled and raised
his eyes heavenward.

Ciudad de Luz occupied a few acres of land enclosed within cement block walls on a high bluff overlooking the city and the river
that ran through its heart. It seemed to Chele that everything inside
those walls had been broken and filthy and infested for a very long
time. Yet the careful geometry with which paths and buildings had
been laid out was still apparent, and sometimes sitting in Hermana
Belen's little patch of garden he sensed the order and tranquility of
the old convent, somehow still separate from the treeless sprawl and
agitation and pollution of the city that was engulfing it.

One of his first jobs was to clear a thicket with a machete, the same
thicket he and the *mesteños* had hacked away at, apparently to little
lasting effect, over a year earlier. But that truly was an impossible task,
at any rate during the prodigious growth of the rainy season and with
the worn machete Padre Jaco had given him. By the time he finally
cut through to the river bluffs the vegetation was already reasserting
itself in the area where he had begun, and the piles of garbage, broken
wheelchairs, rusting appliances, waterlogged mattresses, and discarded
medical supplies he had briefly exposed to the sunlight were already
vanishing again beneath a claustrophobic jungle of thorns and vines
and towering saw-blade grass.

For the longest time he couldn't get oriented. Pathways were narrow tunnels through the bush, indistinguishable from one another.
One path might deliver him into the nuns' compound, where in the
bleak devotion of Hermana Belén and her novices he felt the op-
pression of eternity and experienced, not for the first time, a fear of
Heaven to counterbalance his fear of Hell. But later, believing he was
on the same path, he emerged into a different compound and came
upon thirty or forty residents sitting down to their slobbery lunch. A
cry went up and a half-dozen people rose from the table and lurched

toward him, whether to drive him off or absorb him into the intimacy of their gibbering communion, he didn't stay to find out.

One path ended in jumbled, broken cement and exposed tree roots on the edge of impassible bluffs. Not long ago, Padre Jaco explained, that path had continued on to what was then the *ancianos*' dormitory. But on the darkest night of the hurricane the bluff had given way and that building tumbled into the flooding river.

Yet God in His mercy had spared the lives of the sleeping *ancianos*. In the hours when the heavens first opened the padre was granted a vision: dread coming on the storm and calamity with the whirlwind. As storm and river raged he and Hermana Belén descended a path that had become a muddy torrent, entered the building, and guided the *ancianos* through storm and flood to more stable ground. All but one, who, taken by a great *susto*, had locked himself in the bathroom and answered their entreaties and prayers with insult and blasphemy. When night fell they finally left him in the darkness of the tempest and returned to their own dark rooms to pray. All night Jehovah's great wind wailed and the fountains of the giant deep burst forth and the windows of the heavens opened, and when Padre Jaco looked out his window at dawn he saw that his vision had come to pass: where the promontory and the building had stood there was nothing but air, and a brown river raging below.

Now Chele stood on broken cement and looked down on a shallow thread of opaque water in a broad, raw bed of rock and debris. Amid the ruins of half-buried buildings yellow tractors pushed rubble about in a seemingly haphazard fashion. The city after the hurricane was like the countryside around San Miguel after a wildfire, a jumble of destruction and decay and vigorous new growth. A constant rumble and booming of wheels and engines, earth excavated and piled up and pounded down, brick and block and rebar rising. Industrial blasts of smoke and dust, jets skimming the distant white ridge of the crematorio and the red gashes where the earth had given way. New skyscrapers—glittering metallic hotels, fortresses of embassies and banks—rising out of the ruin.

That was what you could see. You couldn't see the miners' intricate network of tunnels beneath it all, still intact and already nearly forgotten again. Or any small and insignificant thing—a huddle of children in a dark apartment, a little boy with an envelope pinned to his shirt, riding a bus alone into those hazy mountains.

Once a month a volunteer doctor came. Chele and the novices brought the patients down to the clinic and lined them up on benches or in wheelchairs in the shade of the building. One at a time, Padre Jaco took them inside for the doctor to examine. Chele stayed outside with those who waited, waving off flies and keeping them from wandering or squabbling or getting into some other mischief. Through the open windows he could watch as much of the examination as he cared to and hear all of it, whether he cared to or not. The padre would run through a patient's symptoms in graphic clinical detail, often proposing his own diagnosis and therapy, suggesting medication selected from his storeroom of donated pharmaceuticals. Usually the doctor would gently correct him and the padre, deferential, would ask for clarification and write in his notebook whatever the doctor said. After a few hours she would check her phone and look out at the line of patients.

"If no one else is critical, I'm afraid I have to go."

"Of course. But there are a couple more, maybe not critical but they are in pain…"

"I don't know how you do this, Padre."

"One suffers to see them suffer, Doctora."

By mid-day Chele and the patients were confined to a narrow strip of shade against the building. He tried to make a little conversation, on those occasions when there was someone capable of conversing. But often there would be a line-up of six or eight patients without a definitive sign of higher consciousness among them, each frozen in position—a unique grimace on each face, a unique arrangement of limbs splayed out or contracted by seizure or paralysis. It brought to mind the paintings of Jesus in diverse paroxysms of suffering in the Via

Dolorosa room at the National Gallery. When he thought of the Via Dolorosa and the Stations of the Cross he was diligent about waving the flies away, but sometimes his mind wandered and he had trouble believing it mattered. Then for a while he might make a competition out of it, just sit back and wait to see which patient would draw the most flies. They were so still at times, an occasional twitch or whimper or ongoing tic, but otherwise this incredible stillness and resignation beneath the furious buzzing of the flies.

Yet there was no mistaking that lack of motion for lifelessness. The opposite was true: the stillness on the outside emphasized the perverse tenacity of the life force within. Lungs whistled and gurgled, arteries throbbed, intestines churned, eyes blinked and glittered. Someone might lose her equilibrium and tilt to the side in her wheelchair, and Chele, lifting her upright, would marvel at the texture of the ancient hide, the fragile bone and strips of ropy muscle pushing at collapsed skin. All of it connected to nerves: in spite of everything these remained pulsing, complex creatures who felt pain and even some shadow of pleasure. The organism insisted on life, no one could say why. God's plans were beyond comprehension and it was useless and even blasphemous to second-guess Him, but still you had to wonder what He was thinking, granting Padre Jaco a vision and removing such creatures from the merciful annihilation of the flood.

Ciudad de Luz did offer a few compensations, even a small luxury or two. For the first time in his life he had a room of his own. At first it was in a bungalow connected to Padre Jaco's residence, but the padre was an insomniac and his restlessness seeped through the plywood walls at night. For most of his life Chele had slept in close proximity to twenty other boys, but the creaking and rustling in the next room now kept him awake. With the padre's permission he moved to the clinic storeroom and cleared a cozy little space in the corner, with a comfortable bed and pillows and a curtain. Every once in a while the padre would open a door and he could hear him just on the other side of the curtain, talking to God and rummaging among the broken wheelchairs and walkers and strange medical devices, clothes, toys, stuffed animals, exercise machines, bottles of chemicals and cleaning products and boxes of donated medicines they hadn't yet transferred to the locked pharmacy next door.

But then Padre Jaco would go away and Chele would have the room to himself, a cool, quiet sanctuary where he could retreat and escape into books. Padre Jaco frowned on literature other than Bibles and religious tracts in public areas, but searching through the donations Chele came across boxes of books, hundreds of books in different languages. In his little cozy hideaway he looked through every one. Some of the English books he could manage, if he applied himself. But mostly he just read in Spanish, indiscriminately, all genres, practically anything he came across could serve as escape.

Emerging into the mid-afternoon heat and glare he found few of the residents rejuvenated by their afternoon siesta. They had napped poorly and were full of inarticulate complaints, feeding on each other's unhappiness. As a group they were impossible to deal with at that hour, and whenever he could he tried to split them into more manageable units.

He got Hermana Belén's permission to gather a small group of *ancianos* for relaxation and meditation in the courtyard in the nuns' compound. Here was a remnant of the lost serenity of the convent: painted cement benches, a well-kept shrine to the Madonna, and a tiny garden with rich black soil, flowers in perennial bloom, and a mango tree heavy with ripening fruit. A little fountain trickled. A radio played somewhere in a back room, where a novice was washing clothes. Beside him in their wheelchairs the old ones worked their gums and rosaries or dozed in dappled sunlight, and sometimes it all came together and hypnotized him so that it seemed that he too had lived many decades and washed up on a small, sedated island of age in a tumultuous sea of youth. Could this be Alvaro's intent: that Ciudad de Luz would act as a kind of antidote to the relentless youthfulness of the Gardens, that the company of the old would have a tranquilizing effect on Chele? Or had he hoped for more? Did he imagine Chele the motherless child sitting at the feet of his elders, absorbing the wisdom and serenity of their accumulated years? Yet most of the *ancianos* sat in their wheelchairs in silence, as if resolved to die with their lips sealed, taking their paltry wisdom into the ground with them. Even when through ingenuity and perseverance he succeeded in getting some to talk, taming and seducing them as he had tamed and seduced horses and children, the result was disappointing. Like the orphans they spouted ignorance and prejudice, old resentments, fantasies of rescue and divine intervention. They fidgeted and whined, slumped in their wheelchairs or fumbled with the brakes, trying pathetically to escape. The one thing they seemed to find reliably soothing was the sound of his voice, but he had trouble thinking of things to say to them. His repertoire of prayers was soon exhausted. Then, remembering the *mesteños* and Harry Potter, he began bringing a book and reading to them.

Thieves and murderers, addicts, pimps, whores, and gangsters, if Padre Jaco was to be believed, the *ancianos* were nonetheless a gratifyingly attentive audience, listening with the openness and wonder of children. Maybe the padre was right—their hearts had been scoured and purified. Or maybe it was mere simple-mindedness. Or desperate boredom. They seemed especially drawn to sci-fi and thrillers, stories of extraterrestrials, conspiracies, prophecies, apocalypse. Also to scientific-sounding explanations of paranormal phenomena, though it was hard to say what they understood of the implications of an imminent reversal of the earth's direction of rotation, or the revelation that the CIA had mounted death rays on the same satellites that beamed telenovelas into peoples' living rooms, or a fractal analysis of Martian craters revealing with statistical certainty that a great civilization had abandoned the red planet within the last hundred years.

Padre Jaco could hardly prohibit an activity which had such obvious beneficial effect on his charges, though certainly he would disapprove of most of the reading material. So Chele opened and closed each session with a prayer and kept a children's book of Bible stories close at hand, to take up whenever the padre, beaming and nodding, drew near.

"Do you believe they understand what you read to them, Hermano?"

Chele shrugged. "They enjoy it."

The padre's smile broadened. "Yes. You see it in their faces, eh?"

Chele did in fact think they were enjoying it, but he didn't see it in the faces. The faces looked dim, distant, trapped in spasms, heavily-medicated or not medicated enough. The padre shadowboxed with a drooling *anciano.* "One can't help it, Brother Chele. One has to take joy in them." The *anciano* flinched, practically slow motion, then chortled and appeared to throw back a couple of trembling punches. The padre patted his shoulder. "Such joy and beauty, Hermano, in even the most humble and destitute of God's creatures. Another paradox."

The unrelenting proximity of the padre's Deity was getting on Chele's nerves. Padre Jaco seemed to see himself as God's sidekick, praising and encouraging and interpreting His actions and motives, while God in turn whispered in the padre's ear, nudging and winking, admonishing and applauding and fist-bumping and patting him on the head the way the padre fist-bumped and head-patted the *ancianos.* You had to wonder if all the pestering wasn't making God irritable. Did He really want to be constantly asked to intervene in such mundane and insignificant affairs? Did He never tire of the company of His tedious saint?

But at least the padre's prayers were not the beseeching, wheedling kind. He didn't believe in asking God for a lot of material things. According to the padre's philosophy, you prayed not for supplies or money or doctors or health or even relief from pain, but for faith and understanding: the faith that your needs will be met and the understanding that whatever you do possess must be, by the logic of your faith, all that you need. If some of the residents didn't quite grasp this they at least seemed to understand the importance of feigning it; few dared to complain or ask Padre Jaco for anything specific, for fear he might revoke their coffee privileges or their reading hour with Hermano Chele.

"Padre," the old nun said, a hint of un-nunlike sarcasm in her voice. "Why do you call him that?"

"What do you mean?"

"Have you heard him say Mass? Take confession?"

"But look at him—he's like a saint."

"A saint is one thing," Hermana Belén said. "A priest is another. Do you know how he arrived here, years ago, when we were still a convent? He was at the gate one morning, unconscious, poisoned by alcohol and who knows what else. Covered in bloody vomit, pants full of his own waste. I took him in, bathed him with my own hands, nursed him."

Gradually Chele was forced to admit that Padre Jaco was a tyrant. A benign tyrant, he continued to hope, as evidence accumulated of how manipulative and controlling and dogmatic the man was. Padre Jaco managed the residents' money, medications, records, contacts with the outside world, and whatever scraps of information reached them. He listened earnestly to the doctor's recommendations and then altered medications according to his own whim. If the doctor was unfamiliar with or disapproving of a donated medication, that was no impediment to trying it out on some passive *anciano*.

In any case, the padre's own assessment of a patient's spiritual needs and opportunities for penance generally took precedence over her prescriptions. The doctor grew exasperated and then angry and finally quit coming, but within a couple of months Padre Jaco had recruited another.

Sometimes at night Chele heard rustlings and banging and wailing in the distance. He heard scuffling sounds just outside his room, a low voice muttering, the grass whispering. The wind, probably. The natural settling and shifting of junk. The night watchman poking around. A tormented loco escaping from his ward to stumble through the darkness. Or some scavenger or predator—wild dog, raccoon, nocturnal zopilote—rooting out unwholesome sustenance. Sisimiti howling into a distant firewind, loping across smoldering bushlands in search of charred flesh.

But in the morning Padre Jaco appeared in the dining area, haggard and unshaven in his rumpled, sweatstained shirt, and Chele wondered how he had passed the night, and what the lunatics who took him aside to babble urgently in his ear were trying to say.

Sometimes he took out his *cuaderno* and added to his list of questions.

> *Padre Jaco: a saint who brings grace and charity to Ciudad de Luz, or a night demon who haunts it? Or both?*
>
> *Is evil a fuel that holiness burns on?*
>
> *Is Ciudad de Luz an example of love, or pity? Pity, or fear?*
>
> *The Law of Supply and Demand—doesn't it also apply to human life, just another commodity, declining in value in inverse proportion to supply?*

At reading hour he sat in the sisters' courtyard, waiting for the novices to come in pushing wheelchairs and leading a shuffling contingent of *ancianos*. But instead Padre Jaco appeared, looking especially agitated and disheveled. He managed a thin smile.

"Hermano Chele. Your people won't be coming for their reading hour this afternoon."

The padre reached up and plucked a couple of plump mangos from the heavily-laden tree. He handed one to Chele and with his teeth pulled strips of peel away from the other, spat them out, and bit into the fruit. "They want to deny a miracle. I won't permit that to happen."

The padre gazed at the tree. A strand of mango pulp was snagged in his front teeth.

"Why such an abundance of sweet fruit in this garden, Brother Chele? Eh? And all around nothing but hard clay, thorns, wilderness." He reached down and picked up a handful of black soil. "All around, a poor and pale soil. Not so long ago, this garden soil was the same, and fruit from this tree bitter and sparse. But God enriches His earth through the most paradoxical means."

He led Chele down a side trail to a construction of two-by-fours hung with sheets of plastic, with a long plastic pipe protruding from the top. On the plywood floor inside was a toilet.

"Tell me what you see here, Hermano."

"A toilet…"

Padre Jaco smiled and held up a mango-stained hand. "You see a miracle."

He took Chele around to the back of the structure, opened a chamber at the bottom, grabbed a handful of black, crumbly stuff, and thrust it in Chele's face. "An eco-toilet! A composting toilet!" The padre was grinning like a little kid. Mango juice had congealed in the stubble around his mouth. "The doctor donated it to us. How inscrutable the ways of God, Hermano. This device converts the foulest of human waste to something rich and beneficial. It makes a clean thing out of an unclean. I've been applying the product to the sisters' gardens, and you've seen the results, eh? But now these old people refuse to use it."

His teeth peeled back another strip of mango peel. "Really," said Chele faintly. "Why?"

Padre Jaco spat the mango peel into the bushes. "They're stubborn. They don't trust the miracle, they don't like the look of it. Never mind the look, I tell them. We walk by faith, not by sight. I reason with them, I reward them, and finally I tell them: it doesn't matter if you like it, if this is where God wants you to shit, this is where you'll shit! But they refuse. They leave their *caquitas* in the bushes and behind the bodega, they constipate themselves, anything to deny God the means by which his garden flourishes. So. God then must deny them a place in His garden. He must deny them Hermano Chele's little stories."

Chele walked out to the very edge of the bluff, where the *ancianos'* dormitory had broken away and been carried off by the flood. In the low afternoon sun, the city below was all glare and shadow. He couldn't make out any detail, couldn't see what he knew was there: the viscous flow of the river, the ooze of contaminants along its shores. The valley of the shadow of death. But in the glare the river might just as well have been a clear, tree-lined stream flowing out of cloud-forested mountains. It must have truly been something like that, not so long ago. There was a big story and surely a madness behind that transformation, from Edenic stream to river of acid and shit. But there was also a logic to it, a meaning and natural manifestation of God's Laws. Just as Ciudad de Luz was such a manifestation—not a place existing in isolation, but connected by the complex flow of events to things far beyond its boundaries.

Somewhere between the burning glare and the silhouetted mountains was the oasis of St. Jerome's Gardens, with its extravagant abundance of children, beautiful and innocent and precious in God's sight. But maybe even God was blinded by the glare. The children were beautiful and innocent but also common as tortillas, and hence cheap, in accordance with God's own irrefutable Laws. And it seemed to Chele that their cheapness was a thing connecting Alvaro's shining Gardens, refuge of hope for the young and innocent, to the City of Light, refuge of despair for the old and forsaken. A place where God Himself supplied all that was needed, down to a composting toilet; where the final calculations of His contradictory formulas were implemented and the last dregs of pity administered by His tyrannical saint.

He didn't ask permission and he didn't say goodbye. Within an hour he was on the street with his duffel bag in hand. Late that evening he was knocking on Alvaro's door. He stood in the entryway and told Alvaro he had learned all he could from Padre Jaco and his City of Light. The universal syllogism of Supply and Demand was now clear to him. Major premise, minor premise, conclusion.

"We're worth exactly as much as our own shit."

Convictions of manifest destiny matured into a darker strain of fatalism. McKeanes fell to addiction and obsession and rage, to fire and flood, freak tailwind, thin ice, frayed cable, falling rock. To homicide, fratricide, mariticide. Their schemes unraveled at the moment of fruition. They died young, married badly, vanished inexplicably. For a time they propagated vigorously enough, but most of their progeny left the canyon, and the rest fell to arguing among themselves, feuding and sabotaging and ultimately communicating only through agents, who first negotiated the division of the land and later patched it back together in what everyone called, with no apparent irony, the Family Trust.

10

COUNCIL

"OF COURSE, THE RANCH is not for sale," Angie said. The family was sitting around the remnants of dinner at Ben and Angie's dining room table. Helen, Lena, Jimmy, Ben, Ben's wife Angie, and their kids, Chloe and Sam. All the living known tribe, not counting Clayton and Opal, old and childless and gone south, perhaps for good.

Several conversations had been going on simultaneously but at Angie's words a general silence fell over the table, everyone's radar went up. Maybe a little shudder of premonition went through some of them, even before she added that a client of hers had nonetheless made a credible offer to buy it.

"How can an offer be credible if there's nothing for sale?"

"People have money, Jimmy. A property catches their eye."

"And the agent tells them, sorry, it's not for sale."

"That's right. And nonetheless communicates the offer to the owner."

"This client is aware there's no access? He knows about the road washout? Bridge closure?"

"Of course she knows," said Angie. "I think those are selling points. She likes the idea of a moat around her castle. That doesn't trap *her* there. The airstrip's another selling point. She's a backcountry flyer, she gets around. Which is how she saw the place to begin with."

"Oh. So this client buzzes us a few times, then calls up her agent and puts down an offer."

"Something like that," said Angie. "And then it's like you said, the agent tells her it's not for sale."

"Great. So why are we having this conversation?"

"It's just a conversation."

They'd finished dinner, cake would come later. It was early spring, a celebration of Helen's 70th birthday, and the most concentrated dose of family any of them had had in years. Everyone was dealing with memory surges and short-circuits, flashes of sentimentality, more sustained upwellings of ancient resentments. An excess of wine. Meanwhile, Angie, regal hostess and mistress-of-ceremony, required a brief summary of their situations and projects.

Angie

She went first, speaking mainly of the situations and projects of her children (who had slipped away somewhere). She touched briefly on her real estate business—reeling a bit, naturally, in the downturn, the entire market was reeling, everyone's sense of security shaken, the properties she represented had lost however many zillions of dollars in hypothetical value. Which they would no doubt regain in time. Some clients just needed calming down. Others needed redirection, to be shown how opportunity arises out of failure. In any case, she had her hands full. The business, the household, the children, Helen's health crisis, the ongoing crisis that was the ranch. But she was managing.

"I'm a pretty good manager. The one thing I don't try to manage is Ben. He does that himself. Or not. Now and then we are granted a sighting. A cryptic message comes in over the wires. Okay, let's just say he's been—absorbed in his work. His Model. I assume you all know about that? The Paper he's presenting this summer at this big international conference? I mean, the conference is in Denver, but I guess there will be some international people there. Anyway it's very prestigious, a career milestone, an honor and a validation, isn't it, Ben?"

Ben

Whether the presentation was an honor and validation or someone was just calling his bluff was still to be seen, Ben said. Anyway, it wasn't as though anything was finished. The Paper was just a progress report. His Model still a work-in-progress.

After retiring from smokejumping, Ben had gone back to school and earned a couple of advanced degrees. Still working in fire, he'd never stopped working in fire. But he'd stopped fighting it; his Model was most definitively not about fighting fire. It was about calibrating an equilibrium thrown precipitously out of balance by one hundred years of fighting fire. Contemporary forests were choking on themselves, a direct result of fire suppression, everyone recognized that. A reckoning was due, was already upon us.

What his research came down to was trying to determine with some exactitude what humans could do to affect that reckoning in a positive way. Those forests were going to burn. You could try to ensure—through fuels reduction, prescribed fire, and judicious, informed restraint of fire suppression—that they burned under favorable conditions. Or you could keep doing your best to extinguish all fire, until finally you couldn't. Then fire would burn under unfavorable if not dire conditions. What people called a catastrophe.

For years now his team had been accumulating data. Aggregating and synthesizing data. They'd monitored, groundtruthed. Mapped burn severities, all sorts of spatial complexities. Quantified fuel load increases correlated to fire exclusion. Reconstructed Holocene fire regimes to infer patterns of anthropogenic fire. Etcetera etcetera. All in the interest of building descriptive, predictive, data-driven models of fire. Scientific fire. Fire you controlled, because you had modeled it with such rigor. Because you had the data.

But they didn't have it yet, not enough. In Ben's spiel—they'd heard all this before—that was always the catch. And the implication, always, was that the data, like the cavalry, were on the way, and a sufficiency of data would ultimately illuminate the truth.

Or maybe, thought Lena, a sufficiency of data would turn out to be more like flipping the high beams on a dense fog: blind reflection, a whiteout.

Jimmy

Angie turned to Jimmy. "How's business?" He looked at her blankly. "The horse business?" she said.

"Sure. It's just that I don't call it that. But the horses are doing fine. Taking the winter off, more or less."

"What about you?"

"Same thing. You know how it is in the canyon, Angie, nothing to do but sit around jerking off." He held up his hands, all calluses and cracks and scars and embedded dirt. "Sorry. But you want me to account for myself? Sure. New corral's about built, plus a sweet little riding ring. I planted a garden. House maintenance: painting, shoring things up, organizing the shop. I helped Clayton thin some timber before he left. Fuels reduction, Ben! We got burn piles everywhere. Trash and slash. Weeds, another ongoing project. Weeds are loving this drought. Loving the unirrigated pasture. I'm still working on getting water in the ditch. One thing at a time, right? No, everything at the same time. Shepherding Mom around, did I mention that?"

"Well, you are the caretaker," said Angie. "I guess you signed up for all that."

"Sure," said Jimmy. "Sure I did. Do you hear me complaining?"

Two years before, at his own instigation, Jimmy had been hired by Helen (by the Trust, technically, though as far as anyone knew the other trustee, Clayton, was not involved) as part-time, live-in caretaker of Upper McKeane Ranch, responsible for the rehabilitation of the long-neglected family property and development of a sustainable business model to carry it into the future. He'd written his own job description. The Trust compensated him with a modest stipend and all the pasture and horse training ground he needed. Jimmy had some skill with horses and had spent time on a polo horse ranch in Wyoming, working for people accustomed to paying twenty or thirty thousand dollars for an unbroken polo pony of good pedigree. This was the inspiration for his business model: a small herd of high-bred horses, people willing to pay extravagant amounts of money for them, and the flood-irrigated bottomland pasture of Upper McKeane Ranch.

He'd bought the horses, a half-dozen yearlings. After that the business model got a little fuzzy. He was still working out the balance—how much of a horse trainer versus breeder he was going to be, versus maybe just a horse rancher? Still working out the part about the flood-irrigated pasture. The Antimony Creek blowout three years earlier had downcut the stream channel by about 5 feet, isolating the ditch from its former diversion point. He and Clayton had gerry-rigged temporary solutions upstream, but problems were ongoing and now Clayton was gone and at low flows very little water made it out to the pasture.

"Well, that all sounds discouraging," said Angie. "You were so enthusiastic before."

"Oh, I still am. I'm fucking enthusiastic, Angie."

"Lack of enthusiasm has never been Jimmy's problem," said Helen.

"Or yours," said Angie.

Helen nodded, pushed back her chair, stood up, and left the room.

Helen

She returned with a shopping bag. Out of it she took four softcover copies of *Crack Between Mountains*, one for each person at the table. "I had 500 printed," she said. "If you want more, just ask." She thanked everyone for their help: researching, organizing, editing, just reading. She'd had her shepherd (she smiled at Jimmy), who'd also been her field crew, he helped her monitor and groundtruth (I like that word!). She'd had her proofreader, editor, publisher (she smiled at Ben). Everyone had helped in his or her own way, even when they didn't think they were helping (here she smiled at Lena), even when they conspired to imprison her here in Ben and Angie's house, leaving her with nothing to do and nowhere to walk but the dull cul-de-sacs in their subdivision. But this had forced her hand, she'd finished the book.

"It's beautiful, Helen," Angie said, flipping through a few pages. "Congratulations." Then she put the book down. "Groundtruthing, let's talk about that enthusiasm."

Helen had always covered a lot of ground. She was a walker and an explorer, accustomed to heading out all day with a knapsack and walking stick (an old ski pole). Her book had come out of her explorations. At one time she'd been reasonably competent at finding her way, but over the past couple of years she seemed to have lost her ability to navigate. Staying with Jimmy at the ranch, she'd wander off and fail to return. More than once he'd had to go out with a headlamp looking for her. Now he refused to take her there, it was too wild, too hard to keep her under surveillance. But even back at her own house there was trouble. She'd go for a walk, a route she might have followed hundreds of times, and hours later someone would come across her out on some back road miles from town, tapping along with her ski pole like a blind woman. Which in a way she was, with no idea of where she was or how to get home. But she just kept walking, not at all upset. She'd go for a drive and something similar might happen, except she'd end up even farther afield. Twice the police had escorted her home.

It was clear she could no longer live alone. Ben and Angie moved her into their spare room, a short-term solution. Angie took her to see a neurologist, she underwent a series of brain scans and cognitive tests. "Which I passed with flying colors. Even the neurologist had to admit I haven't completely lost it, not yet."

"It's something that hits her out of the blue," said Angie. "She's out on a walk, and then—"

"I realize I have no idea where I am. My geographic memory is gone. Houses, trails, streets, landmarks, I draw a blank. I can't remember the place, how I got there, how it connects to any other place. I have no *mooring*. I asked the neurologist. *Unmoored*, is that a diagnosis? And apparently it is."

"It turns out she has a recognized syndrome," said Angie. "It has a name, anyway. 'Topographical disorientation.'"

"And a secondary diagnosis," said Helen. "'Peripateticism'. Aristotle had it, apparently."

"Well, I think that wasn't necessarily a clinical diagnosis," said Angie. "I think the neurologist was making a little joke."

"It's not as bad as it sounds," said Helen. "It's not a fog. The opposite of a fog, actually."

"You don't seem anxious, anyway," said Jimmy. "That's good."

"Is it?" said Angie. "She's 70 years-old, alone, and 'unmoored'. Maybe a little anxiety would be appropriate? But it's true she's not losing it. We went over all the different brain scans, electrolytes, chemical balances, and so forth. Basically the lights are on and burning brightly, the neurologist said. What the MRI did show was a little blip, a dead zone somewhere in the hippocampus."

"Her hippocampotamus!"

"Thank you, Jimmy. Anyone else have a little jokey comment they need to get off their chest? Okay, this area of the hippocampus helps control for spatial orientation and navigation. And for whatever reason, in Helen's brain it isn't lighting up. She may have had a small stroke. A seizure. A genetic trigger that just shut it down. Nobody knows. They told her to take a baby aspirin every day. That's it. They have no cure. The patient has to compensate. Find a mooring."

"Her words," said Helen. "The neurologist. You need a mooring."

"More structure," said Ben. "More security."

"Somebody watching out for her," said Angie. "Right now it's us. But long term, we hire someone to stay with her. Walk with her, talk with her, live with her. A caretaker, that could be a mooring. But Medicare's not going to pay for it."

"And Mom has no money," said Ben.

"She has assets. Which currently are bleeding money. A slow bleed, but still."

"This is a birthday party!" said Helen. "We don't discuss money at birthday parties."

"Can we discuss your MRI?" said Jimmy. "That flat line in your hippocampus? I've been looking into this stuff. You know who else gets a flat line? Monks. Yogis. Praying nuns, people like that. You scan the brain of a person in deep prayer or meditation, you'll see a zone in the hippocampus that looks exactly like Mom's. Thick. Dense. Calm. What's that tell you?"

"That it's time for cake?" said Angie, heading for the kitchen, where Sam and Chloe were already clattering around.

But Jimmy was on a roll. "Thick and dense? Or a window into God? The monk, the shaman, what is it they seek? A unified field, right?

No borders, no walls. No coordinates. *Topographical disorientation.* *Spacelessness.* Those people have no location. Yet they feel the presence of God. Does this mean that God also has no location? Or that He's everywhere, every location? Or what if it's *God* who's lost? And if you want to find him, you have to be lost too. Unmoored, wandering the territories. Like Mom, the calmest person at this table, have you noticed? So maybe we should honor that, instead of dragging her back into our space/time prison, where territory is just another thing you measure out and buy and sell."

"*Spacelessness,*" said Ben. "Is *that* a clinical diagnosis?"

"It's real," said Jimmy. "Not tangible, but real."

"Well, maybe it's time to talk about something tangible." Angie stuck her head back in the room. "Something that might actually be helpful to the situation, maybe?"

"I don't know that anybody's ever talking about anything tangible," said Helen. "But I'm not arguing about the caretaker. Except I don't like that word. It sounds so—terminal. I'd prefer—I don't know, a minder, a keeper? A walker. Which sounds like a dog walker, but really, it's practically the same thing, to hear you all talking. But what's happening in the kitchen, those children are about to do something desperate. Angie, something tangible, quick! Cake!"

In fact, two tangible things did come out of that family reunion.

The first was the silver chain link necklace, with a tiny inlaid malachite locket, that Ben gave Helen as a birthday present. He put it around her neck and clicked the clasp.

"I didn't even get a look at it," complained Helen.

"You can see it in the mirror," said Ben. "It's nice, you'll like it."

"It's quite snug."

"You'll get used to it. Think of it as more than a necklace, Mom. Think of it as security. Medic-alert. Your name, addresses, phone numbers are all engraved on the back."

"Dog tags! You just fastened dog tags around my neck."

"In a way. Next, a dog walker, right?" He didn't tell her the code that would unlock the clasp. Or that inside the locket was a GPS tracking chip, so that with a glance at a screen any one of them could know at any time where she was.

A mooring.

The second tangible thing was Lena's job.

Lena

When it was her turn to report she gave the briefest possible summary of her situation. Maybe she'd had too much to drink. Maybe she just wanted a different situation. Yet not just her mother's story of disorientation and confinement but everyone's accounts and diagnoses and excuses, everyone's *projects*, suggested to her the inexorable grinding down and playing out of things, the narrowing of horizons, the inevitable and permanent loss of bearings and moorings.

Cake was eaten, the conversation drifted, Ben took a phone call and disappeared into his study. Twenty minutes later he had not returned. When Lena stuck her head in he was hunched over a keyboard, his face too close to the monitor, scrolling through long columns of numbers and graphs. Ben who always had his nose to some grindstone or another.

"Ben. I'm wondering if you could help get me a job."

She just blurted it out, an idea that had barely occurred to her. He answered without looking up. "You have a job. You were just telling us what a great job you have."

"Well, I'm thinking I need a change."

"You're imagining—what?" His fingers rippled over the keyboard. He glanced at her briefly but at once his eyes went back to the screen, flooded now with fields of color. What *was* she imagining? An escape from the traps she'd constructed for herself? The return of the prodigal daughter? An airplane spiraling into a canyon wilderness? Suddenly she felt stupid, a supplicant only dimly aware of what she was asking for.

"I don't know. Fire lookout or something."

"They hardly staff those anymore. Basically, they're obsolete."

"Just working in the woods somewhere, then. Trail crew. Fire crew."

"You see yourself swinging a Pulaski? Sucking smoke? Packing 80 pounds on your back?"

"Or one of your survey people, data loggers, whatever."

"We have a hiring freeze right now. And I can't hire my own sister. Who has no science background, no tech or woodsy background... "

"I've got a woodsy background. You have to go back a ways, but... "

The colors on the screen had resolved into polygons, gridlines, some kind of map. Ben was all about maps, all about bearings and moorings. No doubt his hippocampus was freakishly enlarged and hyperactive.

"I was under the impression you had a lot of stuff going on in Seattle. Residencies, internships, fellowships. Relationships."

"Ships and more ships, that was your impression?"

"So what happened? They sailed, or what?"

"I guess. Well, some of them sunk. Anyway. Now I'm thinking of moving back out here."

That got his attention. "*Why*?"

There was no way to account for herself. Not even to herself, let alone to someone like Ben, absorbed entirely in his own universe and incapable of imagining the extent to which she lacked organization and direction in her life. How easily she lost focus, how precarious the sequences of her logic. How she could lie on her bed reading and give herself over entirely to visions and apparitions coming out of what she read. The semi-legendary band of McKeanes wandering into their canyon. Her father's plane banking over the geometric patterns of their settlement. Her mother sorting through rockpiles and charred timbers, extracting artifacts, compiling elegies and diatribes.

"No single reason. Family stuff, partly."

"*This* family? So... that means you're going to stick around and start helping out with Mom?"

"Ben. This is how you do a job interview?"

"This is a job interview? You expect me to get you a job? Out here? In Fire?

A few weeks later he called her.

"I talked to some people. It turns out a fire lookout position is opening on the district. You could apply. Front and center on the Maginot Line."

When she hung up she googled it.

MAGINOT LINE: 1: line of defensive fortifications built before World War II to protect the eastern border of France but easily outflanked by the German blitzkrieg.
2: any line of defense that inspires a sense of security and confidence but that fails miserably.

11

TRUE FAMILY

Alvaro's beard now had streaks of gray. It must have begun to turn long before Chele had left for Ciudad de Luz, but in his memory it had never been anything but jet black. Alvaro said things were more or less the same but his beard was just one of many things that seemed to have changed during Chele's six-month absence. Alvaro was hunting down orphans more energetically than ever and there were many unfamiliar faces. Even kids Chele'd grown up with were somehow different.

Or maybe it was him. Six months at Ciudad de Luz, there was no explaining to anyone that experience, never mind the experience that had precipitated it. Nobody seemed to know what had happened between him and Tania and Alvaro, though there were undercurrents of speculation that he did nothing to dissipate or contradict or even acknowledge.

But now Tania was gone. Expelled, either before or after calling Alvaro *pendejo* and *maricón* and telling him in extravagant language to fuck off, then taking up her knapsack and walking out of St Jerome's gates in a cloud of glitter and down the long road to the highway and stepping onto the first bus she could flag down. Gone. That was the story, already a myth. Alvaro said only that she had left under difficult circumstances but that perhaps it was for the best. From Paola he heard that she had gone to live with her aunt in a town near the coast, but that maybe things hadn't worked out.

The horses drifted about, feral again. He wasn't sure he had the patience or desire to win them over one more time. For what? Alvaro had a point—if he had a gift it was wasted on them.

Alvaro called him into his office.

"Your horses have gone kind of wild again."

"They don't remember me."

"They might come around. Or maybe not. Maybe you don't have time for horses now." He handed Chele an envelope. "Your diploma. We said a year at Ciudad de Luz but I think six months is enough. Congratulations." They shook hands. "Now what?"

"I was thinking… University?"

"Always an option," Alvaro said, in a tone that suggested it wasn't. Then he offered Chele a job. A real job, not an internship or work study or anything like that. He'd no longer be a child under anyone's care, Alvaro said, but a paid adult employee of St Jerome's, working with a team on a new project out of the social worker's office. Alvaro didn't yet know what the position would be called. It would involve computers, information management, but it wasn't just a desk job. He would be responsible for planning and logistics. Detective work. Search and rescue. He'd be an observer, a scribe, a record-keeper. A chaperone, chauffeur, bodyguard.

The more Alvaro talked the more it sounded like he was just making it up as he went along, but of course Chele said yes.

The new project was called the Family Awareness Project. The team was Alvaro, the social worker, and Chele. They gave him a computer and a little cubicle in the social worker's office and put him to work on the Database. He'd never heard of the Database and now suddenly they were talking about it all the time. The social worker sat him down at the computer and taught him a password that until then only she and Alvaro had known and together they scrolled through the fields of the Database, which told, in rows and columns, numbers and check-marks, the known stories of the kids he'd grown up with. Important dates, diagnoses, legal status, behavior issues, medications, grades, baptisms, first communions, past residences, names and addresses of known and possible relatives. Not a narrative or story so much as points along the arc of a story, scaffolding to hang a story on. Very little scaffolding, in some cases. Half the fields might be blank. Chele's job was to fill them in.

Some of it came down to careful documentation and record-keeping, the social worker said. A lot of that information might be somewhere in a kid's file, in reports or forms or scribbled notes that no one had ever found the time to sort through and enter in the Database. There would be false leads, mistakes, contradictions. He'd have to crosscheck everything.

Or the file might be nearly empty, the forms all blank. Some kids were foundlings, nothing was known of their origins. Others had passed through multiple relatives and caretakers, with no record kept. Surely they had family somewhere but the family didn't know where they were or didn't care or had forgotten they existed. If you asked the children they might say nothing, or they'd make up some story or just say something that made absolutely no sense.

Chele sat in his cubicle and crosschecked, organized, compiled, deciphered, interpreted. He took notes while the social worker questioned teachers and caregivers and sometimes the children themselves. He found his own name in the Database. Most of his fields were blank. He found Paola Torres, more blank fields. There was no entry for Tania Torres.

Some days he rode a bus into the city and went to the National Archives to scroll through registries on government computers: birth, death, and marriage certificates, real estate titles, voter registration and tax forms, criminal records. He came across his own birth certificate, identical to the copy he'd already seen. His mother's birth certificate. Like his, with a single last name—Cruz—and an empty space where the father's name was supposed to go.

He looked but did not find a death certificate for Maribel Cruz.

The Database is looking better, said Alvaro. You did some good detective work. Now we've got a little to go on. More names. Pieces of family, or anyway places to look for pieces of family.

Then he and Alvaro got in the Mazda and went looking for the pieces and places. They found an aunt in jail, a mother in a homeless shelter, another on the street, another in a hospital psych ward. They made their way through neighborhoods that were more or less like *Colonia El Porvenir*, his grandma's old neighborhood. They knocked on doors of apartments as bleak as hers, or worse. They went deep into the campo, long drives over mountain highways and back roads, traveling on smooth asphalt, broken asphalt, gravel, dirt, mud. Sometimes they just left the truck and hiked the last few miles through forest or bush to some hamlet or *rancho* clinging to the mountainside in the mists, far from any grid.

Every place they visited was poor, unless it was dirt-poor. They entered dark houses that were little more than huts, that made his grandma's house in San Miguel seem almost luxurious. Sometimes the families were warm and welcoming, excited to hear news of children they'd lost track of in the tumult and difficulty of everyone's lives. Or they might be suspicious, even threatening. Chele stayed in the background. He took notes, or tried to. The talk could be wearisome and repetitive, misfortunes and excuses recounted in a wandering fashion and an excess of detail. He did not always pay close attention. But Alvaro did. You could tell by his questions and comments that he was not impatient. He was truly listening, truly empathetic. And no matter how dismal the house or sad or unpleasant the people or discouraging the conversation, he would come around to the same question: when could he and Chele bring the children to visit their family? Just to get acquainted, or reacquainted; it didn't have to be lengthy and it didn't have to be more than that, just a visit. But he said it deliberately, with emphasis—*to visit their family*—as if the visit had already been agreed to and it only remained to schedule it.

Chele almost always drove on the return trip. They might briefly discuss whatever had just happened and then Alvaro would speak quietly for awhile into his phone, a report that Chele would later transcribe and file. Then Alvaro would turn the radio up, too loud to talk, recline the seat, and almost instantly fall asleep, dead asleep, and Chele would just drive.

He reached over and turned the radio down. Alvaro growled in his sleep.

"Tío Alvaro.

After a minute Alvaro sighed. "What, Chele."

"It's like a six hour drive back."

"I can drive some."

"I'm okay, for tonight. But then—we're going to come *back*? Turn right around and bring kids all the way out here, twelve hours on the road, so they can meet—*them*?"

"That's the point. Family awareness, they're not aware until they meet the family. You thought it was just about the Database?

Maybe that was what he had thought. Or maybe he just hadn't thought beyond the Database, hadn't actually considered what the Family Awareness Project might really be about or where they were going with it. So. Was it about removing children from the sanctuary Alvaro had created and putting them in the backseat and driving them over endless mountains to present them to an unhappy family who didn't actually want to see them and who could offer them nothing but a graveyard for their dreams?

He said as much to Alvaro, straight out. But Alvaro said that if that was all a family could offer then maybe the sooner a child took a walk in that graveyard the better. If she were lost in a dream of a family that didn't exist then the sooner she got a good look at the family that *did* exist, the better. Why had they had gone to such lengths to locate and contact these families? Not to hide but to *show* them to the children: look, forget about whatever you've been imagining, this is how they really are. That was the point. That was the *obligation*. Yes it could get ugly. Yes some visits would be disasters. But maybe even a disaster would turn out to be a success. To see the true family, kill the dream family: success.

PFVS. Proyecto Familiar de Verdad y Sueño. What Chele came to call, in his own mind, Alvaro's blandly-named Family Awareness Project. True Family, Dream Family. The whole operation seemed crazy. They would leave the Gardens at dawn, Alvaro behind the wheel, at first, though later Chele did almost all the driving. The two of them in front and up to five kids squeezed into the backseat, washed, brushed, combed, and gelled, dressed and slicked up the best they could manage. Full of nervous and excitable talk, or too nervous to talk.

Sometimes the trip was short but often they would travel for many hours, always over or around or through mountains. They never stopped to admire scenery. Alvaro wasn't interested in scenery or landscape or geography, other than the geography of poverty: rancho and barrio and shantytown, places wracked by general and particular calamity.

The visit itself might last less than an hour, everyone sitting around on plastic chairs in a sparse room that smelled of bleach, urine, animals. A corrugated metal or thatch roof, rough cement or dirt floor, chickens and goats nosing in and out of a half-open door. Sometimes the children had a history with the family they were visiting, sometimes they were complete strangers. In either case, conversations tended to be awkward. Alvaro facilitated a little but not as much as he might have. Again, Chele said almost nothing. He was there, Alvaro had told him, to observe and record. To fill in a few more fields in the Database, maybe. To learn to read between the lines, even when there were hardly any lines. And because he had come out of something like that himself.

In his mind, he'd added a new field to the Database: *Transformación: Familia de sueño Δ Familia de verdad.* Because sometimes he saw it happen, exactly what Alvaro was talking about: dream family disintegrating as children confronted the grim lives of their actual family, saw how poorly they lived, how little they had to offer, and how in both body and spirit they often repudiated the values the children had learned, or supposedly learned, at St. Jerome's. There were kids who got some clarity out of this, a reconciliation with their situation, choices, opportunities. Others just became more unhappy and resentful. And a few abruptly left St. Jerome's and went to live with their true family—a different kind of transformation and reconciliation.

And a successful outcome, by Alvaro's fatalistic logic. A disaster's a success. And maybe, by the same logic, a success might be a disaster.

True family, dream family—everyone was exhausted by the convergence. There was very little talking on the return trips. It was usually dark and Alvaro's night vision was not so good, so Chele drove. Alvaro might shift around to talk briefly with the kids in the backseat but soon he would face forward and turn on the radio and everyone could finally just disconnect and sink into their own private space and do their best to absorb the aftermath of the family visit. Process whatever had happened or not happened. Or maybe none of it had been surprising or informative. Dream or true family, maybe it didn't make any difference to them, they just wanted the thing to be over. Maybe they were carsick, not that you could tell until after the fact. They were mainly silent pukers, the most you heard was the rustle of a plastic bag. A second or two later a stench filled the vehicle, then a window went down and plastic bag and stench were gone.

Chele, of course, could not disconnect. He was driving the mountain highway at night, one hundred percent attentive, wakeful, focused. Lethal obstacles appeared out of nowhere, randomly. Vehicles, cattle, horses, burros, dogs, rockslides, branches, whole trees, dirt piles, potholes, checkpoints, soldiers, bandits, drunks. His eyes were constantly scanning: the road immediately in front of him, the periphery, and the farthest illumination of the headlights and into the darkness beyond, where a piece of metal or reflective eyes might catch a glimmer of light. *His* night vision was excellent, his reflexes true and quick. He was fluid and fast with shifting, braking, steering. Alvaro had praised him for all these things, Alvaro trusted him, their lives were safe in his hands.

Yet at the same time he *was* disconnected. Their lives were in his hands, yet this was when he felt most distant from the kids in the back seat and even from Alvaro asleep on the seat beside him. When he felt most self-absorbed. He was supposed to be learning empathy.

But maybe what he was learning was how to separate from empathy. How to separate in general. Part of him was driving his people out of the mountains and over the twisting highway and safely back home; another part was traveling at a reckless speed away from them, farther into mountains, where people had been living and dying for thousands of years. And still the mountains were wild. Even the settled valley bottoms between cordilleras were wild, or on the very edge of the wild. The cultivated fields and pastures, the black cattle with great curvy horns and humped backs, the elegant snow-white birds perched on the cattle's backs, the coarse sawblade grass beyond the pastures. Wild.

But at last the mountains did end. They went over a final cordillera and descended to the coastal plain and the dirt road joined the gravel road and then a blacktop highway which they followed into a richer country. Anyway it had made some people rich. Old fruit company towns, plantations of sugar cane, African palm, banana. Patches of remnant forest. Then at last the highway ended, then the land, and he got out of the truck and walked onto a jetty and stood in the sunlight looking out on a sea so brilliant and immense he might have been gazing into the face of the sun itself.

There was a road map in the truck that sometime they used to plot out their route, but mostly Chele found it to be not so helpful. The map was static, while the landscape constantly morphed. The landscape was elastic and sinuous, like the roads themselves, and mostly he found the way by trial and error, small clues, the erratic memories of the children and the cryptic directions of the inhabitants. By his own improvised blend of logic and intuition. It turned out he had a knack for just *feeling* his way, for asking the right questions and inferring the right answers.

Gradually he began to assume more control of the *PFVS*. He was doing almost all the driving now, by day and night. He still conferred with Alvaro and the social worker, but most of the planning, route finding, record keeping, and data entry he did himself.

It wasn't about the Database. But still in a way it was. The Database at least was a measure of *something*. Names, numbers, some were accurate. *Familia de sueño* Δ *Familia de verdad*. Success or failure.

He was driving. Everyone else was asleep. He turned the radio down.

"What about my mother?"

Alvaro mumbled something.

"Did you ever even look for her."

Silence. Finally Alvaro sighed. "We had no time. There was no one to do that job. Nothing, really, to go on. We knew she had AIDS, that was about it. There was no treatment back then, Chele. When the drugs came along they weren't available to someone like her."

"You had more than that to go on. You knew she had a business on Calle Cortez."

"We knew she was starting one. That she claimed she was. A clue, if it was a clue, we saw six or eight years after the fact."

"What kind of business, do you think?"

"Who knows, Chele?" Alvaro sighed again. "I doubt she was selling *chicles*."

"Well, now there is," said Chele, after a pause.

"What?"

"Time. Somebody to do the job."

Alvaro was silent, that was the end of the conversation. But Alvaro's silences could mean different things. Chele took this one to mean, go ahead and look.

Calle Cortez was a noisy street of small *tiendas*, bodegas, hotels and *pensiones* and cafes. Sidewalks crowded with shoppers, street vendors, beggars, loiterers and no doubt thieves, he kept his hand on his wallet.

"Do you know Maribel Cruz?"

He asked at street stands and stores and cafes. Sometimes the storekeeper would think about the question, or seem to. Sometimes his mother's name would be shouted to the back of the store. But the answer was always no.

"She has a business around here."

"What kind of business?"

He moved down the street, in and out of stores. Past groups of men smoking, smirking.

"Come back at night, kid. That's when the businesswomen are out."

He came back at night. But was it even the same street? The stores and cafes were closed—not just closed, gone, disappeared behind corrugated metal barricades rolled down across their facades. But other doors and passageways had appeared; he was certain they had not been there before. Colored lights were strung along corridors and over entryways leading into bars. People—men, boys his own age, or younger—drank in silence or shouted at each other over the music. On the streets and sidewalks it was also mostly men. But women and girls looked down on the street from porches and doorways and open windows. Three girls came down and, arms linked, planted themselves in front of him to block his path. One reached out, stroked his arm, murmured something. Another disengaged herself from the others and stepped up close and breathed words straight into his face, he didn't understand but he understood.

"Do you know Maribel Cruz?" He didn't wait for an answer, just pushed past them and kept asking the question, all down the street. *Does anyone know Maribel Cruz?*

Voices and laughter followed him. *We don't know that girl, forget her! Hey baby, my name's Maribel!*

At the corner he turned off the street and fled the neighborhood. Later he scolded himself for panicking, not finishing the job, not asking the right questions or even pursuing the tiny openings he was given. *Me llaman Maribel!* He returned to Calle Cortez—the daylight street, no colored lights or shadowy alcoves, just people selling fruit and barbecued meat, waiting for buses, going in and out of open storefronts, here and there a glimpse into courtyards and patios of exhausted-looking women scrubbing clothes and nursing babies and alternately scolding and ignoring the children running wild around them.

He made a few more inquiries for Maribel, just throwing the name out in a random neighborhood of a city of a million names. He'd seen a fair number of them, combing through archives and registries. There were plenty more to sift through. But the low-hanging fruit had all been taken and that job now seemed increasingly futile, he could spend days with nothing to show. Which meant no one would know the difference if sometimes he did something else entirely. Skipped the archives, wandered the downtown streets. Revisited the National Gallery, the National Museum. Sat on a bench in the *Parque Central*, watching the street children huddled on the steps of the Cathedral, like trash swept into a pile and left there, there was nowhere to discard it. Hung around the malls beneath the glass towers, under the eyes of security men with automatic rifles and bulletproof vests. He didn't dare enter the stores but did stop to gaze at the impossibly expensive stuff in display windows, and at the reflections in the windowglass of expensive-looking people walking past. 'Walk'—a poor word for the way the women conveyed their bodies along the crowded sidewalk, their flow and undulation. Their scents washed over him in waves. He picked one out and followed her through the crowds, for long city blocks shadowing a stranger with no intention or plan and seemingly no will of his own. Finally she entered a building and the enchantment broke. Then he looked up at an unfamiliar neighborhood and, suddenly ashamed of his senseless stalking, found his way back to where he'd started.

So his thoughts were already deep in the city and its labyrinths when Paola came to him with Tania's letter. He read it that night in his bunk, by flashlight. She was living again with her sister and the *mareros*. Other situations had become toxic and she'd had nowhere else to go. But the situation with the *mareros* was also toxic, and dangerous, and she was asking for his help. She had a plan. She'd heard Alvaro had given him a car. She would be waiting the next evening at eight o'clock in Morazán Plaza, and in God's name and the memory of the affection she prayed he still felt for her she begged him to rescue her.

GROUNDTRUTH

The McKeanes came into the canyon, a small but more or less unified band, in the beginning. They prospered briefly, grew in number, then began a long decline. Now there is no band, though the dwindled and scattered members still have a sense of belonging to one. Their home-steads—the word itself is archaic—have slid steadily toward ruin. And yet. To some what those ruins suggest is not so much failure as new pos-sibility, new worth and beauty ingrained in decay.

12

THE MAGINOT LINE

THE MONSOON WAS COMING. Summer's denouement, the fire look-out's moment of truth. Often as not a dry monsoon, in the Perdu country. Lightning, wind, heat. Little or no rain.

¿Piensa usted que va a llover?

She imagines clouds materializing out of a vacant blue sky. Sailing toward the mountain, billowing, flattening, darkening, multiplying, merging into a single black cloud, sweeping across the highlands and over Indian Mountain. She imagines an electric storm in the skies above and around her and over the earth below, thunder and lightning on the mountain, the ghostly blue light of Saint Elmo's Fire shimmering in her window ledges and on the borders of her retinas. She sits on her insulated stool in deep darkness and sudden blazing light, wheeling the firefinder around and sighting at places where lightning strikes the ground and where later, by daylight, she might see a tiny ribbon of smoke rising. Then radios in locations and descriptions and waits for planes and parachutes to appear in the sky and firefighters in yellow Nomex to spill out over the ground.

Her voice on the radio sets all that in motion, but she herself will never leave the tower, never get near the fire. For the old-time fire lookouts it had been different. When those men—all men, in those days—spotted a smoke, they too would radio in, but only to advise the ranger that the lookout would be out of service for a time. Then they'd grab a shovel or Pulaski, toss a couple cans of beans in a knapsack, and plunge off the mountain to single-handedly extinguish the fire.

That was the myth, anyway. How often anything like that had happened was open to question. According to Ben the whole story was open to question. It was a story of ecological delusion on a massive scale. The delusion of the Maginot Line: thousands of fire lookouts strung across the low and high mountains of the West, guarding a territory fully infiltrated and under siege from all directions. But they kept calling in the firefighters, who kept putting out the fires. Winning battles, and so losing the war.

Now those battlegrounds were blackened, or in flames, or soon to go up in flames. The forest was drying up and choking on itself and the old lookouts were mainly abandoned—forgotten, torn down, burned up. Or standing as relics and reliquaries, artifacts of nostalgia. Only a few were still manned, Ben said. Womanned. A few people still peering through binoculars and firefinders, still calling in smokes and strikes, still acting as though the war could be won.

Think of yourself as a Japanese soldier, he told her. Marooned on your forgotten Pacific atoll, taking potshots at distant Allied ships. Genuflecting to a fallen emperor.

The monsoon failed. The sky remained pale and empty, the country dry and dull under a thin coating of dust. Hot winds sent golden waves of cheatgrass rippling up out of the canyon and the river breaks. Indian Mountain became an island refuge—for water, wildlife, chlorophyll. A few patches of dirty snow, tinged with pink algae, clung to the steeper north-facing gullies. On dry, rocky soils on the high ridge, wildflowers held their bloom though long and rainless days. Lena gathered bouquets, a bouquet on every windowsill, every drinking glass a burst of flowers.

Columbine, lupine, cinquefoil, penstemon, valerian.

How exactly am I genuflecting? she wanted to say to Ben. What potshots? Mid-August and she hadn't seen a smoke or so much as a distant flicker of lightning. Scanning, was that genuflecting? A form of devotion, at any rate. Disciplined, repetitive, focused, an endless surveillance of valleys and ridges and horizons, where only the light changed and no sign was ever revealed and very little happened that she could see.

Pienso que nunca.

Then, suddenly, there was something. A man emerged from the trees and stood on the slope directly below her tower, looking up at her, or at the glare coming off her windows. He had a startled look, as if only this moment he'd become aware of the firetower directly above him. He wore high black boots and multiple layers of baggy clothing. A holstered pistol was strapped to his leg and he carried a frame pack and held a large plastic bucket in his hand. Through the glass she saw that it was full of morel mushrooms. The pack as well, maybe. The binoculars brought his face right in front of her, half-hidden beneath a full black beard and the shadow of his hoody. But still she could make out a violent twist or deformation in his features. He lifted his head and she saw that his eyes were wild, the eyes of a fish hauled out of the depths to the surface, dilated and bulging in the sudden pressure drop.

She went out on the catwalk and stood by the railing and folded her arms across her chest and stared down at him. Nodded, slightly. Not a greeting. State your business, mister, and move on. Or just move on. But she didn't speak. He put a hand up to block the sun, or her gaze, or both, then turned and took rapid, limping strides down the open slope and back into the forest.

So. She had practiced looking hard at things, and twice now— mountain lion, mushroomer—had turned back a threat with nothing but the implacability of her gaze. But how real a threat? The lion was one thing, the mushroomer, another. Her first and only visitor of the summer. With bucket and pistol and ruined face he had made a solitary crossing of the deep forest, eyes fixed on the fungal ground, and then emerged into the sunlight and looked up to see a watchtower looming and a baleful woman looking down from her parapet.

In a way he bore a resemblance to her father. A crazy thought that just came to her, maybe because he'd emerged so randomly from beneath the forest canopy her father had so randomly disappeared beneath. Or because he resembled what her father might have become, had he survived his last flight and presumed crashlanding. A forest dweller, hooded and dark. Misshapen bones, eyes popping out of his head, sleeping in caves, feeding on roots and fungi.

She was twelve the spring he went missing. Clayton heard his plane take off and begin to climb—upriver, a side drainage? He hadn't paid attention; the comings and goings of Ethan McKeane were not his concern. But that was the last anyone saw of him. No Mayday call came over the radio, no sighting of wreckage or trail of smoke, no images, no trace on any radar. No clue.

There was nothing particularly suspicious about the circumstances. It wasn't unusual for a small plane to go down in those mountains. Winds could be erratic. Sudden downdrafts, tailwind bursts, thunderstorms. The air thinned in summer heat. A pilot might not get the lift it he counted on, flying low or skimming a headwall or landslide. Killing the engine so he could hear the wind, the river.

If you have control with power, you have control without.

The supply helicopter brought a care package from Angie. Chocolates, cheeses, fruit, a bottle of wine. A corkscrew, a letter. She put the food in her little fridge and stashed the wine and corkscrew on the shelf beneath the firefinder. Then she opened the letter.

> *Just a quick note, no time for more. Hectic summer, full schedule every day. What happened to turning kids loose with a pocket knife and a peanut butter sandwich and letting them muck around in a ditch all day? Ha! Chloe and Sam wouldn't know what to do. But they are very good with their phones. They keep close tabs on your mother, are on her in a flash whenever she steps over her boundaries. Thanks to them, we manage to keep her in the neighborhood. But keeping her in the neighborhood is a very temporary solution.*
>
> *Ben showed me a picture of your lookout. I have three questions.*
>
> > *1. do you have to go down those stairs every time you piss. Or what.*

2. *do you ever see any people. Talk to people.*

3. *what's it like at night. All alone at the top of a mountain, I can't imagine.*

The wine is exquisite. It needs to breathe!

Angie

1. She pissed in a can with a good tight lid. Kept the can out on the catwalk and once or twice a day went down and emptied it in the outhouse. Otherwise she used the outhouse directly or just the ground far from the lookout, so as not to attract mountain goats, who were drawn to urine salts and could get aggressive.

2. She saw a lot of airplanes, full of people, presumably, did that count? Tiny bright specks that crossed the sky and vanished before any sound reached the earth. The sky paled in the thickening and multiplying of their contrails.

At one time she had lived in cities those planes connected. Now no word of them reached her ears. Did she talk to people? She heard people talking, over the radio. Occasionally she spoke with them herself. Routine weather reports and check-ins with Dispatch, messages she passed along to field crews, slightly more conversational exchanges in the evenings with other fire lookouts on distant peaks.

But people were, after all, part of what she'd wanted to get away from. Take a sabbatical from. People and their incessant, repetitive voices. The noise they generated. Mostly she talked to herself. Or to the birds, or her Spanish tutorials, remote human voices that she echoed, over and over.

> *¿Qué tal tu nuevo trabajo?*
> *¡Fantástico, es un puesto estupendo!*

> *¿Te gustaría cenar conmigo esta noche?*
> *Lástimamente no puedo, ya tengo otra cita.*

So no, Angie. Never face to face and talking back and forth with an actual physical person, except when the helicopter descended briefly with provisions and over the engine roar and the beating of rotors she exchanged a few shouted words with the firefighter who unloaded them.

3. At night everything is reversed.

At sunset, a full color gradient across the sky. Yellows and oranges and reds in the west, in the east a darkening daytime blue, deepening to purple and then black on the horizon. Venus rising, crescent moon, scattered stars and planets, and finally above the silhouetted mountains a blaze of celestial bodies, cycling, spinning, revolving. The great vertiginous tumbling of the heavens, that she'd almost forgotten, a city dweller blind in the bubble of her own light.

On nights of no moon, the absolute darkness of the land. At most a faint glow or flicker beneath the trees somewhere far below, suggesting a human presence, a campfire or cabin light. On the far horizon a queasy phosphorescence, the Smudge.

She flips a switch and outside it all goes black; inside, full exposure under a humming yellow light. The lookout now the lookin, a blind city unto itself.

Outside, a silence as absolute, at first, as the darkness. Silence, a conduit to deeper spectrums of sound. The tumble of air molecules through the mechanisms of the weather station. The low throb of far-off engines. The faint reverberation of rivers coursing through canyons. The currents and upwellings of the electromagnetic ocean.

Sometimes she heard coyotes yipping, or wolves howling. Once, a sudden echoing boom, like thunder. She went out on the catwalk. No further sound, no flicker of lightning on any horizon. A gunshot, then. It might have originated from any direction, any distance, for any reason or for no reason. People had guns, they shot at targets, animals, the sky. At each other, at themselves.

At night—late, when she couldn't sleep—she read *Crack Between Mountains*. She turned on the light and sat up in bed and burrowed into the dense, cluttered pages, infected with weird time warps, loops, blocks. Maps she struggled to align with her own. Genealogies that tangled, frayed, looped around, descendants who seemed to morph into their ancestors. The narrative sprawled, tunneled, dead-ended. Then you were in a different tunnel.

But the tunnels led to stories. She dug them out, another excavation.

The story of Ledorah, where her namesake Galen McKeane, trailing sheep on Red Mountain, had prospected a deposit of ore-bearing rock, named his new claim after his wife, and incorporated a mining company under the same name. Then—with the help of encouraging assays, an enthusiastic geologist's report, and (he said) the lyrical cadence of his wife's name—he persuaded a group of investors to finance the construction of a mine, road, camp, and gravity-powered aerial tram line to carry the ore from the Red Mountain saddle to a stamp mill to be built on a flat above the Perdu River, two and a half linear miles and seven thousand vertical feet below. The refined gold would be packed out by mule train to Confluence Bar and the river road.

For many pages *Crack Between Mountains* examined the reasons this scheme failed, beginning with fraudulent appraisals of the ore's value and ending with the sudden collapse of a tram tower, killing two workers. By then the camp had become a town with dozens of rough buildings, the mines had been working for a year, and a huge pile of ore waited at the saddle below Red Mountain for the completion of the tram to carry it down to the yet-unbuilt mill. Then the tower fell and the story devolved into a muddy narrative of suits and counter-suits, changes of venue, accusations, recriminations, defamations, warrants, all coming to nothing when Galen McKeane—star witness, defendant, and litigant—abandoned Ledorah—mine, boomtown, investors, wife—and fled to Confluence Bar, where he hid out in a drift mine tunnel and was buried in the rubble of an unexplained explosion and cave-in. One scenario, anyway. But no dead body was recovered and consequently there were sporadic rumors and unsubstantiated sightings of a living one, in Mexico, in Honduras, in the company of politicians, soldiers, miners, women, coming out of a restaurant or hotel or mine tunnel, or going into one.

The story of the McKeane Ditch, the oldest irrigation ditch in the county, first thing the homesteaders built when they came into the canyon. They worked non-stop all winter and spring, drilling, blasting, cutting, milling, excavating, and by June were taking water from Antimony Creek and moving it over a mile by earthen ditch and wooden flume around talus slopes and cliffs to water new hayfields and orchards on Confluence Bar. For a few years the ranches thrived, growing produce and meat for the miners. But when the tower collapsed the miners moved on and there was no one to buy meat and produce and little point in moving water through ditches or putting it out on fields. Confluence Bar became a derelict place, barely inhabited.

Then floodwaters cut into the banks and shifted the gravels in Antimony Creek, and someone noticed a yellow gleam in a freshly exposed beach. Beaches like that were buried everywhere under the cobble, where over the millennia gold from the eroding ore of the Ledorah lodes had washed down, settled out, and concentrated. Or so the McKeanes decided.

The extraction of the Antimony Creek placers was a violent enterprise that stretched out over generations, waxing and waning with the oscillations of the gold market, the enthusiasm of investors, and the energy and attention span of the miners. They had been ranchers and farmers but now turned their irrigation ditch to a new purpose, going at the gravels first with tremendous blasts of water from hydraulic hoses and an elaborate infrastructure of reservoirs, channels, screens, filters, and settling ponds, then churning up the bottomlands with a forty foot dredge, which now sat abandoned among the gravel beds and tailings ponds they created out of that floodplain.

The story of Olympus Springs, Josie McKeane Pratt's luxury spa on the mountainside high above Confluence Bar, at the hot springs that all the maps called Poison Springs. A name given by a passing fur trapper, spooked by the sulfurous mists rising from a cleft in the mountainside and unaware that people had long considered the thermal waters a rejuvenator and a preservative. With gold fever simmering, the Indians dispersed, and miners and a few settlers still moving into the Perdu country, Josie and her husband Lothar Pratt filed a homestead claim in Poison Gulch and set out to revive and profit from the historic reputation of the springs. Sulfur not as poison but as tonic. They would divert the waters of both hot springs and cold creek and create private soaking pools in the natural grottos of the gulch, consecrated to the pleasure-seeking gods of ancient Greece. On terraced slopes above they would build a luxury hotel and restaurant. There would be rock gardens, fountains, waterfalls, pale marble, blue Mexican tile, teams of white horses pulling coachloads of enraptured patrons up and down the Ledorah Road.

But again the storyline muddied, and Lena lost her way in a convoluted account of the collapse of the mining economy, construction and marketing difficulties, territorial and contractual disputes, floods, landslides, and the passions and betrayals that marked the tumultuous marriage of Josie and Lothar, culminating in the murder of Lothar, found floating in a bathtub at the hot springs with a bullethole in his forehead, a literal bloodbath, while Josie and her infant baby, like Galen McKeane, just vanished.

The story of the Golden Throat Mine, a single shaft Caleb McKeane spent thirty years blasting into the mountain straight across from Josie's tubs, where he'd soaked for long hours, contemplating the bedrock on the far side of the gulch and intuiting the trajectories of the quartz veins running through it. His tunnel never deviated more than a degree or two from its original line—aimed, he was convinced, straight at the mother lode. A conviction that never wavered, though perhaps it did. He was hauling a truckload of ore off the mountain when his truck went into a long skid, spun around slowly, teetered on the edge of the hairpin, and dropped—accident, sabotage, or suicide?—a thousand feet into the spring flood of the Perdu River.

Lena fell asleep with her reading light on and the book open on her pillow and these calamitous stories churning in her head. In the end she didn't know how much of them to believe, how loose her mother might be playing with her facts. An occupational hazard, no doubt, when you wrote about dreamers and bullshitters like the McKeanes. You might become one yourself. Dreamer, bullshitter, feverish miner tunneling into libraries and bookshelves, thrift stores, junkyards, desks, crawl spaces, sheds and attics. Excavating homesites, gravesites, dumps, mines, camps, bringing to the surface and into the light all this material, then using it to reconstruct—reinvent—a history of the Perdu River McKeanes. Patterns that keep repeating. Protagonists walking out of their own stories. Tracks leading into empty skies or underground or beneath the forest canopy, the only character left on the page is the ranch.

And maybe that was about to disappear too.

13

CHISPA

Vamanos, Chele.

He got up and went with Alvaro and they walked and walked. Their longest silence yet. Finally Chele understood that Alvaro wasn't going to break it. So he started talking, and didn't stop until he had told him everything.

He began with Tania's letter. He should have taken it straight to the incinerator and burned it to ash, and with it whatever role she'd imagined him playing in her telenovela. Her reality show, her *sucesos*. Or maybe it wasn't hers. Maybe the script was written by *mareros*. The next scene was when they would drug him, kidnap him, put him up for ransom or sell him into slavery. Or just take the Mazda and leave him in a ditch with his throat slashed, body full of bullets, cock and balls stuffed in his mouth.

Vivo bajo un peligro grave. Mañana te espero en el Morazán, te suplico que me rescates.

I'm in grave danger, rescue me. A telenovela script, but the *mareros* were real, true family. And what if she was finally seeing them for what they were, finally breaking free of her dream family, the big brother *mareros* with their honor codes and revolutionary fervors and fleeting tenderness and outlaw charm? If she wanted to make that conversion and he had the means to help her, wasn't it his obligation to do so? Wasn't that Alvaro's own creed, the fatalism at the heart of the *PFVS*?

Familia de sueno Δ *familia de verdad.* Failure Δ success.

At dusk, alone and without saying a word to anyone, he drove the Mazda down to the gate of St Jerome's Gardens. He spoke to the *guardia* and the *guardia* unlocked the gate and swung it open and Chele drove out of the Gardens and down the winding road to the highway and across the darkening plain, past the perpetual flame of the crematorio and into the city and its valley of the shadow of death. Which wasn't a shadow at all but a dim and poisonous light. He kept descending, all the way to the foaming, stinking river, where in the lowest neighborhoods streets narrowed and darkened and the density of buildings further compressed the streets, distorting and amplifying sounds of engines and voices. In diminishing crowds people hurried past, seeking what refuge they could find before night fell. The sky disappeared. A ceiling closed over the emptying streets and it seemed to Chele that the descent continued, that he had entered the forgotten network of tunnels beneath the city.

How do you find your way through a mine? Bumping over winding, hemmed-in passages, praying they don't squeeze in on you entirely or drop you into some unmarked pit or caved-in tunnel with no exit. He'd thought he knew the city but now recognized nothing. In his childhood rescue fantasies he had always known exactly where to go and had gone there and found the girl and swept her up on the horse and escaped. But now he just weaved and wandered, turning onto random streets and arriving at Morazán Plaza more or less by chance. The maze of dark passageways and low buildings and cement walls glittering with glass shards ended and suddenly there were trees, he was looking at great trunks lit by yellow streetlights, at pathways and benches, dry fountains, a stone horse rearing up beneath a stone Liberator.

Beside the statue the girl rising from a bench looked very small. She wavered on the sidewalk, then veered into the street and yanked the passenger door. He unlocked it and she tumbled in with a wave of perfume, her shoulder bag clunking on the floor.

"Just get the fuck out of here, Chele. They'll cut your balls off."

He sensed a further commotion in the park but kept his eyes straight ahead and hit the gas. The tires squealed. Tania slouched low in the passenger seat. Chele hunched over the steering wheel, too scared to look in the mirrors, and drove.

He turned onto side streets, sped through a neighborhood—more squealing tires, little fishtails as he took the corners—and emerged onto another boulevard. Now Tania sat upright, clutching her shoulder bag and grinning at him.

"Don't tell me fucking Alvaro taught you to drive like that."

"That's not how I drive."

That low, slurry voice. She'd done something weird to her hair. Bleached it, frizzed it, dyed it? Headlights, streetlights flashed over her face, like showers of stars or sparks.

"Where are we going?"

"Just drive."

"Where? What's going on, Tania?"

They were on a street with bars, music. On the sidewalk people gathered around little fires, discotheque lights strobing behind them.

"Let's go dancing. I bet you've never been to a club. About a thousand people squished around you. The music really *loud*. You can't talk, can't get away, all you can do is *dance*."

"Tania. You said you had a plan. I'll take you where you need to go, if it's not too far. Then I need to get back."

"You look different, Chele. Older. Do I look different?"

"You did something to your hair. What's that on your face, more glitter?"

"Yeah, more glitter. Not just on my face."

"What's in the bag?"

"You like it? It's a really nice bag, huh, a Gucci, see? A present."

"Tania. I'm not supposed to be here. I took a big risk. I have to get this truck back."

"Sure, you've got a curfew. Tío Alvaro is waiting up. Stop calling me Tania."

"Stop calling you Tania?"

"I have a new name. Everybody gets a new name. I'm Chispa. Listen, do you ever think about telling Tío Alvaro to go fuck himself? That you're sick of being his fucking *taxista*?"

"The truck has to get back. It's not up to me. So. Where do you want to go?"

"It's a nice truck. What's that all about? Last I saw, you're riding up to old Alvaro on a smelly old horse. That needed a bath. Then he turns around and gives you a truck."

"He didn't give it to me."

"You're driving it." She giggled. "Shampoo, make-up, toothbrush. Pills. Stuff in my bag."

"What kind of pills?"

"Like, for headaches, cramps, don't be so nosy, Chele. Body lotion. Creams. Scents."

"Nothing illegal?"

"Define illegal. Sanitary pads. Condoms."

"Tania. Are you *carrying* something? You're like, somebody's mule?"

"Oh, sure, Chele. *Soy mula.* This is how you talk to girls? Well, fuck off. I'm carrying a hair dryer. I'm carrying a change of panties. My name is Chispa."

He pulled over before the interchange at the *periférico*, the freeway that encircled the city.

"Tell me where you want me to take you."

She looked out the window while he read aloud from road signs the names of towns.

"I guess Chalamanca. You could take me to Chalamanca."

He'd never heard of it. It wasn't on any of the signs.

"Towards the border. *Frontera* town. Not far. You take a side road. The Chalamanca highway. My aunt lives there."

"How far is not far?"

"She *lived* there. I don't know now. Or we just blow through Chalamanca. Straight through to the border. You've been to the border? Never? Well, there's nothing there. Which is the point, right? The point is, get to the other side. Another country, another border. You just keep crossing. And every border you go over, you're that much closer to being free. To being rich."

Along the Chalamanca highway the houses were all dark. Maybe the electricity was out, or the lines didn't reach that far. There were no other cars on the road.

"This is a highway? No pavement, no signs, it's just a dirt road."

"There's highwaymen," said Tania. "So it's a highway. They put rocks in the road. When you stop they come out and steal your car. Kill you, if they get the urge. Nobody drives this road at night."

So how did the highwaymen stay in business? He figured the highwaymen were a myth but then quite possibly so was Chalamanca. He still hadn't seen a sign for it. Maybe the whole thing was a setup. Maybe she'd just invented it on the spot. He'd asked where she wanted to go and when she opened her mouth those were the easy syllables that came out. *Cha-la-man-ca.* Maybe it was the name of a place in one of her telenovelas, a chateau or fancy resort, some enclave where rich people conducted their affairs and intrigues and betrayals.

Or maybe it was real. Maybe her world was larger than he'd imagined, large enough to contain some remnant of family in a little town back in the hills. He decided to believe that was mainly true, if only because he couldn't think what else to do with her. He couldn't just drop her at a street corner or bus station. For sure he couldn't take her to St. Jerome's, proof that he'd violated Alvaro's trust. For absolute sure he couldn't take her back to Morazán Plaza, where *mareros* were waiting to cut off his balls.

The road descended to a river. At one time a bridge had spanned it, but now only abutments remained. Tire tracks crossed the sand and disappeared into black water. He drove straight into the ford, the Mazda surging blindly, headlights streaming water and shining on the tire tracks that emerged from the other side.

"You got balls, Chele. So tell me something. Why are you still a virgin? You are, I know it. You've got awesome balls, you can't stop staring at my tits, and you're still a virgin."

They climbed away from the river again and came out on a hogback ridge. The road wound along the narrow crest, deep blackness on either side, while Tania chattered on about the *mareros* and their apartment and locked doors and secret passwords that weren't as secret as they thought. But not really explaining anything about her life as far as Chele could tell, what she'd done, who she'd done it with, just going on about how claustrophobic and barren the apartment was but behind locked doors were many rooms, vaults, passageways that went deeper into the building and even into the street and the city than she was supposed to know. But she knew.

"Stop, Chele."

"You said *don't* stop. The highwaymen..."

"Yeah, I'm not worried about those fuckers. Come on, I'm about to pee my pants!"

She tumbled out the door, taking the bag with her. He turned the lights and engine off, heard her pee gush, then trickle, then the rustle of clothes. Her low voice in the darkness.

"Coast is clear, if you want to piss too. Or whatever. Got you covered."

He got out. The air felt warm and humid; they were still on the ridge but must have gone down farther in elevation than he'd thought. Approaching the coast, and the border. He stood on the side of the road, looking into the darkness below. Somewhere a dog began to bark. He unzipped, maybe he did have to piss.

Or maybe he just had a hard-on, too hard to piss.

"There's houses down there," Tania said. "People *live* there. *Sin luz. Sin nada.*"

He gave up on pissing, wrangled his dick back into his underwear, zipped up. Then began to slowly move around the vehicle by feel, his hand on the warm engine hood.

"They just sit around. Try to find each other in the dark. Or hide from each other. Or... "

Her voice trailed off. He heard only breathing, the bag rustling, dogs barking. Felt warm, moist air coming off a distant ocean. Smelled ocean, green plants, earth, flowers, Tania. Saw, or imagined that he saw, the shape of her body sloped back against the engine hood in the darkness.

There was an explosion and a streak of orange light. He dropped to the ground behind the truck. The explosion echoed and reverberated, dogs barked madly in the valleys below, and Tania came around the front of the truck toward him while he scrambled away from her along the ground, trying to keep the vehicle between them.

"Hey." She was giggling again. "Hey, goddammit, Chele, I'm not shooting at *you*! I'm not shooting at anything! I just reached into the bag, the fucking thing just went off on its own."

"Guns don't 'just go off on their own.'"

"What do you know about guns? You know about machetes. You know about horses."

"Just put the gun away, Tania. Please."

"Chispa."

"Whatever. Put it away. People heard that for miles. Listen to the dogs."

"Yeah. Everybody's awake *now*. Holy shit, they're thinking, it's the fucking *highwaymen*."

He heard more rustling—the gun going back in her bag, he hoped. Cautiously, he moved towards her and the front of the truck. She spoke, a whisper.

"He just kicked me out. I didn't do anything. I didn't want to leave. He just wanted me gone before you got back."

"That's not what I heard."

"That's what happened. But it doesn't matter. You know what we are, Chele? We're survivors. We're fucking gonna make it. Against the odds. Forget Chalamanca. We'll just take the truck straight across the border. Head north."

For a moment it seemed plausible. Or at least for a moment he allowed himself to imagine what it would be like, to throw off everything and drive across the border with Tania, across many borders. To lie with her on a mattress in the back of the truck. On a blown-out bed in a bottom-end hotel. On a Mexican beach under the stars, with the waves pounding.

"We can't take the truck over the border. We don't have papers. For one thing."

"So we lose the truck. It's too big anyway. Too visible. We crash it over the side of the mountain. Dump it in the river. Steal some horses. Ride to the border."

"Why do you keep talking about the border? What are you doing with a gun?"

"Oh. Well, I guess I don't know that yet, Chele. What I'm going to do with it."

Silence. Darkness. Was she drawing closer to him? Her body swaying, voice almost too low to be heard.

"*Si quieres, te lo mato.*"

"What?"

"You heard me." More silence. Then: "The truck's awesome. But sometimes a girl likes to feel a horse between her legs, you know what I'm saying?"

He got back in the truck and started the engine and turned on the headlights. She stayed leaning against the hood, holding her bag to her chest. Panties, condoms, gun, what else. Something taken from a vault, from behind locked doors. Something that would make her rich, once she crossed enough borders.

He'd heard her. Barely, her voice lower and sloppier than ever. But he had heard.

If you want, I'll kill him for you.

He put the truck in gear and edged forward, pushing her off to the side. Then stopped and waited. Finally she opened the door and got in, sniffling.

The road wound endlessly along the ridge. She kept sniffling. "Are you crying?" he said. "Oh, shit. Don't start *crying*, Tania."

"I'm not fucking crying, Chele. Maybe I just got something up my nose."

After that he drove in silence. But her words echoed in his head. *If you want I'll kill him.* Or maybe, *I'll kill you.* Maybe the gun was pointed straight at him the whole time.

He stopped when they came to the outskirts of a village.

"This is Chalamanca? Your aunt lives here?"

She didn't answer.

"Look, this as far as I'm going, okay? I'm turning around. You can stay here or I can take you somewhere else. But not the gun. Not the bag. The bag and the gun go out the window."

The truck idled. Tania sniffled. No one moved. Finally she opened the door and got out and shut the door and spoke through the open window, he could barely hear.

"I would never do that, Chele, okay? Never." Definitely crying. Then she walked up the road toward a street of shuttered houses, no lights, no spark, a chorus of dogs barking.

A deadly trap narrowly averted, or a rare opportunity squandered? All the drive back to the city his mind went back and forth but could not make that determination. Alternating currents had pulsed through him all night: desire, then fear and even revulsion, then desire again— for Tania, or for some promise of ultimate freedom that Tania represented? But in the end fear had cancelled out all that and he remained, never mind his awesome balls, a virgin. But he could not stop thinking of what she'd said. *Te lo mato.* Then: *I would never do that.* Alvaro had kicked her out without cause, to keep her away from him—could that be true, or even partly true? He could not stop thinking of the shadow of her body, slouched against the warm engine hood in the warm ocean air. The sound of her voice, her breathing, the way her mouth did something sexual to every word that came out of it. By the time he reached the outskirts of the city the pulse of desire had strengthened into a current, flowing out of a place low and deep in his brain to overwhelm all other currents or any thought that might have developed into an objection when he swerved off the *periférico* and again entered the labyrinth.

A man stepped out holding a sign. '*PARQUEO*'. He turned the Mazda into a dirt lot. The same man appeared at his window with a piece of paper. Chele took the receipt and handed him the keys and hustled along the street. Bars and pool halls, red and amber street-lights, sketchy hotels. Girls and women in windows and doorways, their faces passing in and out of light and shadow or just staying in shadow while their voices went out into the street—soft hisses, whistles, babytalk. He veered away toward a deeper voice, sloppy and hoarse like Tania's, and came up against a face of jutting bones, heavy makeup, stubble shadow. Thick mascara, thin disguise. He turned and fled and the low voice went high, shrieking falsetto laughter at his back.

A woman stepped out of the shadows and greeted him warmly, as if there were already some intimacy between them. He hesitated. She took his arm and fell into step with him. Was he looking for something special? Something sweet, or maybe spicy? I'm looking for my mother, her name is Maribel Cruz. He didn't say it. She jostled against him as they walked. Her leg rubbed his leg. Her breasts swelled out of her camisole. She touched his face. She was a few years older but he wanted her older. Tania in ten years, if she survived all her border crossings. She steered him into the open door of a *pensión*. They stopped in the hallway and she told him her price. Chele took out his wallet and gave her money and she took his hand and led him down the hallway. A man was watching TV in a tiny room. He handed her a key and she led him down another hallway and unlocked a door.

The room had one small window, too high to see out of. A bed, a chair, a single dim orange light bulb. In the rust-colored light she watched him watching her take off her clothes.

"Do you know Maribel Cruz," he said.

"*Quita la ropa, corazón*".

He took off his clothes. She pursed her lips at the chair where she had put her own. "*Cúelgala.*" He draped them over the back of the chair and went to her. She was still wearing her bra, nothing else. He put a hand on her breast. She let it rest for a moment, then gently lifted it off. "*Para la criatura.*" For the baby, little creature. She moved his hand slowly down her stomach and put it between her legs and pressed, hard. "*Para ti.*"

She pulled him onto the bed on top of her, whispering or just breathing into her ear, crushing his face into her neck. He heard a ripping sound next to his ear—a condom packet, she'd torn it open with her teeth, had it on him in a second. There were a dozen distractions: bumping and rustling and voices in adjoining rooms, a buzzing reggaetón bass, fingers digging hard into the back of his neck, smells of mold and bleach and her perfume and sweat and the perfume and sweat of men who had been on top of her before. Yet he was not distracted but rather incredibly focused—on her warmth and wet-ness, the thrust of her body beneath his, the heat of her breath, slur of her voice. The smell of her skin, beneath all the other smells and more potent than any of them. He knew that prostitutes faked their enthusiasm but hers did not seem fake. The slippery heat was real, her urgency was real. He swelled against her, drove himself deep into her. Then he orgasmed and suddenly none of it seemed real and he wanted it to stop. But it wasn't stopping. She ground her hips against him, her arms and legs squeezed him, she would not release. Her voice still in his ear, more urgent, more obscene. The back of his head in her grip, squishing his face into her neck so he could hardly breathe.

He wrenched his head free. Her head was up and she was look-ing past him, the expression on her face weirdly disconnected from the sex prattle sputtering out of her mouth. Urgent, but the urgency was about something else. He turned his head to see a hand with-draw through a hole in the plastered wall behind the chair where she'd had him leave his clothes. With a violent twist he broke free of her hold and pushed himself off her and off the bed and grabbed his pants. The pockets were empty. He dropped the pants and yanked open the door and was out in the hallway, naked. The door to the next room was open but there was nothing there but a bed, a chair, a small hole in the wall. No one in the hallway. At the end of the hall-way the clerk in his tiny room, smoking a cigarette in the TV light, not looking at him.

Back in the room the girl was working her way into her jeans. She didn't react to Chele's furious accusations or even look him in the face. The condom—he'd forgotten it—fell off his shrunken penis onto the floor. She curled her lip. "Pick it up." He picked it up, disgusting, humiliating, dropped it in the trash, grabbed her arm. She wrenched away and called out and in a second the clerk was standing in the doorway. He stayed there while Chele got dressed. The girl slipped on her shoes and was gone.

In the street, a few girls managed some few half-hearted hisses. The transvestites jeered silently. He made his way back to the *parqueo* where he'd left the Mazda. He had no ID, no driver's license, no money to pay the attendant. He cursed the girl, the desk clerk, Tania/Chispa, and especially himself, his own stupidity and misfortune.

But he was only beginning to understand the extent of it. He couldn't remember where he'd parked. The narrow streets that dead-ended at the black river, the low, dirty buildings, it all seemed identical. He retraced his steps, circled a few blocks, looked for an address on the receipt the attendant had pressed into his hand—but it was just a generic receipt, no address, no business name. An absence that nonetheless clarified things. No address, no name, no sign, no attendant, no vehicle—just a few mounds of garbage and a couple of drunks collapsed against a wall in the otherwise empty lot where an hour earlier he'd left Alvaro's Mazda in the hands of a thief.

He told the whole story to Alvaro. How he had taken the Mazda and told some lie to the guard and driven to Parque Morazán and swept Tania up from right under the noses of the *mareros* and driven over mountains to Chalamanca and left her there with her bag, her gun. Then driven back to the city and into Barrio Colón and left the truck in what he thought was a *parqueo* and gone with a woman into a room and asked if she knew Maribel Cruz and taken off his clothes and put them on a chair and let her pull him to the bed and looked up to see the hand in his pocket and when he went back to the *parqueo* it wasn't a *parqueo* and the Mazda was gone.

The next morning Alvaro called him into his office. The Mazda was a complete loss, he said. There would be no insurance payment, not when the driver of his own volition drops the keys in a thief's open hand and walks away. So Chele would have to pay for it—about $40,000, how would he earn that kind of money? In the meantime the theft would have to be reported. The police would ask questions. They would draw their own conclusions. Statutory rape, kidnapping, accessory to drug trafficking, reckless endangerment of a minor: he might be charged with any or all of these. But maybe that didn't matter. No doubt the *mareros* had already convened their own kangaroo court. What would Alvaro say to them, when they came looking for Chele?

He had no answer to Alvaro's questions. But they were just rhetorical questions, Alvaro already had his answers. He spoke many languages. He knew people in business and government and NGOs. In black markets, rehabs, training camps, guest worker programs, smuggling rings, underground railroads. He had a line on border crossings, identities, papers, contracts, work.

Work. 24/7, 365 days a year, until you pay off the forty grand, Alvaro said. *Qué Dios te acompañe.*

News and business of the outer world penetrate the high walls and narrow horizons of Perdu Canyon in random and sporadic bursts. Deep in his canyon blind, the solitary seizes on these bits of information and works them with his mind, as with hands and tools he works his placers. He paws and probes at them, distorts them, fits them into a context of his own devising. He has no other context for them, no immunity to the toxicities embedded in them, and sooner or later he's taken by some hot surge of madness, as the Indians fell to smallpox and venereal disease.

14

VIGILANTES

S HE HEARD THE WAILING and bleating and tinkling of bells for days before she saw the sheep.

She got so she scarcely noticed it, a remote background sound like a river or ocean or far-off city, until a change in wind or abrupt silencing of the birds brought it to her attention. Over time it got louder and more constant, but still it took her by surprise when the sheep came swarming out of the woods and spilled over the open slopes below the saddle. A great mewling and yammering of sheep, punctuated by the barking and yipping of dogs. Hundreds or thousands of sheep jammed up on the mountainside and just a couple of little border collies trying to keep them organized, nipping and wheeling and running at stragglers.

A sheepherder on horseback rode up with a couple of loaded pack mules. He dropped the lead, kicked his horse into a gallop, and charged at the gridlocked sheep. He waved his arms, hooted, yelled, whistled. Still yelling, he jumped off the horse and ran fierce and dog-like at the sheep himself.

She'd vaguely known the sheep were coming. But she was unprepared for this noise and dust. The barnyard smell already in the air, the sudden trampling of her green island refuge. Renegade gangs of lambs—not so lamb-like, actually, already nearly as large as their mothers, dirty fleece snarled with sticks and leaves and caked manure—marauded up towards the tower, mowing down the grass and the last of the summer flowers, until the dogs took notice and ran them back toward the saddle.

From inside the cab she watched him through binoculars. He was young, practically a boy. Patchy wisp of a beard, stubby ponytail jutting out of his baseball cap. Skin the color of dust or maybe it was dust, laid over a sheen of sweat. He unloaded and unsaddled the pack animals and turned them out with the sheep to graze. Then set up his tent, a big canvas wall tent that might have been white once but was now about the same color as the already trampled ground and dry grass and brush surrounding it. He unpacked an ungainly hunk of black metal that turned out to be a small wood stove, brought it inside the tent, and fitted it with a stove pipe inserted through a reenforced hole in the tent wall. He went down into the trees and returned with armloads of firewood he stacked outside the tent door. He shifted gear around, arranged ropes and straps, messed with a saddle. He moved in among the sheep and snatched one up and pinned it to the ground to slather something on its underside. He played a little with the two dogs. Then he perched on a rock outcrop above the grazing sheep, the dogs sitting below. Another dog, huge and white, appeared and sat apart from them.

All this time he hardly glanced her way. As if the fire tower were invisible, or just of no interest to him. He inhabited a separate realm of solitude. Yet one thing they had in common: they were both once iconic figures now marginalized, obsolete. The fire lookout pacing her catwalk, repeating her transects, scanning the static world. Genuflecting to the dead emperor. The sheepherder migrating over the last of the nomadic range with his mules and woodstove and smoky canvas tent, pushing his sheep band up deep-worn driveways into the same summer pastures where sheepherders had been camping and grazing sheep and bedding them down for a hundred years. A different generation of herders now, Peruvians and Mexicans where there had once been Basques and Scots, but the exact same line of sheep, though possibly rebred and reengineered in some way.

At sunset she stood on the catwalk and watched the sheep bed down: dogs running and barking, herder charging about and shouting and whistling and waving his arms, sheep bleating and scrabbling about in panicked confusion. A haphazard-seeming operation, but somehow the sheep ended up in a concentrated mass on the hillside.

The sun blinked out over the horizon. The herder and his small dogs vanished. His tent sat solitary in the dusky glade, a little column of smoke rising from the stovepipe, the sheep clumped on the mountainside, the big white dog sitting on a rocky outcrop above them.

In her mother's book was a black and white photograph of a couple of rough-looking McKeanes standing beside a tent in their sheep camp, maybe a hundred years ago. The tent the herder had just set up in the aspens looked about the same. Sheep, dogs, horses, about the same. Only the herder—brown skin, black hair, gaudy Andean hat— was different. And the white dog.

The McKeanes had been out of the sheep business for many decades by the time her family was living in the canyon. But her father leased their irrigated pasture to a rancher whose band grazed it for a few days in August.

The sheep band first appeared to them as a dust cloud high on the canyon rim. They'd track its progress coming down Indian Ridge until it disappeared behind the ridge into the Blue River canyon. Later they heard tinkly bells and faint, mournful cries, then a long column of trotting sheep and a fresh cloud of dust came churning up the river road. Sheep, herders, horses, and dogs jammed up on the far side of the river, squeezed across the bottleneck of the bridge, and finally spilled into the pasture.

Later, another long plume of dust materialized farther down the river road, trailing a speeding, rattling pickup. The rancher, bringing supplies to his herders. He drove across the bridge and straight out into the pasture and parked cockeyed with the door hanging open and stood by the corral counting the sheep the herders drove through the chute.

In the evening, the rancher stood with her father in a field, talking and watching the herders bed the band down. Lena came out on the porch in pajamas and watched, too: herders shouting and whistling at the dogs, dogs barking and running at the sheep, sheep bleating and milling about in disarray. Then from across the meadow a single herder came running, full tilt and long-strided. He whooped and shouted. Two dogs raced in the same direction on the far side of the band. For a moment it *was* like a race, with a roiling mass of sheep dividing the three racers. Then a kind of pattern emerged, a choreography. The sheep began to run in a single direction, deflected by dogs and herder toward a tightening center. The band contracted, sucked in outliers, and gradually took on the form of a perfect, fluid spiral, as if subject to the same laws of physics that create spirals everywhere—in shells, crystals, leaves, flowers, cyclones, airplane trajectories.

That was the image that stayed with her: the sheep turning toward an infinitely dense and turbulent center, the dogs rounding on them, the herder sprinting in high rubber boots across the rough ground, shirt open on his bare chest, shirttail streaming behind.

But was that a true memory, or something she'd dreamed or enhanced in her childish imagination? That infinite spiral might have been an optical illusion, or a fluke. In any case, now on Indian Mountain there was nothing like it—only a messy scramble to bed down, no choreography.

For three days and nights the herder camped on the saddle. During the day the sheep disappeared, moving out behind the ridgeline to graze the open dry meadows to the east, returning only in the evening to their camp and bedding grounds. But still she heard faint cries all day. Still their smell was in the air, and the tinkling of bells, or some echo of bells. Still it felt like a violation, a siege. She left the tower only to go to the outhouse, once to the spring for water and a bath, and once to gather fresh flowers for her bouquets, though most had been trampled or grazed and she returned with only a handful of gentian, budding out in pocket meadows too wet for sheep.

Embedded in the wailing and baaing she became aware of a human voice, calling. Maybe it had been calling for some time. She stepped out on the catwalk. The herder stood at the base of the tower. Two lambs were missing, he said. He made circles out of his fingers and held them before his eyes, and she understood that he wanted to climb up the stairs and look for them through her binoculars.

The sound of someone else's boots coming up her stairs, first time that summer. Another person on the narrow catwalk, also the first time. For several minutes he looked through the binoculars, in all directions, including into the far and certainly lambless distances.

"I don't see nothing. Maybe they hide. They playing."

"Sure, they're kids. I'll keep an eye out."

"You like fruits?"

"Excuse me?"

"Which you like—peach, pear, pineapple?"

"Well—I like them all. *Me gustan. Todos.*"

He lit a lantern inside his tent and she watched the distortions of his shadow against the canvas as he moved about. In the meadow the sheep were bedded down in random clumps. The white dog sat on the dusky slope above, motionless, almost luminescent, it might have been a block of white granite left behind by the glacier.

She turned on the lights and it all vanished. Nothing in her window but her own reflection: a woman sitting alone in a small illuminated cube, in the center of an immense darkness. She got out pencils and paper and sketched vaguely, the beginning of a self-portrait? She put on water for tea, lit a fire in the woodstove, stepped out on the catwalk. There was no light in the sheepherder camp. No light anywhere, other than her little room at the top of the mountain. She went back inside and sat with her tea and watched her reflection, not drawing.

Then she heard it again. Boots on her stairs.

When she opened the door he was standing on the catwalk, wearing a dirty fleece coat, Andean hat, and headlamp. He had a can in each hand. They exchanged greetings. Then it was a bit of a standoff. He nodded, smiled, gestured vaguely with the cans. Should she take them from him? What is it? Fruit cocktail! Many fruits!

She invited him in. He had to stoop, coming through the door. Suddenly the room seemed very small. In the warmth of the stove potent smells blossomed—animals, pine sap, food, smoke, sweat, what else?

She took the cans from him and put them down on the table and took his coat and hung it on a nail by the door. Were all the smells coming off the coat? His other clothes weren't much cleaner but he did look freshly bathed. Coatless and canless, he did not seem so large, just slightly taller than her. His little stump of a ponytail still damp, little wispy sideburns, patchy boy beard. But his face not really boyish, just softened and rounded inside the soft wool border of his alpaca hat.

She served the fruit cocktail in her only two bowls. It was sweet and delicious. In English and Spanish they repeated the names of the fruit. *Durazno,* peach; *piña,* pineapple; *pera,* pear; *uva,* grape; *cereza,* cherry.

Cúal fruta te gusta más?

A mi me gustan todas.

He looked around the room. *"Bonita casa. Vidrio y cielo. Y flores."*

Glass and sky and flowers—the very last of them, your little lambs trampled the rest. No point in saying that.

"Did you find them?"

"Find…?"

"Your lambs!"

"Oh. Sure." He waved a hand, as if to say, never mind the lambs. "They come back."

So maybe there hadn't been any lost lambs, maybe that had just been an excuse to come up in the tower and ask what fruit she liked. She had him sign her guest register. First name on the page. *Primer turista, yo.* Well then, how about a tour? Kitchen, dining room, bedroom, living room, office. In the center the firefinder: mysterious, iconic, archaic. Her hands, fidgeting on the shelf beneath it, touched something smooth and hard.

¿Te gustaria probar una copa de vino?

A line she'd been practicing all summer. She delivered it flawlessly, didn't wait for an answer, had the bottle out, found the corkscrew. Ripped off the seal, pulled the cork, waved the bottle around.

"It has to breathe." For about five seconds, sorry, Angie.

She took two cups off the shelf. Coffee mugs, sorry again, Angie, the glasses are all holding flowers. She poured the wine, handed him a mug.

The wine was exquisite, truly. Her first taste of alcohol in two months. The sheepherder tasted his, then stared into his mug. First ever for him, maybe?

"De dónde vienes?" Peru, she guessed, the sheepherders often were. And that hat.

He was looking at the firefinder. "Firefind. How…?"

"How does it find fire? Magic! But it's not working, I haven't found any. What's 'sheepherder' in Spanish?"

"Pastor."

"Fire lookout?"

"Guardia, supongo. O centinela. Vigilante."

"Vigilante!"

"Como yo. Vigilante de animales. Una yegua, dos mulos, tres perros, dos mil borrega."

"Pero solo un pastor."

"Solo uno. Pero me cuentan por dos."

She tried the question again, in English: "Where are you from?"

A one word answer was all she was looking for. But his answer when it came was many words, a rippling flow of Spanish that amazingly she understood, or partly understood. But what question was he answering? Where he came from, as in, what country—the question she thought she'd asked—or where he was coming from right now, with the sheep? Origin story or travelogue? Or both? The story of a journey, at any rate, or journeys. A wandering in the wild and on the edge of the wild, in solitude and in the intimate company of animals. One mare, two mules, three dogs, two thousand sheep. The hunters— *los cazadores*—trailing behind, in darkness. *Coyote, oso, lobo, león.* In the sky the scavengers, *cuervo, zopilote.*

Y más atrás solo Dios sabe. Los mareros, supongo.

Crossing mountains and rivers, blackened ground, shattered rock. Bright forest, sunless forest, ghost forest. Bodies heaped along the smoky road. The road a city street, canyon, tunnel, mineshaft, river, flood. Endlessly winding. Hand always on the wheel, headlights a tunnel his eyes stare into. A girl on the seat beside him. Her voice in the dark, her body. Her bag. Her gun.

Su voz. Su bolsa. Su cuerpo. Su arma.

The girl vanishes. The truck vanishes. He vanishes. Then:

En primavera a la borrega le cortamos el pelaje.
Sacamos los testículos y se les comen los perros.
Peladas pastan en los cerros.
Y nadie se queja. Nadie deja de trabajar. De vigilar.
Y hacen una bulla en la montaña como el mar.

Her comprehension came in waves and troughs. She understood everything, then nothing. Zopilotes were buzzards. *Mareros* she didn't know. She wasn't minding his smell at all. She poured more wine, had Angie spiked it with something? Was it the wine or something else flushing those words from his mouth and granting her this unexpected understanding, or bits and pieces of understanding, or an illusion of understanding?

We take out their testicles and feed them to the dogs.
No one complains.
We make a sound in the mountains like the sea.

The pure sounds of the language, his voice, the strangeness of his words, or her understanding of them. Even with the meaning frayed the sounds were beautiful. She felt a tremendous sense of peace, listening to his voice, watching him, just being in his presence. She became aware again of the reflection in the window, on the edge of her vision: two faces now, brown and white, boy face and girl face, leaning towards each other in the light and shadow, framed by absolute darkness. *Chiaroscuro.*

"*Y ahora?* Her voice practically a whisper.

"*Mañana, al río. Bajamos, cruzamos, subimos. Otra montaña. Otros ríos. Cuatro pasos.*"

"*Enseña.* Show me."

They stepped up again to the firefinder. But now he fell silent, looking at the map. She put her finger at the center—Indian Mountain, *aquí estamos*—and traced out the sheep driveway, as best she could remember or guess the route. Long winding ridge, deep desert

canyon, at its bottom the McKeane Ranch, an oasis. Geometric, isolated, the rare shelter it afforded. *Un refugio*—something she'd never
called it in English. Then, climbing away from ranch and canyon, the
topographical distortions of the Ledorah Road. Fault line, suture line,
cliff band, in and out of drainages, past grottos, sulfur pools, mineshafts, bathtubs, ore piles, ghost towns, fallen towers.

Was he getting any of it at all? He seemed to be concentrating,
listening— but maybe not to her? His dogs had begun to bark. She
broke off the babble. Now the sheep were raising their voices. He
stood, reached for his coat.

"Something come around. Hunter. *Lobo*, maybe. *Coyote. Oso. León.*
I go."

He shook her hand, thanked her, went out the door. She hesitated
a second, then followed. He'd turned on his headlamp and was starting down the stairs. She went after him.

"Do you often see them? Wolves? Mountain lions? You look back
and one's following?"

He mumbled something and kept going down the stairs. Sure he
saw them. Shot them, probably. Wasn't going to talk about it. Had to
go.

"That happened to me," she said, still following. "Well, first I *felt* it."

He waited at the bottom of the stairs. "You felt."

"Following me. A lion. Then I looked back and *saw* it."

She came off the stairs and they stood facing each other. She
squinted, shaded her eyes, blind in his headlamp. He turned it off.
Then—in Spanish, with dogs barking and sheep wailing, standing she
didn't know how close to him, it was so dark—she told him about her
backwards walk along the knife ridge. How the cougar appeared and
stalked her, how with fierce staring eyes she held it at bay. How it disintegrated into bones and light beneath the aspens.

There was no telling what he heard or understood of it, if she was
even saying what she was trying to say. But there were other things she
wanted to ask. If his family knew where he was. If he had a girlfriend
or wife somewhere. Or somebody. Where were his people, how did
they communicate? She wanted to tell him about the Maginot Line,

the last Japanese soldier. But there was no time for any of it. He spoke, practically under his breath, a few words she didn't understand, his voice low, soft, peaceful, coming out of the dark.

Siento paz, she whispered. She leaned in to kiss his cheek, did they kiss cheeks in South America? Or wherever he was from. But then to her own astonishment her lips brushed his cheek and kissed him softly on the mouth. Then she turned and hurried up the stairs.

For the second time that summer she was awakened by a booming sound she thought at first was thunder.

She rolled out of bed, pulled on her pants, and went out on the catwalk. The sun was rising into a cloudless sky. The sheepherder camp was empty. Sheep, dogs, horses, tent, herder—all gone. The booming echoed, a slow fade. Not thunder.

Later a horseman appeared on the far side of the saddle, leading a mule with something on its back. Even at a distance she could see the upright posture of the rider, the brightness of his hat. The earflaps flapping with the gait of the horse. She picked up the binoculars and saw strapped to the mule the limp yellow body of a cougar. Blood on its mouth, the great muscular tail swinging against the trotting mule's flank. In syncopation, or so it seemed, to the rhythm of the earflaps.

A male, definitely.

The horse crossed the saddle and climbed toward the tower at a fast trot. It stopped below her and the herder looked up.

She couldn't speak. But she must have been shaking her head, there must have been a terrible expression on her face. Immediately he jerked back on the reins and turned the horse. Both horse and mule resisted, dust rising all around them. "Sorry!" he shouted. Then he was riding back the way he'd come, ignoring or not hearing her calls, a hard trot across the saddle and out the ridge trail, earflaps flapping, cougar tail bouncing, broken rhythm.

She spent one more day in the tower, with the wind rising. *Casa de vidrio y cielo.* House of glass and sky. A campfire ban had been issued.

Tell your campers, the dispatcher said. A joke, there were never any campers. Well, there had been one, but he was gone.

She went down to the saddle and studied the sheepherder's camp. A rectangle of flattened grass where his tent had been, orbits of dusty ground around the trees where he'd tied his horses. The stubbly meadow carpeted with sheep shit and smelling like the coat she'd hung by her door. In the dry aspens the wind made a sound like a stream flowing over pebbles. She came upon a fresh carving. Another naked woman? A woman not naked? Or some hieroglyphic of a woman. Or not a woman at all.

She returned to the tower and took out her pencil drawing, the self-portrait she'd begun the night before. She sketched in another figure, then tried to complete it with pen and ink. Black and white, shadow and light, girl and boy, or reflection of girl and boy. She couldn't do it. That image that had seemed so compelling in the night was lost, dissolved, a dream.

His signature in her guest log was illegible. He'd told her his name but she didn't remember.

When they shook hands she'd felt his callouses, thick and hard. But the softest any man had ever grasped her hand.

He was blind to her map, couldn't point to where he'd come from or where he was going. Couldn't tell her the names of any place he'd been. So what had he told her? A story of a journey? *Cuatro pasos,* four steps. Or four passes. One sheepherder, *un pastor,* though he counted for two. Alone, not alone. One horse, two mules, three dogs, two thousand sheep. He fed their testicles to the dogs. In the darkness behind them the hunters: *coyote, oso, lobo, leon.*

And behind them something else, only God knew.

That night a bigger wind came up and blew a gale into the morning hours. At sunrise buzzards were circling over the saddle, more than she'd seen all summer. They swooped and wheeled in the diminishing wind, appearing and disappearing behind the ridge.

She packed a knapsack—food, water, map, radio—and started down her knife ridge trail, not looking into the gully where magpies and ravens and buzzards were gathering. She came out onto the sheep driveway, here not so much a trail as a swath of pummeled and trampled ground on the broadening ridge. She took giant striding steps downhill and came down softly on the inclined ground and in this way almost effortlessly lost thousands of feet of elevation she would have to turn around and regain in the heat of the afternoon.

A senseless plunge off the mountain. Following a sheepherder with no expectation of overtaking him and no idea what she would say to him if she did. She could tell him about the campfire ban. Tell him: I forgive you for shooting my cougar. Not that she could be certain it was *her* cougar he'd shot, and anyway hadn't sheepherders been casually shooting cougars for generations? That was just what they did. And the cougar survived, prospered even, a constant unseen presence in the forest. A totem. She could tell him that. Keep killing cougars if you must, the Cougar will always be there, until you kill every last animal you can never kill the totem.

But what a sentimental idea that was. And what a fool she'd been. Intoxicated, infatuated, she'd romanticized it all: cougar, sheepherder, solitude and companionship, language, meaning, lack of meaning. Everything, down to their reflection in the window, a Renaissance painting. Chiaroscuro! Rather, all shadow and no light, no symmetry, no communication, their only commonalities their isolation and obsolescence—not a connection but a mutual disconnection.

Te lo mato.

His response to her cougar story. Three words that had practically swept her away, coming out of the night at the bottom of the stairs, his mouth so near she felt as much as heard them. Felt and heard their sound—the beauty of it, not the distinct words, not their meaning. His voice in the night, the peace she felt, that was their meaning.

Then she'd covered his mouth and any more words that might have come out of it with her lips.

But now, with distance and in the light of day, words and meaning came clear, though she had to think about it, parse the grammar. Indirect object, object, verb. *Te lo mato*—I'll kill it for you. Present tense, as if it were happening now. *Te*, the intimate pronoun, wrapped up in a promise of killing.

She kept descending, drawn on by the faint, distant wailing of sheep, though by early afternoon she'd decided it was only wind she was hearing. Then she rounded a point and heard something else, the sound she'd been straining for all summer. The river. There it was far below, a thin stream in a rocky bed out of all proportion to the depth and magnitude of the canyon it had cut. Looking downriver, she could see the bend of the confluence—Perdu River, Blue River, Antimony Creek. All coming together, though not exactly as her mother had described it in her book, a fresh configuration of nature. Not exactly as she'd remembered it in that vision from her father's spiraling plane, or as she'd tried to describe it to Chele: a geometric oasis, a refuge, what else had she said?

The view she had now was oblique, half-obscured, the mixing of the diminished streams not dramatic, and, certainly, the configuration of nature no longer fresh. The ranch was about as dry and brown as everything surrounding it, other than the narrow strips of green along the rivers. A little patch of garden, some trees in the orchard that might still be alive. Dry pasture. No smoke or dust rising, no animals or people or anything moving. The same collection of dead machines as ever.

She studied it for several minutes, then turned away and looked down the ridge. And saw her first smoke of the summer, streaming out of the trees in tattered white ribbons just below Coyote Point, where the ridge dropped away abruptly on all sides.

She was too deep in the hole, couldn't get a radio call out. She started back up the ridge in the heat of the high sun, practically running at first, but then plodding, sweating, gasping for breath. Her calves were burning. By the time she had climbed far enough to connect with a repeater the smoke had consolidated into a black, boiling column.

The dispatcher's voice was flat, terse.

"That smoke was reported a while back, Lena, by one of the field crews. Couldn't raise you on the radio. Jumpers are on their way."

In the days that followed she mainly stayed in the lookout, under another kind of siege. She monitored the radio, kept an eye out for spot fires, and watched the smoke plume grow, the planes and helicopters circle. She tracked the progress of the fire on her maps, the drainages that had burned or were burning or were likely to burn next. Tried to figure out which were the four passes he would go over, and was the fire anywhere near them.

She finished reading *Crack Between Mountains*. History or fiction, elegy or smear? *The McKeanes came into the canyon, the last Jeffersonian yeomen.* But you never found out where they came from, or what happened to them when they went away. Stories petered out into fragments, contradictions, rumors: the story of Galen and his mine, the story of Josie and her tubs. Or just stopped cold. The story of Ethan and his plane, told in a single paragraph near the end of the book. How he had filled his fuel tank from barrels sitting on the edge of the strip where his plane was parked, below the ranchhouse of the kinsman who more than once had threatened to kill him. Then taken off and was never seen again.

Accident, sabotage, or suicide? The end, in any case. But not necessarily the end, the way Helen told it. The plane disappeared, Ethan disappeared—not really an end. Rather a disappearance so unexplained it left open the possibility of a reappearance. Topographical disorientation, could that be an explanation? He'd brought his plane down in a part of the world he did not recognize and where no one recognized him. Where he had no mooring.

But more likely he'd simply miscalculated his fuel, or the fuel was tainted, or he'd had some other mechanical or aviation problem, and somewhere over the mountains and canyons not far from Confluence Bar had lost power and gone down, maneuvering through atmospheric and then boreal layers on a silent glide—*if you have control with power, you have control without*—to crashland in a swamp or pocket meadow and—okay, not likely—emerge from his plane brain-battered, amnesiac, disoriented, lost. But alive.

The smoke plume grew and towered over her until finally it collapsed and dissolved into the sky everywhere, smoke and Smudge coming together and obscuring her view so she could no longer see fire or aircraft or any land beyond the immediate slopes and escarpments of Indian Mountain. Her close scrutiny of earth and sky had in the end yielded only blindness. She put away her books and maps, computer, papers, pens and pencils, and waited for the sensory compensation that comes to the blind. But there was only the sting of smoke in her throat, the buzz and whine of invisible aircraft, the sputtering of the radio, and the dirty, impenetrable white of the midday sky, relieved only by the deep blue of the gentians opening on her windowsills and at the horizons by a faint orange glow, as if just beyond the curve of the earth fire were burning everywhere.

II

As for the earth, out of it comes bread
But beneath it is turned up as it were fire...
—Job 28

No man becomes a prophet who was not first a shepherd.
—Mohammed

15

SISIMITI'S FIRE

THE DAY AFTER HE SHOT the cougar and brought it to Lena in her tower, Chele finally trailed the sheep off Indian Ridge and down to the river crossing, a full day late for his resupply rendezvous with Oscar, the Peruvian foreman. But he'd kept his promise. Killed as promised. *Te lo mato.* The words escaping from his mouth into the tiny space that separated them at the bottom of the stairs, in the long, frozen moment before she breathed her answer—*siento paz*—and with the same breath kissed him.

The second kiss of his life. Only their lips touched. But he felt without touching the contours and textures and heat of her body.

The dogs barked incessantly as he made his stumbly way back to camp. The euphoria of the wine and kiss faded and he was left with a sour taste in his mouth and a thickness in his limbs and in his mind. The barking grew more urgent at his approach. In the meadow the sheep were restless, anxious, crying out. He quieted the dogs and took up his rifle and walked a wide loop around the band, scanning with his headlamp. He heard nothing, saw no movement, just the faint white shape of Lobo on the far side of the band, the glint of his nocturnal eyes.

He turned off the headlamp and watched and waited with the growling dogs in the darkness, only a sliver of moon. Something was out there, crouched in deep shadows beneath the aspens.

Coyote, oso, lobo, león.

Y más atrás solo Dios sabe.

The light in the lookout tower remained on. She felt peace, she kissed him, she left her lamp burning late into the night, a beacon and still-open invitation. He turned away from it. If he went to her now his sheep might well be slaughtered, perhaps the dogs as well, the peace she felt would be shattered.

Finally the light went off and the moon sank behind mountains and then the night seemed bleak and endless. The hobbled mare and the mules thumped in the grass, the dogs kept a deep growl going, the sheep surged in the darkness, and Chele sat hunched in his coat on a rock, rifle in his lap and hat pulled over his ears.

Vigilando, it came to him naturally. This vigil like and unlike the vigil he'd kept on the hillside above the girls' dormitory, with horses ghosting along the paths and Alvaro pedaling up on his bicycle. *Who's your girlfriend, Chele*. No one. No *one*, he longed for some aggregate or abstraction of them all.

It was still dark when he began to break camp. By sunrise he was on horseback, skirting broken cliffs and spires, following a long file of trotting sheep in and out of gullies, bells tinkling, lambs wailing, ewes calling to their lambs.

The horse and mules went skittish. The dogs growled low, dropped to their bellies. He followed their gaze to the near ridgeline.

A cougar sat on a rock in the full sun, watching the sheep pass. Then it turned its head and looked straight across at Chele. He met the cat's gaze and held it even as he dismounted, reached for his rifle in its scabbard, raised it, and sighted through the scope.

At the bottom of the stairs she'd told him a story, with some urgency in it. *Al reves*, she'd kept saying. Something backwards. He kept thinking of the Sisimiti's feet. But of course her story had nothing to do with the Sisimiti. It was about a cougar, she saw it everywhere, watching her.

Te lo mato.

He hadn't been thinking about Tania. Yet those were her words, practically the last thing she'd said to him, her voice coming out of the darkness on the Chalamanca road. Then those exact words had come out of his mouth, standing face to face with Lena in the darkness on Indian Mountain. And Lena had heard them as a promise that brought her peace.

For you, I'll kill it.

A promise. As if cougar-killing were something he did as a matter of course, when in fact he'd never even seen a cougar and had fired a gun to kill, or maybe to kill, only once, one week earlier, one bullet, blasting away in a pre-dawn delusional panic at the wall of his own tent.

He'd killed chickens, that was it, cutting their throats with a kitchen knife. Tania had sneered. *Sangre de gallina no me hace nada.* Yet cougar bloodletting also seemed to be strangely empty of adrenalin or awe. He fired the gun. The cougar opened its mouth to scream but made no sound, or the sound was lost in the explosion of the gunshot and the brief stampede and cacophony of sheep, horses, dogs. The cougar convulsed in silence, tumbled from its rock, lay still. Blood spurted, then oozed onto dirt and rocks to dry in the sun.

A cougar had appeared and he'd killed it, as promised. Extraordinary, a miracle. But a miracle that took place in a vacuum. No one had seen it, nothing would come of it. The gunshot would echo inside his head, inside her head, maybe, distantly. He would trail the sheep away and the zopilotes would swoop in from empty skies and Lena might walk out the ridge and see that he had kept his promise. And then rode away, gone, forever.

He dismounted, unpacked a mule, and scrambled down into the gully and then up the slope to the dead cougar. He dragged its heavy body down crumbling bluffs on one side and worked it up a slope of loose, jagged rock on the other. It snagged on rocks and trailed blood and gave off a terrible smell of wildness and death, but somehow he managed to get it to the trail and up on the protesting mule.

When he rode up to the firetower she was standing on the porch looking down on him. Her face was strange. Contorted, mouth open but no sound coming out. Like the cougar, screaming a silent scream. She turned away and went inside. He waited, but it didn't seem that she was going to come back out. Humiliated, defeated, he rode back the way he'd come and rolled the cougar's body off the mule into the same gully he'd dragged it out of, then repacked the mule and rode hard to catch up with the sheep and dogs.

It was too late in the day to make it all the way down to the ranch where the Peruano would be waiting. He made camp at a point where the ridge steepened and the sheep driveway descended into woods that were already dark. There was no pasture, no water, hardly any flat ground. He unloaded the mules but kept the packs intact and bedded the sheep down hungry and thirsty. He built a small fire and heated a can of soup for dinner, then stoked the fire for warmth and light and laid out his sleeping bag on horse blankets near the coals. Like Lempira, the guerrilla *cacique* and trickster, who'd also led his band deep into the mountains and built remote ridgetop campfires. Signal fires to lure the Spanish into the mountains with their great horses and heavy armor and guns, only to find bloody signs on the rocks and cracked bones in the smoldering pit of a fire and the Indians vanished into dark woods below or waiting in hit-and-run ambush behind the rim of a rocky gulch.

He drifted in and out of sleep. His fire sparked and popped. The forest creaked, groaned, breathed raggedly in the wind. Rivers sounded far below. The dogs growled low and unknown creatures rustled in the woods, unless those too were just sounds of the wind.

A thudding and crashing in the brush woke him. He sat up, or dreamed he sat up. Looking across a dark gulch, he glimpsed for a split second the flicker and glow of another fire, or fires. An obliterating shadow passed before the flame and he slipped back into a half-sleep distorted by fire dreams: torches and embers, the crematorio smouldering, trash fires, shadow figures lurching on the edge of firelight.

At dawn the wind was calm and his fire cold. But the smell of smoke and ash lay over silent woods and it seemed to Chele that he had spent the night in a waking dream or in the company of ghosts, wandering, like him, through a country of exile and emptiness.

The sheep too had wandered in the night and were now scattered among the trees and open slopes. The dogs, distraught, led him to some clumps of bloody wool and then to two disemboweled lambs, killed by a predator—a bear, he guessed by the sign—not two hundred meters from where their shepherd lay hypnotized by campfire coals, dreaming of the fires of Sisimiti and Lempira.

What was the achievement of the indigenous
warrior Lempira?

Lempira survived. Until he didn't.

He left the dead lambs where they lay. He and the dogs rounded up the band and set off down the steepening ridge until it dropped away in cliffs and rockslides and the driveway wound off the ridge and down through forest, then out into easier, more open country. The sheep spilled over slopes of dry, yellow grass, the dogs yipped and jostled along their flanks, and Chele, leading the packstring behind and smelling of woodsmoke and blood, drove his wailing band into the canyon. They forded a shallow river and descended past black cliffs onto the great bend of a larger river, where the sheep turned onto a narrow bridge and on the far shore and through a haze of heat and dust he saw his grandmother stepping onto the deck to meet their charge.

Until then his hallucinations had mainly been aural, triggered at night by the echoing silence inside his tent and throughout the day by the relentless bawling of sheep. An oceanic sound, he thought, though he knew little of oceans, despite having grown up on a narrow strip of land squeezed between the two largest bodies of water in the world. But it wasn't until his work with the *PFVS* took him to some Caribbean seaside towns that he heard the sound of the surf—a sudden, startling crash or roar at times, at others a muted background. Only gradually did he become aware of the deeper reservoir of sound contained within it: not the washing of waves against the shore but a tumult of voices and engines, the world trying to speak to him from beyond that strip of surf-battered sand.

The sheep sounded nothing like that ocean. Yet their voices too were incessant and inescapable, they too rose and fell in intensity and transmitted an undercurrent of sounds that would otherwise go unheard. All day on the mountainside the sheep cried out to one another, and beneath that swollen and pitiful racket he heard bird calls and distant automobiles, electronic beeps and hums, airplanes, music, bells, water, wind. But more than anything he heard human voices, the murmur and drone of a background conversation. Sometimes the tone grew urgent, as if someone were speaking directly to him, summoning him. But always the message was lost in the babble or carried off in the wind or reabsorbed by the bawling and bleating of sheep.

That was a sound he'd first heard not from the animals themselves—his was mainly a sheepless country—but from his own friends and housemates, when they learned that Alvaro, rather than just expelling him as expected following the disaster with Tania/Chispa and the stolen Mazda, had set him up with a job in the States. Out West, working with horses—not, as he had once fantasized, as a cowboy riding the range, but as a sheepherder. The culmination of a series of rewards and punishments imposed on him over the years. Reward and punishment, carrot and stick, achievement and fuck-up—it seemed that he and Alvaro had gone back and forth like that forever, condemned to a certain rhythm and symmetry, a strange dance or combat. And then Chele had fucked up beyond all previous fuck-ups but in the course of fucking up had also achieved something semi-noble: a rescue, however flawed, of a girl in distress, which Alvaro had never openly acknowledged but in his begrudging way had recognized, tapping into his vast network of connections to improvise this ingenuous and perverse punishment that was, like all his punishments, simultaneously an opportunity.

Chele was expelled, exiled, and at the same time presented with a version of the American Dream—a thing for which respectable and humble people worked and saved for years, abandoned their families, risked their lives in hostile territories, turned their fate over to mercenary coyotes, dodged helicopters and infrared and militias and cartels, lived indefinitely in fear and uncertainty. Whereas he, a fuck-up of an orphan kid with no money or family, was simply handed a plane ticket, a visa, and a contract he had no choice but to sign.

Ingenuous and perverse. Alvaro had either given him a chance at redemption or thrown him to the wolves. And indeed at times he thought he heard wolves howling, though he had not been plagued by them as some of the herders were. Oscar said that when he started as a herder there had been no wolves, they had been helicoptered into the heart of the wilderness and quickly multiplied, viciously slaughtering sheep and bringing new misery to the lives of the sheepmen. But so far—now into his second summer on the job—this had not been Chele's experience. He had led his band through the country of the wolfpacks without incident, beyond an occasional remote howling at night. Perhaps the wolves truly feared his great white dog, Lobo. The name itself a defiance. Or perhaps they had taken his measure and decided to leave him alone, at least until they could engage him purely on their own terms.

But still there were nights when he hardly slept, the wolfpacks of his own brain marauding. And real bears, real lions and coyotes stalked his sheep through a country largely empty of people, a thousand square miles and not so much as a settlement, just the occasional camper or backpacker, hunter, mushroom forager, woodcutter, drifter, outlaw, pilgrim. Long nights in a canvas tent, or longer ones wintering over in a trailer at the Armstrong Ranch, deep in the river canyon. Mostly in the company of other herders but lately alone, a rifle by his side, dogs at the door of his tent, a horse, two mules, and two thousand ewes and lambs bedded down outside.

No women. The irony of that. Wasn't it his obsession with a woman—a girl—that had got him into this? Or her obsession with him. Now there would be no women, for weeks and even months on end. The Peruano confirmed it. If he saw a woman without a man out there, she would be ugly. If she wasn't ugly it meant she was a *bruja,* a sorceress. He wouldn't be the first sheepherder to encounter a *bruja* in the bush, or to lose his sanity to her cruel and unattainable enchantments.

Oscar talked about *brujas* in the same straightforward way he talked about sheep and horse care, predators, woodsmanship. Maybe he was just being provocative. In any case, no women. Yet at times Chele was aware of something female and sexual in the landscape, a heat or moist chemistry the earth itself gave off. A feminine voice murmuring within that background clamor of androgynous voices. Sometimes he would just lie down in a patch of warm sun and give himself over to a terrestrial embrace. And sometimes the chemistry changed and the country became another kind of female: cold and dangerous, remote, unknowable, denying.

But in over a year on the job his self-discipline and confidence had grown, and the landscape too had seemed to gain grandeur and to imply in its grandeur some destiny and purpose, as if in his wanderings with the sheep he was traveling toward something of great worth.

And then a flesh-and-blood woman—not ugly, not a witch—had turned out to be a part of it. He'd climbed her tower, talked with her in two languages, drunk her wine, told her his story, pieces of his story, or tried to, it was too much, impossible for him to explain or for her to understand. But she'd responded with her own story, also impossible to understand. Yet between them, somehow, there had been an understanding. She felt *peace*. She kissed him, sealed a covenant.

Which he fulfilled. He shot the cougar. And it was at that moment of fulfillment that destiny and purpose evaporated. There was no understanding and now there would be no peace. There was only the oceanic bawling of sheep, reaching a fever pitch, the wail of a storm-driven sea, as the sheep entered the canyon and caught the scent, or memory, of green pastures on the far side of the river. They quickened their trot, rounded the last curve, and pounded onto the wooden planks of the bridge. Where on the far side the ghost of his grandmother leaned on her walking stick and waited to be swept away in the stampede.

At the last second the current divided and the sheep streamed around her. She held her ground for five seconds, ten maybe, then was slowly turned and caught up in the roiling stream and carried back to shore, stick waving, white head appearing and vanishing in the dusty mid-day glare, like a tuft of freshly-washed fleece sinking and rising amid the filthy coats of a thousand sheep.

He spurred the mare and trotted hard after them. Beyond a wide gravel bar the dogs were turning the sheep through an open gate into a field. His grandma was nowhere to be seen. The horse and mules hurried across the bridge, eager for pasture. On the far side he saw Oscar coming down a dirt road on an ATV.

"*Profe*," the foreman greeted him. "You're late."

16

TROJAN HORSE

THE NIGHT HE LOST his mother Jimmy McKeane barbecued on open coals an entire chinook salmon, captured in flagrant violation of fisheries regulations in a trap rigged in a pool in Antimony Creek, a trick he'd learned from the unrepentant poacher and scofflaw Clayton McKeane. By the time the fish was done, Helen had fallen asleep on the bed he'd set up for her in the old homestead cabin that served as tool shed and workshop, and after trying not very hard to wake her he sat down on the sagging couch on the front porch of the ranch house to a luxuriously solitary feast.

His old yellow lab, Trevor, slept noisily in the corner. The sheep band that had invaded the pasture that afternoon had mainly settled down. Every once in a while a lamb bawled, a bell tinkled. On the porch table, Helen's GPS monitor beeped softly and blinked its reassuring red eye. Her icon—some kind of insect shape, blue fly, mosquito—flashed on a map of Confluence Bar on the screen. Like a nightwatchman waving his lantern, ten o'clock and all's well. Jimmy kicked back, sipped a beer, and had taken maybe two succulent bites of fish when the sheep dogs started barking and Trevor lifted his head and growled and a moment later Caleb McKeane, who thirty years before Jimmy was born had driven a truck loaded with four tons of ore off the hairpin on the Ledorah Road and dropped a vertical quarter mile into the floodwaters of the Perdu, came hobbling up the road to ask if he had any more of that salmon.

Jimmy was slightly intoxicated, and Caleb already a hallucinogenic presence on the porch. All day Jimmy had gone in and out of the house, veering from one never-finished project to another, and each time he navigated the narrow channel through the mudroom clutter he felt some unnerving sensation he wasn't able to put his finger on until mid-afternoon, when he finally stopped to take a hard look at all the junk that had accumulated through natural processes in the mudroom over the years, with the recent addition of the junk he'd brought up from the shop to make room for Helen, after she refused to sleep in a house so abandoned and at the same time so haunted by multiple specters of the past. He peered into the jumbled depositional layers—shovels, axes, snowshoes, cracked hoses, broken ski poles, cans of dead paint, trowels, sprinkler heads, boots, coats, toys, fishing rods, straw hats, cowboy hats, baseball caps, plastic buckets stained with blackberries harvested a quarter century ago—and through the gaps between these objects his eyes connected with the eyes in a photograph that had been hanging on that wall since they were kids. One of the few known likenesses of their ancestor the hardrock miner Caleb McKeane, who three quarters of a century earlier had lived in a legendarily primitive state in a cabin at his Golden Throat mine up at Poison Springs, poaching venison, stinking of sulfur, and greeting the rare arrival of a visitor with a blast of his 12 gauge. The visitor could decide whether it was fired in salutation or warning and take his chances accordingly. Caleb spent twenty years tunneling into the mountain, extracting just about enough gold to keep himself in cigarettes, amphetamines, and nitroglycerin, before he took the exit off the hairpin. That at least was the story Helen told, in part at least substantiated by this picture on the wall: a hunched, subterranean creature emerging into the light, deep-set, heavy-browed, and frankly demented eyes glaring out of a thicket of hair as if at the same demons that populated his tunnel.

After that, every time Jimmy went through the mudroom he felt Caleb's eyes on him, though from most angles he couldn't even see the wall behind all the junk, let alone a photograph hanging on it. And now in the fading light he found himself looking over the porch railing at those exact same eyes, set in a scratched and bug-bit face that glistened darkly with sweat and stubble, dirt, sap, ash.

Caleb's eyes, not Caleb's face. Not Caleb's dirty red smokejump-er's knapsack, not Caleb's voice—well, of course he'd never heard Ca-leb's voice. But this voice he'd been hearing all his life, most recently four days earlier, when he'd picked Ben up at his basement office and driven him to the airport to fly off to his conference—a last-minute favor to Angie, who had to run kids around and tie up loose ends and prepare for her own journey. Why couldn't he take a taxi or some-thing, Jimmy wondered. He could, Angie said. It would just be nice if you gave him a ride.

But when he got to the office Ben hardly glanced up from his com-puter. While he waited, Jimmy had a look around the basement. He made his way through a warren of desks, chairs, tables, computers, boxes, cabinets, regular printers and oversize printers, copy machines, fax machines, shredders. Walls covered with maps, posters, diplomas, photos, plaques, certificates, commemorations. He ventured farther, and in the near darkness got a sense of an even denser concentration of furniture and machines and files; a sense that he'd stepped into a vault where such things waited for complete obsolescence and use-lessness if these had not already come to them.

During the drive out to the airport, Ben hardly looked up from his phone. When they got to the passenger drop-off he didn't imme-diately get out of the truck, but instead insisted on showing Jimmy a sample of his presentation on his phone. Graphs, maps, photos, video clips, diagrams, illegible text, all flashing by senselessly on the minuscule screen. About the only thing Jimmy caught was the title: *A Stochastic Model for the Restoration of Anthropomorphic Fire on a Watershed Scale.*

"A model. As for the real thing…?"

"Oh, we get that, sooner or later. We know we'll get fire. The ques-tion is, on whose terms. And the idea is, the better the model, the more the terms are ours."

"Stochastic?"

"Yeah, that's basically a recognition that it's never going to be *abso-lutely* on our terms. The model incorporates the inherent randomness of its variables. Randomness is programmed into its algorithms. There are no predictions, just probabilities. Hypothetical scenarios."

"Oh. Well, anyway, congratulations. So the paper is—*a paper?* Published? Or—also hypothetical?"

"No. Not published and not hypothetical. Look, this is what I've been working on for the past ten years. It's incredibly data-rich. Totally not hypothetical."

Then he took up his suitcase and laptop and was swept into merging streams of pedestrian traffic and sucked through corridors and tunnels into the airport. Only to be spat out four days later below the porch at Upper McKeane Ranch. He dropped his pack practically on top of Trevor, who barely stirred, and fell onto the couch. Jimmy went to get a beer and a plate of salmon.

"You want a fork or something."

Ben was staring at the monitor. Glowing numerals, blinking bug, little beeps.

"What in the holy fuck is she doing down here?" he demanded through a mouthful of fish. He jabbed a fishy finger at the monitor. "Look at this. She's a hundred yards from here. She shouldn't be a hundred miles. A hundred yards. What? The barn? The outhouse?"

"The shop. I set her up out there, that's where she's sleeping. I brought down a mattress, some furniture. She loves it, sleeps like a little kid. Twelve, fourteen hours at a shot."

"That's great. She slept a lot at my house, too. Which was our agreement. Our agreement was, she stays at the house, until we work out her situation."

"Absolutely. But look. Angie's gone, bringing the kids to camp, taking care of clients, whatever. You're at your conference, or so we thought. Lena's not available, as usual. So suddenly it's me babysitting Mom, again. Okay, fine. But not at your house. I need to be here."

"Why?"

"Why? I'm the fucking caretaker. I have work."

"What work?"

"What work. Fuck. Irrigate, for one thing."

"I don't hear sprinklers."

"Well, the system's still down. I'm fixing it, that's why I was in town, remember? Running around buying hose and pipe and whatnot. I stop by your house to say hello, next thing I know I'm giving you a ride to the airport. Next thing, I'm getting guilt-tripped and shanghaied by your wife. *It's only three days Jimmy. Your mother, Jimmy.*"

"Seems like you've been working on that irrigation system for quite a while."

"That's right. And there's still no water in the ditch."

"So why is that? Maybe because that ditch is no longer viable? Because the whole construct of this ranch is not viable, and never was? Because your projects are all fantasies, totally unrealistic, just like everything anybody's ever tried to do here?"

"Yeah, maybe. Isn't that fucking fantastic? We own one of the last places on earth where being totally unrealistic is still… *viable.*"

"This explains why you disable the alert on the tracking software and bring her here?"

"I enabled it again, once we got here. Took a new central waypoint. That shed where she's sleeping. Safety zone radius is the same, about a mile."

"You can't count on GPS in the canyon."

"It's working. Mostly. And even when it's not working it works, you know? Like one of those doggy shock collars, conditions her to recognize boundaries. And respect them, maybe. Eventually. If she pushes it, well, you might not know right away, if the satellites are out of range. But eventually they come around. And then, if she's out of bounds, the alerts go off, you know right where she is, you go there and corral her, walk her home, she goes to bed. And stays there, for awhile. But I have a question for you. Two questions. What are you doing here? And where the hell did you come from?"

Ben waved his hand vaguely.

"Sure, the sky, you're a smokejumper. I will say you look the part. Ashy, dirty, charcoaly. You smell like smoke. Or is that mud? Maybe you landed in a swamp, never found the fire."

Ben was studying the monitor.

"That happen often?" Jimmy said.

"What?"

"I don't know. Miss the target. Drop into a lake or something. Dangle in a tree until somebody cuts you down."

"Oh, all the time. In the cartoons."

"It *is* kind of a cartoon, right? Macho superhero throws himself out of an airplane. Parachutes into the flames to save the forest. Over and over, you did that how many times? You miss it?"

"You don't exactly 'parachute into the flames.'"

"You don't exactly save the forest, either. There's more beer if you want. Whiskey too. Roxanne left some weed, if you're up for that. High test."

"Hmm. Where'd this salmon come from?"

"The river. Before that, the ocean. Before that, the river."

"Poaching a deer is one thing. But salmon..."

"I don't call it poaching. Subsistence. This fish was all spawned out, just about dead. That's why it tastes a little beat-up, sorry."

"Tastes fucking great. Seventy-six. Times. Throwing myself out of an airplane to parachute into the flames and save the forest. Or so it says on the plaque they gave me when I retired. Seventy-six times saving the forest, by disrupting its most fundamental ecological process. That part they left off the plaque. So Roxanne was here? You and Roxanne are still..."

"Still. Anyway, she visits me sometimes. Maybe she just likes running around buck naked at the ranch. You know who else you look like? Crazy old Caleb McKeane. You got Caleb's eyes, Ben."

"Caleb's eyes."

"That picture hanging in the mudroom our entire lives? Ancestor Caleb? The miner? You better take a look at the eyes."

"I remember the picture. Not the eyes, specifically."

Which got Jimmy thinking: what specifically did he remember about the eyes? He'd been feeling them on him all afternoon, but the eyes themselves he'd barely glimpsed, or imagined he'd glimpsed, glinting out at him from beneath that deep twilight of clutter. The rest of the photograph, the context for the eyes, was unseen, though so familiar he could imagine it clearly. Yet he couldn't say when he'd last noticed it, really *looked* at it. Couldn't say why, if Caleb's gaze was so potent and spooky, it had only come to his attention when buried beneath such a phenomenal quantity of junk. As if the eyes were visible only when hidden. As if to be present Caleb needed to be entombed.

But in a way Caleb's eyes were not the point. Whether he had or hadn't noticed Caleb's eyes before wasn't the point. The point was, he hadn't noticed *Ben's*. The point was, when had Ben's eyes ever looked like this?

"Mad scientist gets out of my truck," said Jimmy. "Rolls his suitcase into the airport, flies off to the mad scientist convention. Couple of days later, wildass Caleb McKeane shows up on my porch begging for dinner. Only it's not Caleb, it's the mad scientist. So. What happened? How do you connect...?"

That things are connected in ways we mainly fail to perceive, over great distances and spans of time, was for Ben a baseline premise of his research and the Model it yielded. It's what his Model was: a web of connections once hidden, now defined, quantified, mapped, projected.

That much Jimmy understood of his brother's explanation as it continued deep into the night: pedantic and free-ranging, abstracted, disjointed, alcohol- and marijuana-fueled. But Ben had already tapped into something. He'd come battered and famished out of the wild, an apparition, pupils burning with a subterranean glow. Unless that was just the reflection of the coals in the firepit where Jimmy had barbecued the salmon, or of the electronic digits on the monitor, dying embers of a fire that gave off no heat, and that never actually died.

Or so it seemed to Jimmy in *his* intoxication.

A massive convergence and divergence of independent vectors. One way of conceptualizing an airport. Each with a unique trajectory. Yet the ultimate effect—the sum of the vectors—is zero, no trajectory at all. So any single vector could enter the convergence zone and never emerge, or emerge undetected. Or with its course slightly altered, ever so subtly deflected.

"We're talking a particular vector here?" said Jimmy. "That has a name?"

Ben got on the plane, went up into the sky, returned to the ground, went from airport to taxi to hotel to brightly lit, crowded conference room. Then the room went dark, except for the glow of cell phones, and above the cell phones, on a podium on the stage, the brighter glow of his laptop. The phones blinked off. He tapped the laptop screen. His paper blazed gigantly on the gigantic screen behind him. His *paper.* Except there was no paper, Jimmy was right about that. No material. Just data, floating in a polychromatic ether streaked by the flash of the laser pointer. Quantifications of the obvious that reveal the obscure. The unknown illuminated through methodical juxtapositions of the known.

"Well, that doesn't exactly give me a visual," Jimmy said. "Of what's on the screen."

Ben stared at him. Caleb's eyes. *"Fire,"* he said. "Anthropogenic fire."

Primordial fire is fire the gods throw down from the skies. Anthropogenic fire is fire stolen from the gods. Promethean fire. Stolen, caged, carried on long migrations and released into places and seasons that had scarcely seen flame. People set fire for the hunt, to clear or freshen pasture, burn out or decoy an enemy. For the thrill of watching flame sweep over the bush. Or, to nurture and protect the land, because they understood the dynamic of forests, fuels, fire.

But those early firebearers were eliminated, overrun by people who believed, or pretended to believe, their own creation story: that they had come out of a Garden where fire had never burned. People who imagined that the open glades and savannas they settled were not fireforged by lightning and humans out of Pleistocene forests but simply created that way, to ease their occupancy. People who imagined they could now purge the land of fire.

And so the human/fire collaboration devolved into the Hundred Year War on Fire, that we know has failed, that we don't know how to end.

Did he miss it?

Some things he missed, others not so much.

He missed the physical strength and skill, the acrobatics, even the grunt work—filthy, hot, smoky, sweaty, no witnesses or glamor, at the end of the day pure exhaustion and the satisfaction of a line well-built, trees properly felled, the fire neatly contained, mopped-up—he missed all that. He missed the companionship and camaraderie, the shared danger, teamwork, pride. Being part of a crew, a cohesive unit.

He missed jumping. Not the jump itself—flinging yourself out of an airplane, that *was* a little crazy—but the long, ephemeral moment after the jump, the space and time between plane and ground. The sudden deceleration of the world beneath an open parachute, suspension between the separate immensities of sky and earth. Suspended animation, animated suspension. The fire a small element in the expanse of territory below, and also a thing of great beauty and significance. A stream of smoke, a short run upslope or firing in the resinous crown of a conifer. But mostly burning close to the ground, vital to the integrity and history of the ground. Working it slowly, piece by piece, as it had for millennia.

Then the smokejumpers descend from the sky and stomp it out.

In their lifetime, the forest had changed drastically. The density of trees was now many times what it had been historically. Half the mature trees were dead, from drought, disease, fire. Ghost forests, littered with standing or jackstrawed snags. On a windless day you could hear the methodical chewing of the bark beetles. The climate in flux, flora and fauna migrating or disappearing, all systems, all biomes in flux. Creeks dried up, blown out. In the jumbled debris you saw the wreckage of check dams, fish traps, gauges, sensors, diversions, hydrographs. *Data.* Yet new data was constantly flooding in—rivers of data, clouds, deep veins, bottomless data mines. Every year his database doubled, quadrupled. Every year, two, four, eight times as many angels dancing on the shrinking head of a pin. More variables, feedback loops, more kinks and confluences and bifurcations in the feedback loops. More moving parts, permutations, possible outcomes. More stochasticity.

Ben stared into space. He took a sip of whiskey. The crickets sang their single note, the lambs bleated multiple ones, the fire flared and dimmed. Far away an owl hooted. Trevor, dreaming, twitched and snorted. Behind it all, the river, a constant.

"So the Model's in flux, too. Which means it's never finished. Never gets out on the ground. There's no action. Action means risk, and risk means blame when things go wrong. Which sooner or later they will. So we're afraid to act; we keep waiting for a perfect model to tell us what to do. But even a perfect model is too risky. Even a perfect model can't tell us with any certainty what's going to happen, if we light a fire, for example, or let a fire burn. On the ground, there's always just one outcome, right? But that's also stochastically determined. Which means a perfect model has a different outcome every time you run it.

"So the Model's in flux *and* in limbo. Everything keeps changing, and nothing happens. And so at some point people start losing interest. They stop showing up at meetings. They get transferred, assigned to another project, retire, wander away. Their desks are still covered with old stuff: maps, thumb drives, sticky notes, reports, binders. Then one day the desk is clear. Nothing but a computer, and somebody new sitting in front of it. Pretty soon I don't know who those people are or what they're working on. I don't know who's on my team, if I even have a team. And eventually it comes down on me, I get the memo. Hey Ben, things are shifting around, we got a new office for you. It's in the basement. You saw the basement."

"The reliquary. Euthanasia ward."

Ben shrugged. "It's what happens with projects, I guess. An idea flares up in the Agency's brain, money pours in, the idea burns bright for awhile. Then it slowly fades out. The money goes away, the fog rolls back in. Institutional dementia takes over, again."

And yet. His Project had survived. Hunkered down in that basement, in an obscure corner of the brain. Dementia working in its favor, maybe. Still enough of a budget to pay his salary and send a bare-bones crew out in the field for a few months every summer, not so much that anyone paid attention to what they did there. Or to what he did in the basement, the tangents and digressions he pursued, how many windows might be open on his screen.

He helped Helen publish her book. Benjamin, a noble name in printing, she effused. Not knowing or just pretending not to know that although it might still take some level of skill to write a book it required almost none to publish one. You could do it online, painting by numbers. What a world, every half-literate fool a publishing house unto himself. Old Benjamin the printer, Poor Richard, groaning in his grave. But Helen said she had no interest in mastering those skills herself, that was why you had children. And as usual the easiest thing was to not argue with her, just do what she asked, do it in the office, on the side, one more window open on the desktop, one more distraction, not unpleasant. At times he even *liked* doing it, liked getting the layout and formatting and cover design just right. Creating a tangible product, never mind how useless.

As for content—well, what did that matter? It wasn't as though he had either the time or desire to critique or proofread. To read the thing at all, for that matter. Probably no one would read it, reading it wasn't the point. The point was the existence of the physical artifact, the Book. Which, thanks to him, now existed. 500 copies.

Benjamin, a noble name in printing.

In the meantime he was tracking her, 24/7. The GPS necklace: another tangent, another physical artifact that had proved unexpectedly satisfying. And hardly distracting, really. He'd programmed an alert to trigger on his devices when she left their yard. Ground Zero. A little window would pop up, map or satellite photo, and he could monitor her moving through his neighborhood, a tiny blinking bug icon in the corner of his screen, tiny chirping sound in the background. But if she drifted outside the perimeter of her Safety Zone—his neighborhood, basically—a second alert would go off, the screen would automatically zoom in on her icon, instead of a subtle blinking the bug would start flashing out an SOS distress signal—blinkblinkblink blink-blink-blink blinkblinkblink—and the chirping would shift to a waa-waaing siren sound. Then he would forward her coordinates to Angie's phone so she could drive out and retrieve her from the back roads she was probably wandering, fending off rattlesnakes with her ski pole. Or if Angie was unavailable they'd send Chloe and Sam on their bikes to escort her home.

So the necklace had worked out. A solution to the hippocampus problem, the topographical disorientation problem, if only temporary. Good, practical, down-to-earth technology, never mind that it depended on satellites out in space.

Another thing he was tracking: the freefall of the real estate market and the increasingly precarious state of his family's finances. Angie said not to worry but if half her clients were underwater how was she staying afloat? Her empire seemed to be unraveling but maybe it was always unraveling. Maybe it had always been a shell game. Or some kind of game. Her business, Angie liked to say, was all about nurturing relationships, a deal might or might not come out of that, you still had the relationship. And now her client—the pilot, her *friend*, really—had made an even more generous offer on the ranch. This time the trustees had taken notice, there had been offers and counteroffers, contracts were being drawn up. Jimmy could throw tantrums and monkey wrenches, but the ranch was going to be sold. It *had* to be sold. One more hole in the ground this family keeps shoveling money into, was what Angie called it, and Ben had to agree. A wishing well, that no one other than Jimmy had any wishes for. Or even plans. They were like landed gentry hanging on as long as they could, impoverishing themselves to cling to the title, the peerage, this singular and worthless distinction. Selling the ranch is unthinkable, Ben said. Until you think of it. Then it just seems inevitable.

"Nothing's inevitable," said Jimmy. "But you were talking about your Model. It's exiled to the basement. It survives. And then—"

"It didn't just survive," said Ben. "It *prospered*. In the basement it could cast a wider net. Add complexity. Add beauty. It could be more flexible, a contortionist. Or, it could go the other direction. *Simplify*. Pursue less convoluted pathways of logic. It could identify a mistake and then—just fix it. Of course, the consequences of fixing it can't be predicted."

"Sure. Stochastic. Guiding principle."

"You know what's stochastic? Where lightning strikes. The kind of fire it ignites. What happens when people fuck with it. Seventy-six jump sites, that's stochastic. Random points in space and time. You could build a model around them. One that actually does something. Embed it in the larger Model, that does nothing. Trojan horse. Link it to real-time data: ground, fuel, and atmospheric conditions for each of those jump sites. When those parameters are close to what they were on the date we jumped that fire, the model triggers an action. Which is really a *reaction*: the undoing of the original jump. The original mistake. Not *fixing* it, it can't be fixed, it's too late for that. But it can be undone. Jumpers go back in, only now they don't carry chain saws and pulaskis, they carry drip torches. They reignite the fire they'd put out before, and then—they walk away. If it rains the next day and puts the fire out again, great, the fire's out. If a cold front comes through and blows up a firestorm, well, there's going to be a firestorm. Anthropomorphic Fire, in the service of Primordial Fire. We light the torches, but fire we give back to the gods."

"Trojan horse?"

"Then out of the blue I get the invitation to present. Which I accept, out of vanity, out of shock, how could I not accept? I wasn't ready, the Model wasn't ready. It was too raw, too fragile, too *complicated*. An octopus. But I packed it into a thirty minute PowerPoint, took it to the conference, put it up on a giant screen in front of a couple hundred people. Eggheads, fire dogs, mad scientists, like you said."

Ben kept talking, but what Jimmy mainly heard was flashy gibberish, more or less the equivalent of scrolling through the slides on his phone in the airport dropoff zone. He was too stoned for this stuff. Or not stoned enough. Plus he had to pee badly. But when he stood up Ben stood too, blocking his exit from the porch, still talking, a dark shape rocking and swaying before the flicker and glow of the monitor and the fainter flicker and glow of the cooking fire, dying in the blackness beyond. Talking, talking, just spewing words. Slurring and spitting words. You want a visual, he said. What's on the screen. Okay. Visualize a cloud of data. Unbearably bright. The material world dims, recedes. Carbon-based beings. Blood, chlorophyll, smoke, fire—it's all gone. There's only data. Data, and the obliteration of data.

He went on and on. Fractal echoes. Genetic tracers. Feedback loop-deloops. Trojan horse. Seventy-six little flame icons flickering on the screen. Jimmy's bladder was bursting but he couldn't break away. The story was building to a climax, maybe. Ben's audience had turned against him. Whispering, muttering. Someone stood up, shouted, he shouted back. The moderator was on her feet, trying to calm things down. Images kept firing past on the screen, he wasn't controlling them, he was just watching like everyone else. Then, sudden darkness. A little blue shape in the center of the screen, a bug, blinking off and on. *Blinkblinkblink. Blink Blink Blink. Blinkblinkblink.* The bug started wailing, or maybe it wasn't the bug. *Waawaawaa. Waaa Waaa Waaa. Waawaawaa.*

He'd seen and heard it before, of course he had. He'd fastened the GPS necklace around his mother's neck, chosen the bug icon, programmed the SOS rhythm, the blinking and wailing, to activate when she crossed over the boundary of her safety zone. So now it was bells and whistles, lights and sirens. Default override of anything else happening on his computer. Default zoom to her location. He'd programmed all that. But he couldn't stop it, all he could do was watch the pixels tumble. This wasn't the first time. In a second the pixels would resolve into his neighborhood, she'd be making her usual break for the hills. And Jimmy, assuming he was paying attention, would round her up.

But when the pixels resolved it wasn't his neighborhood. It was in the mountains somewhere. Canyons, rivers, a settlement. Dirt roads, fields, rock piles, orchards, house, barn. *Confluence Bar.* Not even. She'd crossed the Perdu River, was headed up the Blue River Trail.

"What the fuck. Why is the alert triggering now, two hundred miles from what's supposed to be her safety zone? What's she doing up *Blue River?* Researching her next book? She's going to trek up the mountain and visit her daughter? Or, is this just another pointless, disoriented walkabout? Is Jimmy with her or where the fuck is Jimmy? These are the questions going through my head. My presentation is no longer there. Or on the screen. It's over. The moderator's trying to say something, house lights are on, people are pissed, they're up and heading for the door. Well, fuck them. I'm already recalibrating. Shifting gears, making a new plan. Back on the mouse, zooming in on that little blue bug. But I can't find it, it blinks off, it's gone. She's walked into too deep a hole, satellites can't find her. Still I keep zooming— to the river, the trail, the ground. But you can't zoom to the ground. The ground blurs, pixelates. Inside the pixels, nothing. *Spacelessness,* brother. Your word. Not tangible but real."

Ben fell silent. His breathing was labored, his breath sour.

"And then?"

Ben rocked and swayed, staggered, almost fell. "And then I came out here. First night I camped on the helispot. Second night, I don't know where the fuck I was. Third night, this is it, brother. Here I am. Groundtruthing. I think maybe I ate too much of that salmon."

He sat heavily—fell—onto the couch. Jimmy lurched out into the darkness to finally piss. He stood for a long time, looking up at the stars and thinking about Ben's voice coming out of the darkness, the weird undulations of his body, the flash and swoop of his hands in the starglow, fireglow, screen glow. Or maybe Ben was pure shadow and he'd only imagined the hands. Maybe he'd mixed things up with a memory of different hands, different voice, different kind of story. One of their father's improvised soliloquies on the violent origins of Precambrian rock or the fissions and fusions of continents or the churning of magma deep beneath their feet. Not explanations or lectures so much as invocations, conjurations. Ethan's voice low, constant, mesmerizing, the movement of his hands intricate and indecipherable, so that Jimmy as a child had stared at the empty kinetic space between them as if into the chasms of the suture zone, where pieces of the world ground up against each other and were sucked under and remade and new alchemies were born.

But what exactly had Ben conjured up between *his* hands? Jimmy still didn't have a visual, still wasn't sure what had happened at the conference, what Ben had or hadn't said, which Model or Models he'd put up on the screen. Finally his pee dribbled to a stop. Silence, not quite silence. The river, not just the river. A stirring in the sheepherder's camp? He went back to the porch. The monitor was dark. He could barely see Ben, now splayed out on the couch, head back, mouth open, emitting little gasps and snores and snorts. He turned him on his side and rummaged up a sleeping bag and laid it over him, then poured a final finger of whiskey and sat before the monitor, beeping softly once again, flaring, glowing. The electronic campfire, stirred back to life. Satellites coming into range above the canyon rim, triangulating their mother's location, a unique point in that cold immensity of space. X axis, Y axis, Z axis, bingo. Coordinates unchanged, blue bug icon unmoved, Helen still at her mooring. "Going to bed," he announced pointlessly to the wheezing form on the couch, and went there, feeling a certain vindication and reassurance and sense that he had, never mind how Ben saw it, complied with his filial duty.

He slept until mid-morning and awoke, slightly hungover, to sunlight streaming through the windows and a dusty barnyard smell in the air. But quiet: no sheep sounds. The sheep boss had complained to him about the dry pasture and said something about moving the band out early; apparently he'd done it. Jimmy checked the monitor. Ben checked it too, when he got up an hour or so later. They had coffee, showers, breakfast, kept checking the monitor. She was still in the cabin, still sleeping like a champion. She slept with the same incredible endurance with which she walked. Sleeping and walking, the two went hand in hand, reinforced each other, different faces of the same obsession. You had to admire it, envy it. How many adults could sleep with such abandon? They marveled each time they picked up her signal and might have gone on marveling all day, if Jimmy hadn't looked up from his second bowl of oatmeal to point out that the receiver, for all its usefulness in telling them her location, said nothing about her condition.

"You mean, for example, is she still breathing."

"I'm not worried about that. Christ, I don't doubt she'll outlive us both. But she has been out there maybe 15 hours. What's she *doing*?"

Yet such was the miserliness of their imaginations, the deep trench of reductionist logic they were stuck in, that the possibility that the receiver might not even be telling them her location did not occur to them until they opened the door of the shop and saw the sheets and blankets in disarray on the mattress, an open suitcase on the work bench, and a hacksaw lying on the bench between the suitcase and the vise. Squeezed in the jaws of the vise was Helen's necklace, cut ends dangling, silver chain and malachite locket twisting and glinting and smeared with something that might have been blood.

"Her hippocampus," Jimmy said. "She amputated it."

17

PROFE

The foreman helped Chele turn the sheep out in the pasture, unsaddle the horse and mules, and turn them out with the sheep. They fed the dogs, set up the tent. They unloaded supplies from the ATV trailer. Then Chele went down to a rocky beach and washed up while Oscar cooked breakfast, Chele's first and Oscar's second of the day. They sat outside the tent on a stump and a camp chair, eating bacon and eggs and bread and drinking coffee. Oscar wanted to know why Chele was a day late getting to the river camp.

"Predator attack," Chele answered, after a pause. "I lost two lambs. I shot a mountain lion." All of which was true, never mind that the actual chronology of events was reversed and there was no connection between them and neither fully explained why he was late getting to camp.

Oscar piled a huge quantity of scrambled eggs on a chunk of bread and shoved it into his mouth. "So, *Profe,* where are the claws? I told you. You shoot a varmint, you bring me the claws. Mr. Armstrong needs the claws. What else you been shooting?"

"Nothing," Chele lied.

"You run into anybody up there? No Indians? Just that *cholo* keeps popping up in your mirror. *Indio de verdad* hasn't been seen up on Indian Mountain for about five years."

The real Indian was Oscar himself. He claimed a direct lineage to Rumiñahui, Atahualpa's general who'd dumped the treasure of the Inca into a bottomless lake so it could never be recovered by the treacherous Spanish. Whereas Chele had no lineage at all. *Chucho*

Americano, Oscar said. Standard-issue American mutt. Casserole with no recipe. A soup made of leftovers, whatever was lying around got thrown in. Still chomping on his scrambled eggs, Oscar leaned in—too close—and peered at Chele. *Veo Cortez. Veo Montezuma.* Cortez, Montezuma, a little George Washington, a little Genghis Khan, a trace of some African—no one remembers *his* name—who thought he was a king too, until he woke up with his black ass chained to a slave ship.

Oscar laughed. He sat back, swallowed his eggs, gulped his coffee. Then fell silent, staring into space. Except there wasn't any space, just the broad canvas wall of the tent, which had housed sheepherders for decades and was impregnated with deep stains of smoke and dirt and grease and covered with patches and caulkings, among them the fresh white patch Chele himself had glued on a few days earlier and which Oscar would no doubt eventually notice, because he noticed everything.

For over a year Chele had been consciously trying to channel Oscar. To be more like Oscar—observant, pragmatic, *present.* Focused on the task at hand: keeping his sheep healthy, fat, and safe, anticipating obstacles and dangers and shepherding the band safely past them. Focused on controlling the runaway trajectories of his thoughts and shepherding *them*, shielding thought from abstraction, digression, superstition, delusion, and whatever fresh disaster might ensue.

> Thoughts become words
>
> Words become actions
>
> Actions become habits
>
> Habits become character
>
> Character becomes destiny

Profe, professor. Oscar had taken to calling him that in the beginning. A way of needling him whenever he came upon Chele fumbling ineptly with a camp chore, or reading a book, or writing, as he occasionally did, in a little notebook. *Lost in your head, Profe? Wondering what the hell your hands are supposed to be doing?* Oscar had the idea, or pretended he did, that Chele had been raised by nuns in a convent orphanage and educated, frivolously, at the university. It did no good to tell him that he hadn't ever gone to college, had barely graduated from high school.

The nickname had stuck, even as Chele, adapting quickly and without complaint to the seasonally changing demands of work and living situations—lambing, shearing, gelding, trailing sheep through the mountains and living out of a tent for more than half the year—had vastly improved his standing with the foreman.

A couple of weeks earlier Oscar had transferred his partner, Raúl, to a band that was having trouble with wolves. A new herder was supposed to replace Raúl but hadn't shown. Gone wetback, Oscar said. "Signed his contract, then wiped his ass with the contract. Contract's just a paper gets you across the border, then you do what you like. Buy new papers, get an easier job, go find your people. Everybody's got people they can run to someplace in this country, that got to take them in. What about you, *Profe*? You scheming on something like that?"

Chele shook his head. "I don't have people, not in this country or any other."

With Raúl gone, he was left alone in charge of an entire band of sheep. A temporary situation, Oscar assured him, while Mr. Armstrong did the paperwork to sign on a new herder. "It's a two man job, for sure. And you're just one man. Not even. Half man, half boy. But as long as you're doing the work of two, you'll get paid for it. Mr. Armstrong said so himself."

The work was unending, but he preferred to stay busy, and twice the pay meant half the time to pay off his debt. In the meantime, instead of another man, Oscar had brought him Lobo. Armstrong was getting the big white dogs for the bands they trailed through wolf country—expensive dogs, but the government, which had brought the wolf back in the first place, was paying for them.

"Wolf won't come near with this big sonofabitch standing by. You hope. But you don't treat him like your normal sheep dog, understand? He's more guard than herd dog. He knows he's here for one thing—*intimidation.*"

The other dogs were border collie mixes, with sheepherding in their blood. They could stop an errant sheep cold just by giving her a certain look. The dog would crouch low, staring, while the sheep stood trembling, paralyzed by the predator eyes locked on hers. Hunter and prey, an ancient relationship turned on its head, the rituals of the kill now rituals of protection.

Lobo was the only animal whose name Oscar used. The others he just called by what they were—*Yegua, Mulo, Perra, Cachorro.* So for Chele they were mainly nameless. They didn't seem to *need* names. Or instructions, they knew what the job was and they just went to work. They liked to work as much as he did. The mules practically packed themselves, eager for the trail. The dogs cocked their heads and studied him, discerning his intentions before he knew what they were himself, and immediately moving to carry them out. He quickly learned the whistles, voice commands, and hand gestures they responded to, and Oscar had to acknowledge that he handled dogs with skill. The horse and mules too, though he didn't say it straight out. "Who taught you to ride?" was another of his standard lines, though Chele decided it was meant less as criticism than as recognition that he had his own style on the back of a horse. Oscar still sometimes called him 'Profe' and teased him about college and the nuns, but it seemed he didn't re-ally mean anything by it, beyond an acknowledgment that Chele was out of place and different than his other herders, doubly a stranger and foreigner in their midst.

Lately he had even made a few overt gestures of kindness. He'd brought him a couple of small guidebooks, to identify plants and an-imal tracks. When Chele came down with a cold, Oscar gave him an alpaca hat, and his next batch of supplies included two bottles of Pe-ruvian *curandero* remedies—one to strengthen the immune system and invigorate the kidneys, and the other, a greenish liquid the consis-tency of phlegm, to slow and thicken the blood and temporarily blunt sexual longing. On the label, a black-haired, bare-breasted temptress gripped the bars of a cage. It was a medicine he prescribed to all his herders, Oscar said, except those who were so old the blood already barely seeped out to their extremities.

Chele'd thanked him and dosed himself with the cold and kidney cure as instructed. The temptress he stashed deep in his kitchen box.

Oscar rendezvoused with Chele every ten days or so, to bring supplies, tell him where to go next, and inventory the sheep. To inventory Chele, make sure he hadn't gone off the deep end with tedium and loneliness. And indeed in Oscar's presence it seemed his imagination was less volatile. Once the foreman appeared he saw no further sign of his grandma. Who wasn't his grandma, of course, wasn't even a credible phantasm of his grandma. His grandma—*his godmother*, even in real life his grandma wasn't his grandma—had been hobbled by unrelenting ailments and moved, barely, with a walking stick and a stiff, scrunched-up, long-suffering shuffle. Nothing like the fluid grace of the white-haired woman he'd seen crossing the bridge, then turning—pirouetting—to be swept back in a current of scurrying sheep.

Though in fact his grandma had also been a little other-worldly like that. Swaying in her skirts and apron atop her little mare, pouring out streams of muttered stories while she cast an eye about for Sisimiti, for Cadejo. Stories that took pieces of botany and history and legend and religion and mixed them up with her own private superstitions and *sucesos*.

Which—apparently he had no choice—were now his.

A few nights earlier, at Rigg Flat, their last camp before they went up on Indian Mountain, something had crossed the dry meadow and stopped outside his tent.

In the lingering twilight of midsummer evenings, Chele, though exhausted, sometimes had trouble falling asleep. He lay awake in the near-dark, smelling tent canvas and animals and remembering Tuctuc and his band of *mesteños*, gathered in the corridor outside the dormitory to escape the night rain. Their smell was practically the only thing that could wake him, back then. Radios blasting, conversation, argument, lights, singing, laughing, cursing, crying, snoring, breathing, farting, creaking, rustling… he slept through it all. Only the horses penetrated his barriers, gliding through night grasses, rubbing up against the edges of buildings and dreams.

He heard something coming towards the tent from across the meadow. The dogs were silent. The horses didn't stir. There was only the clear, crisp sound of something large moving through dry grass. A human gait? Or…? Then stopping outside the tent, just a few feet away. Then, absolute silence again. He took up the rifle. He waited. Finally he unclenched his throat.

"Who is there?"

English had never sounded more guttural and empty of meaning. He called again, louder. The silence outside continued but that sound kept echoing in his head until it seemed not to have originated in the grass outside his tent but rather in some separate and private space that now also enclosed him. How long did he lie in the dark listening, praying? Waiting for the intruder to further declare itself. Man, beast, or spirit? Hunter, messenger, tattooed assassin? At last he took a deep breath, gripped the rifle, and lunged out of the tent into the starry night, where the dogs barely stirred and the tent was a pale, solitary form in the undisturbed grass.

The next night was the same. Again he lay on his cot in the silent dusk and heard someone or something crossing the meadow. Again the sound stopped just outside the tent; again the animals did not stir; again he spoke and received no answer. In the long silence he lost track of the origin of the sound—had it in fact come from outside the tent, or from… somewhere else? He'd tracked its progress with the rifle and now the rifle was pointed toward the place where the sound had stopped and without coming to any conscious decision he squeezed the trigger.

There was a great explosion and a bitter smoke and he was thrown back against the cot. Dogs barked, sheep bawled, horses lunged and whinnied. But when he ventured out with rifle and headlamp he found nothing in the grass: no blood, no tracks, no glint of luminescent eyes, only a bullet hole in the tent wall and a burning smell that stayed in the canvas for days.

There was no way to share any of this with Oscar, of course. He could no more confess to Oscar that he'd shot through his tent at some unseen, ghostly intruder than tell him he'd just spotted a spirit woman from his childhood crossing the bridge with the sheep. The foreman didn't deal in that kind of ambiguity, would waste no sympathy on a herder unable to distinguish between ghosts rustling around in his memory and flesh and blood creatures that could threaten his sheep. He might tease about *brujas* and enchantresses, but Oscar's mind would never trick him like that. His mind was literal and concrete and fixed things unembellished in their places. Oscar liked things mapped out. He kept trying to map out the cougar shooting: location, time of day, possible witnesses. There was nothing to tell, Chele insisted. The cougar lay on a rock and watched the sheep pass. He'd shot it. The body fell into a gully.

"You got the right to shoot," Oscar said. "The *responsibility*. You see a cougar, you shoot. Shoot first ask questions later. Don't ask questions. Don't advertise. Just bring me the claws. Mr Armstrong needs to see the claws."

"I didn't advertise anything. I fired one shot. Nobody saw."

"But not a wolf. You don't shoot a wolf, unless you catch him in a killing act. Even then. Government paid more than a thousand dollars for your big white dog there. Why? Not to protect sheep, nobody cares about the sheep. Or the sorry little brown kid running around with them. They pay to protect the fucking *wolf*. Dog keeps the wolf away from the sheep, keeps the herder from shooting the wolf, is the idea. You shoot a wolf, there'll be no end to the shitstorm."

"I haven't even seen one. Heard them a couple times, I guess."

"All right, then. In a way it don't matter. Sheep are about done in these mountains anyway. Every year they shut down a couple more allotments. Sheepman's a fossil, going the way of the wool sweater. That coat you're wearing, you call that fleece? It ain't fleece. Sheep wear fleece. You're wearing plastic. They grind up soda bottles. Coca-Cola, Fanta. That hat's the only real fleece you got. Peruvian alpaca, *de calidad*. In my country those hats go way back. The Inca had one, maybe. Old *abuelo* Rumiñahui wore a hat like that, not much else. A damn loincloth, fighting the Spanish in their helmets and armor, on horses. But he held them off, for awhile."

"Like Lempira."

"Lempira?"

"Lempira was a Lenca cacique who unified Indian resistance against the Spanish invaders and successfully defended, for a time, the great rock fortress of Cerquín."

"Is that so? Thanks, *Profe*."

"He was a warrior and a shaman. A trickster. He had visions that showed him how to trick the Spanish, steal their horses, burn their haciendas. Until they tricked *him*. They got him to come out into the open for a parley. Then they shot him."

"Yeah, that's about right. Fucking Spanish."

"It was a long time ago."

"Sure. But nothing's really changed, huh? *El colonialismo vive aún aquí.* You're still sneaking around the woods like that old *indio*, anyway. Up on Indian Mountain with a rifle, horses, sheep. Poaching cougars, dumping them in a ditch. Indian Mountain, what's that all about? What Indians? Nobody remembers them, or what they called the mountain. But you can be pretty sure they had a better name for it. Indian names are always better. Spirits, visions, something that *happened*. A *story*. Just one word, sometimes, but a pretty good story." He rattled off something in Quechya. "Not bad, huh?"

"I don't know. Sure."

"Yeah. You know what it means? *Placewheretheprofeshotacougaranddumpeditinaditchandforgotabouttheclaws.* See, a story."

"I didn't exactly *forget* the claws."

"Whatever. Anyway, there's still Indians up there. Indian ghosts. That aspen grove you camped in? The sheepherder carvings? Those are Indian *artifacts*, mainly. Mexican Indians, South American Indians, but still. Archaeologists come around, photographers, tourists. It's practically a museum up there. But you leave those trees alone. Modern day herder carves something, anything, his name or his girlfriend's name or any of her sweet spots or his own sorry-ass hard-on, nobody's gonna see a cultural artifact. It's all graffiti to them. Ghetto shit, vandalism. *Prohibido*. Mr. Armstrong'll hear about it from the ranger. We'll get a visit from the Forest cop, not the archaeologist."

Chele grunted. The foreman was staring at him.

"All right, then." He poured himself another cup of coffee and stared Chele down some more. He laughed. "You damn well better have carved something. You owe it to them ghosts. Tradition going back to *los bascos*. Sooner or later you got to do it, understand?"

Chele, confused, grunted again. Oscar continued: "We all do. I did. I gouged my name in one of those trees, about twenty years ago. Maybe you saw. Maybe you couldn't tell. Those carvings mutate. You carve something, then the tree takes over. Sap bleeds out, tree grows, your carving cracks and stretches. That tree gets old enough, it just *swallows* the letters, chews them up, maybe a hundred years after you cut them in."

"There was a witness," said Chele.

"What?"

"The lion. I showed it to the girl in the tower. The *vigilante*."

The Peruvian peered at him. "I thought nobody saw. You said it fell into a hole."

"Nobody saw that. Maybe she heard the shot. Anyway I dragged it out. I put it on the mule and took it up to her tower."

Oscar waited.

"It had been stalking her, that's what she'd told me. I showed it to her, so she could see it was dead. Then I dumped it back in another hole."

The Peruvian stared even harder. "*De veras*. You shoot a cougar that's lying on a rock watching the sheep pass by, like it's watching a parade. Then you haul it—a full-grown cougar—out of the ditch and up on the back of your mule. Then take it up to the firetower to show a girl you been talking to. A girl. And then you drop it back in the ditch. That's how it happened? Was the girl pretty? Was she impressed?"

"She was pretty. I don't think impressed."

Chele had loved the camp in the aspen grove, a far less somber and foreboding place than the dim coniferous forest. Beneath an open canopy, leaves trembled in the smallest wind, keeping sunlight in motion across tree trunks and ground. The younger trees offered up bark as smooth as skin, as bright as blank white paper. Here and there messages were carved into the soft wood: initials, names, dates, hometowns, an occasional blunt obscenity or crude pictograph. Horses and dogs, human figures, nudes, genitalia.

But mainly the carvings had seemed melancholy and a little haunted, even the sex ones. A commemoration of times past, of ghosts, the dead. A museum. As Chele drifted from tree to tree he'd recalled drifting from room to room, painting to painting, around the sunlit colonial patio of the National Gallery—a similarly diffused light, with a similar hushed reverence and sense of the lost past. Except the National Gallery was an inclosure where armed guards stood watch over sanctified works of art hanging in isolation from everything around them, while the carvings were primitive scrawls and the grove open and borderless, a conduit to other places.

In the evenings a kind of magic light came through the aspens, so that the ground itself seemed to glow and the pale amber light that fell on the carvings lent a solemnity and even sacredness to the names of men who had passed this way before and to the names of towns and villages and family they'd left behind in some other country to which perhaps they had never returned.

But that light also exposed a falseness in the carvings, the nudes in particular. It exposed a loneliness so profound and permanent that no memory of an actual woman was left to the carvers, only these caricatures. Or maybe caricatures were all they'd ever had. Maybe they'd never seen a real woman naked in a clear light, and so had no choice but to carve blindly and stupidly.

But Chele *had* seen a naked woman, with exceptional clarity and in a different kind of transformative light. He remembered precisely her long-striding legs, the perfect symmetry of her body, weaving among debris piles and river mud in the aftermath of the flood, while beneath a wild tangle of hair her head pivoted slowly to hold him in her gaze. He remembered her lines, her *alignment*. A geometry that might be reproduced, carved into wood with just a few simple lines.

Not a masturbatory gouging in the flesh of a tree. Not a mess of blurs and shadows like the nude in the National Gallery.

Do you ever make pictures, Chele? Naked ladies?

He stopped before a smooth, pale trunk. He took out his knife.

He'd spent way too much time on his carving. Trying to get it right, though well before the light faded he saw it was no good. The thing was harder than he'd thought. Not the mechanics of carving or the steadiness of his hand, but the steadiness of the image in his mind. Was he trying to rehabilitate the nude in the National Gallery, or capture the naked lunatic crossing the intersection? Or Tania on the night road to Chalamanca—not naked at all, but leaning back against the warm hood of the Mazda as if she were?

Opposing lines—the erect, sensual symmetry of the naked lunatic; the slumping, sensual slouch of the might-as-well-be-naked Tania. No way to reconcile them. He ended up with a mess. Finally he put away his knife and went back to camp. He bedded the sheep down and checked on the stock. He walked out the ridge and back in the long twilight. Darkness, when it came, would last only six or seven hours. There was nothing left to do except maybe read a little in bed, then sleep.

A light went on in the lookout tower, a quarter mile away. He took it as an invitation.

The foreman had some business with the caretaker. "Take a break," he told Chele. "When I get back we'll inventory. Then I'm hitting the road, it's a long haul out of here."

Oscar disappeared and Chele, exhausted, lay on his cot and slept. The tent was stuffy and he awoke drenched in sweat. He got up and went outside. Oscar was sitting in the shade with his back against a tree, writing in a notebook. A letter, he said.

"To your wife?"

"My daughter. She's fifteen. Acting up. You know how girls start acting up."

"Yeah. Sure."

"Last I was home she was a little girl. Princesses and unicorns. Now she's strutting around practicing her idea of being a woman. Pretty soon she's done practicing, it's the real thing. That's what she thinks. You gotta try to slow her down, *viejo*, my wife says, get her thinking not so crazy about sex. A real, old-fashioned letter from her *papi*, maybe that's what she needs. Paper letter, no screen, she holds it in her hands and has to read it. Oh, sure. Fuck. How do you write a letter to your daughter about sex?"

"I don't know. Tell her about chastity?"

"Chastity!"

"'The virtue of using the gift of sexuality in the right way, whether one is single, married, or vowed.'"

"Okay, I'll tell her that. Tell her I got this sheepherder wants to teach her about chastity, a little trick he learned from the nuns."

"When will you see her next?"

"Oh, I see her all the time. On the screen. In the flesh, it'll be another year. Three months home leave, every three years. Same as you. That's how it's been for me and her, her whole life."

"I guess you sort of get used to it, huh."

"You think? What you get used to in Peru is having no work. No money. Me, I'm sending a paycheck home every month. My kids are healthy, wearing nice clothes, living in a nice house. They got a big TV, computers, bicycles, the works. They'll go to college, like you, because their daddy's five thousand miles away with his arm up a sheep's cunt. That's how it is, *Profe*. Family life, modern time. You had a different idea?"

"No. I don't have ideas about family life."

"Bullshit. You got ideas. It's just they got nothing to do with the way things really are. Look, I know about orphans—in Peru there's plenty. Parents might be dead. Or living halfway around the world, Spain, Italy, working like slaves, sending a little money home. Maybe starting up a fresh litter of kids, first batch got to grow up more or less on their own. That's how it is."

"Capitalism, huh. Globalization."

"Globalization my ass. *Orphanization*, is what that word means. Means there's nothing special about being an orphan. Millions of kids making their own way in this fucked-up world. Falls on one kid to pack a mule train, trail sheep through the mountains, scratch a hole in the ground to shit in every morning. Another's walking across Mexico to the Promised Land, turns out to be a desert where they take his *mochila* and his shoelaces and tell him to get lost. Another, all he's got to do is drag his ass down to the Western Union and sign for his cash. So. You rested up, *Profe*? Let's get this done. We're way down in a fucking hole here and it gets dark early."

They inventoried the sheep. They herded the band over near the corral on the edge of the pasture and the dogs pushed them toward the chute while the foreman stood on the bottom rung of the fence, silently counting. Chele stood next to the chute shoving them along, one at a time in the oceanic noise and the dust. He wasn't gentle. Sheep took a lot of punishment on these long migrations, that was just the way it was. Stupid and docile creatures with no will of their own, they were also surprisingly tough. Not noble beasts, individually, but with sheep it wasn't about the individual. It was about the band, a single shape-shifting organism flowing through the mountains, leaving in its wake only dust and trampled vegetation and little pellets of shit.

But when you broke it down like this, one sheep at a time, that organized intelligence dissolved. These were just cells they were counting. Two thousand wailing units. To pass them all through that corral took a long time. Sheep by sheep, an unending repetitive motion that when he glanced away his eyes transferred to the landscape. Pasture, mountains, trees, clouds: any static thing stared at could be set in motion and sent streaming off toward a corral chute somewhere. Meanwhile the sheep kept coming and he kept grabbing handfuls of wool and shoving them along. It felt like some kind of trance. Through the swirling dust he could see Oscar's lips moving as he counted, his voice inaudible over the wailing and keening of sheep and the jangling of bells and thudding of bodies against the boards. You could be pretty sure Oscar wasn't hearing the ocean or falling into any kind of trance.

He was counting, and at the same time inspecting every animal for limping gaits, sores, infections, general lassitude.

How many, he said, jumping down from the fence, and Chele had to admit he hadn't kept count. The foreman spat in disgust. *Profe* got his head in the clouds, can't do the math. Thinking so big he can't think. But as usual his derision was mainly an act, because according to his own count the two lambs killed at his bivouac camp were the only animals Chele had lost, the best record of any herder that summer.

They opened the corral gate and let the sheep back in the pasture. Not that they'd find anything to eat there, the Peruvian said. Every year this grass was poorer. Now it looked as though it hadn't been irrigated all summer. The caretaker blamed the floods that had washed out the ditch and diversion dam. Well, that was three years ago. He blamed the drought, creek so low he couldn't keep water in the ditch. There were pieces of new pipe along the ditchline and coils of new hose lying around, but the ditch remained high and dry. The pasture where the sheep were supposed to stay for four days they'd already grazed down to stubble.

"So I'm changing the plan. You're moving on. No layover. Sure, you need a break, but there's no help for it. You move out again tomorrow, and Mr. Armstrong pays for just one day of pasturing. I already told the caretaker."

Oscar squatted down to scratch a map in the dirt, a sign that his departure was imminent. Always before they parted, Oscar, using whatever materials were within reach—rocks, twigs, pine cones, clumps of dirt, animal dung, a stick tracing lines in the dust—would sketch a map of the sheep driveway: the river crossings, passes, ridges, mountains, swamps, ghost towns, landmarks and hazards and prominent features Chele would encounter in the days ahead. *Poison Spring. Pico Rojo. Ledorah. Antimony Pass.* "That's the first one. Ten days, four passes. Then we meet up again."

Chele squatted beside him and committed the map to memory. Memorizing, the easy part. Following the main driveways was usually straightforward enough, they were worn so deeply into the earth, plus he'd traveled over them the season before. But at times he'd find himself plunging through blind forest, trying to reconcile his memory of Oscar's diorama with the actual physical country he was traveling through. Then it felt more as though Oscar had blindfolded him, spun him around once or twice, and pushed him off in a general trajectory he would follow until the Peruvian appeared once again, to trace another map on the ground and deflect him in a new direction.

Ten days, his longest solo stretch yet. Four passes, Oscar repeated. The fourth one the highest. It's the wild you're heading into now. *No hay nada.* Where you been up to now, that's the *civilized* part of this country. Then he stood, brusquely shook Chele's hand, got on his ATV, and rode across the bridge and away from the ranch. Chele squatted down again and in the softening light continued to stare at the map—not for the paltry information it conveyed, but because those sticks and scratches in the dirt preserved for a few hours the sense of another human presence in the canyon.

He went to bed well before dark. He dreamt he was riding Tuc-tuc across a meadow strewn with boulders. The boulders morphed into huddled groups of sheep that rose up when Tuc-tuc bore down on them and moved in whatever direction the horse moved as it tried to avoid them. Boulders and sheep multiplied. He'd head Tuc-tuc into what seemed to be a clearing, just a few low shrubs and rocks. Then the shrubs and rocks would rise up as sheep, the horse would turn, the sheep bump into more sheep, small clumps of sheep coming together in bigger clumps while the horse desperately tried to find a way around them and the sheep desperately tried to get out of his way.

A dream of frustration, but the effect was mainly slapstick. Then the dream changed. He was on foot now, trying to make his way not across a mountain meadow but through dense, thorny bushland that seemed somehow familiar. Somewhere dogs were barking. Frustration shifted to anxiety, vague familiarity to recognition. He was busting through the wildland that lay between the pathways at Ciudad de Luz, trying to get to a clearing where Padre Jaco waited for him. Through a web of brambles he could see the crooked shape of the man, ministering to the dark soil beneath his mango tree, or to some afflicted soul at his feet. His strong, coarse, menacing hands, working through the decomposition of things.

He got up well before dawn, lit the lantern and stove, made coffee. The dream—the nightmare—came back to him. Padre Jaco. He might well be dead by now. Or overtaken by his own demons and addictions, that small pocket of evil he could not drain now burst, seeping through his body. Or simply aged and declining in the natural order of things, among the gibbering himself. Ciudad de Luz—a nightmare, yes, but the truth was for Chele it existed as a place of consolation and refuge. A failsafe and a kind of insurance, was how he had come to think of it. If he ever faced a disaster too terrible to endure, ever faced absolute and permanent defeat, he would return to Ciudad de Luz and, like Padre Jaco before him, do his final penance. The ultimate punishment and redemption: living out a cycle of identical days, serving the wretched and the discarded, driven by a faith so extreme as to be indistinguishable from despair.

He broke camp by first light, saddled and packed the stock, and moved the sheep out, eight thousand little hooves obliterating Oscar's diorama and the tracks of his ATV. On horseback he followed the band up the dirt road, past dry fields and silent buildings, sagging gates and fences, weedy vegetable garden, swollen zucchinis, overripe tomatoes, an old dog watching from a porch hedged with vines and yellow roses.

"Hallo!"

It was the old woman from the bridge, standing in the doorway of a cabin near the road. In one hand she held a hacksaw. The other tugged at something around her neck.

"I need you to help me cut this off."

A command, not a request. Then she went back inside the cabin, as if certain he would follow.

18

BONEYARDS

Their technology had failed them. They had failed their technology. It amounted to the same thing: GPS necklace dangling bloodily in the vise, Helen unmoored, again. Wandering as God meant her to wander. Or so Jimmy had blathered drunkenly at her birthday dinner. *Spacelessness*. Another thing he'd blathered, a made-up word, though maybe it meant something. A casting off of moorings, an adaptation to age and mortality and the pitiless way the world kept changing into a more incomprehensible and unwelcoming place. Better to cut the moorings. To occupy not one location on a degraded planet, but no specific place at all, or the entire universe at once.

In any case she had slipped away, right under their inebriated noses, leaving no track they could see in the dry soil around the cabin or the freshly sheep-trampled road.

He left Ben to search close at hand while he set out on the ATV, a wider recon loop around Confluence Bar. First, Upper McKeane: past the drying garden with its unharvested bounty, the empty cabin, the ponderosa grove, the now-deserted sheepherder camp. Past his most recent projects—the never-used horse corral and riding ring, already incubating a fresh crop of knapweed and Russian thistle. He bumped across the lower pasture, stinking of sheep as it would for weeks, though the sheep had been here less than 24 hours. He could still hear their faint wailing far up the Ledorah Road. Then he turned down the low road and crossed the bridge to the Blue River side and got off the ATV and looked around for tracks in the sheep-trampled ground. Nothing. He turned back across the bridge to head up the ditchline, detouring into the boneyard at Lower McKeane to pick up the ATV trailer with the hose and pipe and cement. Might as well get some materials staged, if he was going to drive all they way out the ditchline looking for Helen. Which maybe sounded calloused, like he wasn't taking his mother's disappearance seriously enough. Wasn't taking seriously the drama—the melodrama—that had played out or been staged in the cabin. Hacksaw, vise, open suitcase, bloody necklace. Wasn't taking seriously her neurological affliction, that ominous flat line on her hippocampus scan.

Well, he wasn't. Something in her hippocampus had flatlined, so what. Other parts of her brain were compensating. Overcompensating. And nobody was tracking that.

The idea that she was lost, he definitely wasn't taking that seriously. This wandering up Blue River that had gotten Ben so worked up—a non-event, from his perspective. Had he even been aware of it? If so, it hadn't worried him. She was always wandering off. And always coming back, or he rounded her up and brought her back.

Anyway, what about this 'topographical disorientation'? More hyperbole. Helen knew her way around Confluence Bar better than any of them. She'd diagrammed and photo-documented the place, excavated and inventoried, measured, counted, extracted, dissected, re-enacted. Sniffed her way out shallow ditchlines somebody'd scratched into the ground three quarters of a century ago, to irrigate a little pocket hayfield or a few fruit trees tucked away in some forgotten alcove or bench, that hadn't been irrigated for decades. Broken into old shacks and sheds and cabins, sifted through pine needles and mouse turds looking for artifacts and clues, hantavirus be dammed. Stalked the floodplain of lower Antimony Creek, taking perverse interest in the wreckage of the hydroplant and diversion dam, the chunks of turbine and headgate half-buried among tailings and old mining debris. Wandered the brambly wild orchards with their mulches of dry-rotting fruit, the vast, fallow garden acreage some manic digger had expanded beyond all sustainability and purpose. Disappeared into back rooms, closets, attics, cellars; sorted through mildewed clothes and fabric, quilts and embroideries, collections of beads and buttons and thread and yarn, shelves of files, books, papers, newspapers and magazines, row after row of canning jars with dark contents and illegible labels and lids swollen with botulistic churnings.

"It was the women kept the place together," she said. "The men hammering away in their boneyards, or up on the mountain chasing obsessions and delusions. But those women had boneyards, too. You have to give them credit for their own obsessions and delusions."

Jimmy had tagged along dutifully the whole time. For him it was a job. Many jobs. Chaperone, chauffeur, bodyguard, research assistant, general lackey. Minder and keeper, by default, until she found a more suitable one. *Jimmy go see what's under that old sink. Jimmy get up on that stool, see if you can pull down the rest of those papers.* Fine. He had the run of the ranch. He had an expense account, a few percs, got to see some things that had previously been hidden to him, and others lying around in plain view that he'd never really taken in. He'd learned some history; parts of it might be accurate. Had he enjoyed himself? Not exactly. Mostly he'd felt resigned, fatalistic, trapped. Lena had long since fled to the coast and Ben was a workaholic with a difficult wife and irritating kids, and so it was mainly left to him to deal with the quirks and demands of their mother's eccentric but harmless little hobby. Harmless? He wasn't so sure.

Sometimes she'd scrunch up her face and hang open her jaw and just stare at a thing for the longest time, some outbuilding or mine adit or piece of rusted-out machinery lying around in the woods or the boneyard. Then come up with a story to go with it, grafted seamlessly, as far as he could tell, onto any number of stories he'd heard before. What he couldn't tell was how much of it might be factual and how much she was making up on the fly. The boneyard being especially fertile ground, in spite of her antipathy toward Clayton. Or maybe because of it. She'd divined all sorts of revelations and confirmations in that expanse of oil and iron, to her it was emblematic and metaphorical and prophetic, whereas to Jimmy it told a fairly straightforward story about the booming and busting of McKeane enterprises over the years, Clayton's in particular.

The boneyard sprawled across an expanse of river gravels and placer tailings that had been levelled by a bulldozer and over time covered with engines and engine parts, plow blades, dozer blades, harrows, winches, cables, logs, stacks of rough-milled boards and warped plywood and creosoted timbers, steel barrels, pumps and valves and fittings, sheets of aluminum, irrigation pipe, culverts, fuel tanks, stock tanks, tires, old snowmobiles, dead trucks and tractors. A water tender. A portable sawmill. A two-seater plane stripped down to the fuselage. Machines to cut wood, crush rock, mix cement, filter gravels. A 40 foot crane standing like a monument or a sentinel, that hadn't budged in at least 15 years. All the heavy and light equipment that Clayton and his predecessors had scavenged from floods or hauled up the canyon and across the river, before the road washed out and the bridge was condemned and gated.

All testimony to a familial madness and to the breadth and ongoing delusion of Clayton's ambition. Not that Clayton himself had ever acknowledged failure or the likelihood that any piece of equipment might never again be put to use. He'd worked as a miner, rancher, truck driver, heavy equipment operator, hunting guide, outfitter, and finally as handyman in a bed and breakfast that might go an entire season without hosting a guest. And still he found a reason to put on his coveralls and rummage around in his junk piles, fiddling with some old piece of machinery until he got it to run, sometimes. And then he *would* find some use for it, which somehow justified the continued existence of the boneyard and everything in it.

As kids they'd made forays into it—a forbidden playground, full of alluring dangers and secrets. Lena especially had been drawn to it and was especially daring in her explorations. She'd climbed all over stuff, the loaders and trucks and fuel tanks and rusty old mining machinery. She'd summited the crane and sat up there giving a bird whistle, taunting Clayton, who never looked up from his hammering and sawing. The three of them played hide and seek, with each other and sometimes with Clayton, who might not know he was playing. They sent Lena in close, she was small and quiet and fast. Her bird calls echoed out of the culvert until Clayton finally did look up. *You goddamn kids get the hell out of my culverts!* He never caught more than a glimpse of her, but she had him spooked. Sometimes he yelled at the culverts when they weren't anywhere near.

In any case, useless or not, there was no alternative to the continued existence of the boneyard. Six years earlier, a hundred-year flood had come down the Perdu, washing out the last three miles of the river road. The engineers determined that the road was in the floodplain and in any case too unstable to rebuild and that the bridge pilings were structurally compromised. So they converted the road to an ATV trail and tank-trapped and gated the approach to the bridge, with just enough room for an ATV to squeeze past. Confluence Bar was now accessible by four-wheeler, motorcycle, foot, or horse. Or small plane, the airstrip was still in place. As was the Ledorah Road, though no longer connected to any other road and officially closed. But Clayton kept it mainly clear of fallen trees and rocks and theoretically drivable all the way over the pass to the Ledorah townsite, where it fingered off into game trails and mining tracks and a sheep driveway soon swallowed by forest.

For awhile Opal and Clayton ran a rough little resort that mainly served hunters. The guests stayed in three rudimentary guest cabins on the high terrace, with views of the river (filtered) and the boneyard (unfiltered). Opal cooked and Clayton took clients on spring hunts in the canyon for bear or cougar, or up the Ledorah Road in the fall to hunt deer and elk out of his spike camp. But the spike camp turned out to be illegal and there were other irregularities and after many warnings his outfitter's license was suspended. Then hardly anyone came to the guest cabins.

But still they eked by. Until Clayton, standing on the bucket of his front end loader preparing to prune trees in the apple orchard, made a long reach for the chainsaw Opal was passing up to him, lost his balance, and fell, his full weight plus the chainsaw coming down on her. She cushioned his fall but when he got up she just lay on her back moaning, lips pressed together thinner and tighter than ever. He eased her onto a piece of plywood, strapped her down, lowered the bucket to the ground beside her, slid the plywood in, and drove the loader back to the yard with Opal riding ahead of him in the jerking and swaying bucket. He maneuvered the plywood gurney into the ATV trailer and hauled her out to the driveable road, transferred her to the bed of his pick-up, and drove her to the hospital.

While the doctors operated on a hip fracture, Clayton crossed his arms and stared down the nurse who suggested his wife might have suffered less had he called an ambulance.

"Government shut down my road. Ambulance can't get to my place."

"A helicopter could."

"Helicopter! For a busted hip?"

But from her convalescent bed Opal broke a long silence to tell Clayton that she was done. The ride in the ATV would be her final trip across that bridge. For once Clayton saw the futility of argument. He returned to the canyon only once, to close the house down, winterize the heavy equipment, and sell or give away his animals. There were no takers for the hounds. The last thing he did before he drove away was to lead them, howling piteously, down on the gravel bar, tie them to a fallen cottonwood, and shoot them.

A few months later a postcard came from Mexico: a photograph of a couple of tourists in bathing suits and sombreros, sitting in lawn chairs on a stony beach, scowling at a flat turquoise sea. On closer examination the tourists proved to be Clayton and Opal. On the back of the card Clayton had written:

> *Couple of beach bums, what do you make of that?*
> *No telling when we'll be back. Opal says never. She*
> *sends regards. I don't say never but I do admit Mexico*
> *is not so bad as expected. For the time being anyway*
> *you are the last McKeane on Confluence Bar.*
>
> *From the second to last one,*
> *Clayton*
>
> *PS did you get those piles burned*

Jimmy had first come to live alone in the canyon during a period of youthful spiritual yearning and seeking, with the idea of spending a winter in seclusion, reading and meditating and contemplating the nature of God. At the end of that first winter he took his Bhagavad Gita and Tao Te Ching and Koran and King James Bible down to the gravel bar and tossed the entire library into the spring flood of the Perdu River. There was no human wisdom that would guide him to God. He would come to God, if he was to come to God, by obscure and circuitous paths. Through working with Clayton, possibly. Clayton: hard, bitter, atheistic, a stony path to God.

So later he'd bewildered everyone, himself included, by becoming something like an apprentice to Clayton. Or accomplice, or enabler. The man was full of narrow opinions and sour resentments and, in Helen's view at least, dangerous malice, though Jimmy did not put much stock in her dark insinuations about the unguarded fuel barrels on the airstrip below his house and the disappearance of Ethan McKeane's plane. But it was easy to see why Ethan had quarreled with him and Helen kept her children away from him and Ben and Lena still had nothing to do with him. Yet Jimmy was more drawn to the man, even to his acidic old wife, than repelled. Opal and Clayton were the true keepers of the flame, the family's last real link to the land, to working the land. The jobs he'd done with Clayton—propping up fences, putting up solar panels, thinning timber, piling slash, fireproofing, keeping the ditch and hydroplant alive—had probably given him more satisfaction than any other work he'd done at Confluence Bar.

And now Jimmy was the keeper of the flame and Clayton was slumped in a lawn chair, watching the Sea of Cortez lap tiny waves against a beach of pebbles. But his coveralls still hung in the barn, his machines still rusted in the rain and sun, his voice still reverberated in Jimmy's ear. Jimmy was getting a little tired of it. He made a perfunctory search of the boneyard, hide-and-seek territory of their childhood. Though now Helen seemed to be playing a more serious game.

"The ranch is going to be sold."

She'd dropped her bombshell on the drive in, breaking a long silence to make her blunt announcement—quiet, matter-of-fact, coming out of left field. *The ranch is going to be sold.* He hadn't said a word, just let the silence settle back in and hold until they pulled up at the end of the drivable road. Neither had mentioned it since.

In fact, it wasn't a bombshell. He'd known something was in the works ever since Helen's birthday party last spring, when, also out of left field and without provocation—but maybe with a hint of something like triumph in her voice?—Angie had announced that the ranch *wasn't* for sale. A few weeks later she showed up in the canyon with her client, a woman. Lean, tan, very well put-together. A few years older than Angie. Or so she appeared from a distance, Jimmy never saw her up close. A pilot. They flew into the canyon in a tiny plane, spiraling down and approaching at just the right angle and landing on the strip as if maybe it weren't the first time. Angie brought her up to the house. She seemed surprised to see Jimmy. For a second he thought—well, he didn't know what to think. He and Angie chatted a minute, about nothing. Her Californian smiled, distantly.

Jimmy had no idea where the woman was from, of course. 'Californian' was what Clayton would have called her, reflexively, derisively, by default—she was rich, beautiful, full of her own self-importance and accustomed to getting her way. Or you assumed all that. Californians—whose actual place of origin was beside the point—were now a dominant presence all up and down the river. Resented, scorned, ridiculed—and courted for the opportunities they presented, for example, the opportunity of converting one hundred years of delusion and disappointment into a formidable amount of cash.

In Perdu Canyon there were still a few homesteaders and recluses scraping out a living up some narrow gulch or side canyon, still one or two working ranches along the main river, but most of the large old ranches and backwoods hideaways had been converted to vacation homes, designer ranches, corporate retreats, survivalist compounds. River stone, lacquered pine, instant aspen glade and piney woodland, lawns, ponds, waterfalls, swimming pools, white rail fences, black horses. Here and there an old cabin or outbuilding left to stand decoratively, maybe renovated for caretakers, who lived a life of decadent and idle servitude, according to Clayton, since the owners were seldom there and there wasn't anything for them to do except wash windows and mow lawns and apply herbicides.

Clayton spat on the ground at about twice his usual rate when he talked about the new ranches. "You see that turf the new people laid down at the Carlson place, Jim? You'd think they were building a god-damn golf course. But it's *just a fucking lawn*. Every Canada Goose in the state's already worked it into its itinerary. Swimming pool's going a little green, you notice?"

"I guess."

"Seen many titties out around that pool? Best start paying atten-tion. But don't get the idea you're seeing something real. It's all fake. A boob job, straight across the board."

Sometimes Jimmy wondered if Clayton had stayed on in the can-yon, with his acres of obsolete machinery and skid trails and stumps and his slavering, bloodthirsty hounds and his hardscrabble titless wife, only to express his contempt for the Californians and their boob job ranches. Which nonetheless, like any boob job, had a *presence*. They were *there*, and all up and down the river the real ranches no longer were. So, which was real?

White fences, black horses, chemical green pasture. A fantastic color scheme, he had to admit. His own expensive horses were cam-ouflaged, nosing out the last palatable stalks of grass on the shadier aspects of Pete's Ridge. Trespassing on the national forest, if anybody wanted to get snarky about it. So arrest the horses. They were basi-cally free agents now, more than half wild, forgetting the little they'd known about barns and hay, saddles, bridles, fences, riders, trainers. And never having learned the first goddamn thing about polo.

The horses had foraged for themselves since January. He'd turned them loose when his hay ran out and hadn't seen them since early summer, when he'd gone up on Pete's to bring them down and couldn't catch a single one. Now he'd about decided they were better off stay-ing there anyway. Which was indefensible, when you considered that a short time ago he'd had such high hopes for them, had put so much time and money into them. But he wasn't trying to defend it, or justify all he'd done and learned on their behalf. He'd learned about *polo*, of all things, added polo to his own stores of knowledge. His own personal database, no algorithms, no science. Rather an accumulation of instinct and clues and small insights and random pieces of information that in the end added up to nothing and answered no questions, certainly not the question of what to do with a band of high-bred horses going feral on the mountainside.

The ranch is going to be sold. Not a bombshell. Rather, a predictable aftermath of Helen finally finishing her book. The denouement, in a sense. Not that Jimmy had actually read the thing, or planned to. But he had a pretty good idea of how it went, he'd helped midwife it into existence. Probably all the more reason to never read it. He'd been out in the field with her, groundtruthing, you might say. Bearing witness firsthand to the facts and artifacts out of which she'd constructed her litany of calamities and more banal failures that had befallen the McK-eanes. The old journals and ledgers, bank statements and contracts and letters of intent, the ore assays and production stats and pedigree charts of sheep and cattle and horses purchased and subsequently sold at a loss. All adding up to this, a heritage of weeds and ghosts.

But presented with the same evidence Jimmy had come to different conclusions, considered different implications. The unexplained purchase of quality horses. Certain cryptic comments in letters and journals. His own conviction that things had a cyclical balance, so that three or four generations after the homesteaders had sold off their horses it was natural that horses should reappear in the same pastures. That an ancestor's vision from a hundred years ago should now come down to him: horses shaking out long manes in a flooded pasture while their owner walked his fences, midsummer grass brushing his thighs, a high-spirited dog running out ahead, high-spirited woman stepping out on the porch, barefoot, bare brown shoulders, shading her eyes as she moves into the sun. At night the bedroom windows wide open, the smell of cut hay and horses, the blended sounds of her breathing, the river, the distant rippling rain of sprinklers.

There was nothing wrong with that epiphany. But maybe the Californians' lawns and swimming pools and boob jobs were less fantastical. Sometimes Jimmy felt less like a rancher or even a caretaker than a janitor, just cleaning up messes left lying around the place. He burned what was burnable; the rest, with no practical way to haul it out, got stashed in the potters' field of Clayton's boneyard. In the pastures sprinkler pipe rusted and weeds grew twice as high as the grass. His horses wouldn't come down off Pete's Ridge, his dog barely hobbled across the yard, there was no woman on the porch. It wasn't going to be Roxanne, she'd made that clear.

"That ranch is a nice place to hang out," she'd told him. "For a couple of days. A week, max. Summer camp. You know why camp is so great? Because it's *temporary*. Nobody *lives* there. Most people have sense enough not to live in a place with no society or internet, barely any electricity, in a hole at the bottom of a mountain at the dead end of a road that isn't even a road anymore."

He took Roxanne home. They parted ambivalently, but they'd been doing that for years. He went by Ben and Angie's to finagle more money out of Helen for materials, then into town to buy cement and pipe and a thousand feet of high pressure hose, high tensile steel-reinforced. He swung by their house again on the way out of town, hoping for a dinner invitation, maybe a couple glasses of quality wine. A miscalculation. Ben was leaving the next day for his conference. Angie had to take the kids to camp. Then she was off on a business trip, whatever that might mean. He got the impression that one thing it meant was that she'd be back with documents for Helen to sign. In the meantime, could Jimmy give Ben a ride to the airport in the morning? Stay with Helen until Angie returned? He had to say yes. But the next day Angie called: something had come up, she'd be gone longer than expected. He would have to stay on.

"I can't. I have to irrigate. My pasture's bone dry."

"I'm sorry. Maybe it'll rain."

"I've got horses!"

"Well, Jimmy, I don't know. You've got a *mother*."

So he and Trevor ended up stuck at Ben and Angie's during a heat spell, which thanks to the swimming pool and the AC wasn't so bad for them but was terrible for the pasture. He and Helen lasted one day, then escaped to the canyon—and from Angie's documents—in his truck. He put her behind him on the ATV for the last three miles after the road closure, Trevor riding in the trailer on top of the cement. He left dog and mother at the house and drove to the boneyard to drop the trailer. The specter of Clayton lurked in the shadow of his old water tender, half-disgusted, half-amused.

"This is how you look after the place, Jim? You *start* irrigating in August?"

"Maybe. Or maybe it's not just about irrigation anymore."

The last McKeane on Confluence Bar. The loneliness was profound. Yet so were the compensations. He was the steward of McKeane Ranch. One ranch, unified. Fields and orchards and gardens, buildings, rockwork, waterworks—everything forged by the pioneers out of the wild, all their dreams and sweat come down to him. To Jimmy it did not seem like the sweat of ghosts. Their sweat was tangible in shacks and rockpiles, in the holes in the ground they had left behind everywhere. Ruins, maybe, but not necessarily carrying a *feel* of ruin. Just as often what he took from the seeming failures and disasters of the McKeanes was a kind of inspiration, a heightened awareness of possibility. A vision not of reclusion and solitude in a dark hidey-hole but of the dynamic oasis the homesteaders had imagined and briefly cultivated. Not a withdrawal from the world but an opening to it, drawing in settlers and nurturing a human community on Confluence Bar and all up and down the river. Farmers and ranchers, builders, herders, gardeners, hunters, fishers, students, teachers, guides, poets, philosophers, children.

A romantic vision, pollyannish for sure. But it wasn't as if he went around talking like that. *It ain't over till it's over*—that was about as pollyannish a sentiment as he was likely to express aloud, in regard to the ranch and any number of other endeavors.

In any case, there was no chance Helen would be lurking around the boneyard in this kind of heat. And nothing, absolutely nothing, could be done without water. He finished hooking up the trailer with its load of hose and pipe and drove up the ditchline to the old diversion.

There were times when Jimmy saw himself as a dogged warrior, working with tenacity and ingenuity against great odds to save the family estate. Other times he was a dilettante who didn't really have to work and so was free to try his hand at any number of frivolous and peripheral endeavors. The horses might illustrate either narrative. The ditch, on the other hand—there had never been anything frivolous or peripheral about the ditch. It was over a hundred years old, the first irrigation project in the county, or so Helen claimed. First thing the homesteaders had built coming into the canyon. She'd devoted an entire chapter to its surveying and construction, the allocation of its water and the bickering and sabotage that ensued. And how nevertheless every summer for a hundred years water was taken out of Antimony Creek and moved a mile and a half by ditch and flume around the rocky point of the mountain to irrigate bottomland hayfields, orchards, and gardens on Confluence Bar.

But no more. Three years earlier, huge thunderstorms had converged on Red Mountain and in half a day dumped four inches on rain on ground too hard-used and fire-scarred to absorb it. The second hundred-year flood, three years after the first. Flash floods, landslides, debris flows, an unprecedented amount of water and soil flushing out the bottom of the watershed, reaming out a new channel for Antimony Creek and cutting off the McKeane ranches from yet another vital connection. A place that had been an oasis—leaves and flowers, riffles and falls, mossy pools, water ouzel, river otter, spawning salmon—was devastated, as bad as anything the dredges and hydraulic hoses had done downstream. Raw mineral earth. Tumbled trees and boulders. Plastic pipe and metal pipe and chunks of cement and timber, the abandoned dredge half-buried in sand and gravel among flowering thistle, mullein, goathead. And the downcut stream trickling through a broad bed of jumbled rock and debris, disconnected forever from the ditch diversion and mangled headgate left high and dry on the stony bank above.

In a way, Jimmy found it beautiful. The hard beauty of sheered-off, unoxidized rock; energy dissipated but also concentrated in the raw creekbed and high eroding beaches. *Shivu* had been here. And now there was a powerful sense of *potential*, something new taking form, you couldn't say what. Perhaps a thing as obvious as, say, a freshly unearthed nugget shining in the gravels. Or perhaps a more subtle exposure.

The only way to get water into the ditch—other than pumping it, not a sustainable or economical solution—would be to move the diversion upstream, to the point where the elevation of the ditch once again intersected the creek. But with the channel cut down to boulders and bedrock there was no way to extend the ditch that far. As a temporary measure he and Clayton had laid pipe, a few hundred yards of six inch PVC pipe just sitting on the cobble of the floodplain or anchored with bolts and cables to boulders or rock walls, connecting the ditch to a new diversion they built upstream out of river cobble and layers of plastic sheeting. Again, unsustainable. Their improvised dam washed away at high flows and at low flows diverted so little water that most just seeped away through the ditch bottom and never made it to a field.

"Ditch has always leaked," said Clayton. "Ethan claimed I was taking his water. I never took more than my rightful half. His just leaked away."

A few hours before Ben showed up, the Peruvian sheep foreman had driven up to the house on an ATV and in pretty rough English informed Jimmy that the band that had just arrived would be heading up to the national forest tomorrow. They were supposed to stay four days but the pasture was very poor; he'd tell Mr. Armstrong to pay for just one day.

"*Dígale pues,*" said Jimmy. "Go ahead and tell him. *Que se vayan, pues. Qúe barbaridad.*" His Spanish was rusty but he was always looking for an opportunity to use it, if only to express to a sheepherder how little regard he had for his sheep. 'Hoofed locusts', in Muir's memorable phrase, which unfortunately he didn't know how to translate into Spanish.

Jimmy knew the pasture was worthless. But it was humiliating for him, scion of the original sheep ranching family—never mind that he hated sheep—to hear it so bluntly stated by a man with no roots or history in the country. A weed. Admitting it was mainly weeds doing the actual work nowadays, ranch work included, real and fake ranches alike. Admitting that 'weed' was a relative term. That he himself was one. Admitting he'd more or less forgotten the sheep were coming. Admitting, finally, that maybe the biggest obstacle to resurrecting the ditch was his inability to think of a good reason for it to still carry all that water and irrigate all those acres of orchard and alfalfa. One band of sheep, four days, wasn't enough. The ponies were no longer a reason if they'd ever been.

So maybe the way to resurrect the ditch was to lower expectations for it. The water right gave you so many CFS but that didn't mean you had to keep taking it all. You could just use a fraction, leave the rest in the creek. Shrink the oasis. Let the gardens die back. Let the pastures go mainly to weeds, the ponies go feral on the mountain.

But keep the ditch alive. Go farther up the creek, into the bedrock narrows, and build a new diversion. A cement dam but it wouldn't look like a dam. It would look exactly like a natural dike, a hardened intrusion of magma snaking through the bedrock and giant boulders and creating a pool that was always full, even when the creek ran very low. The pool would feed a new diversion, headgate and screened pipe hidden beneath more artificial rock, buried pipe running the length of the ditch, no water would seep away. But he wouldn't need much water, just enough to keep a few sprinklers going at Upper McKeane. To maintain a modest garden, a few fruit trees, a few acres of pasture. So when their mountain meadows dried up the ponies might get a whiff of chlorophyll and come home, if only for a visit.

But where the pipe came around the point, at the boundary between Upper and Lower McKeane, he'd build another small dam. Create another pool. Put in a valve, run a hoseline down to the gravel bar, and take out a little more water. Just enough water, just enough head, just enough pressure to wash out a sluice box of ore.

The air had gone hazy. He smelled smoke, vaguely, heard distant sounds: engines, voices. Sheep wailing, a helicopter? Or maybe just the river running over its rocks. Helen was not likely to be found skulking around this sunblasted wasteland either. He unloaded the trailer at the washout and drove back along the ditch, still keeping an eye out for her, when he thought of it. At the last second he swerved off the ditch track and turned into Lower McKeane—to check the airstrip, he told himself, in the interest of a thorough search. But really just for kicks. To raise a cloud of dust skidding and fishtailing and weaving around the junk—dead refrigerator, smashed culvert, tangled roll of barbed wire, rusty cement mixer, old steel barrels—he'd dragged out behind the ATV and distributed randomly yet strategically around the airstrip. An obstacle course, a joyride. Joyride on an ATV; in an airplane, impossible. There would be no more trespass landings. The same small plane had buzzed the place a few times in the weeks since, like an angry horsefly. Angie too was upset. Her client was losing patience. She'd suspended her offer, pending clean-up of the airstrip. Well, she has no say in it, Jimmy said, it's a private strip. When she shows me the title I'll move the stuff.

He raced around half-heartedly, then left the airstrip and continued past the bridge turnoff and around to Upper McKeane. Best get back and see if Ben had turned anything up, or if he'd even looked around or was too hungover and exhausted to look around, after thrashing his way over the mountain and spending a couple of nights lost in the bush and a third at the ranch, getting far more wasted than he had the stamina for. A misadventure entirely set in motion by Jimmy, inadvertently, of course, when he took Helen into the canyon. It was true that he'd promised not to do that. But that was before they had the GPS tracker. What he hadn't considered was that when she did wander her GPS would trigger an alert not just on the screen he was monitoring but on Ben's devices as well. That an alert would go off at such an inopportune moment, not just disrupting Ben's presentation but *sabotaging* it, exposing the empty pixels at the heart of the thing… well, naturally he hadn't considered that. It had been upsetting for Ben, of course. Only, he didn't seem *that* upset. Maybe because he'd already sabotaged it himself? Put his seventy-six jump sites up on the conference room screen and launched into a rave about Anthropomorphic

Fire and stochasticity and his Trojan horse plan to send smokejumpers back into the woods to reignite the wildfires they had previously
extinguished. If in fact he had really said all that, or any of it. If his
audience was still paying attention. If they hadn't already walked out.
If the Trojan Horse was anything even remotely real, or just another
of Ben's ironic mindfucks gone completely off the rails.

Jimmy stopped on a low bluff and looked out over the gravel bar,
not that he expected to spot her sneaking around that barren cobble
field, either. A few small sand beaches here and there, patches of wil-
low and cottonwood trying to get a start. Little mounds of gravelly
soil sprouting thistle and mullein. Tailings and waste rock: what Ethan
McKeane's placer drifts had coughed up over the years. The drifts
themselves were almost impossible to locate, even when you stood
right next to them. At best they might look like an animal's burrow,
dark and closed, trickling water.

A person might hide in one of those holes. But not Helen. She
hated the drifts, hated the idea of anyone going in there. Those claims
were forfeit, she said. No one had worked them or shored them up
or even gone inside for fifteen years. The river was doing the recla-
mation work, the earth itself closing them off. No one was ever going
in there again.

She was wrong about all of that. Jimmy, not the shifting earth or
flooding river, had closed off the tunnels. He'd engineered little cave-in
and blockades, piled brush and sticks around the entrances to look like
flood debris. Then squeezed and wriggled around it and gone inside.

Beyond the entrances, the tunnels opened up some. Inside, they
were surprisingly stable and cohesive—mixed alluvium, everything
from clays to large cobble, practically cemented together. But disap-
pointingly short and straight. That network of braided channels and
abandoned meanders must have only existed in his imagination, or in
his father's imagination. The drifts did have a moist smell, and a few
little pockets of ancient beach, and at the end of one he came across
rusty tools—shovels, pick, rock bar. He hauled out a few buckets of
gravel and sand and carefully washed it in a pan at the river, old-school

prospector style. He had to look hard for it, but a bit of yellow color was left in the bottom of the pan.

That was the second epiphany, that more or less replaced the horse epiphany. *He could work his father's mines.* Ethan's tunnels were still open to him. He wasn't afraid to go inside them, go to work there. Go deeper, to where the gold was lying. The dark, the depth, the closed-in space—he wasn't afraid of it. He was a little afraid of the overburden, the weight of unsolid earth above him, but surely that was a healthy and not a crippling fear.

Like the horse epiphany, this one circled back to what the homesteaders had begun. Except the horses had turned out to be not a completion of a circle but a disconnected arc of it, the circle far too wide to be closed. It might someday come around to horses again and it might not. This circle was simpler, tighter. His father's mines, the pioneers' ditch, two dozen bags of cement, a few thousand feet of hose and pipe. The foundation of a more modest and sustainable economy on the ranch, with expectations more in line with what might actually be achieved. No expectation of a bonanza. No intention of spending all his daylight hours underground or working the sluice box. No ripping into the land or poisoning the water or sucking the creek dry.

He'd just borrow a little water from the creek. Then every once in a while push a wheelbarrow load of gravel and sand out into the light, dump it into the sluice box, take up the hose, flush the gravels back out on top of the bar or into the river, and filter out a little gold.

He'd gone back in a dozen times now. He brought a few timbers down to reinforce any potential weak spots, then flooded the darkness with a high-powered headlamp and began digging up the gravels in earnest, in a reverie, with a smell of fossilized streambeds in his nostrils and a map of ghost channels forming in his mind. Yet it was always a great relief to surface. To follow the wheelbarrow out onto the daylit earth, where a live river twisted and gleamed between rocks glazed by the sun. Thinking of his father surfacing behind *his* wheelbarrow, emerging into a world that each time must have seemed more unbearably bright, unbearably disorienting and strange.

Then he'd climbed into his plane, taken off, disappeared.

A little ore was coming out of the mines. A little water flowing in the ditch. The horses were still out there. He and Roxanne hadn't split. The ranch had not been sold.

It ain't over till its over.

"So how did it go? Any sign of her?"

"No. Plenty of tracks, none of them hers. How about you."

"No. Nothing."

"You want some dinner? Leftover salmon?"

"*Nothing*, really." Ben lay on the couch, speaking to the ceiling. "Pastures are empty. No sheep. But didn't the sheep just get here? No horses, either. What happened to your ponies?"

"They're around."

"Not even any horse sign. Your ponies don't shit?"

"It has been sitting out all day. I'll heat it up. The salmon."

"There's nothing for them to eat, why would they? I took a walk out the ditchline. I did see something there. Pipe, hose, about 20 bags of cement. What the fuck, Jimmy."

"What do you mean, what the fuck."

Ben sat up. "I mean what the fuck are you planning to do with 20 bags of cement?"

"Well, I'm building a dam."

"A dam."

"You saw what a mess it is up there. How everything's gerry-rigged. And still not working. Can't hardly get water out of the creek, or keep it in the ditch. So I'm piping the water, and I'm building a diversion pool to keep the water level up. To make a pool, you need a dam."

"Jimmy. *It's a salmon stream.* You can't just build a dam in a salmon stream."

"A little dam, it won't block fish passage. Fish will love it, they love pools. I'll stain the cement, texture it. It'll look like part of the bed-rock. Nobody will even know it's there."

"Fishheads snorkel that creek. They'll see it."

"They won't care. They'll be too busy counting fish."

"You have a permit for this?"

"A permit."

"You want to build a cement dam. On a salmon stream. On the National Forest. You need a permit. Many permits."

"Well, it's not on the National Forest. That's our land. I'm pretty sure it is. Right on the boundary, anyway. Depends which survey you're using."

"Which survey. Jesus. Which—it doesn't even matter. It's not going to be our land. We're *selling*, Jimmy.

"Not yet. Nobody's signed anything. Sale hasn't closed."

"Papers are just waiting to be signed. Trustees have agreed to the terms."

"Yeah, well, where are these trustees? Clayton's in Mexico, somewhere. Helen we don't know where the fuck she is, or what the fuck she might be doing there."

Jimmy was looking at the wall map. "You said you camped at a helispot? Where was that?"

"Spur ridge off Indian Mountain. Blue River side." Ben got off the couch and went over to the map and put a finger on it.

"That looks like line of sight to the summit. Did you wave to the lookout?"

"Sure I waved. Didn't see her wave back."

Jimmy went outside. He walked up to the cabin and looked around by the porch and stood in the doorway looking at the unmade bed and the open suitcase and the severed necklace dangling in the vise. He thought for awhile about the mechanics of that. He left the cabin and walked up the road, squatting now and then to study the dusty surface, pounded by thousands of cloven hooves. And other tracks he hadn't noticed or fully considered before.

He went back to the house. Ben was looking through the cupboards.

"Maybe I'll just open a can of beans or something," he said.

"I know where she is."

"You know where she is."

"Ledorah Road. Poison Springs. Josie's Tubs."

Ben stared at him. "Those old bathtubs up at the mine? Nobody's hauled them out of there yet?"

"She has a thing about the hot springs. She wants to spend an entire night sitting in one of those tubs. Arthritis therapy and vision quest all in one. She keeps pestering me to take her, I keep putting her off. So I'm thinking she just busted out and went on her own."

"That's what, eight or ten miles up the road."

"Or maybe not on her own."

"No shade. It was a hundred degrees today."

"Right. And Helen decides she's going to go sit in a hot springs. Got a problem with that?"

"Only that it's crazy. Even for her."

"Sure. But she's desperate to get out. To go for a walk, a really long walk. No collar, no lead, no safety zone. And then along comes this nomad walking past her door."

"What?"

"Think, Ben! The sheepherder! He rides up, on his way to … wherever, he's always on his way to somewhere. She gets *him* to cut off her collar. He pulls her up on his horse and she's gone, no tracks. Except there are tracks. I went back just now and took a closer look. On top of all the sheep tracks, in the dust. Horses, boots."

Ben took a can out of the cupboard, opened it, plopped the contents into a pan, turned on the burner.

"That's crazy. But it is crazy. So maybe. She could have. So what do we do?"

"Well, we drive up and get her."

"In the dark? Up that road, on an ATV?"

"We'll take Clayton's Jeep. It's got good clearance, decent tires. Narrow wheelbase. A plowblade."

"That Jeep still runs?"

"We'll get it running."

"Is that road even drivable?"

"Might be some tight spots. Trees down. We'll throw in a couple of shovels. A chainsaw. Take it real slow. We can talk. You can finish your story."

"My story."

"About the mad scientist. He goes off the deep end at his confer-ence. Loses his mother, his audience, takes a dive into the pixels. Next chapter: he walks up to my porch begging for a plate of salmon. We haven't heard the part about how he got here. Pixels to porch, how'd it happen?"

19

THREE BATHS

CHELE LEFT THE HORSE and mules standing in the road and followed the woman into the cabin. The logs were old, settled; the place *smelled* old, dry, decomposing. There was a bed, a chair, a workbench. She stood next to the workbench, holding a hacksaw in one hand and the silver chain of her necklace in the other. Both hands were lightly streaked with blood.

"This thing. It's strangling me. But I can't get it over my head or unfasten it and you see what happened when I tried to saw it. So I would like you to please do the sawing."

She handed him the hacksaw, sat on a stool, and laid her head on the workbench next to a vise. "Clamp it," she said. The chain was not so tight—not exactly *strangling* her—but when he closed it in the vise only a little space remained between her neck and the vise. Blood seeped from a shallow cut on her neck. He felt a stickiness on the handle of the hacksaw. He did not want to saw downward on the chain so close to her neck, so he removed the blade from its frame and held it by either end and began to gently saw upwards and away from her. She watched his face and not his hands as he worked, her head held a little askew, tilted sideways, jaw hanging loose. But the tension still in her neck, helping her hand keep the chain taut. Finally the blade cut through and the two ends of the chain fell away and dangled in the vise.

She lifted her head off the workbench. "Oh, thank you! Thank you, Mister...?"

"Cruz. Mister Cruz." Not that anyone had ever called him that. "Chele." He found a box of tissues and a water bottle on a table beside the bed and cleaned up the blood.

"Well, *gracias*, Chele Cruz. I'm Helen." She shook his hand. He moved to open the vise but she stopped him. "Leave it. It'll give somebody something to think about."

He took a step toward the door. "I go. I have sheep—"

"Yes, you go! But there must be another man with the sheep? Or coming along behind?"

He shook his head. "Mr. Armstrong short-handed. Only me."

"I see. Well, they won't get lost. There's only the one road."

He said goodbye and went out the door. He was halfway across the yard when she called from the cabin doorway for him to wait, she was coming too.

The road was narrow and deeply rutted. It climbed steeply out of the canyon, winding in and out of dry creeks and around promontories and outcrops, twisting and turning back on itself so that their direction of travel was constantly shifting and it seemed the world was no longer fixed in place but tilted and wheeled around an axis that moved with them. In places he had to dismount and lead the stock around rockslides and washouts and over fallen trees and branches and remount on the other side. But it was awkward and pointless to ride while this old woman poked along beside him with her ski pole, so finally he just got down from the horse and led the stock. Slowly they moved up the road. Eventually he persuaded her to ride, but she couldn't tolerate the jostle and jarring of anything like a trot, so still the mare just shambled along.

Never in more than a year of sheepherding had he been separated from the band. But now it was just a dustcloud moving away from them, high up the mountain. To care for the sheep was his sole duty and responsibility. He had no responsibility, none, for this old woman who without explanation had attached herself to him. Yet how to get her off his hands. He could not very well make her get off the horse he'd just made her climb up on, then hop on himself and ride away, leaving her to walk alone up an abandoned road in the blazing sun on her way to God knows where.

She'd given him her ski pole to carry. There was a bit of *deja vu*: an old woman on a slow horse, talking, while he plodded along beside carrying her walking stick. She was nothing like his grandma, but still, *deja vu*.

She was talking about the road. Not much of a road, she said, it didn't connect to anywhere. But it had a name. The Ledorah Road. And a history, the sheep were a part of that. They'd pioneered it, blazed the first trails up the mountain into the high summer pastures. The road followed. She went on and on about it. Who had built it and why—for sheep, gold, timber, water. How long ago, why it was abandoned. It was all a little hard to follow. All about the road but nothing about where she was going on it.

"Señora Helen, uh, *perdón*. Where is your destination?"

"My *destination*?" As if the question were absurd. "Well, for now, Josie's. The Baths."

"You have a bath?"

"Three baths. Cold water, hot water, cold again. There's a little resort up there. A luxury spa, ha! What about you?"

"No! No bath."

"I mean your destination! Where are *you* going?"

The Peruano, squatting in the dust beside his pinecone and sheep turd diorama, had recited a dozen or more names. But somehow Chele couldn't spit any out. He gave a vague wave of his hand. *Más allá.* Farther along.

They'd climbed high above the canyon bottom. He could see where the rivers came together—the smaller one he'd forded above its gorge, and a piece of the bridge he'd crossed over the larger river, where he'd had that fleeting vision of his grandmother, swept up in a river of sheep. The ranch with its dry pasture. The pine grove he'd camped in. The corral where he and Oscar had inventoried the sheep. Sheds, barns, houses. The little cabin where he'd sawed off her necklace.

He'd seen the separate parts, passing through, but here was a more complete perspective. Also more unreal and abstracted, not unlike

one of Oscar's dioramas. But the place was larger and more complicated than he'd imagined. Spur roads and trails and tracks snaked out
through little side valleys and over low divides, along ponds, wood-
lands, dry fields, wild gardens and wild orchards, to end at a broken
stone wall or pit or the ruins of a house or barn. Other buildings were
not so derelict but neither did they look exactly occupied or cared for.
Everywhere were piles—rocks, dirt, slash. Stacks of wood and metal.
Old machinery, dead-looking vehicles. An airplane with no wings. An
excavator of some sort, half-buried in sand and gravel in the creek. A
long, level strip of brown grass and bare earth, with more chunks of
metal and machinery scattered across it.

Un refugio, Lena had called it.

"No cow," he observed. "No horse."

"No. It's not that kind of ranch."

What kind was it, then? It didn't matter, they were leaving it behind. Rivers and canyons, leaving them behind. Canyons opened to
mountains, mountains to a wider sky. A thin stream of black smoke
rose up. Helen on the horse was talking, talking. For sure there was a
language barrier but her meaning was obscured by more than that. She
kept talking about a family, *the* family, the McKeanes. They owned or
had owned everything: the ranch, the road, the earth that was riddled
with holes. Caves, tunnels, crevasses, grottos, gulches, mines. They
owned boiling sulfur waters and therapeutic mudbaths, rejuvenating
and corrupting at once. Their schemes unravelled at the moment of
fruition. They fell to addiction and hot surges of madness and rage.
They died in unburiable ways.

Her sentences did not sound like normal sentences. More like rec-
itations, incantations, like parables out of the Bible or some other book
of ancient prophecy impossible to grasp. But what prophecy? Surely
some disaster? The earth riddled with holes—of course he thought of
San Miguel. A grotto, a gulch—that was the blackwater stream at *Colonia El Porvenir*, trickling through its ravine beneath a barrio built
of sticks and poles. The red ground hard and dry and cracking, until
the hurricane rains came and the ravine filled with muddy water and
the softened earth turned to a torrent of liquid mud.

The therapeutic mudbaths of the poor.

But wasn't he supposed to be channeling Oscar? Who would never let his mind go to a place like that. He'd stop up his ears to these *bruja* stories, curse her, ride away, be done with her.

But to Chele they did not seem like *bruja* stories. More like the fragmented stories of his grandmother, confiding some intimate knowledge which he'd always failed to decipher. Or not even talking to him, just casting her words out over the earth for whatever being, animate or inanimate, might be listening.

A track led off the main road into a deep draw. The heat was brutal. Clouds of steam or mist rose from the shadow. He heard water running, smelled a strange and bitter smell. It took him a moment to identify it. *Azufre.* Another moment to recall the English word. Sulfur.

She'd dismounted. "This—your destination?"

She didn't answer. Anyway he had to keep moving, faster. He pointed up the road. "The sheep. I catch them up."

"Oh yes, you *will* catch them up! But first, you need to prepare yourself! You need to rest, and get out of the sun. You need *medicine.*"

Twenty minutes later he was in deep, cool shade, squatting in the middle of a creek on a submerged rock ledge, behind a curtain of water. The waterfall *loud*, the air so moist he might have been breathing underwater, inside this small, dim room of rocks, moss, ferns. This cold, wet, roaring place.

But how had it happened? The heat had something to do with it, his thoughts confused by too much sun? Or that sulfur smell, somehow drawing him off the road down into this cleft in the earth? An evil smell, seemingly, but maybe not purely evil... Or maybe Helen's words, her voice, the rhythm of her *bruja* incantations. Murmurings of deep shade, medicinal waters. A luxury spa. Gardens and fountains, stairways cut into stone, white marble, blue tile, grottos, pools, baths.

All in ruins, he'd understood that much. So he'd expected—what? Wild gardens, maybe, dry fountains. The skeletons of bathhouses, broken steps descending into caves and grottos, the baths overgrown with algaes and swamp weeds.

Baths, not bathtubs. Not six stained, unremarkable bathtubs lined up on a cement slab on a narrow flat scraped out of the steep, scabby hillside, above a rocky gulch and stream. A few similarly excavated flats nearby, occupied by half-built structures half-fallen over, or by nothing. Old junk scattered about on the hillside and in the gulch—mining junk and construction junk and the random junk of what must have been somebody's daily life. Plumbing junk: plastic buckets, hoses, valves, fittings, pipe. A black hose gushed sulfury water. He followed it around the hill to a springbox, hot springs bubbling out, streaming over terraces of pale rock to the creek below.

All of it out in the open, on the exposed mountainside. No grotto. Far below, where the gulch dropped away off the mountain, there might be grottos.

She picked up the hose and begun to fill a tub. Talking the whole time. Pieces of story, outlandish, no context or explanation. The gods of ancient Greece, Aphrodite, Dionysus, played a part. A man stalked the grottos, piece of rope in one hand, knife in the other. Blood ran over the stones. A tower was involved. A woman and a baby got on a train. A miner came out of the earth, fell through the sky, black water closed over him and he was gone.

She filled two tubs, then dropped the hose. He helped her down the steep, skittery bank to the creek, not easy for her or him. There had been a path but it had washed out since she was last here, she said. They came down to a pool among boulders and small waterfalls. She began to undress. He put a hand in the creek.

"Cold! You bath here?"

"Bathe. Absolutely." She was down to her bra and underpants. Again, like his grandmother. Her ritual of purification, sitting in her underwear in the silty river shallows. Her swollen legs, their purple, knotty veins. Now Helen was about to do the same? Only this water was freezing. And she was taking *off* her bra and underpants.

Another second, third of the week. Second time in his life he'd been kissed, fired a gun, looked straight-on at a fully naked woman. Once again, a second that had little in common with the first. The naked lunatic had crossed the intersection with perfect symmetry, perfect balance, perfect smoothness; naked Helen hunched over, her flesh lumpy, saggy, blemished, She probed tentatively with her ski pole and leaned shakily on it as she stepped into the pool and made her way slowly out to deeper water, then lowered herself into it up to her neck. Then looked back at him, and waited.

He took off his clothes. Not his underwear. Then stepped out over the rocks and took a great, gasping breath and sank into the pool.

The coldest water he'd ever been in, incredibly cold. He couldn't breathe. His heart clenched, his skin stung. He closed his eyes. When he opened them she'd vanished completely. There was only the empty, clear pool, with the waterfall pouring into it. When she reappeared he didn't see where she'd come from. She did that a couple of times, appeared, disappeared, before he figured out that she was going behind the waterfall. Finally she emerged and made her way to shore. He started to follow but she turned, raised her ski pole, pointed it at him, turned him back. So he took a deep breath and went under the pounding waterfall, too. And entered a roaring, mossy room, half water, half air.

First bath.

The second was in a tub, hot and sulfury. *Hot.* His skin burned, the heat as painful as the cold, at first. Then the burning passed and it felt wonderful. Wonderful to just sit, and not on a horse. Not moving. Not thinking. He lay back in the tub and just *felt* the cleansing water on his skin, pinesap and dirt and lanolin dissolving in sulfurous mist and heat. The springs bubbled, the creek cascaded in the gulch below. Pure, self-contained sounds: water, wind, birds, faint buzz of insects or a distant airplane. The most tranquil moment he'd known in months.

Siento paz.

"Which tub do you suppose it was?"

He sat up. She was looking over the rim of her tub at him. "Which tub?" he said.

"That she was sitting in! Nursing her baby, when she shot him." She made a pistol out of her finger and thumb, pointed it at him, brought the hammer down. "That he fell into, while she slipped out with the baby. That he *died* in, bled to death in. Bloated and rotted in."

He didn't know what to say to that so he said nothing. He sank deeper into the water. For the first time in a long while he thought of his Book of Questions, stashed among his old *cuadernos*, compilations of useless and obsolete knowledge, in a storage room somewhere at St. Jerome's Gardens. The Book of Questions was also useless and obsolete, long-abandoned, half-forgotten. Yet questions continued to arise.

> *What was that ranch even for? Was she the rancher? Or what?*

> *What was with the necklace? Why had she made him cut it off?*

> *Was this bathtub her destination? Did she have a destination?*

> *Why, even close up, did she still remind him of his grandma?*

> *And of who else?*

Another list. Things Helen and his grandma had in common.

> *aged wanderers*

> *back road travelers*

> *walking stick*

> *tellers of confusing stories*

> *horse women*

> *water women*

> *medicine women*

"Little boy blue!"

Her voice seemed to come from far away. Sing-songy voice, teasing voice? He sat up.

"Come blow your horn! Sheep's in the meadow, cow's in the corn."

He knew the English nursery rhyme, the Scandinavians had taught it to him when he was little. But his sheep! They were not in any meadow but up on the desolate mountain, with predators maybe closing in and only the dogs to protect them.

Where is the boy who looks after the sheep?

She laughed—at him? He laughed too, for no reason. But the question was real, no joke. Where was he, the boy who looks after the sheep? The boy who had been a seed and a nucleus and then was turned out into exile and even in exile had remained a kind of nucleus, orbited by an entire constellation of animals, finding them pasture and water and leading them over mountains and canyons and keeping a constant vigil against predators who thumped invisibly in night woods and who might be just as inclined to sink their teeth and claws into him.

Where *was* he? Something had happened to him out on the long sheep driveway, between the sulfur waters of Josie's Tubs and the bottom of the stairs at the Indian Mountain fire lookout. Between his second naked woman and his second kiss. A chaste kiss, completely unlike the first. There was only the brief touch of a woman's lips, a single moment of warmth, softness, moisture. Then he was released again into dryness and cold. He stumbled back to camp, huddled on a rock, a deep chill came into his bones. At dawn he broke camp in a hypothermic trance and shot the cougar in a confusion of purpose and fled the mountain and bivouacked restlessly beside a campfire, Lempira's fire, Sisimiti's fire, and descended to the canyon in a dust-cloud of sheep and a hallucinogenic fever.

How could the kiss have been chaste, then, with that as its aftermath?

He heaved himself out of the tub. Rejuvenated, or had a sulfurous venom seeped into his veins? He stood over her. "I'm leaving."

She made a sound. Still humming, maybe? Or a long sigh or moan—of pleasure? She lay back, her head barely out of the water, eyes closed. The water supernaturally clear, a lens that focused on and magnified black moles and skin tags, blue veins, sunspots, birthmarks, bruises, scars, hair. Flaccid, pale skin hanging from her arms, flaccid breasts undulating in the ripples like protoplasm, ghostly jellyfish.

Watery revelations of flesh, of bodies. Physical bodies, it seemed he'd always been studying them, tending to them. Children's, old people's, animal's bodies. Female bodies, male bodies. Their commonalities and differentiations, their beauty and grossness and decay, their injuries and scars and remarkable utility of form and feature. Their vulnerabilities, their resilience.

"I think none of them," she muttered.

"What?"

"They must have got rid of that tub. Pushed it off into the gully. Buried it under tailings." She opened an eye. "I would like you to fill those two buckets and bring them back up here."

"I have to leave."

"Of course. But please bring my bathwater up first. And pour it over me. I'm not risking my neck trying to get down to the creek again! Third bath will have to be a shower."

He scrambled back down to the creek, filled the buckets, and set them on the shore. Behind the high embankment he couldn't see Helen or the tubs, just the spring box and terraced rock the springs themselves must have laid down over unmeasured time. The rock itself waterlike, rippled and fluted. Petrified water, glowing as if with its own light, or some light within the deeper rock beneath.

On the other side of the gulch, a great fan of completely different rock—sharp-edged, shattered, opaque and glittery at once—spilled off the mountainside and into the creek. The bloodstained tub, the Mexican tile, the grottos—buried beneath, perhaps? Above, at the top of the rock fan, a black shadow. A cave, the mouth of the mine that had disgorged the tailings, and then the miner, who then fell through sky and into black river water?

"Chele Cruz! My bath!"

He took up the two buckets and powered up the embankment, not spilling a drop. He went over the last rise into a windblown cloud of sulfury steam and practically ran her over, standing there right in front of him, naked, waiting for her bath. He was still wearing underpants but he *felt* naked. He set down the buckets and put on his jeans. Then picked a bucket up and poured it slowly over her head. She shut her eyes, sucked in her breath. He picked up the second bucket. The wind blew furiously. Water streamed off her face and blew back into his. He poured and the wind blew all the harder, trees and bushes bending and waving wildly in the gale, everything blown away in streams and tatters: leaves, water, smoke, steam, whatever she was shouting at him through streams of sulfur water.

She got right up in his face. *Take. Off. Your. Pants.*

He shook his head. "I just put on. I need to go."

"Yes! But first, your third bath. You finish on cold, that's how the medicine works! Take off your pants. Go back down to the creek. Get under the waterfall. Stay there. The water's freezing, but it won't kill you. The opposite. Let the cold pass *through* your skin. It drives the heat in deeper. Cold and heat, they work together. You can keep going all night."

He did as she said. Barefoot, he skidded and scrabbled to the creek. He took off his pants. He stepped into the pool and stood ankle deep in the water and looked down the gulch and out across the canyon at an immense and cloudless sky, only slightly smudged where the windblown strand of black smoke hit some kind of atmospheric ceiling and dispersed.

"Chele Cruz!"

She was staring at him from the high embankment. "You haven't always been a sheepherder."

"No! One year."

"And before?"

"Before, no, not sheep. Other things. Never sheep."

"So what happened? How did a boy like you end up in a place like this, all by himself with two thousand sheep?"

There was no easy answer to that. Maybe she wanted to hear the hard one. Maybe he wanted to tell it to her. But not now, in bad English, standing in his underpants in an icy creek with his sheep gone up the mountain.

"I need work," he shouted. Easy answer. His feet were freezing. "I need money."

"How much do they pay you to shepherd two thousand animals?"

He told her. He took a deep breath, lunged toward deeper water. "What if you got twice that, to shepherd one more?" He went under the icy water.

20

GROUNDTRUTHING

THE LEDORAH ROAD WAS BLOCKED by rockslides, slumps, fallen trees. Some the Jeep could squeeze around or blade to the side but others they had to clear as best they could with shovel and Pulaski, rock bar, chainsaw. Then ease their way over the top, the Jeep swaying and tilting at an angle that, fingers crossed, was not quite steep enough to roll. Or they'd clear debris from the outer edge of the roadbed and sneak around the toe of the slide, tires clinging to the very rim of a black precipice that, fingers crossed, was not too undercut to hold their weight.

Ben was loving it. Jumping in and out of the Jeep, grabbing up a tool, digging out a mudslide or cutting out a fallen snag or rolling a log or boulder out of the way. Work, it had to be done and you just did it, no bullshit.

Jimmy felt energized, too. Working like this, side by side with his brother, when was the last time that had happened? And he liked the driving, threading the needle again and again, more exhilarating than nerve-racking. More skill than luck. But a little bit of luck.

Once or twice he stopped and set the hand brake, in case it worked, put a rock behind a tire in case it didn't, and squatted down and in the light of his headlamp studied the tracks in the road: a windblown blur of thousands of sheep tracks, superimposed on them here and there a horse or boot print, also blurred but not yet erased by the wind.

"She's up there, for sure. We'll catch her at the tubs."

Just below Caleb's Corner a big snag had come down and was hanging over the road, blocking passage. Ben studied it, limbed it, topped it, made the final cut balanced high on the embankment. The log fell, rolled, went over the side. After several long seconds they heard it careening off the cliffs below. If it made to the river they never heard the splash.

Ben held the saw high, let out a triumphant whoop, and jumped down from the embankment.

"I'm still wondering what happened inside the pixels," Jimmy said.

"What are you talking about? Nothing ever happens inside the pixels."

"Helen's bug crawls onto your screen. Flashes, wails, disappears. You zoom in. All the way, *you're* inside your pixels. Spacelessness happens, remember? But then what? How'd you get out? How'd you get from the pixels to—here?"

At Poison Springs the row of tubs sat empty on a cement slab above the gulch. Jimmy left the engine running, headlights on, brake on, tires blocked, and they had a look around. Enamel, travertine, rebar, all glistening in the headlights. Air stinking of sulfur. Fresh horse sign beneath a tree, fresh splashes of water on cement and rock. Fading prints of bare feet. Water the only sound: the stream running over rocks, the eternal bubbling of the hot springs.

On the far side of the springs, what remained of Caleb's cabin clung to the edge of a ravine clogged with dry-rotted timber, mining machinery, vague lumps of iron rusting under the moonlight. Another McKeane boneyard, farther along than Clayton's, though one day Clayton's too would be like this: hard surfaces softened, sharp lines and edges rounded, returning to the earth. Absorbing more light than it reflected, sucking in light like a black hole.

But even in broad daylight Josie's Tubs gave him the creeps. Helen had some mystical idea about what happened when you stewed in that water for an unnatural length of time but Jimmy wasn't buying it. If he sat in one of those tubs for long he invariably found himself thinking of Josie's husband Lothar Pratt, who had soaked longer than anyone, according to Helen. The way she told it, Lothar was raging around with a whiskey bottle and Josie lying in a tub with her baby on her breast when she told him flat out the baby wasn't his. Lothar grabbed a knife and came at her in a fury and she shot him point blank in the face with a little pistol wrapped in her towel. When he fell into the tub she slipped out, leaving him lying in the water with his head lolled over the side and blood and brains dripping out onto cement and travertine. And the baby never stopped suckling the whole time. You assumed she was making that last part up and maybe the rest as well, since there were no witnesses and no one knew what became of Josie McKeane and her baby after she walked down to Confluence Bar and out the river road and caught a ride with a neighbor to the railroad junction.

Days later the neighbor found the note in his truck.

> Lothar Pratts lying in a tub up at the hot springs.
> No hurry he is dead

Jimmy liked hot springs, in general. But he didn't like Josie's and especially he didn't like it in the middle of the night, with moonlight and headlights glinting off tubs and steam and random junk lying in the bottom of a blown-out gully where runoff from abandoned mines and sulfur hot springs came together, a confluence of unwholesome histories and effluents.

"Okay, she *was* here," he decided. "But this wasn't her destination. Maybe there is no destination. Or, the destination is never the point. The point is, the vision. Maybe she sat here long enough to have one. And the vision was: herself, walking away from the ranch. Not selling it, not keeping it, not occupying it. Just… *walking away*. Walk and keep walking, a walkabout. With a sheepherder, perfect, he's on a perpetual walkabout."

The road wound in and out of the drainages incised into the eroding flanks of Red Mountain. Long tunnels of brush closed in. Branches scratched and whipped their arms and faces; the Jeep had no doors or windows. Then the brush was gone and the road a narrow rock ledge, no obstacles. Just vertical cliffs rearing up on one side, obliterating darkness falling away on the other.

"By taxi," Ben shouted. "Airplane. Car. Helicopter. Bushwhack."

"What?" Jimmy shouted.

"In that order," Ben shouted. "How I got here. Go down the Blue River trail, that was the plan. But I ended up bushwhacking."

They had to shout over engine noise, whining belts, rattling tools. Jimmy leaned over the steering wheel and peered into the tunnel of headlights, praying they wouldn't come across some impassable obstruction or blowout that would force him to back down the road to a spot wide enough to hazard a turnaround. Praying that the headlights would in fact lead them, as expected, to their mother. Expected but not guaranteed. Okay, maybe he was starting to feel a little anxious, a little less certain it was all going to work out.

They stopped to clear a slide. Ben kept talking while he shoveled. They were far enough from the idling truck that he didn't have to shout.

"Helicopter was already in the budget. Annual site visit. QC. Groundtruthing. Which could mean a lot of things. I could be setting up a new monitoring site. Calibrating sensors. Checking up on the field crew."

"You have a field crew in Blue River?"

"No! No sensors, either, no study site, nothing. But nobody knows that, nobody's that curious. But apparently I did have a mother there. There she was on the big screen, her little blue bug crawling up the Blue River trail. Blinks, disappear, like you said. I'm already closing the laptop, I'm out of there, already gone. Already putting together the plan. Which is simple: she's making a run up Blue River from the bottom; I'll come down from the top and catch her.

"So. All morning and into the afternoon I'm on the move, taxi, airplane, car, helicopter, just a quick stop at the house to grab my pack. All the time I'm downloading maps and data to my phone and making arrangements with the helibase and by midafternoon I'm strapping myself into a helicopter. Which is when my phone starts going off again. Her GPS is back on line, her little bug's flashing out its coordinates. Which are no longer changing. She's not moving and she's nowhere up Blue River. She's back at the ranch. Safe and sound, presumably.

"Okay. So maybe Jimmy *is* paying attention. Maybe you'd chased her up the trail and turned her around? Or maybe she'd turned on her own. Whatever. But a search and rescue is still in order. The rescue part for sure. Somebody needs to rescue her from the ranch. From her babysitter. From the *canyon*, before she goes in too deep and gets lost in it for good. Somebody's got to take her back to civilization and not let her out of sight until she signs the papers that need to be signed and the notary seal comes down—*boom!*—and the sale finally closes and we're done. We're free. And rich, relatively."

They'd shoveled about halfway through the slide. For awhile they worked in silence. Then Jimmy said:

"So you ride to the rescue. In a helicopter. Which drops you at a helispot on top of a mountain fifteen or twenty miles from where you know she is."

"There was no closer or easier place. Has to be on a ridgetop, any-where else around here is too steep and too rough, too much forest. "

"Ben. We have an airstrip at the ranch. Plane can't land there, for the moment, but there's plenty of room for a helicopter."

"Can't put a helicopter down at a private strip without authoriza-tion. And who the hell would you ask for authorization, there is no authority. Anyway at the helibase they don't like last minute changes on project work. You don't want anybody to start asking questions. And the plan was still going to work, the Blue River trail was still go-ing to work, I thought. That trail is a pretty straight line to Conflu-ence Bar. All downhill, I figured it would take me a day to hike it. So I spend the night on the ridge, right on the helispot, flattest place for miles, then first thing in the morning I bushwhack down to the trail. Which, it turns out, is impassible. Brushed over, blown-out, buried in blowdown."

"Well, that isn't exactly *news*. That trail's been abandoned for years."

"Okay. I guess that's a piece of information that didn't make it into the database. But it got everything else right. I had the entire *water-shed* downloaded—basically, a synthesis of every study, every analysis, every mapping project anybody's ever done in Blue River. I have this new app, specifically for cross-country travel. *Pathfinder.* You feed it all that data, and the program sifts through and maps out the cleanest possible route to your destination. Fantastic.

"So. I delete Blue River Trail from the database. I tell Pathfinder: take me to Confluence Bar. Pathfinder recalibrates, gives me a new route, takes it about a second. The best possible route—contouring out of Blue River, weaving around brushfields and blowdown and cliffbands, angling up and across tributary valleys and basins to come out on Indian Ridge, then following the old sheep driveway off the ridge to come back down into Blue River just above the confluence.

"The best possible route, algorithmically, but still pretty rough going. Gullies, steep sidehilling, doghair thickets. Brush and blowdown. No surprises, though—it's all in the database. Which is what's so cool. The *ground* I'm walking on is a physical manifestation of the *datafields* Pathfinder is simultaneously displaying in maps and tables on my phone. The ground a vindication of the data and vice versa, a beautiful symmetry, a mirror, chicken and egg.

"And one more thing that went wrong with the plan. Running Pathfinder like that sucks a lot of battery power. Pretty late in the game, I realize my phone it running low on juice. I start shutting things down but it's too late. Phone dies. Okay. No big deal, I got a solar charger, spare batteries, paper map. Only, turns out I *didn't* have any of that, I'd packed in a hurry and stuff got left out and I hadn't exactly prepped ahead of time. I did have a radio, for emergencies. This wasn't one. I knew right where I was and where I was going. For the past twenty-four hours I'd been poring over maps and photos, it was all more or less imprinted on my brain.

"And for awhile I kept it all straight, I *did* know where I was—which fork of which creek, which old landslide or burn scar I'm weaving around. But then it all starts to shift and blur. Scale gets slippery, resolution fades, topo lines are turning into a tangle of Mobius strips in my head. Pretty soon I'm off course, wading through heavy brush, climbing over huge downed trees, almost impossible to move. Impossible to stay oriented. Zoom in, zoom out, recalibrate, where the fuck am I? And at some point the map in my head just burns out, switches off. That part of my brain runs out of juice, like my phone. Then I have *no* understanding of where I am, where I'd been, where any place is relative to any other place. My geographic memory is just—gone.

"*Topographical disorientation.* I'd always figured it was mainly bull-shit, right? Always assumed that on some level Helen was just fucking with us. But now suddenly I understood. The pathology is real. A hereditary condition, maybe. Maybe I've had intimations of it for years. Brief episodes, it always passes. But now it was staying with me, and hitting hard. I was *unmoored*, exactly as she'd described it.

"And just like her I wasn't hating it, wasn't anxious, wasn't pan-icked. Remember what she said? *It's not a fog, it's the opposite of a fog.* Exactly. It's more like coming out of a fog. Into some clear, open space I'd almost forgotten about. No maps or models, no algorithms, no coordinates. No data. I'm disconnected from all that, all the usual abstractions. And maybe this will allow me to finally *connect*. To— well, I don't know. But I kept thinking of something you said. What if it's God who's lost? And if you want to find him, maybe you have to be lost, too."

They got back in the truck and bumped over the slide. It was about this point in the story that Jimmy started getting intimations, too. Not of topographical disorientation, the pathology—he knew right where he was, about twelve miles up the Ledorah Road, going in and out of rockslide corridors funneling off the side of Red Mountain—but of a more familiar sense of bewilderment. Here he was, once again listening to one of Ben's stories and not really getting it, any part of it—the setting, the sequence of events, the events themselves, what was real and what was not real. Once again, no visual. Ben was more energized than ever but his energy had taken kind of a scary turn. Sometimes he shouted even when they were far from the noise of the Jeep. Or his voice dropped practically to a whisper and Jimmy had to stop whatever he was doing and lean in close to hear. The story was starting to sound like a dream but Ben never said it was a dream. He said he made camp in the dark, in the only flat place for miles, on half-dry ground on the edge of a marsh. Built a fire. A *fire*, why? Well, to heat his dinner, of course, but also for light, comfort, consolation. Because it was such a powerful thing, this single flickering light on the land, in the center of a great darkness. A sacred thing. Sacred fire, sacred darkness. Sacred, immense, doomed. Earthly darkness, a relic. On timelapse satellite cams you could watch the extinction happening. Light consuming darkness, the fringes of the continents blazing ever brighter, light spreading inexorably into the heartlands and the wildlands as well.

And that too was firelight. Woods burning, everywhere on the planet. The ancient forests of the Jurassic and the Miocene, extracted from a long burial and slow metamorphosis, then transported, refined—flash-metamorphosed—and, finally, burned. A controlled burn, deep within furnaces and engines, there had never been a burning more controlled. And never a burning more out of control.

He gathered a huge pile of firewood and extinguished the darkness with his own blaze, then got in his sleeping bag and lay watching his fire burn down to embers. He slept—was it sleep? Or were his eyes wide open, full of fire? Aboriginal torches, lines of creeping ground-fire. His ears full of wind and voices, other sounds. The falling of the great trees, the wailing and thundering of the great herds, a rumbling and a moaning in the depths of the mountain. Something breathing in the shadows just beyond the firelight. A beast not fully human loping away over the dry marsh.

He stood and followed. Or dreamt he stood and followed. Was he also carrying a torch? The creature stopped, looked back. Then hurried on, barely a shadow and then only a sound, a heavy body breaking through the brush. Upslope and through a thicket of trees he saw a second fire, flickering, flaring, glowing, vanishing. He stared hard but now there was only a blackness over the uninhabited earth. Above, a million points of light, shedding absolutely no light on the ground.

He awoke at dawn to a campfire of cold ash and the smells of smoke and the musk and dung of animals. No sense of where he was or what had truly happened in the night versus what he had dreamed or otherwise invented. The Pleistocene firestarters. The great herd passing. The beast not fully human. The extinguished flame.

He packed his sleeping bag and ate a little food and started walking again and came out of the trees onto an open ridge, the sun rising over a world that was purely mountainous, endless peaks and ridges seen in great clarity and radiance. But at his feet a deep canyon, three canyons, the dark crack where they came together still in shadow.

A confluence. A mooring.

Geography snapped into place. Topographical disorientation, instantly cured. Or, another way of putting it: this singular state of being was once again lost to him. He knew exactly where he was and the arrangement of things around him. He saw that the ground was trampled and shat-upon not by the great herds of his Pleistocene visions but by a band of domestic sheep. That the land smelled not of wildness but of the barnyard and the feed lot. The sun rose further and on the high horizon he saw the silhouette of a great, ancient, skeletal tree. But he knew instantly—because geography had snapped into place—that it was not a tree. It was Lena's firetower, that had been looming over him while he scrabbled around the mountainside below without ever seeing it, until now. Or had he looked straight at it many times without comprehending what he was seeing? Which come to think of it was how it generally was when you looked at Lena: what you thought you were seeing was never the thing that was really there.

He thought back to their conversation in his study. *I'm wondering if you could get me a job. My ships sailed. Some of them sunk.*

Or maybe she'd just wanted to jump overboard? He'd stared at her, waited for her to explain herself.

No reason. Family.

She was jumping ship for family? And this was how she did it? Went up in a firetower on a mountaintop no one in the family would ever approach? Except him, here he was. He could call her on the radio, invite himself for breakfast. Or just drop in, cold call, surprise!

Or maybe it wouldn't be a surprise. She was a Watcher; maybe she'd been watching for the past day and a half as he'd floundered around on her mountainside. He felt her eyes on him now, felt her presence even as he turned his back on the firetower and followed the sheep track down off the ridge and into canyons and forests.

It took him all day to get off the mountain. He was weak, sore, tired. Out of shape. He forded the Blue River where the sheep had forded and followed their track to the confluence. Darkness had fallen by the time he crossed the Perdu River bridge and limped up the road toward the house. Pale ghosts in the pasture morphed into clumps of sleeping sheep. The sheepherder tent, another pale ghost: the same tent, maybe, that had gone up beneath the ponderosas every summer of their lives, like a thing immune to all the changes that had happened in the world.

21

FOUR PASSES

EMERGING FROM THE CONFINES of forests and canyons into a high, open country, Chele held deep in his belly the ice cold energy of the waterfall and the heat energy of the molten earth. Josie McKeane's vision—grottos and fountains, marble pools, Mexican tiles—may have never been realized, but the restorative power of her hot springs was real. He could tap into it all night, ride a horse, walk all night. His head was clear, his body strong and clean. Cleansed by sulfur, rank and purifying at once.

It was the first he'd traveled at night. Under a foreign sky, rising wind, stars and moon spinning, foreign mountains wheeling around him like the sky. The Peruvian's map was useless. He could distinguish no landmark or reference point. The country was formless shadow and dim silhouette, with the wind gusting and the animals nervous and a red glow pulsing faintly behind black ridges.

They began to hear a sound. Not the river. An engine. Far below, headlights swept out across the darkness, disappeared, appeared again, wound in and out of the drainages.

Finally the vehicle caught up with them. Chele led the stock high on the embankment so they wouldn't spook. Helen waited alongside the road. A stripped-down Jeep, no doors, jerked to a stop. Two men were inside. Over the rough idling of the engine Helen and the driver exchanged a few shouted words. Then she turned away and began walking up the road again. The Jeep moved with her, the man still talking, shouting. She walked and did not answer. The Jeep stopped and backed up and the driver leaned across the seat and called out to Chele, something else he didn't catch, possibly in Spanish. The Jeep ground into gear and lurched forward again, passed Helen. Chele led the pack string back onto the road, then saw that the Jeep had turned around and was coming back down. It stopped as it approached Helen and the driver leaned out and started talking again but she just kept walking. After a minute the Jeep again moved forward and he had to scramble to once more get the stock up off the road.

The Jeep stopped below him. *"Dice que va arriba,"* the driver shouted. *"No quiere regresa."* He waved his hand vaguely. *"Quiere con usted. No quiere con nosotros. Qué barbaridad!"*

Chele didn't answer. *Qué barbaridad,* the man repeated. Then switched to English. "She says you're taking her with you. That you have an agreement."

Chele, straining to hold the lead, thought about that a second. "Yes," he said.

"Says you've agreed to look after her. She's paying you for it. Plus, she's going to *guide* you. That's the agreement, she says."

"Yes," Chele said.

"Well, she can't guide. She gets lost. And she has no money. So you're not getting paid."

"Is okay."

"No gear, either. No food, tent, sleeping bag, toothbrush, *nada.* Maybe a toothbrush."

"Is okay. No problem."

"Oh, there will be. There can't *not* be problems. But fine. She's an adult. You have an agreement."

The Jeep moved forward, then stopped. The man leaned his head out the window.

"Keep your eyes open, you might see some horses up there. Runaways. They might come around your mare."

"The last of the Perdu River McKeanes," said Helen, when Chele caught up with her again on the moonlit road. "So far as we know."

One of the dogs kept appearing on the road above, cocking her head, imploring. He whistled her back up toward the sheep. It was well after midnight and six or eight miles beyond Josie's Tubs when they came to the place where the sheep had finally stopped and bedded down in scattered clumps above and below the road. He unsaddled the stock and made a quick camp under the stars. He gave Helen his cot and sleeping bag and wrapped up in horse blankets in the middle of the road, in the wind, and slept a little. At dawn the wind was still blowing and he took the dogs on a wide sweep of the mountainside and managed to get the band more or less back together. When he returned to break camp, Helen had put away her bedding and was going through the commissary. Looking for coffee, she said brightly, and breakfast!

They did in fact have an agreement, negotiated, to use the word loosely, as they'd traveled up the road from Josie's Tubs, under a rising moon. I would like to propose a verbal contract, she'd said, and pretty much all he'd done was listen until she stopped talking and then said yes.

He would agree to take on a certain responsibility for her, no more and no less than his responsibility to any individual sheep. Her words. In return, he would receive compensation far more generous than his sheepherder wages. And she would do her share of camp work, plus serve as guide, at least until they passed beyond the country she knew well, the country of the McKeanes. *You'll cross four passes*, Oscar had told him, and now the Ledorah Road left the canyons, skirted the shoulder of a reddish mountain—Oscar's *Pico Rojo*—and climbed steadily toward the first. In the distance, thin streams of smoke rose up into an otherwise featureless sky.

They came across rusted shells of trucks, old tractor tires, strands of rusty cable. Junk, Helen said. But it told a story, about the men who built the road and cut down the forest and raised up an instant town of hotels and boarding houses, stores, taverns, brothels, stables. Who dug the ore and hauled it to the pass and put up a tramline to move it to the canyon floor.

The wind carried off her words. Sheep poured through a rocky gap, disappeared. The smoke streams multiplied, converged, thickened, darkened. Silhouettes of dead trees lined the ridges. On the far side of the canyon a more isolated silhouette, tree-like but larger than the surrounding trees. A tower, he decided, though he could distinguish no features. No girders, no cabin, no stairs. No porch where Lena might be watching with binoculars as he climbed to the pass and disappeared.

He held up a hand, both hands, opened his arms to her. Then turned away from canyons, ridges, tower, smoke, and followed the sheep over the divide.

They skirted a great sprawling pile of shattered rock and came down into a basin where a dozen or so wooden buildings stood, or collapsed, among mosquito-buzzing thickets of pines. The ghost town, Ledorah. They came upon open pits, dry ponds, piles of rock and rocky soil. Had the miners built the town on ground they were already mining, or mined it as an afterthought? He approached a cabin, a dark wreck of logs and sheet metal amid the pines. One wall heaved up atop a gnarled tree root; another sank away beneath soil and pine needles and its own decomposition, so that the building leaned not at any single angle but in a precarious twist, a slow vortex of ruin. The door hung open on one hinge. Old mattresses spilled their stuffing onto a floor covered with cooking pans and dishes, broken furniture, tar paper, carpet pieces, books, papers, animal droppings, pine needles, sand, branches, dried mud.

How long since anyone had lived in that place, or even stepped inside? Yet to Chele the ruin did not speak so much of the building's abandonment as of its occupancy. This was more or less how people lived. He'd seen it, taken kids to visit family in houses that weren't in much better condition.

On the near ridge the sheep wailed. A distant engine droned. Between the droning and the wailing he heard Alvaro's voice.

You came out of something like that.

The sheep had moved past the ruins onto a low ridge, grazing where they could. Helen was poking through a pile of old bottles on the far side of the building.

"What about—hotel? Stores? The bars, the, the…"

"The brothels? Well, what do you imagine a brothel looks like, Chele?"

She gave him one of her slackjawed stares, as if she knew what he imagined. A woman watching from a shadowed doorway, a pimp smoking in the TV light, a hole in the wall just big enough for a hand to slide through.

"Maybe this was one. Four walls and a roof and a mattress tossed on the floor, what else did they need? Imagine the misery of those girls' existence. But everyone's existence was miserable. This was a terrible place. Under snow eight months of the year, swamps and mosquitos and blackflies and a burning sun the rest of the time. No trees, they'd cut them all down. They worked all the time in the snow, mud, dust, sun. People got hurt, sick, died, couldn't be buried in the frozen ground. It was bleak, Chele! And for what? It was all about wealth, supposedly. Well, where's the wealth? There is no wealth."

They followed a trickling headwater stream past more tailings and rubble up to camp in a high, dry meadow. Fire had killed most of the trees but the grass was good. They took a day to regroup and rest and feed before crossing over the second pass. The wildest country yet, Oscar had warned him. *No hay nada.* Yet this part of it, at least, had not always been so forsaken.

They came upon the occasional overgrown road or trail, sometimes a fallen-down cabin or a more mysterious construction decaying beneath the trees. He'd point into the shadows at some unlikely amalgamation of wood and iron, pulleys and rusted gears—*what was that for?*—and Helen would peer at it and come up with an answer that to Chele seemed less an explanation of the contraption itself than yet another apocryphal story about the people who'd built and used it.

Here and there were blazes slashed into trees, cairns, more cryptic arrangements of rocks. Tombstones, a tiny cemetery? But Helen said no. There is no burial ground, no gathering of bones. The bones are scattered.

Beyond the second pass they encountered fewer traces of a human presence, and for long periods they walked in silence. Helen rode only when she tired late in the day. Mostly Chele stayed with her at the rear of the band, keeping the stragglers moving, but when the country was open and easy enough he untied the pack string and free-trailed the mules and, leaving Helen to walk alone, moved up on horseback to patrol the flanks and make sure the band was staying on course, not that he was any longer certain of the course.

The sheep churned up and obliterated all sign of whatever had gone before them, but game trails and tracks went off into the woods, so he had some idea of the creatures that had passed that way. Small animals like marmots, squirrels, foxes, grouse. Also deer, elk, coyote or maybe wolf, maybe bear, maybe cougar. With the help of Oscar's guidebook he'd learned to recognize certain tracks, but in the dry soils they were hard to read, interwoven and superimposed on one another and then seemingly altered as mud dried or dust blew around, or as if the ground itself chewed and half-swallowed them, the way the aspens chewed and swallowed carvings. He saw what looked like a couple of isolated prints, larger than a moose and nothing like a moose in any case. His grandmother, seeing a track like that in the barren, colorless soil of San Miguel, would have leaned out over the neck of her little horse and sucked in her breath in a long hiss. *¿Ves? ¡Huella de Sisimiti!*

His grandmother. Who wasn't his grandmother and who in any case was gone, taking her angels and demons with her. Yet still Chele thought of the Sisimiti. Of the ignorant and superstitious culture that had created him and then, even when the world changed and the Sisimiti became a relic and practically a caricature, couldn't quite hunt him down and put the apparition to rest.

He'd never felt he belonged to that culture. But what Alvaro said was undeniable: he had come out of it. It was a thin primer beneath the heavy coat of culture Alvaro had painted over him. And when pieces of Alvaro's culture flaked off maybe that primer was what was left.

They stayed mainly in forest, ascending a broad valley and then turning up a side creek until they came out from under thinning trees and made camp on a high grassy bench, just below the third pass. For a long while much of the view had been blocked by trees and nearby mountains. But now they'd gained elevation and distance, and from this high camp they looked out on a seemingly endless layering of ridges and peaks and the canyons between them.

One small piece of it was on fire. That stream of thickening smoke they'd seen from the first pass was now a great white plume, roiling into the sky and spreading low over the ground, with a deep darkness at its center. Two small planes circled. He might have been hearing them for some time without really registering the sound. But now came a louder thrum of engines. The planes circled higher. A larger plane lumbered low over the ridge and flew straight into the smoke. A dense red mist came out of its belly and drifted over the trees. The black smoke flattened and spread low. The big plane lifted, banked, and disappeared behind the ridge.

Helen went to bed right after dinner, but once the sheep were set-tled Chele hiked up to the pass. To get his bearings, he told her. He sat on a high rock and looked out on the darkening world, the many ridges he and his animals had crossed, the shadows between them that were the deep canyons they had descended into and climbed out of. The tiny silhouette—not a tree—at the crest of a long ridge on the far side of the nearest and deepest canyon. Somewhere down that ridge he had bivouacked, lost two lambs, passed a night of fire and ghosts. And now behind the ridge the sky was filled with smoke, no longer a rising plume but a great spreading cloud, pastel tints glowing and fading in the sunset. A tiny airplane circled, caught a last high ray of sun, and disappeared into the dusk. The cloud flattened and began to collapse over the canyons. Smoke and shadow merged into the same darkness and finally he saw the fire itself, or pieces of fire, flickering, pulsing.

Lempira's fire, Sisimiti's fire.

Chele's fire.

Helen stood shivering in the early morning, but when he began to gather firewood she stopped him. No smoke signals, she said. "What do you suppose all those planes are scouring the country for? And that fire lookout, over on Indian Mountain? Maybe she wasn't paying attention before, but you can be sure she is now."

"She always pay attention," he said.

"Sure. It's just a question of, to what." She stared at him "You saw her? Spoke with her?"

Chele jerked his head, barely.

"Well. She's another one, you know."

"Another...?"

"McKeane. I've been telling you about the dead ones. But there are still live ones, too."

So now he had her name. *Lena McKeane*. Otherwise nothing, not even a stick figure silhouette on a distant ridge.

Beyond the third pass they descended into a thickening smoke and it became more difficult to keep the band together. They came upon sudden escarpments, thickets of trees or brush a sheep might penetrate but not a horse, forests where fallen trees lay criss-crossed three or four deep, no country for horse or sheep. The sheep would jam up at an obstacle while the dogs kept the pressure on from behind until finally the band splintered and sheep streamed through bottlenecks where they could. Then the splitting streams would merge again or maybe just keep subdividing. Sheep were all over the mountainside, stringers of sheep plunging through the trees in the dust and smoke, the wailing of sheep and barking of dogs passing like an echoing wave through the forest that was silent before their passage, and silent afterwards.

Helen's stories also split and merged and split again. Echoed, meandered, veered off on wider tangents, became increasingly fantastical and contradictory even as they reworked the same ground. Crucial background information it seemed she just left out, as if assuming he knew things he had no way of knowing.

But still he was left with a sense of a history he was somehow caught up in, of the presence of people or ghosts moving inexorably toward a dark fate never fully revealed, even to them. Of a river that never reached the ocean but instead filtered into the black sands and fractured rock of a desert plain, among the wreckage of ancient canoes and flatboats. Her stories were full of wreckage. The truck loaded with gold that missed a turn high on the Ledorah Road, hung for a moment in the sky, plunged into the river torrent far below. The wreckage of towers, ghost towns, ghost miners vanished into Mexico, beyond Mexico, dying in unburiable ways, killed by fire and flood, thin ice, frayed cable, freak tailwind, falling rock. By the hand of mercenaries, assassins, a lover's hand, by their own hand. By the accumulated debaucheries of their lives.

"Debaucheries," Chele echoed. A new word.

"You name them. Intoxications, fornications. Rages and addictions."

He thought of his grandmother's afflicted fingers fumbling with her rosary beads.

> *Are we praying for my mother.*

> *We're praying for you. That you don't grow up to be an addict and a fornicator and a blasphemer like your forefathers.*

Some stories just broke off, no ending. Or ended almost as soon as they began. Or had multiple endings.

> *A sabotaged airplane crash-lands in the spruce bottoms.*

> *Ending #1: The pilot crawls away through the muck and disappears amid the trees.*

> *Ending #2: In a cockpit overgrown with moss and vines a shattered skeleton still clings to the rusted controls.*

Riddles and parables. *Sucesos.* Things that happen, or not. Inventions of his own misunderstanding. Listening to her was like reading a book with half the pages missing, you had to fill in the spaces. But he was accustomed to missing pages. To lessons that came at him piecemeal and never cohered. To archiving in his memory long strings of disconnected facts that might not be facts at all.

What became of the builder of the Ledorah Road

> *He was killed by a fatal madness and the accumulated debaucheries of his life.*

What are the properties of sulfur

Sulfur heals, imparts strength, endurance, excessive passion. The smell stays on the skin for days, weeks, maybe forever.

What was the achievement of the hardrock miner Caleb McKeane

He drove his truck through sky and water and parked it on the stony bottom of a river.

Helen's voice weakened. She fell silent for long periods. To fill the silence—and remembering the question she'd asked him at the hot springs, still unanswered: *how did a boy like you end up in a place like this?*—he began to talk. To tell his own story, which he'd never told anyone. He'd tried—and failed, miserably—to tell parts of it to Lena. To Oscar, but Oscar had heard something else, had deflected his stories with jokes about college and the nuns, though beneath the jokes there had may have been some kind of understanding. And now he found himself telling Helen, as if in his own words, a thing Oscar had once said to him: how although the sheepherders were strangers in this country, with no connections to any place or person, it was they who connected the country to itself, lowland to highland, season to season. No one lived as close to the land as they did. Without buffers or distractions, no television or computers or screens of any sort, nothing but a layer of canvas between them and the country, the animals, the seasons, the night.

At camp he began to hobble the mules as well as the mare, afraid that her presence would no longer be enough to hold them. They thumped and snorted through the night. In the distance arose a sound like the wailing of sheep. But nearby the band was silent. The dogs rustled, paced, growled. When he stepped out of the tent he felt their eyes on him in the darkness. Demanding an explanation, or straining to communicate some critical piece of information beyond his skill to decipher.

Lobo vanished for long stretches of time. Then appeared hunched on a rise, wads of burrs and sticks tangled in his fur, watching the band with yellow eyes. Chele put out food for him but did not approach. Lobo, the Antiwolf.

The smoke plume was somewhere behind them. Swelling, contracting, they saw it sometimes in the afternoons and evenings, when the smoke that settled over them at night finally lifted.

He began to worry about food. They were down to a little rice and pasta, a chunk of cheese, dried fruit, nuts, a few cans of soup, handfuls of huckleberries when they came across them. But there was plenty of meat, no one would go hungry.

The Lord is my shepherd, I shall not want.

He caught up a lamb and tied its legs together and took it into the woods and left it on the ground, bleating, while he went back for the rifle. That Psalm was intended to comfort and reassure. But now it was the righteous voice of Padre Jaco he heard. *We shall not want, Brother Chele.* By which he'd meant: We *cannot* want. Our faith and desire is in the providence of the Lord; what we want is exactly what we have been given.

He spoke silently to the lamb. *You want the thistle pasture, the smoky air, this bullet.*

He hung the dead lamb from a tree and cut its throat, letting the blood run out onto the pine needles. He skinned and gutted it and left the guts and fleece on the ground, appeasement to the wolves and coyotes. They roasted the meat in the Dutch oven, buried with coals in the ground. *Borrego al hueco.* Then sat around a small campfire and ate it, what difference did a little smoke make, with the sky already so full of it.

Even before Padre Jaco's voice started distorting it in his head the Psalm had begun to irritate Chele. The persistent metaphor of sheep in the Bible irritated him. Sheep: simple-minded, fatalistic creatures, that was what Jesus wanted? He himself wanted to be a *shepherd,* sitting on a hillside protecting and nurturing his flock—until the day he pushes them through a chute to the abattoir or leads them out in the woods and pulls a trigger?

The Lord is my shepherd, I shall not want.

When the smoke lifted they could see planes they'd been hearing all day pass overhead. A helicopter flew low, spooking the animals with its terrible roar and clatter. Spooking Chele—were they looking for *him*? Was he a fugitive, cowering beneath trees and smoke? But how was it even possible to hide? There were technologies to penetrate opaqueness, to see without seeing. Sensors of heat, motion, fear. Drones and satellites, silent and invisible, suspended in sky and space, detecting signals you didn't even know you were emitting.

Round satellites, floating in space like Eyes of God. And if satellites were God-like, might God be something like a satellite? Not a shepherd as the Psalm would have it, a constant presence and guardian of his flock, but more of a distant, dim satellite orbiting in space, uninterested in the petty affairs and transgressions and supplications of individuals, focused instead on larger patterns and abstractions, probabilities, codes, infinite numbers.

Alvaro said that if you tried to visualize God you always came up against paradox, and here was one: he felt closer to God when He was distant and drifting. It made Him easier to love. It made the consequences of His syllogisms and algorithms easier to accept, if you considered that God Himself had never bothered to do the math.

Que Dios te acompañe. Alvaro's final words to him. And maybe God was with him; maybe he was walking in the company of God. But was it still possible to feel God's presence if you were no longer certain you believed in Him?

Well, he didn't believe in the Sisimiti, either. But still he felt a presence.

The smoke thickened further. The morning sun was a flat orange disc in a white sky. He couldn't tell where the fire was burning or where sounds were coming from or what the sounds even were, sometimes: wind, a falling tree, ravens, sheep, wolves, coyotes.

Be thankful for the smoke, she said. Trapped smoke means a trapped fire. When the smoke lifts, watch out. That's when the fire makes its run.

There was a prodigious hatch of insects, everywhere the air filled with small white gnats, sinking and rising. No, not gnats. Tiny pieces of ash, sinking more than they rose. A thin skiff of ash lay on the ground, on the horsepacks and the horses themselves, on their arms, hair, faces.

Resting on a log, Chele looked across a smoky meadow and saw large animals gathered on the far side. Elk? Horses? When he stood they drew back, vanishing in the smoke as the horses at the Gardens had dissolved into the night.

He saw the *loca desnuda*, striding through the cluttered woods exactly as she had strode across the hurricane-ravaged street.

He saw Tania, leaning back against a fallen tree. Then she too went into shadow.

Hallucinations. *Willful* hallucinations, it was easy to summon them up. And reckless, no doubt, when what the situation called for was a clear grasp of what was really happening and a mind free of futile visions and longings. Going through his dwindling provisions, he came across the *curandero* remedy Oscar had given him, to diminish desire. Now he took a slug of the bitter, viscous stuff and found that it worked as promised—by unleashing in his bowels a terrible diarrhea that sent him bursting out of his blankets a half dozen times during the night. In the morning he poured out the contents and, taking one last hard look at the black-haired temptress, breasts heaving behind her prison bars, flung the bottle into the bushes.

They went over the fourth pass in a thick smoke, no wind, nothing visible beyond the nearest rise of the ridge and the sheep trotting out ahead. They'd veered off the Peruvian's map. He had no reference points, no way of knowing whether this was the right pass or whether it was even a pass at all. They didn't descend but rather just contoured around the broad crest of a ridge. The skeletons of dead trees emerged from the smoke. Pale, twisted trunks and limbs, dry and hard as fossils. Yet the image that came to his mind was the disheveled line-up of *ancianos* and *enfermos* waiting for the doctor outside the clinic at Ciudad de Luz. Their frozen, spastic poses amid the swarming flies. Another image: the fourteen paintings in the Via Dolorosa Room at the National Gallery, illustrating the distinct physical agonies of Jesus at each Station of the Cross. Paintings he had gazed at for a long time—at first because he felt obliged to set an example, then in a sincere effort to muster pity for a suffering over 2000 years old, before moving on to study with more genuine interest the painting of the reclining nude.

The mid-day light was a pale orangeish glow, the sun a small glaring eye straight overhead. Their throats were raw from breathing smoke. Helen had begun to cough. She grew hoarse and he had trouble hearing her above the rising noise. Ewes bleating for lost lambs, lambs crying for their mothers, helicopters and planes passing low overhead, a dull roaring in the distance she said might be fire. Oceanic noise, again. Voices and engines. The Peruano had said this was the highest pass, from here he would see everywhere he'd been. But in fact he could see nothing beyond the rise of the nearest land; canyons and mountains on all sides were lost in smoke. Yet even in the claustrophobia of the smoke he *felt* the sucking vertigo of those distances and depths. As if the smoke itself had depth, as deep as any far horizon or arc of the night sky. And the ground as well—in leaf and flower, wood, lichen, soil and rock he saw depth and layering, decay and renewal, a simultaneous wearing down and thrusting upward. The natural, fundamental structure of things, first revealed to him in the architecture of *Colonia El Porvenir* when he was a small boy walking up the muddy street with Alvaro, then again from the overlook above the Gardens, from the river bluffs at Ciudad de Luz, and now from this smoke-blind mountain pass. The new layered upon the ruins of the old, layers multiplying and expanding even as they simultaneously compressed and contracted. The old subsumed by the new and then rising up again, so you kept glimpsing the world you'd left behind in the strange new world you were about to enter.

You could use a guide, Helen had said, and in the beginning it had seemed she really did know the country. But now it was apparent that she was as lost as he was. They were back in dim woods again, had she led them there? Or had he, reflexively seeking cover? They kept trying to follow drainages up into the higher meadows but were turned aside by cliffs and narrows. The open country seemed out of reach. The sheep driveway had long since splintered into game trails that led nowhere in particular, like the unsigned trails worn into the hills above St. Jerome's Gardens. In the vague hope that it might trigger in Helen some memory or understanding of a way through, he told her about Oscar's map. Told her about it and then, because it was impossible to explain in any other way, got down on his hands and knees and scrabbled around reconstructing it as best he could on the ground, in the original language. A vocabulary of twigs, lichen, deer shit, sheep shit, pebbles, pinecones. She sat in the dirt next to him, giving no sign of recognition as he recited aloud the names of places exactly as Oscar had, a pronunciation that rendered them even more remote and wild, further situated from the known world.

How did a boy like you end up in a place like this?
You're born into a brothel with a deadly virus in your blood. You kill a black zopilote with a random stone, upsetting some fragile balance in the world. You stand on the poisoned ground of the crematorio—a seed, a nucleus—drawing a flock of human zopilotes into terminal orbit around you. You look across a flooding river at your grandmother's neighborhood and see instead a swath of raw, red earth, bodies washing up on the muddy shore below. You ride up to Alvaro on a horse soiled with your own semen. You stand on the bluffs where the *ancianos'* dormitory had tumbled into the river, with any number of fresh calamities radiating out from your feet. You return children into the arms of disastrous families, with no inventory of the disasters that ensue. You rescue and then abandon a lost girl on the

Chalamanca highway. You hand your car keys to a stranger, follow another stranger down the dim hall of another brothel, maybe the same one into which you were born.

You start a forest fire, lose half a band of sheep, lead an old woman off the map, into the smoke.

Naturally he felt dread, he felt remorse, but he also felt, implausibly, a kind of euphoria. He felt liberated and unweighted and transformed, even as he rode blindly through the smoke at the exact pace of an after-dinner *bajando la comida* walk with Alvaro. A pace that exhausted and exasperated, accompanied by a silence that sooner or later forces speech from your lips.

Even a disaster is a success.

Helen stopped. "What did you say?"

He shrugged, kept moving. He'd spoken aloud without meaning to. What he'd said wasn't something he could explain, not in English or any other language. Not without cataloging all those disasters he'd witnessed or precipitated. The City of Light, the *crematorio*, the *Proyecto Familiar de Verdad y Sueño*. St. Jerome's Gardens: a place where an orphan could grow into a horsetamer, mentor, acolyte, detective, rescuer, cougar killer, woodsman, navigator. An arsonist, a *guerrillero*, an outlaw? A survivor, anyway, so far. For all the wrong reasons Tania had been right about something—he was a survivor, not because he could ride a horse and swing a machete but because he'd learned how to extract from disaster a tiny kernel—a seed, a nucleus—of success.

"What do you mean, Chele?" Helen persisted.

Eventually he had to make some kind of answer. "There's millions of orphans," he said. Stalling for time, once again more or less repeating something the Peruano had told him. People had children. Then the parents died or went away and the children had to feed themselves, teach themselves, smuggle themselves over borders. Or get snagged on them, swept up against a border and stuck there. But sooner or later a few break through—another thing Oscar had said. Never mind the *Migra*, electric fence, wall, helicopter, satellite, infrared, desert, snakes, coyotes, drug-runners, militiamen. *Culebra, coyote, traficante, vigilante.* People find a way through all that. They metamorphose, go beneath the radar. Never mind how sophisticated the radar, there's always an unsophisticated way to get beneath it—wasn't a backcountry sheepherder proof of that?

Helen nodded, as if all this made sense, connected things. And maybe it did. Maybe connections were all around and it was just a matter of recognizing them. Connections between horses, overlooks, wandering old women. Between St. Jerome's Gardens and Ciudad de Luz and the broken-down ranch at the confluence of rivers that eventually trickled out into desert rocks. Between flooded labyrinths beneath a disastrous city and the dry pits and tunnels the McKeanes had excavated.

Connections between his grandma's *sucesos* and prayers—*I'm praying you don't grow up to be a fornicator and a blasphemer like your father and your grandfather and all their fathers before them*—and Helen's stories of an entire family of fornicators and blasphemers. Family stories of fuck-up and transfiguration, of disappearance and separation and a genealogy that was also a labyrinth and tangle of connections: between the McKeane who trailed the first sheep into Antimony Basin and the McKeane who put up a row of bathtubs on the mountainside and vanished with her baby on a train and the McKeane who abandoned his mines and towers and woman and children and went underground and emerged from other mines in Mexico and beyond Mexico and the McKeane who sank a dry tunnel a quarter mile into the mountain and drove his truck another quarter mile into the river and the McKeane who stockpiled heavy equipment on the wrong side of a condemned bridge and sabotaged the airplane of the McKeane who crashlanded in a swamp and the McKeane who walked backwards along a stony ridge with a cougar following and the McKeane—*the McKeane*—who went feverish over a fleeting kiss and shot that same cougar and lost his sheep and set fire to the forest and wandered in the woods with the McKeane who'd clamped her necklace in a vise—

"*Tú también.*"

"Excuse me?"

The likeness was suddenly obvious. The eyes, voice, mouth. Lena.

"You're one, too."

"One what?"

"*La familia. Los McKeane.*"

She was silent for a long time. Then: "I wasn't born one. But I'm one now, yes. By marriage. By contagion."

"I was born one," Chele said.

22

EMBERS

"How are we going to explain this?"

"Explain what?"

Jimmy hunched over the steering wheel, straining to see whatever was just beyond the short reach of the headlights. High beams didn't work. They were coming down on the hairpin, and on the emptiness beyond the hairpin. Caleb's Corner.

"There's papers she needs to sign," Ben said. "We need to keep her safe and sound and get her out of here and back home so she can sign them. How are we doing? Well, first, we get wasted like a couple of teenagers. We lose her. We drive out of the canyon looking for her. We find her. And then... we let her go. Up a dead end road in the dark with a sheepherder kid who may or may not speak a little English. People are going to wonder why we let that happen. And I don't think we have an explanation."

A rock face loomed over one side of the road, the void pitched out beyond the other. Jimmy could feel Ben's eyes on him in the darkness. Caleb's eyes. The grade steepened and he moved to downshift. Good old granny gear, you wanted to just crawl around that hairpin. But the transmission wouldn't budge. He jammed the stick around trying to find the sweet spot, force it or ease it, all the time pumping weak brakes while the Jeep bore down on the hairpin in neutral and the headlights tunneled off into blackness and Ben just kept talking.

"We *let her go*. Catch and release. Why? Well, she has an *agreement* with a sheepherder, he's going to be *her* shepherd. Oh, and she's going to be his guide. Topographical disorientation, no mention of it. No mention of the ranch she's selling, the escrow docs waiting to be signed."

They came down hard into the turn. At the last second the gears synched and the Jeep skidded and lurched back and they crept around Caleb's with everything under control, plenty of buffer, just the lightest foot on the brake. Now he could relax, a little. Now he could glance at Ben, or into the darkness that enclosed him.

"Not like that."

"What?"

"That's not how we explain it. We say—not that we have to explain anything, but if we did, we'd say, well, pretty much what Mom just said to us: this is goddammit the plan we all of us agreed on. We agreed she'd hire somebody to chaperone her. Well, she hired him."

"How old do you think that kid is? Is he even eighteen?"

"Sure he's eighteen. He's an adult. She's an adult. Consenting adults. They do what they want."

"Okay. I'm still wondering what our explanation's going to be."

They drove awhile in silence. Then Jimmy said: "Here's what I'm wondering. You're at a conference, in the middle of a once-in-a-lifetime presentation. You go full-on maverick, you're burning down the house. Then, you get a cryptic signal from your mom's GPS. She's lost in the woods, or so you decide. You walk out on your own crazy presentation. You catch a last-minute helicopter ride, because suddenly you've got to find her. Except you don't, because it turns out she isn't lost. But still you keep going. You thrash your way out to a ridge, fall asleep in front of your campfire, have weird dreams, hallucinate wildfire, mastadon herds, a bogeyman. And a couple of days later the fire is real, the house *is* burning. How do you explain *that*."

Driving up the road earlier in the evening, Jimmy hadn't noticed the forest fire across the canyon. At first they were too deep in the hole; later his attention was on the road, the rockslides, the abyss. Not until after they left Helen and started back down did he look out and see anything beyond what the headlights illuminated.

"Holy shit."

A half moon was sinking over the mountains to the west. The stars were coming into their own as the moonlight dimmed, but the land everywhere was dark, dark, other than a point directly across the canyon, where a deep red glow backlit the ridgeline trees, and fire flickered and flared on the black mountainside below.

"Ben. You seeing what I'm seeing?"

"I see it."

"Holy shit."

The road demanded his full attention but still as they descended he stole a few glances at the fire, trying to figure out where it was burning. Indian Ridge, he couldn't tell which drainages. But flaring up, still active even at night, that was how warm and dry and windy things were. When they dropped into the inner canyon the horizon closed in and pockets of fire blinked off one by one and by the time they came around Caleb's all the land was in darkness and you wouldn't know there was a fire burning close by, except for the smell in the air.

"Not like that," said Ben.

"What?"

"That fire. That isn't how I'd explain it."

"All right."

"I don't have to explain it."

"Well, how'd it start? There was no lightning."

"You sure about that? You're down in a hole at the bottom of a canyon, how would you know what's happening way up on the mountain? Fire can start in lots of ways. Lightning. Campfire. Cigarette. Spontaneous combustion. Could be a holdover. Could be somebody's cooking drugs. All kinds of people are sneaking around out there. Where'd that sheepherder come from, did you happen to notice? Or you just looked out the window and there he was, tramping through the property with a couple thousand sheep?"

Jimmy didn't say anything. In fact, he had just looked out the window and there he was.

"For me, lighting a fire would be a conscious act," Ben said. "I would be conscious of having done it. And the truth is I don't know what happened. There's stuff we just can't know. Subconscious stuff.

It was a weird night, there was a lot of subconscious. It can get *weird* up there. And fire is definitely a part of the weirdness, that's just the way it is."

The most amazing thing about that explanation, Jimmy thought, was how pedantic Ben managed to sound delivering it. A scientist, spelling out the obvious logic. *Lighting a fire would be a conscious act. I was not conscious of it. Ergo, I could not have lit it.* When in fact nothing about it made sense, there were at least two or three separate fallacies in as many sentences. Which for a scientist seemed like a lot, until you considered that this scientist had recently taken the form of crazed Caleb McKeane, emerging from the night to beg for a slab of salmon. And before that he was a Pleistocene nomad, hypnotized by coals, dreaming of torches.

Jimmy had been around the western forests for any number of fire seasons and had an idea of what was likely in store. A sky full of planes and helicopters, trucks and engines and heavy machinery all over the roads, yellowshirts tromping through the woods, cutting down trees and scratching in firelines, calling in retardant strikes and bucket drops, scouting roads and trails and GPSing every elk wallow or trickle of water or potential fuel break or safety zone.

Not one of them seeing the ground like he saw it, knowing it like he did. Every dip or rise in the ridge, the character of each creek, where streamflow was likely to dry up late in summer. The built trails and the game trails, the secret alcoves and blind canyons and pocket wetlands where no one ever went. The really rough places where no one *ever* went, too choked with brush and dead and down timber and doghair thickets that would never grow into timber. The bone-dry, nearly vertical brushfields and grassfields in the interior canyon, broken up by shale outcrops and talus dumps that some cowboy fire boss might get the idea to tie into a fireline so he could try his hand at a burnout, God help him if the wind turned. And the wind was always turning.

What Jimmy knew, how he'd come by that knowledge, would be of no particular interest to those firefighters. The fact that he'd walked or ridden or driven nearly every square foot of the country, hunting and fishing, looking for antlers or arrowheads or berries or mush-rooms or game, would not be of interest. Helping Clayton clear trails or set up a camp or cache. Or just wandering, feeling connected to something big, if only by virtue of living in a big place and coming to some small understanding of it, though what possible use that under-standing might be to anyone was one more thing he couldn't explain.

Morning light caught them by surprise. Apparently it had taken all night to drive up the Ledorah Road, turn around, and drive down again. Dawn came on slowly, never making a full transition to day. A thick smoke had settled into Perdu Canyon. The sun rose pale orange and wobbly and cast only a muted light on the world. They stopped now and then to look around, though they couldn't see far in the smoky air. And what were they even looking for? Spotfires? Horses? But any fire was still far away, and his horses no doubt farther. Up in the high country, searching out some cool patch of meadow or shaded grove. Those horses wouldn't see a bottomland hayfield till winter, if then. What were the chances they'd ever see the manicured polo grounds they'd been bred for? And who's loss was that? Polo, a stylized horsemanship executed on homogenized fields before spectators who rose at half-time to ritually drift over the grass, chardonnay glasses in hand, flattening tiny divots with their boot heels. He felt nothing for polo, how could he? What had he been thinking? What hypnosis had *he* been under?

Maybe raising horses for a different sport he might have had a chance with them. An Indian polo with no spectators or boundary lines or groundskeepers, an anarchic gallop across anarchic country. Maybe then he would have maintained his ambition and focus. Or maybe that was exactly the kind of animal he was raising—not a horse that lived on scientific diets and training regimens and raced up and down a field in pointless pursuit of a ball, but one that ate sticks and leaves and survived by speed and cunning and the constant goading of fear, outrunning wolves and cougars and ten thousand years of do-mestication up on Pete's Ridge.

Clayton's network of disintegrating skid trails materialized out of the smoke on the steep slopes above the ranch. They heard but did not see the first planes, circling the low end of Indian Ridge. A helicopter came jackhammering up the canyon, too much sound to squeeze between the narrow walls. They looked for it to emerge from the smoke at the river bend but instead the sound revved up, then diminished and cut out, and when they came down onto Confluence Bar the helicopter was sitting on the airstrip amid Jimmy's obstacle course of junk and firefighters in bright yellow Nomex were jumping down from it. On the edge of the strip a man, wearing not Nomex but the same pair of filthy orange coveralls that had been hanging on a peg in the barn for the past year, sat hunched and scowling on an ATV, watching the hotshots unload and barely glancing over when his Jeep pulled into the yard.

III

If only we too could discover a pure, contained, human place,
our own strip of fruit-bearing soil between river and rock.
— Rainer Maria Rilke
(Duino Elegies)

The world is made of fire.
— Pers Merlicht

23

IN FIRE

THE GHOST OF Ethan McKeane appeared to his widow as she and Chele descended in a helicopter onto the airstrip at Confluence Bar, where the drab, dry, seemingly abandoned fields and buildings they had looked down on two weeks earlier from high on the Ledorah Road had been transformed, or at least disguised.

The strip had been mowed and the junk Jimmy had spread across it was gone. Clayton's wrecking yard of rusty old metal and machinery and stacks and piles of *stuff* looked about the same, but the fields and tailings ground and gravelly floodplain of Antimony Creek sparkled and shone with new metal, new colors, new machinery, new stuff. A couple of small airplanes. A lineup of pick-up trucks and SUVs and fire engines. Earth-moving machines, fuel tanks, portapotties. Fire-fighters in bright yellow Nomex shirts and red hardhats. A tent city of many colors spreading across the brown pasture, weightless nylon rippling in the breeze like the flags and banners of a midway.

But amid all the color and commotion her eye went straight to Ethan's ghost, leaning into the gale of the helicopter rotors on the edge of his old airstrip. She recognized him immediately—not so much his physical features as his bearing, his expression, his *aura*, though Ethan had been dead now twenty years and she saw him for just that one moment through the multiple distorting lenses of the helicopter window, her helmet's tinted visor, and her smoke- and dust-ravaged eyes. Then he disappeared behind yellowshirts and a cloud of dust and chaff and grasshoppers kicked up by the whirling rotors.

And so her long walkabout ended. One minute she and Chele and the animals were trudging through smoky forest as they had trudged for days, and the next the forest opened and the smoke lifted and they could see flying overhead the planes and helicopters they'd been hearing for so long the sound had fused with the muted roar of the unseen fire. And the aircraft saw them. A plane circled low. A helicopter came in just above the trees, pivoted, and hovered straight over them, screaming and clattering and blowing up a storm of pine needles, branches, dust. Dogs and sheep scattered howling and wailing into the woods and were gone. Helen scrunched herself up low on the ground, while Chele fought to hold the panicked stock and the firefighters rappelled to the ground to rescue them.

She was not sorry to be rescued. Her skin was dry and cracked and raw with sores and scrapes and insect bites. Dark veins throbbed in her thighs and calves. Her bones were grinding against one another. Finally she had walked enough, walked herself to satiation and beyond, to exhaustion and very nearly debilitation. The journey with Chele and the sheep, which had begun as a grand adventure, a liberation, had ended in smoky claustrophobia beneath the trees. Hundreds of square miles to wander in but ultimately the paths of the great coniferous forest had turned out to be as constricted as the sidewalks and cul-de-sacs of Ben and Angie's subdivision.

Chele wanted to stay with his animals but the firefighters said the flames were too close. The wind was rising, dropping embers and scattering fire. The animals would have to make a run for it on their own. Already the pilot could see sheep and dogs heading toward the ridge, upwind of the fire, where they might be safe, for the moment. The firefighters shouted all this over the noise and wind of the hovering helicopter, while they were helping Chele unsaddle the stock and rigging Helen up in a helmet and sling to be hoisted into the sky. She tumbled into the helicopter and someone strapped her into a gurney, while the sling went back to the ground for Chele.

Now, still strapped to the gurney, she lay in a bit of shade on the edge of the landing strip at Confluence Bar amid a general bedlam of radio static and airplane noise and vehicles driving and stopping and boots passing close to her head.

"What's going on?" The man she spoke to was unshaven and brown. He spat a dark, thick glob into the thistles and shrugged.

"Cluster."

"Cluster...?" She waited. His eyes invisible behind sunglasses.

"Cluster*fuck*, ma'am."

A young woman—one of her rescuers?—knelt beside her and strapped a blood pressure cuff to her arm and said something about a hospital.

"I don't need a hospital."

"We have to get you checked over. You've been through a lot. Breathed a lot of smoke."

"I'm fine. Just get me off this thing. Then I'm walking home."

"You're a long way from home."

"Half a mile. Where's the boy who was with me? The sheepherder?"

The girl released the blood pressure cuff and stood up. Helen closed her eyes. When she opened them a group of yellowshirts was approaching. One crouched beside her, introduced himself, and started asking questions. Wanted to know was she in pain, did she know who she was, where she was, what day of the week it was. She closed her eyes again. Then a familiar voice was asking the same questions. She opened her eyes. A second yellowshirt loomed over her, squeezing her hand and looking hard into her face.

Ben, last seen as a slumping shadow in the passenger doorway of Clayton's Jeep.

"Do you know who *you* are?" she answered. "Do you know where my sheepherder is?"

A thing at his belt buzzed. He muttered an apology and stood up, was gone. Another yellowshirt knelt beside her, patted her shoulder. It took her a moment to recognize Lena, looking awkward and incongruous in baggy firefighter clothes. Playing dress-up. But colorful for once. Brighter, better-illuminated.

"Oh my god, Mom, how are you? We've been so worried."

"Where's Chele? My keeper, where did he go?"

The glare was intense. She kept closing and opening her eyes. More people knelt or leaned over her and asked more questions, or the same questions. Finally they unstrapped her, let her sit up, gave her a rehydration drink and an energy bar and bits and pieces of information.

The fire has jumped the canyon and is burning in mountains on both sides of the river.

The Indian Mountain lookout has been evacuated, it may have already burned.

The river road and the bridge have been reopened to provide access to back country roads and to the fire camp.

Her vitals were good. She wouldn't be medevacked. For the time being she could go to Upper McKeane to rest and recuperate.

Angie was sending some papers for her to sign.

She felt another hand on her shoulder and turned to face—*Jimmy.* At least there was some expectation of seeing him here. At least he wasn't wearing a yellow shirt, didn't squeeze her hand or pat her shoulder or ask outlandish questions. He just helped her to her feet and led her over to an ATV and she got on behind and he began to drive slowly away from the airstrip, while she considered how exceedingly strange it was to encounter first their father's ghost and then her three children in this canyon they'd fled together so many years before, and whether that pointed to a calculated scheming on their part or to the work of an Unseen Hand or merely to an improbable coincidence.

Then she saw him again. Ethan's ghost. Standing on the side of the road, looking straight at her as the ATV slowly passed by. But now, close up... he was like but unlike Ethan. Ethan aged, maybe, or a vision of how he might have aged. Stiffened and stooped, furrowed, spotted, scaly. A lizard, a buzzard. But some familiar quality of expression, a bitterness deeply engrained yet finely-tempered. Then she recognized the buzzard. She was staring open-mouthed at the last man to see her husband alive or dead, the volatile, unapproachable Clayton McKeane.

She gripped Jimmy's waist and they drove on, past the fire camp and Clayton's junkyard and through the open gate into Upper McKeane and down to her cabin.

"You could stay in the main house, if you want," said Jimmy.

"I don't. Jimmy. Where is he? Chele. My—the sheepherder."

Jimmy started driving off, then stopped. "Look, I wouldn't worry about him. Really. When you're ready, come up and take a shower. I'll rustle you up something to eat."

Everything was exactly as she'd left it. Her bedding tangled on the mattress, clothes and toiletries spilling out of the suitcase she'd left on the work bench. Her necklace still clamped in the vise on the workbench, beside the hacksaw Chele had used to cut it free of her neck.

She undressed and lay down. The bed felt wonderful. She was thankful for that—to be off the ground and lying with a bit of real padding beneath her hip, inside a shelter of pine logs that gave off a musky, earthy smell somehow evocative of the canvas sheepherder tent she had slept in so many nights.

But the truth was she could no longer trust her sense of smell. At one time she had prided herself on it, in some ways the most powerful and discerning of all her senses. But now it was drying up like so much else. Desiccation, the expansion of deserts, a steady accumulation of losses: such was the natural order and general expectation of things. Yet still she dared to hope for some small compensation.

But this sudden loss of Chele she had not expected. He was just gone, no warning or explanation. He had not wanted to be rescued, hated abandoning his animals—might he have gone back up the mountain to search for them? Or was he in trouble? Under suspicion, something to do with the fire? Had the firefighters snatched him up and taken him away for questioning? For accusation, imprisonment, deportation? He had no connections, no family—how would he defend himself?

She had failed to live up to the terms of their agreement. She was supposed to be the guide, but when they were returned in the helicopter to the place she knew best she had looked away, distracted by bright colors and metals and the sudden apparition of Ethan's ghost, who of course wasn't Ethan's ghost but possibly his murderer, or so she'd insinuated in her book, though in fact she had no proof or even evidence beyond the most circumstantial. There was no way to resolve the question of Ethan's disappearance and presumed death, just as there was still, nearly two decades after she'd left him, no way to resolve the question of their marriage. She'd taken their children and walked out of the canyon, out of the marriage. The most courageous, definitive, resolute act of her life, and in the end it hadn't resolved a thing. The marriage least of all. For years that continued, a purgatory. They couldn't figure out how to finish it off or revive it, how to live together or apart. Whether theirs was a love story or some other kind of story.

During that time, she hadn't returned to the canyon for more than brief visits. Ethan would fly out to stay with them in town, at first for extended periods, though as his restlessness increased the visits grew shorter. Often she had only the vaguest idea of where he was. Either flying around the backcountry or holed-up at the ranch, presumably. Literally holed-up, burrowing into rocks. Underneath the ground or far above it. The ground itself, the entire blue-green surface of the planet, he mainly abandoned, until ground and sky slammed together and the life was crushed out of him. Again, presumably. Another definitive act resolving nothing, unless making something permanently irresolvable could be a kind of resolution.

A knocking broke into her reverie. She got up, wrapped a towel around her waist, and went to the door. But it was only two firefighters wanting her permission to take some 'structure protection' measures on her property—limb trees, set up sprinklers, assess hazards and fuels.

Helen stared at them. A pair of young women, girls, at once intimidating and ridiculous-looking in their firefighter clothes, high leather work boots, complicated masculine accessories dangling from belts and straps—tool pouches, radios, work gloves. Whereas she stood before them more than half-asleep, braless and unbathed, wearing a t-shirt and a raggedy towel over blown-out granny underpants, with a sleep-drugged stupefaction on her face, probably.

"Fine," she said, starting to close the door. But the girls kept talking. Edging around the door, peering into the room, telling her their names and the name of their squadron or battalion or whatever it was. Asking about the sheepherder she'd been traveling with. How had she made his acquaintance. How would she characterize their relationship. Could she reconstruct the route they had followed over the mountains. Had she observed him engaging in any unorthodox on-the-job behavior.

"This isn't a good time," she said, closing the door. She went back to bed. But now she couldn't sleep. What did it mean, a pair of bumptious girls sticking their noses into her cabin playing at detective, trying to get her to talk about Chele? For one thing, it meant they didn't know much themselves. They didn't know where he was. Which meant he was still free.

But still she regretted sending them on their way with their questions unanswered.

How had she made the acquaintance of the sheepherder? That she might have answered just by opening the door a little wider and pointing to the necklace in the vise.

How would she characterize their relationship? Well, not as a relationship with a sheepherder. To her he was a shepherd, an important distinction. *Pastor.* And she in turn was his employer, camp helper, guide. All relationships still evolving, too fresh to characterize at all.

Could she reconstruct the route they had followed over the mountains? Only by getting down on her hands and knees and assembling out of whatever scraps lay at their feet a diorama of a landscape they would never reconcile to their maps.

Had she observed any unorthodox on-the-job behavior? What could that mean? The job itself was unorthodox—he was working for her and simultaneously working for Armstrong. She had asked him only to look after her with the same care and diligence he extended to any other member of the band, no more and no less. But in the end she'd required far more. An impossible job, even for a young man of such wide-ranging ability and adaptability, such extraordinary perception and imagination. An orphan, he knew nothing of family. But that hadn't stopped him from imagining one, from assembling out of broken strands of genealogy and coincidence an origin myth all his own.

I was born one.

Of course, in his mind it wasn't a myth he'd assembled but a truth he'd uncovered, embedded in the logic of the family history she told and in his fragmented understanding of his own origins. The abandoned mines of San Miguel and their degenerate gringo miners. His lost mother and unknown, degenerate father. The ambiguous shade of his skin. The fateful juxtapositions of things widely separated in time and space that seemed to mark his path. Tunnels, roads, driveways, grandmothers, signal fires, refuges. All signposts, clues, if barely. If more magical thinking than logical deduction.

But she hadn't tried to argue with him. An orphan and a mongrel, he could make a theoretical claim to any number of families. If he wanted to belong to this one they would make room for him. For all their faults, the McKeanes had never been an exclusive tribe; anyone who wanted to join badly enough could probably just join. She herself had joined *without* even really wanting to, certainly without knowing what she was getting herself into. And now look at her. Matriarch, trustee, heiress, poised to exchange an unused—unusable—property for a sum of money large enough to provide for the financial well-being of her descendants as well as her own comfort and security in her failing years. As Angie had so persuasively put it.

But now, lying in bed in the oldest building on that property, her body finally still, eyes closed, breathing calm, it seemed to her that Angie's argument was not, after all, so persuasive. What use did she have for a large sum of money? What use to her was anything on Angie's cluttered list: investments, portfolios, legacies, vacations, houses, servants, specialists of all kinds to wait upon her and ease her passage into decrepitude?

The *elimination* of clutter, not its accumulation: that was the primary task of the old. And maybe a compensation. More space opened up. Space for everything, including sleep: the small, sweet compensation of lying down and floating into sleep on a wave of optimism so

disproportionate to her circumstances it might well signal the onset
of dementia.

She napped every afternoon, escaping from heat and glare and
smoke into a bottomless sleep that split the day in two and altered
time, whether by increasing her number of allotted days or using them
up faster, it was impossible to say.

With age it becomes increasingly difficult to adapt to new situations and learn new routines. But Helen at seventy was experiencing
the opposite. She squatted by an open fire, roasting the flesh of an
animal she'd just helped slaughter. Her teeth and fingers ripped meat
and fat off bones she then tossed to dogs who gnawed and growled in
the darkness at the far edge of a circle of firelight, all she saw of them
was the glint of eyes, teeth, saliva. She leaned into an ice-cold creek
to scrub grease and ash and charcoal from her hands and face. She
slept through the night on a sagging cot in a canvas tent and woke
in the morning wondering if Chele had slept at all. She *walked*, no
one trying to stop or rein her in, all day long on a trail of sheep dung
through smoky, borderless forests, with dogs and horses and a sheep-
herder/keeper by her side.

She'd adapted to it all. And now she was adapting to new patterns
and routines: back and forth between Upper and Lower McKeane, between private cabin and public fire camp, between sleeping and waking. The multiplication of days; the compression—or expansion—of
time; the constriction of territory, or its liberation.

The territory: the McKeane Ranch, upper and lower ranches. Not
a square foot more; the surrounding Forest, with wildfire still far away
yet burning in all directions, had been closed to the public. But she
was free to wander all over Confluence Bar itself—her own property, after all, though now occupied by this alien settlement that had
risen up in a matter of days and would be dismantled in even less
time. Impermanence, a defining quality of a fire camp. But not only
a fire camp. Was there any meaningful distinction between the pre-
fabricated, temporary structures of the camp and the long-vanished

teepees and salmon-drying racks and fire pits of the very first settlers? Or for that matter the soon-to-vanish constructions of the ones
who followed—cabins and corrals and barns, fencelines, flumes, stone
walls and foundations and outbuildings? Only that those had been
around for long enough that a person—having been around for a
good deal less—might mistake them for the place itself, rather than
artifacts of yet another short-lived occupation which would also one
day disappear.

But for now fat-tired trucks squeezed past each other on the
roads, helicopters and airplanes rattled the canyon walls, generators
thrummed into the night. People hustled in and out of meetings,
stared at screens, muttered into satellite phones and radios. Crews
assembled and stood by, moved gear around, cleared brush, cut fireline, rolled out hose along the dry bed of the irrigation ditch and set
up pumps and sprinklers to deliver water to fields that had not been
irrigated for decades. Vans and trucks and crewcabs crept down the
Ledorah Road, returning from graveyard shifts and spike camps closer
to the firelines. In the dim and smoky light, with their picks and shovels, headlamps, hardhats, blackened clothes and skin, they might have
been miners, returning from the diggings in Antimony Basin.

She wandered into Clayton's junkyard. Heaps of old lumber and
metal, stockpiles of dead machines. Dead, yet some flow of energy
seemed to come out of them. Did she only imagine a vibration, a high-
pitched hum? The iron graveyard working like a reactor core, fueling
the surge of activity around it, the dead metal charging the living?

Beneath an ancient water tender a light flashed. Clayton crawled
out, wearing a headlamp. He straightened, stood erect, stared at her.

"This old thing's got to pass inspection, Helen. They're wanting to
lease it from me. Wanting to drive it up and down the mountain with
all the other trucks they keep bringing in on the road their engineers
said was undriveable, over the bridge they condemned."

His headlamp blinded, a terrible eye of Cyclops. And she without
so much as a burning brand to thrust at it.

"Must have got the engineers to take a second look. *Sure* that bridge
is bad? *Sure* that road can't be rebuilt? Well, maybe it can. Maybe you

can get an engineer to *un*condemn a bridge as easy as you got him to condemn it in the first place."

He flipped off the headlamp.

"I hear Angie sent in the papers. They got a notary down there at the camp. Soon as you're set, Helen, we can go down and sign."

At last she found her voice.

"Not yet."

The first words she'd spoken to Clayton McKeane in fifteen years.

From her own children she learned nothing. It was Clayton who told her the fire had started in a direct line of sight seven miles from Indian Mountain and burned twenty acres before the fire lookout even got on her radio. That investigators had traced it to a campfire up by Coyote Point, with abundant sign of sheep in the surrounding woods. That aircraft had spotted a band of horses running wild ahead of the fire on Pete's Ridge, and later a small scattering of sheep corpses in a burned-over clearing in Conway Basin. That they didn't know where the sheepherder was. They'd brought him in on the helicopter, took their eyes off him ten seconds, he was gone.

"I'm standing right there," said Clayton. "Yellowshirts running ever which way. Walking all over each other on their radios. You looking for that Mexican boy? Well, he went thataway. Sent 'em on up the mountain."

"You saw him go up the mountain?" said Helen.

Clayton shook his head. "Saw him go down on the gravel bar. With your daughter."

She'd always thought of Clayton McKeane as a purely destructive force. But now, close up, he didn't seem capable of doing half the damage she'd attributed to him. He didn't even seem big enough, physically. He must have shrunk with age, lost mass or maybe concentrated it, like some tightly coiled machinery buried in his junkyard. His Cyclops eye taking in information, then holding her in its gaze while his soft, rasping voice transmitted it.

Yellowshirts come on a second fresh campfire up on Coyote Point.

Sheep keep straggling in to Armstrong Ranch. Dogs too. No horses, no mules. No herder.

Ben McKeane's sitting in a tent punching numbers into a computer, telling everybody what the fire's going to do next.

Yellowshirts all over the mountain, fire popping up everywhere, and Jimmy McKeane decides the thing most needs doing is for him to get down under the gravel bar and start digging up placers.

Some evenings you might see Lena walking on that gravel bar too. Then all a sudden you don't see her. You get up early enough in the morning, might see her walking back.

In the pastures outside her window the firefighters rolled out hoses and kept sprinklers going night and day. Helen fell asleep to the pulse of that artificial rain, the smell of rain on dry summer grass.

When she awoke, the rain was splattering against the window. A wind had come up in the night. She turned on the light and dumped out on the bed the packet of documents Ben had brought her. An extraordinary convolution of language, thick paste of words and ideas, both antiquated and modern! Location and area, rigidly defined. Invocations of latitude and longitude, azimuth, angle, distance. Water rights, mineral rights, claims, deeds, easements. A dozen different places where she was to sign or initial and so relinquish the one hundred year-old claim of the McKeanes to the measured land.

How was it possible to have such power in your name? The documents didn't say but she knew it was mainly rock the McKeanes owned, or little deposits of soil derived from that rock, or brought in on one flood to be carried away on another. The oldest rock on the continent, Ethan had boasted—falsely, for all she knew. Yet he seemed to have infected her too with his raptures of deep geologic time, undermining her ability to navigate her own small span of time, or take seriously a contract which claimed the power to own and transfer ownership of that rock and soil.

She had no idea what the hour was. Middle of the night, early morning? But there was no going back to sleep. She put the papers away, dressed, went outside. The smoke had cleared out. The sky was a bottomless swath of stars, framed by dark canyon walls. For the first time since she'd left the high country she saw fire, a subdued glow pulsing at the edge of the breaks.

She walked up the road toward a string of bobbing lights and the soft thud and scatter of falling earth. A rumble and grunt of voices, the ring of metal striking rock. A crew was lined out along the ditch, digging and scraping at the ground. A headlamp beam flickered over her and did not stop. No one looked at her.

Invisibility: that could be a compensation.

She turned back down the road toward the river, passing the sheep-stinking pastures and the empty sheepherder camp and coming out on the low, rocky bluff above the gravel bar. Fireglow—maybe the light of dawn?—reflected off a lowering ceiling of sky. But with sunrise came a strange reversal: the black, moonless, transparent night gave way to a daylight that was smoky and opaque. And here was yet another compensation: she could see through that opacity. A human figure crossed the bar and vanished, swallowed by rocks. Then a vaguer, smokier figure emerged from the gravels, like some underground creature drawn to light and the smell of dawn. By the time she descended the bluff and begun to make her way across the bar that figure too was gone, if it had been there at all.

She stood beside a low mound of tailings at the mouth of one of Ethan's mines. His handiwork, one of the tiny gashes he'd left in the earth. Which the earth, in its slow, inevitable way, was closing. But for now it remained pried open with precariously balanced timbers. That shoddy-looking construction had been Ethan's deliberate strategy to protect his claims. No one in their right mind would go into a hole like that, he'd said. She'd had to agree. But now on the outside were new-cut timbers, hand tools lying about. A smell stung her nostrils, urine or musk, like the outside of an animal den. But from the darkness came a flow of cool, moist air.

"Jimmy!"

No echo, her voice swallowed instantly by the dark. She called again, and again, throwing different names into the hole.

"Lena! Chele!"

Something stirred. Nothing *seen*, the mine was pure blindness and darkness. But she sensed a movement forward, just beyond the reach of daylight. Then her attention was drawn to larger movements in the distance. Yellowshirts were coming across the bar. She hissed into the mine.

"Go back!"

She stood still, waiting for them to pass. Invisible.

"Mrs. McKeane. We been looking for you."

"You don't want to go in there, ma'am. Closed site. Hazmat."

They were looking straight at her. Invisibility, another impermanent state.

They shined a powerful beam into the mine. It passed beneath the archway of timbers, across piles of rock and deeper rubble within.

"Are you alone here? Were you talking to somebody?"

"No," she said. "No one." Then, because that lie did not seem convincing, she lied again. "I was calling to my dead husband. His ghost."

The man clicked off his light and touched her arm.

"Fire's spotted into the canyon just upriver, Mrs. McKeane. We can't hold it. Winds are shifting, cold front's coming through, faster than we'd anticipated. We're pulling out of the canyon, it's just too dangerous down here. We got a stage III evacuation order, effective immediately. The ranch, the camp, everybody. Ghosts can stay."

She allowed him to keep his hand on her elbow all the way back to the house. Everywhere firefighters were at work, packing up tents and trucks, rolling up hoses, spraying foam over buildings and burn piles. They worked steadily, intently, full of serious purpose. No one standing around with his arms crossed, spitting into the thistles. *Cluster.*

They paid her no attention. Yet among those anonymous, lumbering, heavy-booted creatures were several who had first emerged from her now diminished and dessicated body. Another astonishing metamorphosis. Not so long ago that same body, ultra-hydrated and elastic, had swollen to accommodate a furious growth, a chemical surge of hormones and cell factories. Then someone had snipped off the final umbilical cord and the next thing she knew her body had lapsed into obsolescence. Babies were suckling at full breasts; then the breasts were shrunken sacs and the babies scattered like shrapnel, like spotfires.

They had a vehicle at her cabin and waited while she packed a bag. She got in and they drove to the airstrip, through Lower McKeane and what was left of the fire camp. Clayton's house and barn were wrapped in a glittery, silvery foil. Clayton himself leaned against the hood of his water tender, smoking a cigarette and watching the evacuation. He too wore a yellow shirt and green pants—when had she ever seen him in anything other than coveralls? He made a scribbling gesture in the air, mouthed a question. She shrugged, pretended not to understand. In any case the answer was the same.

Not yet.

She was strapped to the seat of a plane. It taxied down the bumpy strip and lifted into the air and for the first time in twenty years she was flying out of the canyon, ascending in a steady, steeply-banked spiral, raptor-like, buzzard-like, blue sky and green forest and black smoke and red flame unwinding above the riparian strip and the settlement hemmed in by river and rock. Fire was burning in forest and grass and brush and seemingly even in rock—not a single front but many separate fronts, converging on Confluence Bar from many directions, while a line of vehicles crossed the bridge and retreated down the river road.

The ranch was going to burn.

Simultaneous with that realization came another one. Or rather, an admission of what she must have known all along. She would not sign. Not yet, not ever. She would not sell. She would remain the owner, even if everything she owned burned to ash, even if the idea of ownership was an illusion and a disaster. The ranch would stay in the family, even if it divided and indebted and impoverished them and made each generation crazier than the one that came before. Even if after a hundred years of possession they still had no practical idea what to do with it. A hundred years was nothing. Let it go down through the generations, let fire shower from the sky, flush through the canyon like a tidal flood, deadly, though it wasn't death she was thinking of as she looked down on the smoldering black earth, but life: fertilization, gestation, multiplication, metamorphosis.

24

SUCESOS

ESS THAN twenty-four hours after the fire camp at Confluence Bar was evacuated, the last yellowshirt stood beside his water tender with a hose in his hands, watching a wall of flame sweep around the canyon bend while embers and rain fell from the smokeblack sky.

The rain came from sprinklers the crews had set up before they left. Unfavorable winds had kept them from lighting the backburn they'd prepared, to clear out lighter fuels on the west side of the house and barn. The east side was already theoretically buffered by dredge ponds and tailings and the metallic sprawl of the boneyard, which had been cleared by a fire crew of fuel cans and other combustible materials. But they must have missed something, or just not anticipated the intensity of the radiant heat and the quantity and volatility of petroleum products that over decades had dripped onto the compacted ground. Within the jumbled, wailing roar of the fire Clayton heard a series of explosions. Dragging the hose, he rounded the corner of his house and was met by a blast of heat and a boiling black smoke. Flames shot up out of the yard and off the roofs of his guest cabins. He dropped the hose, ran to the far side of the house, and ducked into the root cellar to crouch in a musty darkness, smelling his own burnt hair and waiting to die.

Hours later he emerged into an afternoon like twilight. His house had not burned. He made his way to the edge of his boneyard. The fire had flashed over it, melting glass and blackening metal but mainly moving on, though an insupportable heat and smoke and smell of toxic combustion remained. He turned away, blackened and nearly melted himself, stumbled across the smoking gravels, tore off his boots and clothes, and threw himself into the river.

Chele Cruz, lying alone and in a sleepless stupor in the cramped darkness of a mine tunnel, heard on a rising wind the wailing of his sheep. He crawled to the mouth of the tunnel and stepped into a hot wind and a smoky glare. The wailing grew louder, wilder. But not until he saw the fire coming around the river bend did it occur to him that he was hearing not his lost sheep but the hunting cry of the Sisimiti, carried on a firewind exactly as his grandmother had described it so long ago.

He fled back underground. The muffled turbulence outside grew louder, deeper, the roar of a stormdriven ocean. So far from any coastline, yet all summer he'd been hearing it—the ocean, and voices and machinery submerged within it. But this was something else. A desert ocean, containing not voices but only the terrible echo of its own depth and emptiness.

For how long did the storm rage? At last it seemed to calm, and he ventured out of the mine into a dim light, onto black ground. On the far shore, beneath a forest canopy of huddled shrouds and dying torches, the earth streamed smoke and held pockets of low flame. Fire glowed and flared in the hills all around. Behind him, ranch buildings crumpled in flames.

Only the river was free of fire. Over smoking rocks and embers he moved toward it. But coming over the last rise, he stopped.

On the beach below hunched the Sisimiti, naked body streaked with ash and charcoal, head swiveling to survey the destruction he had wrought. Chele dropped back into a swale and retreated to his tunnel. His grandmother had described a lumbering, loping creature ranging over the barrens, huge backwards feet, a brute penis swinging through the ash. But now in the aftermath of a great fire Chele had seen him close-up: a lewd old man, stiffened and hunched-over, stringy muscles, bony haunches. Shoulders sprouting ash-colored hair. Raw, spotted skin. Zopilote head pivoting on a wrinkled neck. The feet facing forward. The penis nothing special.

Confluence Bar burned over in a wind-driven wall of flame impervious to all fire lines and retardant bombardments. Yet the fire's destructive force was not equal or absolute. Two of Clayton McKeane's guest cabins, some outbuildings, and much of the equipment and materials in the boneyard were destroyed or damaged. But the main house and one cabin escaped the flames if not the smoke. The barn at Upper McKeane burned, and the wind tore off the foil shield the crews had wrapped around the house there so that it also burned to the ground. Yet the homestead cabin—Helen's cabin—though surrounded entirely by blackened ground, did not.

Most of Clayton's burn piles, perversely, did not burn.

Cooler weather and September rain slowed the fire; it smoldered on the mountain for a while until more rain and finally snow put it out. Gradually the McKeanes began to drift back to Confluence Bar. When it was a fertile oasis they'd abandoned and nearly relinquished it. But now, fire-blasted and ash-covered, it drew them in.

Helen was the first to stay. Her cabin was more cramped than ever. Before the evacuation Jimmy had moved furniture and boxes down from the house, so all their eggs wouldn't be in one flammable basket, he'd said. That had turned out to be prescient; everything left in the house or barn was burned or smoke-damaged beyond hope of salvage. She rearranged things so that the bed was accessible, put a couple of chairs near the woodstove, and made space on the workbench for a kerosene lamp, a small camp stove, and books and writing materials.

It was enough. She did not feel confined. She had all of Confluence Bar to wander over, territory liberated by fire. But in fact she scarcely left the area of her cabin. Strangely, she no longer *felt* much like walking, had neither the energy nor the desire. As for topographical disorientation—she wondered if she might have been cured. Or if her condition had entered a new phase, new symptoms, if more than the hippocampus might be involved. If immobility was neutralizing it?

In any case, she had a very good sense of exactly where she was in the world. She felt *planted*, hyperconscious of space and topography. Topography had been stripped by fire of its green mantles, its ornamental flourishes and disguises, and the elemental form of the world exposed. Everything inessential had been turned to ash: forest and bush, pasture, fences, buildings, gardens, dumps, ruins, documents, artifacts. The rubble of dead people's lives—all turned to ash. Though not before she'd scavenged and sifted through it; triaged, classified, chronologized. Shaped it into a book that gave the dead a stability and coherence they surely hadn't possessed when alive.

In which case, wasn't her book a misrepresentation of their lives? And why had she spent all that time on the dead, when there were yet the living to contend with?

Sometimes it felt like she might be the sole inhabitant of Confluence Bar. But she knew crews were camped in the vicinity, rehabilitating fire lines and cleaning up their camps. And Clayton was around, though at first she saw little of him. But gradually he began to stir himself.

He began with the clean-up—finishing what the fire started, he said. He made great piles of half-burned, rain-soaked lumber and other barely combustible materials, doused them in diesel fuel, and set them aflame a second time. Then left them to smolder under low November skies. He sifted through his boneyard, crawling over and under vehicles and machinery, sorting, rearranging, salvaging. He felled burned trees and skidded the logs to his landing and stacked them there, though it wasn't clear what else might be done with them, since even with the bridge and river road still open the charred timber was of too little value to justify the long haul to a mill.

Sometimes at night she heard the sound of a diesel engine working up at the log landing. She heard back-up beepers, chain saw, nail gun, drill, generator, compressor, heavy objects bashed around. Headlights swept out across the gravel bar and the river, and the sky above the landing took on a steady fluorescent glow, lit up now and then with bursts of bright bluish light.

In the morning all was quiet. When she walked up to the landing she found it deserted. She stared for a long time at a fresh arrangement of logs, boards, hardware, metal, ropes. Another random pile? Or an intentional design, somehow reminiscent of the pioneer contraptions she and Chele had come across half-buried under fallen branches and pine needles in the dimly-lit woods beyond Ledorah, whose purpose she had also been unable to explain?

Her children were in and out of the canyon at unpredictable intervals, checking up on her, bringing her food, supplies, herbal concoctions, supplements, medicines. Sometimes they lingered for a bit of conversation. She could never recall much of what was said. The energy they brought into her cabin was the energy of static, or of smoke. The energy of spotfires, smoldering out to nothingness in the duff, never without some risk of blowing up into a conflagration. They harbored their own secrets and private epiphanies, gestated their own outsized and impractical ideas. Morphed as she herself was morphing, you couldn't tell into what. Small, incremental mutation, or sudden transfiguration? Chrysalis to butterfly, tadpole to frog, hard round seed to leafy plant.

But where was the boy who looked after the sheep?

A fire crew cleaning up and reseeding fire lines found amid ashes and cracked and blackened cobble on the far end of Confluence Bar the charred remains of a knapsack, a pair of boots, and a melted belt buckle—all determined to have belonged to the sheepherder Chele Cruz. Evidence—not proof—that he had been caught up in the fire and killed. He must have cast off his burning clothing as he fled to the river, and the river had carried away the final proof.

Helen listened with downcast eyes but remained silent. She had the proof. She had heard the story from Jimmy and Lena, and later from Chele himself. Who was Chele no longer.

When he got out of the helicopter on Confluence Bar he was numb, dazed, in shock. All around him a great noise and commotion, vehicles and firefighters on the move. Someone touched his arm. *Sígame,* she whispered. He recognized the voice before he saw her face. He followed her away from the airstrip onto a dirt road. An ATV pulling a trailer came up behind them. The driver was the man who'd driven the Jeep on the Ledorah Road. *The last of the Perdu River McKeanes.* The ATV jerked to a stop. *Sube,* Lena said. He got in the trailer and a tarp came over him and the ATV started moving again. At first the road was smooth but the ride got bumpier and bumpier until finally it seemed they were just driving over rocks. They stopped and the tarp came off and he got out. She was pointing at a pile of rocks. *Métete*, she said. He saw the hole in the rocks, and crawled in.

But the burned clothes and pack? A red herring, placed in the path of the fire by Lena as the evacuation was underway, to throw any investigators off the scent. Except not really a red herring, because in fact the sheepherder, the orphan Chele Cruz, *was* lost. Gone. The boy Helen sometimes saw out on the gravel bar in the evening or early morning hours, or far away across a field, talking with Clayton or one of her children or just staring across the burned-over land or into the spark and glitter of low sunlight on the river—that boy was someone else.

He sometimes came to her door under the cover of dusk. His hair was cut short, a buzz. No ponytail or little beard. The clothes were different. When she called him 'Chele' he didn't respond. That's not even a real name, he said. Call me Mateo.

She spent the winter in the three month shadow of the mountain, tracking the short arc of the sun across the canyon walls, studying the blue light that seemed to emanate as much from the snow as the sky. Never had she been so glad to see snow. In one snowfall the scorched ground vanished and the canyon became beautiful again, perhaps more beautiful than ever. The smoothness and simplicity of burned-over fields and hills, now covered with clean snow. The stark and bitter beauty of black trees, standing against that pure whiteness.

Her winter walks were short, solitary affairs, mainly quiet—the background sound of the river, the echoey croak of a passing raven. She saw the tracks of animals in the snow but few animals. Here and there she came across boot tracks, mostly Clayton's, and the tracks of his machines—plow truck, snowmobile, tractor. Sometimes she waved to him across a snowy field, or he straightened from some task in his junkyard to stare and finally lift a hand or call out a greeting. Once— by accident, it seemed—they found themselves face to face, passing each other on the road. Then Clayton surprised her, first by speaking, then by the content of his speech.

"I got ahold of your book, Helen. Read it. Every word."

Possibly the most astounding thing anyone had ever said to her.

"I'm in agreement about the burial ground."

She just looked at him. He kept talking. He said he had a plan to capitalize the recovery and rehabilitation of the ranch. That the trustees should meet to discuss it. That they might as well meet in town, at the bank.

Again she was speechless. Finally she said: well, what about Mexico? What about Opal?

Opal, he answered, after a pause. She was always pining for a Mexican honeymoon. Turns out what she wanted was a Mexican divorce.

At dusk Mateo sometimes visited. Mateo, she called him that to his face, when she remembered, but it was awkward, in her thoughts he remained Chele. He was still keeping a low profile, spending the daylight hours mainly in the mine. It wasn't so bad, he said. Comfortable temperature, decent airflow. Jimmy and Lena brought him clothes, food, water, mattress, sleeping bag, flashlight, battery-powered lantern, and books, many books, and it felt not so much claustrophobic as comfortable and safe and also strangely familiar; he might have been back in his refuge in the storage room at Ciudad de Luz, burrowing into books while Padre Jaco rattled and raged with his demons outside.

Behind his living space the tunnel narrowed and Chele didn't follow it farther and so never saw the end. It was as if there was no end. What he did see, on even the blackest night, no moonlight or starlight, was a strange, inconstant light in the tailings rock at the mouth of his tunnel, that seemed to come from deep inside the rock or from very far away, like starfields glowing and glittering and abruptly going dark.

Then he remembered the incandescent tailings on the outskirts of San Miguel and the idea of subterranean connection took hold. *How does a boy like you end up in a place like this?* Was he saying that the mine tunnels had something to do with it? That what seemed like a dead end had a crack that opened onto another tunnel, and another, the tunnels beneath San Miguel connecting to the tunnels that had channeled floodwaters and mudflows into the city and then to the tunnels the McKeanes had blasted into their mountains or burrowed out beneath ancient riverbeds? So that an ancestor buried in a drift mine cave-in at Confluence Bar could emerge from a mine in San Miguel with a packet of gold and a lust made insatiable by his long passage underground. And so he'd left many descendants but only one had found his way back, through entirely different portals and passages, a surface rather than underground realm, trails and back roads and highways, horses, trucks, buses, cars, and the last road he drove seemed to go underground, a mine tunnel he followed until it bottomed out at a cement wall and a dark river and he parked the truck and gave away the keys and when he came back there was only the cement wall and the stinking river. A dead end.

But there was a crack in that one too. He had gone through and come out on the sheep driveway, that had led him to Lena in her tower and to the cougar and the ranch and then to Helen and over four passes and into a wall of smoke. Another dead end. And the crack in that one was the crack of his bloodline, his new understanding of who he was and of his inheritance and the ancestral home and refuge he had come back to, upon which might be projected some remnant or vestige of the refuge he had come out of.

His English was vastly improved. But it was a fantastic English, practically delirious, and she couldn't tell if this was what he was truly describing or if it was just her imagination running away with whatever she understood of his words. But for a while, sitting in the low lamplight of her cabin listening to his quiet voice, it all seemed clear and true. The three separate but interwoven strata: mines and tunnels; roads and trails; bloodlines. The portals and passageways through them, between them. The refuges. Somehow it all made sense.

But after he left and she blew out the lamps and lay down to sleep the sense went out of it. Connections dissolved, cracks and portals closed, all that was left to her in the black night were isolated images. The grandmother riding her little mare through tailings and scablands and patches of bitter herbs. The zopilote children at play in a pale and poisonous dust. Lempira's signal fire, Sisimiti's firestorm. Shadow horses moving through night grasses, the black-bearded man emerging from deeper shadows between dormitories. Mango juice drying in stubble on the padre's chin. The cougar opening its mouth to scream but never screaming. The raw red earth that had turned out to be so soft. The naked woman gliding across the intersection, eyes locked on the boy watching from the open window of a waiting car. The girl's slurry voice coming out of the night. *Te lo mato.* Lena's low whisper coming out of a different night. *Siento paz.*

The river swelled with snowmelt, ran thick and brown from mud-slides and ash. Helen, lying in bed listening to the churning and roil-ing of water and rock, was thankful to be on high and solid ground, until she started thinking about where that ground had come from. Gravel bar and alluvial fan, Confluence Bar had been transported by floods and landslides out of canyons and gulches slashed into moun-tains rising 7000 vertical feet above her. 7000 feet, she knew exactly how far and how high that was. She had measured it out with her grinding joints, climbing with Chele Cruz out of Confluence Bar and over four passes into a country of smoke.

Any part of it might soon be washed away. Antimony Basin and Ledorah, the Ledorah Road, Confluence Bar itself—it was all on the brink. Antimony Basin she'd seen with her own eyes—stripped, soft-ened, and raw even before the firestorm came through to burn and reburn everything in its path. Now nothing was left but ash and burnt sticks and unprotected black earth. A rapid snowmelt or hard thun-derstorm would take it down to the bone.

Lying on the edge of sleep in her cabin at Upper McKeane Ranch, listening to the crack and roll of thunder high up the mountain, Helen had a vision of the next hundred-year flood. Rain fell for days in sheets and pounding waves on melting snow on Red Mountain and Ledorah. The humps and piles of earth the McKeanes had dug up, the charred wreckage of all they'd built and quickly abandoned, was flushed out of its basin and sent churning down gullies and through the canyon of Antimony Creek and out across the delta at Confluence Bar. The flood cut new channels and filled in old ones. Water backed up behind debris damns and submerged the broken headgate and spilled into the McKeane Ditch. Within minutes, a torrent gushed around the point of the mountain. Water poured out of multiple breaks in the flume and ditch bank and flooded everything below: roads, pastures and orchards, sheep camp, boneyard, the ruins of burned-out buildings.

When at last the brown waters receded, her cabin at Upper McKeane was perched high and dry on the edge of a new cutbank of Antimony Creek and she was looking straight across a wide, shallow creek at what was left of Lower McKeane Ranch: Clayton's boneyard, house, and outbuildings, clinging to an island between the Perdu River and split channels of the creek, above a shoreline buried in mud and logs and flotsam washed down from Antimony Basin.

And Clayton McKeane just went on living there. As the water dropped he put up slapdash bridges and crossings, to be carried away in the next flood as the island itself would soon be carried away. From atop her cutbank she watched him moving along his cluttered shore. Salvaging, scavenging, prospecting. She waved and called to him. If he called back his voice was lost to the wind and water and tumbling rock.

Or it was lost because it was a voice out of a vision. When she opened her eyes and looked out her window she saw no island, no physical rift between Upper and Lower McKeane. No flood, not yet anyway. That spring, at least, the snow melt was gradual, the rains gentle. Stream and river channels mainly held. The McKeane Ditch and Ledorah Road still clung improbably to their mountainsides. When the wind blew, and sometimes when it didn't, a tree might be heard falling in the woods. But most of the burned trees still stood, inert skeletons, shiny and black, while the hammering of woodpeckers echoed through the needleless glades.

But on the ground it was as though a long siege had been lifted. Suddenly it was obvious how the dense forest had long robbed the earth of life, blocking sunlight and pumping water from the soil. Now in a new abundance of light and water green shoots emerged from the black ground and root crowns of charred shrubs. Soon much of the ground was covered with a thick, succulent foliage, and later the foliage with bursts of giant flowers—lupines, sunflowers, monkey-flowers, fireweed, thrusting out on long, leafy stalks toward the sun and the bees.

Elsewhere, fire had seared an impermeable seal over the soil and few plants sprouted. Yet even here the ground yielded life and color: low, primitive compounds devoid of chlorophyll; fungi pushing up through powdery white ash; slimy, iridescent crusts of molds and algaes.

Out of brown needlecast in the burnt forest came a prodigious sprouting of morel mushrooms. Commercial mushroom pickers arrived, setting up camps along the river road, in turnouts or small flats and beaches beside the river. They crept up the road in vans and pick-ups, beater station wagons and old SUVs, low-slung highway cruisers. Loners, drifters, tweakers. Forest people out of the northern woods, nomadic families, immigrants and refugees. Small bands of quick, watchful men; women wearing sarongs and rubber boots, baskets of mushrooms balanced on their heads, silent babies bound to their backs. Then if you looked across the river you could see how the outside world had slipped into the McKeanes' crack between mountains. You could feel the weight of countries shift, see the blood mix. See how even as the blood mixes there persists this division into wandering tribes.

Early in spring, Jimmy moved into the spare room in Clayton's house. He talked of working again with Clayton, of fence repair, salvage logging, of building a new diversion in Antimony Creek and blasting a new ditchline into the bedrock of the narrows. Of building a new log house on the foundation of the old. But almost at once he disappeared back under Ethan's placer drifts. Then the morels sprouted and he too emerged from underground. The gold wasn't going anywhere, he said, neither were timber, ditch, fences, the countless things lying around the place that needed fixing. But the mushrooms would last only a few weeks and not be seen like that again for years. Little buds of sexual flesh erupting everywhere out of the ground, where dark filaments, secret webs of mycelia, underlie and nourish the daylit world. Awakening in us obsessions and desires only partially explained by the fact that a person could make three or four hundred dollars a day just wandering through the forest harvesting them. Dried, they were a high value product with a long shelf life and negligible shipping weight or volume—exactly the business model, Jimmy pointed out, that made sense for McKeane Ranch. Ignoring the fact that it was all so ephemeral. He went out in the burn all day and returned with fifty or sixty pounds of cut morels in plastic cartons strapped to his back-pack frame. He dried them in the sun on sand and gravel graders bor-rowed from the boneyard, then stored them in paper bags crammed on top of the boxes in Helen's cabin, to be sold in winter or another year, when there was less of a glut and the price improved.

The canyon morels hatched tiny, pale worms and grew flabby and coarse. The pickers moved up to the higher country, where the mush-room bloom was invigorated by an early summer monsoon. Jimmy did not migrate with them, but now Clayton said it was too hot to work outside under the high sun, on black ground that gave off heat as though it still held fire. So Jimmy went back under the placer drifts in earnest.

But evenings and mornings he was out in the fields and along the roads, training his puppy. His old dog Trevor had run off during the fire. Except Trevor couldn't *run*. Which was maybe another reason Jimmy avoided above-ground work: too many charred bones lying around.

But he loved his new pup. A terrific little mutt, he said: one part Australian shepherd, one part border collie, many parts breedless tramp and scavenger. Totally wild and totally trainable, she was go-ing to make a great mountain dog, a great herd dog.

What would she herd? Sheep, maybe. Horses. Children.

Lena put up a tent near the blackened grove by the old sheepherder camp and went to work on the long-neglected garden. Her summer amid stunted trees and short-season flowers on Indian Mountain's rocky ridge had stirred up in her a longing for deep soil and growing plants. She rebuilt the deer fence and the compost bins, tilled in old manure from the corrals, and planted long rows of vegetables. The ditch was dry but she ran a hose from the domestic spring box to water her seedlings, though the flow would be inadequate for summer irrigation.

Her vegetables were off to a spectacular start in the ash-fertile soil, under warm sun and spring rain. But why such a big garden? How would she water it in summer?

"Something'll work out," she said, glancing at the sky. Where water comes from.

Sometimes she was gone for days on end. It came out that she was taking flying lessons. Flying, another longing stirred up during her summer on Indian Mountain, reading Helen's book and looking down on the canyon flyways, up at a sky streaked with contrails.

But why flying lessons, when she had no airplane and no hope of the money to buy one? She shrugged and looked again at the sky. Where airplanes come from.

Ben set up his office in Clayton's remaining guest cabin. He brought in computers, antennas, solar panels and satellite dish, and spent most of his time inside, working. It wasn't clear if he was working on his old project or a new one, or whom he was working for. If the people who came around to speak with him were his people, if he still had people. He said he was hustling to set up systems, to get the office running on autopilot and get himself out in the field. Things are happening so fast out there, he said. For years there had been a kind of equilibrium—unsustainable but static, he hadn't understood *how* static, how little had yet been set in motion. But now a trigger had been pulled and a thousand dormant processes activated. Old data was obsolete, models useless. Probability tables, predictive algorithms—complex, elegant, meaningless. It was all scorched earth. If you wanted to see how things played out you had to be in the field, observing. *The Field.* Look at Darwin, he said. Five consecutive years in the field, no distractions, and out of it he brought forth a new vision of the world. It was humbling to think of Darwin, his extraordinary powers of observation and synthesis, though it was also true that by modern standards and capabilities Darwin's datasets were minuscule, his tools primitive and crude. Yet wasn't it those very limitations that had allowed him to see so expansively?

"Ben and Darwin," said Jimmy, sitting at the workbench sorting mushrooms. "Now there's a pair."

In June, Angie, Chloe, and Sam appeared and set up their tents on the bluff near Lena's. What can I say, Angie said. I guess we love camp. We love sleeping in tents. I guess maybe we'll spend the entire summer in these tents, we have no plan.

But the children said they hated camp. They sulked, nursed grievances, hardly emerged from their tents. Meanwhile Angie spent little time in hers, and no one believed she had no plan. The ranch sale had been pushed to the back burner, but someone had to keep tabs on all these people coming around—rehab crews, insurance people, scientists, arson investigators. Someone had to go through the books, catalogue and inventory what had been lost and saved. And still there was her business to manage. The real estate market may have contracted but that only meant it was poised to expand. It meant clients were all the more anxious, properties and clients alike all the more in need of maintenance. Of inspiration, visualization, epiphany. On the one hand there was bankruptcy, natural and unnatural disaster, foreclosure. On the other, windows of opportunity, points of leverage, new horizons, new wealth.

She came and went, mostly driving in and out of the canyon. Once she flew in with her client, the pilot and would be-buyer of the ranch (though she'd withdrawn her offer). She was here not as a client but as a friend, Angie said. They walked around Confluence Bar, talking, laughing, taking pictures of each other and selfies together. Ben never came out of his cabin. It was terrible what the fire did, Angie said, but now that it was greening up the property might still have a certain attraction, diminished of course, for the right person, under the right circumstances. But the idea of hanging around focusing myopically on any single isolated property, rigidly defined by stationary bound-aries—that wasn't right for her business. Her business required flex-ibility, mobility, the dissolution of boundaries.

As the summer wore on her absences became longer, her visits more fleeting. Chloe and Sam, of course, had to stay behind. By now they had emerged from their tents and begun to wander about, ex-plore, play. They just needed a break, Angie said. From schedules, structure, screengazing, surveillance. The four Ss, she said. They need independence and responsibility, time on their own and in the care of adults not their mother. Why was it assumed the mother always had to be at the center of things? Those kids had a father, too. They had an aunt, uncles, great-uncle, grandmother. All here on Confluence Bar, a village, isn't that what it takes?

Chloe and Sam began to transform their encampment on the low bluffs. Confluence Bar seemed barren, scoured by fire, but somehow they kept coming up with materials: boards, poles, chicken wire, bricks and tarps and pieces of fabric. They built walls, a door, a sort of roof, put up flags and banners, gates and archways, annexes. Where were they coming up with all this stuff? But then it became obvious: they were ransacking Clayton's boneyard and his unburned piles. Their fort spread tentacles and outposts and passageways across Conflu-ence Bar. Into Lena's garden, to blend with vines and trellises and disappear beneath towering corn and sprawling squash. To Clayton's boneyard, where it incorporated his culverts, steel drums, dormant machines. To his log landing, where the children spied on him as he worked. They prowled around his pits and piles, crawling over and under logs and boards, climbing, scrambling, scampering, swinging, balancing, hiding.

Pits and piles? Or balance beams, obstacle courses, bridges, slides, swings, towers, mazes, tunnels, forts?

A playground.

Early in summer, against all expectation and for the first time in years, water flowed in the irrigation ditch and flooded the farthest pastures and orchards on Upper McKeane. Night breezes carried the sound of pump motors down from the narrows of Antimony Creek, and sometimes a light bobbed along the ditchline or swept out over the pastures. Clayton McKeane, roaming about with shovel and head-lamp, flood irrigating with water sucked from the creek into the ditch by pumps and hoses left behind by retreating fire crews. Fire salvage, he said, equipment abandoned to the flames within the boundaries of his property, and therefore rightfully his. He would have irrigated by broad daylight if it weren't for the fierce summer sun, which, ever since he rounded the corner of his house into the blast furnace heat of his exploding boneyard, he could not abide.

The night water flooded Lena's garden. Lettuces, peas, greens, and strawberries gave way to peppers and corn and tomatoes, beans climbing on tall poles, squashes and melons swollen and sprawling over the ground. Sometimes in her daughter's presence Helen was overwhelmed by an olfactory surge. Sunlight, soil, sweat, pollen, chlorophyll. The girl's hands were calloused, but the skin on her face soft and radiant as a child's. Helen took another breath, got a second wave of smells. Rivers and moss, deeper soil, damp rock, underground streams, sulfur.

The same smells were on Chele—Mateo—when he came bringing food, news, stories. His English was now close to fluent. I practice a lot, he said, with my coach. She's a good coach, said Helen. Pretty good, he said. But listen to her Spanish, you'll see I'm better.

Now he came by daylight. Because he wasn't afraid, he said. He, Mateo, had nothing to fear. Mateo was no sheepherder, fugitive, arsonist. Only… a helper. *Un ayudante.* He helped with everything. She saw him out in the roads and fields, alone or with her children or grandchildren or riding around on Clayton's backhoe or in his truck, helping dig out foundations, repair fences, move pipe. Build piles, tear down piles. Scoop up old horse manure, dump it on Lena's garden. All work that was new to him, he said. But in a way not. An ayudante, another thing he'd been before.

And so he came back around to the cyclical and interconnected nature of things. The tunnels, again. The fusing and blending and pollinating and cross-pollinating of things far apart in space and time, the wide and abundant scattering of their seed. There were millions of orphans, the Peruvian had said. Kids making their own way in the world, blown around in the wind or stuck against a border fence, like so many plastic bags caught in the chainlinks. Then you look closer and it really is just plastic hanging there. The orphans disappear, go into tunnels, portals, passageways. Emerge into a canyon, a crack, a crucible. A refuge, bare but fertile ground.

* * *

In the full heat of summer Helen is wilting. She hardly leaves her cabin. Towels tacked over the windows keep out the harshest daylight, but lying on her bed in the afternoons she can feel black heat seep through the walls. Jimmy's dried mushrooms give off a potent stench in the warm, closed air. Her visitors complain but she doesn't mind, after awhile hardly notices, it might as well be her own smell. Chloe and Sam are simultaneously attracted and repelled. Sometimes they don't even come inside, or they don't stay. Or they might burst in, Sam scrambling up on her lap to study the convoluted topography of her face, to tug and poke at her loose, fungal flesh. Chloe, lately grown so distant and watchful, stands back. Wrinkles her nose, sniffs the air, gazes at her grandma not with childish delight but with a more adult curiosity, suspicion, even. Wondering, what kind of grandma is this, what kind of mushroom?

The mushroom grandma gazes back, wondering herself. What kind of orphan? What kind of seed, what kind of nucleus?

In the evenings she pulls the towel back and opens the window to let in light and cool air while she writes in her notebook. Sketches for a new book? A sequel to *Crack Between Mountains*? An epilogue? Or no kind of book at all, unless it's the kind Chele wrote, pages no one will ever read stashed at the bottom of a locker, questions without answers. *Sucesos*, things that happen, or not, she can't say why she's writing them down. Out of habit, maybe, a compulsion to collect and hoard, to harvest from the wild and preserve in the dimness of her cabin these small fruiting caps, sprouted from some fibrous, tangled, immense underground organism.

And yet she too feels a sense of urgency. Everything's changing so fast, surely Ben's right about that. Soon the earth will wear a fresh disguise of leaves and branches and this brief revelation of naked form will be lost. Fresh migrations will fragment these stories of the living McKeanes, fresh convolutions of the earth will obliterate them. Nothing stays the same or in one place for long. A person might find a temporary mooring—a mine, a cabin, a strip of soil in the bottom of a canyon—but all around is a restless geography of suture zones, thermal bulges, continents adrift. The geography of Chele's ocean, Lena's ocean, where nothing is moored. No fixed location of place, no fixed chronology of event, no fixed link between place and event. All things surging in all directions, like Ben's airport vectors, canceling each other out so that the ultimate effect is directionless, motionless, and, finally, calm.

In the flooded pastures, grass grows lush and tall out of blackened stubble, and at night elk and deer and fine-boned wild horses come out of the hills to graze. Except no one has actually seen the horses, their presence is inferred from a few clumps of what might be horseshit. Out of horseshit rises rumor of horses. In the canyon there is, as ever, a brisk trade in rumor. Illegal mining, stolen timber, grazing trespass, arson. Infidelity, divorce, abandonment. Drug deals, blood feuds, territorial disputes and alliances and vigilante justice in the mushroomers' camps. Cycles of desire, disillusion, decay. Hot surges of madness. Fresh configurations of nature. Enchantments, metamorphoses, darker strains of fatalism.

> *Government workers have removed Ben's files and computer hardware from Clayton's guest cabin. Ben continues to work there, sitting with his laptop at a bare table. The satellite dish still in place, the data still streaming.*

Following the meanders of prehistoric streams beneath the cobble, Jimmy has come upon a paystreak of fine-textured gold.

Mushroomers report a sighting, somewhere in the shadow of Red Mountain, of the wreckage of a small plane, just visible among blackened rock and burned-out vegetation.

Clayton and Jimmy have gone up into the narrows of Antimony Creek to drill dynamite holes into the bedrock, to mix and pour cement.

Angie leaves her children under the care of "the village" and travels with her client to look at properties in Italy, in Spain.

Oscar the Peruano arrives in a pick-up, pulling a horse trailer. He and Mateo ride up the mountain, looking for sheep, horses, mules, dogs, the airplane.

Clayton takes his backhoe out in an abandoned hayfield and digs three rectangular pits, side by side.

Mateo and Lena disappear for days on end. Gone up the mountain, still searching for animals, airplanes? Or beyond the mountains, to cities and borderlands, a different search and rescue?

Chloe and Sam run about with tangled hair, barefoot, blackberry-stained, half-naked, feral. They built cooking fires anywhere they like on the still-blackened ground, fry eggs stolen from wild geese, barbecue corn stolen from Lena's garden, hot dogs stolen from Ben's little refrigerator. They speak into their phones as if there were connectivity. They sleep in their forts, or Jimmy's tunnels, or Clayton's boneyard.

Ben appears on the porch of the cabin. His computer is a relic, he says. The satellite dish, also a relic. Where are my children, he says. Where's Angie?

A man with a salt-and-pepper beard tours the property with Chele/Mateo. They walk very slowly, silent at first, but once they start talking they don't stop.

Low in Lena's belly a small swelling appears.

She writes it all down. Visions and rumors, or things that really happen? In any case, all founded on the most precarious of foundations. The shifting sands and gravels of Confluence Bar. The fantastic delusions of Chele. Money that doesn't belong to anyone. Where's the money come from? A question Padre Jaco answered with a beatific smile and a heavenward gaze; that was all Chele ever got out of him. But somewhere there had to have been a bank. Always there's a bank. In the case of the McKeane Ranch, all the money belongs to the bank, or the ranch itself does; they were living off an equity loan, the ranch was collatoral, fully mortgaged. For the time being Clayton's fuel tanks were full, there were spare parts, materials, everyone was on the payroll, things were happening. *Sucesos.*

But the snake was eating its tail. Angie's Californian—her zopilote—might get her claws into the place yet. It might become like the other ranches, a toy for the rich, a farcical parody of itself. But that too would be ephemeral. Sooner or later it would be swept away in a flood, overrun by one of those catastrophes which are just the normal course of events that happen on earth, the calamity stories Ethan told the children when they were very young, how the world that seemed to them so fresh and eternal would be annihilated, split and blown apart, melted, obliterated by fire, dust, rising oceans, he was telling this to five-year-olds. And so a sense of doom and impermanence pervaded their lives from a very young age. Ethan claimed this was a necessary perspective and also liberating; he said it was a strange sort of comfort, and not merely a cold comfort.

But that was his framework of time, never hers. She hears machines, children's voices, water running. *This* is the time she's living in—the present and the near present, the foreseeable—or imaginable—future. She imagines clear water coursing through the old ditches, flooding pastures and orchards, turning turbines, washing gold out of the placers. She imagines giant flowers blooming in the wetlands beneath skeletal black trees, tropical birds flashing in the new foliage. A school of wild salmon holding in the deep, clear pool where Antimony Creek empties into the Perdu. She imagines new buildings—dormitories, mess hall, classrooms, playgrounds—rising over the ash. Burial grounds dug into the earth beneath it, receiving bodies: hers, Clayton's, whatever bones might be brought down off the mountain.

She imagines Lena and Chele emerging some morning from beneath the river cobble or descending from a night journey to the sulfur baths to walk along the gravel beach, trailing behind them a raggedy string of children they have borne or salvaged. And on the high bank, in the sparse shade of a fire-scorched pine or peering croneishly though a gap in the curtains of her cabin window, she imagines a single *anciana* watching those children, her presence altering in subtle but crucial ways the flow of space and time around them.

Those children might find themselves, like Chloe and Sam, both attracted to and repelled by this old woman and her musty little cabin. One or two might gather the courage to sneak up to her window and peer inside. Then they'll find they can't easily break away. They'll feel the pull of an underground atmosphere, thick with fungal gases and webs of mycelia. Ripe with fertilization, gestation, multiplication, metamorphosis. A place where vital materials are sequestered and distilled and an intricate network of fibers, tunnels, cracks, and fissures undermines the solidity of the surface world.

But she is not yet that *anciana*, those children are not yet present. For now it is only the McKeanes, living and dead, who show their faces at her window. When she tries to bring them into focus the faces shatter and dissolve—*pixelate*—as if cracking into tiny pieces under immense interior pressures: obsession, disillusion, the pressure of holding opposing forces in precarious balance. The pressure of making constant adjustment to failure. Yet for an instant in those faces she also glimpses a radiance and an optimism unlooked for in people making such adjustments. Which is how McKeanes have always adjusted to failure—by immediately turning their attention to new and more outrageous hopes.

That's how things appear by day. At night everything shifts, and the fragile logic of the daylight hours gives way. Headlights wind slowly up the darkness of the Ledorah Road. In a weak moonlight, shadow figures pick their way across the gravel bar and vanish among rocks.

The grass rustles with wind or the passage of large animals. Other shadows swim the river, clatter and snort on the far bank. The Sisim-iti skulks about, shovel in hand, redirecting the flow of water. Peering into people's windows with his Cyclops eye. Later the grass is still, but over Lower McKeane the sky glows with a lurid industrial light, and from the boneyard comes a clanging, clanging, clanging.

By dawn the clanging has stopped. But when the sun strikes the canyon rim there's the distant sound of an engine. A small plane rounds the bend, approaching Confluence Bar on a kamikaze trajec-tory. The engine cuts out. In the sudden silence Helen hears birds, riv-ers, bells, wind pouring over the plane's wings. Then the engine coughs and fires, the plane lifts, skims the ranch buildings and the standing black snags, dips a wing, and banks into the downstream bend.

No one sees the face of the pilot.

Acknowledgments

I'm grateful to the many readers whose critiques, questions, and encouragement helped fuel the writing of this book over years of gestation and evolution, crafting and recrafting. Particular thanks are due to Greg Michalson, whose careful readings and insightful criticism identified any number of flaws in an early version and helped the story find its path. Two readers, Phoebe Hershenow and Mike Kane, have been with it since the beginning, reading numerous drafts and helping shape the book in a significant way.

Early in the process I received two literary fellowships from the Idaho Commission on the Arts, and I'm grateful for that encouragement and recognition of the potential in those early drafts. More recently (2022), an excerpt was awarded first place in "Write on the River" a writing contest for residents of central and eastern Washington. Again, thanks for the recognition and encouragement. Thanks to Peter Donahue for coming up with the title, to Perri Howard for helping me envision the maps, and to Max Hershenow for website design, the Fireland Press logo, and for transforming my primitive map sketches into something beautiful. And many thanks to Sarah Bennett for her skill and patience in the book's design and layout.

About the Author

Nick Hershenow is the author of *The Road Builder* (2001 Blue Hen/Penguin Putnam), which won the Western States Book Award for Fiction in 2002. He lives and writes in central Washington state and works part-time as a preschool teacher/outdoor educator. But for two decades very different jobs took him flying, driving, riding, walking, and bushwalking into urban mazes, rural backwaters, and the front and back country of Idaho, Washington state, Honduras, and Ecuador. Those places and experiences inspired and inform the writing of *Groundtruth*.